CB

086 350 079 X05 93

DENIS GIFFORD

THE **COMPLETE** CATALOGUE OF **BRITISH COMICS** INCLUDING PRICE GUIDE

DENIS GIFFORD

THE **COMPLETE** CATALOGUE OF

BRITISH COMICS

INCLUDING PRICE GUIDE

Webb & Bower

EXETER, ENGLAND

First published in Great Britain 1985 by
Webb & Bower (Publishers) Limited
9 Colleton Crescent, Exeter, Devon EX2 4BY

Designed by Malcolm Couch

Production by Nick Facer

British Library Cataloguing in Publication Data

Gifford, Denis
   The complete catalogue of British comics.
   1. Comic books, strips, etc.—Great Britain
   —Bibliography
   I. Title
   016.7415′941   Z5956.C6

   ISBN 0–86350–079–X

Typeset in Great Britain by Keyspools Limited, Golborne,
Warrington, Lancashire

Printed and bound in Hong Kong by Mandarin Offset
International Limited

Contents

PART ONE   6

Introduction and History

What is a Comic? – The First Comics – Adult Comics – The Comic Boom
Comics – Comic Strips – Comic Heroes – Comic Artists – Coloured Comics
Comic Specials – Comic Supplements – Giveaway Comics – The Golden Age: the Thirties
The Dark Age: the Forties – Comicbooks: American and British
The Silver Age: the Fifties – Library Comics – The Television Age: the Sixties
Reprint Comics – Underground Comics – Current Comics – Errors and Omissions

Collecting Comics

First Editions – Special Editions – Runs and Bound Volumes – Specialized Collections
Collecting Comicbooks – Comic Curiosities – Comic Supplements
Comic Spin-offs – Rare Comics – Collectability – Buying and Selling Old Comics
Condition of Comics – Caring for your Collection

PART TWO   17

Illustrations

PART THREE   113

How to Use the Catalogue

The Catalogue – Reference Books for the Collector
Magazines for the Collector – The Association of Comics Enthusiasts

PART ONE

Introduction and History

What is a Comic?

Comics have been such a familiar part of the everyday scene for so long that the question 'What is a comic?' would seem purely rhetorical. But as a browse through the many illustrations in this catalogue will quickly prove, comics have progressed through many styles, shapes and formats before settling into the standardized product to be found in any newsagent today. Even the once basic requirement of a comic, the strip cartoon, may no longer be the creation of an artist: some comics have replaced pen and ink with photographer and model. The word 'comic' itself has changed its meaning too. In the early press guides and trade reference books, the classification 'comic' refers to such humorous publications as *Laughable Dialogues*, which carries no illustrations of any kind to relieve its columns of text. *Punch, Judy* and their many satirical followers were also classified as 'comics', and such magazines will not be found in this catalogue. Nor will *Adventure, Rover* and the many other boys' and girls' weeklies, which are properly described as 'story-papers'. These essentially text publications cannot qualify for inclusion, despite their colloquial classification as 'comics' or 'story comics' by both newsagents and readers from the 1940s.

The First Comics

The history of comics as we know them could not begin until the advent of mass education and cheap printing in the late nineteenth century, but there are several remarkable prototypes to be found in the earlier era of lithographic printing when caricaturists produced sheets and folders of political and social comment. The earliest known of these to be regularly issued as a fortnightly tabloid of cartoons and strips was published in Scotland, *The Glasgow Looking Glass* (No 1: 11 June 1825).

The first publication to meet the criteria of a comic and lay down a formula that would hold good for some seventy-five years was *Funny Folks* (No 1: 12 December 1874). Originally designed as an eight-page pull-out supplement to the Christmas bumper number of *The Weekly Budget*, publisher James Henderson evidently realized he was on to a good thing with his tabloid scrapbook of cartoons and humorous text, for *Funny Folks* immediately became a weekly paper in its own right, running for twenty years and notching up 1614 editions. Its success inspired the engraver and publisher Gilbert Dalziel to issue the most famous and popular of all Victorian comics, *Ally Sloper's Half-Holiday* (No 1: 3 May 1884). It was an assured success, for it starred a character whose comic-strip capers had been amusing readers of *Judy* since 1867.

Adult Comics

Ally Sloper and his comic companions were all designed to be read and enjoyed by adults. Most of the cartoons were comments on current events in the news, and the *Half-Holiday* in particular had a preoccupation with saucy ladies of the variety chorus. There was no market for a pictorial publication aimed purely at children (outside religious and Sunday-school magazines) since Victorian children had virtually no money of their own beyond the Saturday ha'penny. However, children obviously enjoyed looking at the funny pictures in father's comic, and by 1896 *Comic Cuts* was regularly running strips 'for the children'.

The Comic Boom

The boom in comics began on 17 May 1890 with the publication of *Comic Cuts* No 1 by Alfred Harmsworth. In layout and appearance this eight-page tabloid was little different from *Funny Folks* and the other comics which had preceded it. Its instant success was due purely to its price, one halfpenny, half the cost of all the others, which was one penny. As rival publishers imitated Harmsworth's ha'p'orth, he too brought out companions, *Illustrated Chips* (No 1: 26 July 1890), *The Wonder* (No 1: 30 July 1892), founding a publishing empire that became the mighty Amalgamated Press, today the even mightier International Publishing Corporation.

Children's Comics

It would be thirty years before a comic deliberately aimed its appeal at children, and succeeded. The earliest attempt, *Jack and Jill* (No 1: 7 March 1885), ran only seven issues before upgrading its appeal to the adult market. Harmsworth's first coloured comic, *Puck* (No 1: 30 July 1904) (see below), had begun as an adult weekly with some pages for children entitled *Puck Junior*. By the end of 1904 characters from this section had moved to the front page and the comic was clearly aimed at youngsters. Ten years later the first comic completely designed for children was published: *The Rainbow* (No 1: 14 February 1914). Its immediate success led to several follow-ups by the Amalgamated Press, while other publishers converted their failing adult comics (*Sparks*, 1914) to children's comics (*Little Sparks*, 1920), much to the bewilderment of regular readers.

Comic Strips

The comic strip (American term) or strip cartoon (British term) is considered the basic element of all comics, but historically this is not the case. Although strip techniques (panels, balloons for speech, captions, etc) were known from the early days of printing and illustration, they only find their way into comics, and come to dominate them, by gradual evolution. The earliest comics are content with cartoons and caricatures: *Funny Folks* has the occasional strip, but rarely repeats a character.

Comic Heroes

The first comic-strip hero was undoubtedly the redoubtable Ally Sloper, yet although his *Judy* episodes from the 1860s were reprinted in his *Half-Holiday* of the 1880s, few new strips were drawn about him. Gradually, recurring characters were introduced into the Harmsworth comics, one of the earliest being Jack B. Yeats's burlesque of Conan Doyle's Sherlock Holmes, 'The Adventures of Chubb-Lock Homes' in *Comic Cuts* (18 November 1893). The most famous of all the early comic heroes was the team of tramps, 'Weary Willie and Tired Tim', created by Tom Browne for the front page of *Illustrated Chips* (16 May 1896). Longest lived of all the comic originals, they remained on page one until the final issue of *Chips* on 12 September 1953.

Comic Artists

The art of the British comic is peculiarly its own. It was founded by Tom Browne, a Nottingham cartoonist, whose clean and simple linework, inspired by the joke drawings of Phil May, was both amusing and suitable to the cheap ink and paper used in early comics. The Browne tradition, a long way from the over-etched exaggerations of Ally Sloper, can be traced right through British comics to the present, via those who emulated him and who were in turn emulated: Percy Cocking, Roy Wilson, Hugh McNeill, Robert Nixon.

Coloured Comics

The first comics were printed in black on white paper, coloured paper soon being introduced as a means of identifying one comic from another: *Chips* was the first, becoming famous for its pink paper. Colour printing came late to British magazines, and the first comic issued in colour was the special autumn number of *Comic Cuts* (12 August 1896). It was a Harmsworth enterprise, designed in the shadow of American colour supplements, and caused the price of that week's issue to be doubled from a ha'penny to a penny. Coloured special editions continued spasmodically until Trapps Holmes issued *The Coloured Comic* (No 1: 21 May 1898), the first regular weekly comic to be printed in full (four) colours. It was not a great success, and was forced to drop colour printing from No 72, excusing the continuation of the title by printing on coloured paper. Harmsworth returned to the challenge six years later with *Puck* (No 1: 30 July 1904), a twelve-page tabloid weekly with four pages in colour. Coloured comics, being more expensive to print, at first cost one penny to the 'black' comics' one halfpenny, and by the thirties cost twopence to the 'black' comics' one penny. (Halfpenny and penny comics were known in the trade as 'black comics'.) All comics were printed letterpress until *Mickey Mouse Weekly* (No 1: 8 February 1936) suddenly startled the world by being the first comic to be printed in photogravure with full colour.

Comic Specials

Special editions of comics have been issued from the earliest time, usually at Christmas. Ally Sloper was the first, as usual, with his *Ally Sloper's Christmas Holidays*, an unnumbered double number that was issued annually separately from the weekly comic, from December 1884. Even before the existence of the *Half-Holiday*, in the days of *Judy*, there was an annual *Ally Sloper's Comic Kalendar* (No 1: December 1875) followed by *Ally Sloper's Summer Number* (No 1: July 1880). Christmas numbers have always had a great appeal to collectors of magazines, journals and newspapers, and Christmas numbers of comics are no exception. They are highly collectable and usually cost more than regular editions. Of equal interest are other special editions – holiday numbers, Whitsun and Easter numbers, birthday numbers, 'Number' numbers (ie Nos 100, 500, 1000, etc) – and those commemorating notable events: jubilees, coronations, royal weddings and victories.

Comic Supplements

The American idea of a comic section as a supplement to the Sunday newspaper was first tried in Britain, in a small way, when *Home Chat*, a women's weekly published by Harmsworth, added a four-page pull-out supplement for young children entitled *The Playbox* (29 October 1898). It was very popular and ran to World War II. Then came *The World and His Wife*, a sumptuous shilling magazine for the family, which introduced *The Monthly Playbox* (No 1: 1 November 1904) as a full-colour supplement. It featured 'Mrs Hippo's Kindergarten', the strip that introduced Tiger Tim. Tim went on to become front-page hero of *The Rainbow* (1914) and continues to appear to this day in *Jack and Jill*. The first comic supplement in a British newspaper was in *The Weekly Budget* for 16 October 1910; it was an American Sunday section specially printed and shipped over. The first newspaper comic supplement originating in Britain was *The Oojah Sketch* (No 1: 8 October 1921) featuring the *Daily Sketch*'s strip character, 'Uncle Oojah'. The boom in children's comic supplements came in the thirties when the *Daily Mail* introduced their 'Teddy Tail' comic (No 1: 8 April 1933), followed by the *Daily Express*, the *Sunday Dispatch*, and the longest running of them all, the *Sunday Post* whose *Fun Section* (No 1: 8 March 1936) is still with us. Lately the first successful comic section on American lines, the sixteen-page *Cartoons*, has been introduced into the *Mail on Sunday* (No 1: 17 October 1982).

Giveaway Comics

Closely related to newspaper comic supplements are the giveaway comics. These come without charge and fall into two categories: the promotion of a product, or of an idea. The earliest advertising comic was *The Ovaltiney's Own Comic* (No 1: 26 October 1935), which was given away each week as a supplement to the comics published in Bath by Target Publications. More offbeat and elusive are the *Merry Miniatures*, a series of small comic-strip booklets given away with every penny or more spent in certain prewar dairies and sweetshops. Recent advertising giveaways included in this catalogue are comic-strip bubblegum wrappers, small comics inserted into cereal packets, and various toy and film promotions. The second category of giveaway comic includes comics designed to promote good health, such as the *Superman* series aimed to discourage children from smoking.

The Golden Age: the Thirties

The period 1930 to 1939 was truly a golden age of British comics. The style of comic drawing, founded in the eighteen-nineties, had standardized in the nineteen-hundreds, and the parallel school of 'Nursery Comics', as those designed for younger readers were classified, developed in the teens. The twenties were a period of development, coming out of the paper shortages of World War I and smoothing out the roughness that still remained in the penny comics as they slowly grew out of their working-class, street-corner readership. By 1930 comics were, without exception, for children, and were being created by artists, writers and editors whose sole aim was to provide quality entertainment for youngsters that would be acceptable to parents and teachers. The nursery market was particularly catered for with care, and such papers as *Tiny Tots* and *Chicks Own* for the little ones, followed by *Rainbow*, *Sunbeam* and *Playbox* for the next group, followed by *My Favourite*, *Crackers* and *Sparkler* for the juniors, are gems of the comic-makers' art. The ultimate comic in this group was *Happy Days* (No 1: 8 October 1938), a photogravure colour comic of superb art and design: the climax to a true golden age.

The late thirties also saw the birth of *Dandy* (No 1: 4 December 1937), *Beano* (No 1: 30 July 1938) and *Magic* (No 1: 22 July 1939), three formula-breaking comics published by D. C. Thomson of Dundee. Their break from the long tradition of the Amalgamated Press ushered in new styles of comic drawing, and influenced AP into publishing their own 'new look' comics, *Radio Fun* (No 1: 15 October 1938) and *Knockout* (No 1: 4 March 1939).

The Dark Age: the Forties

The war years were bad ones for comics. Paper shortages, acute after the Nazi defeat of Norway, killed off many of the famous prewar titles: *Puck*, *Tiger Tim's Weekly*, *Joker*, *Jester*, one by one they vanished from the newsagents, often without even an editorial farewell. Even Thomson lost *Magic*. However, while the law now prevented the launching of new titles on a regular basis, it did permit the publication of unconnected one-shots. The first to take advantage of this was Philipp Marx, a refugee, who issued *The New Comics*, in two undated, unnumbered editions. These were such a sell-out among comic-starved children that he was soon issuing a new title almost every week. Many other new, small publishing companies followed suit, sometimes issuing numbered comics, more often issuing strings of titles with connecting prefixes: Martin and Reid with their *Jolly* series, and later (for these restrictions continued long after VE day) Paget Publications and their *Paget* prefix titles. During this period comics were printed on any kind of available paper, including stiff beige cardboard and even silver paper. The author, as a youth and tyro cartoonist, bought and saved each of these comics, and in the course of research discovered that almost none of them was deposited for copyright with the British Museum. Consequently, this catalogue with its illustrations provides the only published pictorial record of this comic phenomenon.

Comicbooks: American and British

The American comicbook developed during the early 1930s as a handy-sized booklet of sixty-four pages plus covers, reprinting in reduced size strips from the Sunday supplements. Originally giveaways, these books began to be sold on newsstands at ten cents and soon became original productions in their own right. These were imported into Britain as ballast and sold in Woolworths and street markets at twopence a copy. Once World War II started, the importation of comicbooks ceased. A distributor who had handled them, Gerald G. Swan, was inspired to produce his own British version of the American comicbook, to fill the obvious gap in the market, and issued *New Funnies* (No 1: February 1940). Its immediate success led to a string of similar comicbooks from Swan, and as the paper shortage brought other new publishers into the field (see above) the smaller comicbook format became standardized for the 'pirate comics', as they were termed by the Amalgamated Press. T. V. Boardman, who had also imported American comics, began to reprint some titles in abridged British editions (*Smash Comics*, etc), and another wholesaler, L. Miller and Son, made a reprint arrangement with the New York publisher, Fawcett (*Captain Marvel*, etc). Other publishers produced original comicbooks but pretended they were American by labelling them '10 Cents': Cartoon Art Productions with their *Super Duper Comics* (No 1: 1946). The 1950s were the boom years for British original comicbooks. Following the banning of dollar imports by the Labour Government, and coupled with the secondary banning of comic imports following the 'Horror Comics' scare, Miller and other publishers of American reprints were virtually forced into publishing natively created comicbooks. The most successful of these was *Marvelman*, which was a British conversion from Fawcett's *Captain Marvel*. British comicbooks died away in the 1960s after reprinting of American comicbooks was resumed. This, too, has now disappeared, save for the American Marvel comics, which have their own UK publication arm.

The Silver Age: the Fifties

As Britain emerged from the austerity age into the Elizabethan Age, comics once again took flight. *Eagle* (No 1: 14 April 1950) appeared with all the sensational effect of *Mickey Mouse Weekly* in the thirties. It was printed on good-quality paper and the excellent artwork was in full-colour photogravure. Its front page hero, 'Dan Dare' by Frank Hampson, became the idol of every space-minded boy. Many other fine new comics followed in *Eagle*'s wake, including *Girl* (No 1: 2 November 1951). A new trend was born, in which comics, which had always been designed for both sexes, were now being designed for separate ones: boys *or* girls.

Library Comics

'Libraries', the trade term for pocket-sized comicbooks, dates back to the Victorian era when old story-paper serials were reprinted in paperback format. The Amalgamated Press issued many such story libraries, but only the *Sexton Blake Library* survived the war. As the printing equipment for these paperbacks still existed, they were used to produce the first library comicbook, *Cowboy Comics* (No 1: April 1950), as an experiment. *Thriller Comics* followed (No 1: November 1951), and soon as many picture libraries were being issued as story libraries were in prewar days.

The Television Age: the Sixties

Comics have always reflected the popular entertainment media: *Film Fun* (No 1: 17 January 1920), *Radio Fun* (No 1: 15 October 1938), and eventually *T.V. Comic* (No 1: 9 November 1951). By the sixties televison had a great grip on children, who were the main market for comics, and comics fought back by concentrating on television characters and themes. *Express Weekly* became *T.V. Express* from 23 April 1960, and the Gerry Anderson science-fiction puppet series had whole comics built around them: *T.V. Century 21* (No 1: 23 January 1965), *Lady Penelope* (No 1: 22 January 1966) and *Joe 90* (No 1: 18 January 1969).

Reprint Comics

Newspaper and magazine strips have been reprinted in book format since the beginning. The first such comicbook was *Ally Sloper: A Moral Lesson* issued by *Judy* magazine in November 1873. The first regular newspaper strip cartoonist was W. K. Haselden, whose annual selections were issued as *Daily Mirror Reflections* from 1908. J. F. Horrabin's *Dot and Carrie* (1923) and *Japhet Book* (1924) followed, with Brian White's *Nipper Annual* from 1934. After the war came other booklets reprinting 'Jane', 'Garth', and a few popular American strips like 'Rip Kirby'.

Underground Comics

Underground or alternative 'comix' originated in the USA as part of a protest movement of young people against the status quo. A few were reprinted in Britain, and several attempts have been made to launch native underground comix. The first was the tabloid *Cyclops* (No 1: July 1970), followed by *Nasty Tales* (No 1: April 1971) in regular comicbook format. Currently only *Knockabout Comics* (No 1: 1981) is managing to survive, thanks mainly to the professional undergrounder, Hunt Emerson.

Current Comics

While weekly titles proliferate in the British newsagents' racks, the comics scene is by no means as strong as it was in the booming fifties. Circulations have shrunk from the quarter- and half-million mark to the 10,000, although old favourites like *Beano* can still top 400,000 a week. Prices of comics have risen from the prewar penny and twopence to an average of twenty pence a copy (four shillings in old money), which may have something to do with their shrinking circulations.

Errors and Omissions

Everything possible has been done to make this catalogue complete, but a number of dates and runs are at the moment untraceable. If any reader or collector can supply any missing item of information, the compiler would be grateful to receive it at the Association of Comics Enthusiasts, 80 Silverdale, Sydenham, London SE26 4SJ.

Collecting Comics

One is tempted to complete the phrase, 'For Fun and Profit', for certainly both are to be had from the hobby of collecting comics. There are few other areas of collecting where a purchase of a penny or two can increase in value a thousand per cent and more in a few years. But few comic collectors are in the hobby for gain; they collect comics for fun and would not part with a favourite issue or a rare number one for twice the top prices listed in this catalogue. There is something special and quite personal about the look and even feel of a favourite comic, which may mean more to just one ex-reader than all the money in the mint. A comic is not merely a swatch of folded paper printed with pictures: it sums up the age in which it was produced, it summons up the very moment in which it was first read. Thus a childhood lost forever comes rushing back as a forgotten comic is glimpsed, taken up, and relished once again.

Yes, pure nostalgia is the prime reason comics are collected. For while today, more than ever, the art of the comic is being appreciated for the comedy and adventure it colourfully depicts, those who collect comics from an artistic or historic perspective are thoroughly outnumbered by the happy nostalgics. And it is for this reason that fashions in comic collecting wax and wane. In the 1930s, when story-paper collecting was the prime vogue, those few specialists who sought out old comics wanted the *Ally Sloper* of their youth, the *Comic Cuts* and *Funny Wonders* they had bought with their Saturday ha'penny. In the 1940s the collecting craze moved into the twenties, when coloured comics like *Puck* were at their peak. In the fifties it was the thirties that were all the rage, the great Golden Age of British Comics when *Mickey Mouse Weekly* was born, and Dundee hatched the *Dandy*. Grown men of the sixties had little to look back to in the wartorn forties, but the Gerald G. Swan comicbooks began to be collected. In the 1970s it was *Eagle* No 1 that became the great nugget to be mined, and at the other end of the social scale, the L. Miller comicbooks. Both shared the theme of science-fiction, which by the 1980s has come to dominate comic collecting, at least with the younger element.

Thus it can be seen that the comics read as a child, particularly between the ages of nine to twelve or thirteen, and duly discarded as 'childish', are the comics sought once again when the otherwise mature person is suddenly bitten by the collecting bug around the age of thirty. This is, for some reason, a predominantly male urge. A psychiatrist could no doubt explain why adult ladies seldom seem to experience the need to recapture the delights of their lost girlhood in this enjoyable way. But for the present we must accept that comic collecting is a masculine hobby, as a visit to any comic mart or convention will bear witness, and indeed the membership of the Association of Comics Enthusiasts also proves. For every fifty male members there is but one female.

First Editions

First editions of novels and books are the most sought-after items to any book collector, and so it is with comics. The first issue of any comic is an automatic collector's item, and within weeks will become worth more than the original purchase price. Any collector new to comics is advised to watch the newsagents' racks and snap up a new number one as soon as it appears. First issues of magazines of any kind have long been collected, so it is likely that from time to time early number ones come on the market, via local second-hand book dealers or auctions. Children also, of course,

11

eagerly buy the first issue of a new comic without thinking of it as a 'collector's item', and these too will find their way into the marketplace after a while.

Special Editions

Christmas numbers, with their snow-laden lettering and highly decorative borders and design, have long been favourites with the magazine-collecting fraternity, and so they are with comic collectors. Bursting at the seams with seasonal, old-fashioned fun, Christmas numbers always seem to bring out the best in artists and editors. They have existed almost as long as comics themselves, for both the early *Ally Sloper's Half-Holiday* and *Funny Folks* issued Christmas numbers in their first years of publication. Christmas numbers are still an important feature of comic publishing and, although some of the more grown-up comics dealing with adventure and war do little more than wish their readers a 'Merry Christmas', the younger comics are almost as snow-bedecked as their prewar predecessors. So, as with number ones, the advice to collectors is to buy all the Christmas numbers as they come out.

Other special editions are birthday numbers, which like Christmas often come every year in a comic's lifetime. These were not so common in prewar days, *Mickey Mouse Weekly* being the first to publish an annual anniversary number. Postwar, *Eagle* and *Girl* had birthday numbers, and although few special features are introduced they make excellent items for a collection not based on runs.

Commemorative issues of comics are also instant collector's items. These are editions marking some public event, such as a royal occasion: the jubilee of 1935, the coronation of 1936, victory (World War II), and of course the coronation and jubilee of Queen Elizabeth II. There were even some comics which saluted the wedding of the Prince and Princess of Wales, which will certainly become much sought after in years to come. Here again the advice is to keep a close eye on your local newsagent.

Other special editions which were particularly popular before the war are Boat Race numbers, and those marking holidays: Whitsun, Easter, summer, bank holiday, New Year. Much missed today are the old time fireworks numbers, often a riot of colour. Other issues involving the publishing history of the comics themselves are numbers celebrating 100, 200, 500, and even in a few cases, 1000, 2000 and 3000 editions. Rather sad, but always worth collecting are final issues. These are highly elusive, except where they have been bought by regular readers of the title as published. The trick to collecting current last numbers is to look for the headline: 'Grand News Inside, Chums!' The grand news is often that next week there will be no issue of comic A, because it is combining with comic B! And, of course, the newly combined comic A and B also becomes a comic worth collecting!

Runs and Bound Volumes

Collecting a complete run of a favourite comic can be almost a lifetime hobby. Usually collectors confine themselves to a single favourite of the past, such as *Eagle* or *Mickey Mouse Weekly*, and it is surprising how frequently long runs if not complete sets of these popular comics come on to the market. The high quality, both of editorial and artwork, and of paper and printing, explains why young readers were often reluctant to throw these comics away, and tended to collect them in cupboards and later move them into attics. It can be great fun searching dealers and marts for elusive numbers required to complete a year or a run, and the joy of actually finishing a set is only lessened by the gap in life now that the collection has been completed. Such collectors often move on to comics which they may not have read as a child, but which were published at the same period, or which are somehow similar to their favourite. *Eagle* collectors often move on to *Express Weekly*, for instance.

Bound volumes have a special appeal. While most collectors prefer each comic to be a single object in its own right, thus retaining much of the appeal it had when first read, there are few who can actually resist the lure of a bound volume. In the early days of comic publishing bound volumes could be obtained from the publishers each year, or were often bound up by local binders for collectors. The Victorians were great ones for binding their magazines in this way and many of these find their way into the antiquarian bookshop trade. Unfortunately comics tended to be tabloid and so made rather unwieldly and hefty books when fifty-two were stitched together. Bound volumes were also produced by publishers for their own reference and editorial purposes. Many of those from the Harmsworth/Amalgamated Press/Newnes/

Henderson/Odhams conglomerate came on to the market when their present owners, IPC, cleared their shelves and sent them to auction. Although many were bought by collectors, these slim red half-year volumes still appear through dealers, and are certainly a good buy. They are especially good, as not only does the binding preserve the comics far better than if they were loose copies, they are also cheaper than if you were to buy the twenty-six copies singly. This is because the price if scaled up precisely would often be higher than a collector would want to pay at one time, and also because many of the comics available in volume form are of less collectable titles: *Jingles*, *Tiny Tots*, *Playbox*, etc. A word of warning: examine a bound volume carefully before buying. Many of them were used editorially and have had strips and even whole pages cut out.

Specialized Collections

Certain collectors, those who are not merely indulging their personal nostalgia, follow a theme. This may be the comics themselves, in other words the history and development of the comic in its own right. To such collectors a comic of any period or title is of interest, unless they wish to concentrate on a period of special interest to themselves, such as the thirties, or World War II. Others favour a more specific theme, such as cinema (*Film Fun* and *Kinema Comic*), television (*T.V. Comic*, *T.V. Heroes*) or even a particular theme within television, such as the popular Gerry Anderson puppet series (*T.V. Century 21*, *Joe 90*) or the long-running serial 'Dr Who', which has appeared in several comics. Others collect a particular artist, such as the prolific Roy Wilson who drew so many fine front pages in the old comics, or the equally prolific Dudley D. Watkins, for many years the mainstay of the *Dandy* and *Beano*. With the development of the adventure strip, and particularly the science-fiction variety, artists such as Frank Hampson and Frank Bellamy are much sought after, and already the younger artists working on *2000 AD*, such as Dave Gibbons and Mike McMahon, have become collectable. Generally, however, it is only the modern comic artists who are collected, thanks mainly to the changing attitudes of many publishers who no longer insist on artistic anonymity.

Collecting Comicbooks

The 'golden age', if one can dare call such a low-quality era golden, of British comicbooks covered the twenty years from 1940 to 1960 when their more exciting models, American comicbooks, were generally unavailable. Restrictions on their import, for economic or censorship reasons, left a gap in the comic market which enterprising printers and publishers rushed to fill. From Gerald G. Swan's first *New Funnies* (February 1940) through to the many monthly, and even weekly, titles of L. Miller and Son, British comicbooks based on the American format were issued in their thousands. Paper restrictions prevented wide distribution, and no complete runs of all the Swan and Miller comicbooks are known. (Like many of these minor publishers, they failed to deposit copies at the British Museum.) Swan comicbooks are very popular with collectors who bought them as young readers, as are the Miller science-fiction and super-hero titles (*Marvelman*, etc). There is less interest in the western titles (*Rocky Mountain King*, etc) but this may grow. Along with these native productions are the many, many reprints of American comicbooks. These are listed in this catalogue, although a purist would not consider them as 'British' comics. However, they are British editions, and often have locally drawn covers and some editorial content. Favourites among collectors are those earlier Miller editions printed in two-tone photogravure, an extremely attractive colour process which is now extinct. Number one collectors are warned to check carefully in the catalogue, as in many cases Miller comics had no 'No. 1' as such, often beginning with 'No. 50'!

Comic Curiosities

The paper restrictions of World War II and its aftermath led to the production of many one-shot (single issue) comics, as new series titles were illegal. The paper shortage also meant that all kinds, shapes and sizes of comics appeared, ranging from pocket-sized folders to comics printed on brown cardboard and silver paper. These curiosities of the comic world are always worth collecting.

Comic Supplements

The newspaper-circulation wars of the 1930s led to a rash of well-produced comic supplements being issued in the *Daily Mail, Daily Express* and a number of provincial papers. Some of these had extremely long runs, and that of the *Bristol Evening World* became the most frequently published comic of all, with a daily edition! Curiously, these supplements seldom come on to the market, despite their enormous circulation. Even the famous *Sunday Post Fun Section*, which has been running ever since 1936, is seldom found. There is an enormous profit to be made by someone who finds a run of these supplements in a Bristol (or Dundee) attic. Incidentally it is interesting to note that these newspaper comics, while drawing their inspiration from the American supplements, modelled themselves on British comics entirely, using many of the regular comic artists. Lately we have seen the *Mail on Sunday* comic supplement, which is very much in the Yankee manner, and which is certain to become a sought-for series in the future, especially as several issues were printed but not distributed due to industrial action.

Comic Spin-offs

Comic characters have been merchandized since the very beginning: Ally Sloper was not only the first comic-strip hero, he was the first to be merchandized. Although spin-offs have no place in this catalogue, they are fun to find and fascinating to collect, ranging as they do from Sloper clay pipes to Dan Dare playing cards and Riders of the Range braces! The temptation to add artifacts to a comic collection is great, especially as they are so uncatalogued and unknown.

Comic artwork is perhaps the most obvious spin-off from comic collecting itself. There is not a lot of it on the market, mainly because publishers traditionally retain original artwork and eventually destroy it. However, some pages and newspaper strips do turn up from time to time via dealers or through the effects of a deceased artist, and these are certainly worth acquiring. One cannot be choosy about artists or characters with so little original art available, but when one chances across a favourite artist or character, the pleasure of owning and framing such a piece is tremendous. Some comic artwork can be purchased at incredibly low prices. For instance, artwork from Miller and Swan comics was unloaded in quantity when the companies closed down and stockrooms were cleared. Already prices have risen from 50 pence a sheet to £5. On a higher plane, IPC unloaded hundreds of 'Dan Dare' colour originals, which were sold by dealers for around £10 a sheet. These can now fetch £50 and more. Newspaper-strip originals are easier to acquire, although 'classic' strips such as 'Jane', the original Dowling 'Garth', Watt's 'Pop' and Monk's 'Buck Ryan' are virtually gold dust. No copies are known as the publishers destroyed the old strips to make room for the new.

Rare Comics

The rarest comics are not necessarily the highest priced. This is because only a few collectors collect from a historic or completionist viewpoint. Thus there is no 'penny black' of the comics world as such. Age does not automatically mean higher value in comics. No 1 of *Beano* would fetch far more at auction than No 1 of *Funny Folks*, considered the first comic. Oddly, No 1 of *Dandy*, so rare that there is no known copy in private hands, would be likely to fetch considerably less than No 1 of *Beano*, several of which exist among collectors. Extremely rare are some of the prewar giveaway comics, such as *Lilley and Skinner's Kiddies Comic*, which was given away with each purchase of shoes from that company. Only one odd copy is known among collectors – not a No 1. Even so, it is unlikely that a copy of the comic would fetch a high price at auction, unless two completionist collectors were to bid against one another.

There are a few comics whose existence is only known by copies on deposit at the British Museum. These include *Frolix* and the several reprint titles issued by Ransom in the twenties. Even rarer are comics not deposited at the museum and known only by mention in trade publications, such as *The Bouncer Comic*, which apparently ceased publication on 14 November 1931, and *Comic Revue*, issued in the week of 13 September 1941. Only one copy of No 1 of *Sparks* for 2 May 1896 is known, a comic unlisted by the British Museum or any contemporary trade publication. But rare as these titles are, their values are not automatically high, as with such comparable hobbies as stamp collecting.

Collectability

All comics are, of course, collectable to someone. But it is one of the curiosities of comic collecting that quality seldom equates with collectability. Probably the finest British comics are those published for the nursery market, from the very young *Tiny Tots* and *Chicks Own* to *The Rainbow* and up to the present day *Jack and Jill*. Yet these comics, attractive and even beautiful as many of them are, fail to interest collectors. Even the nostalgia angle fails to work its magic here, for almost every comic collector must have cut his comic teeth on these popular titles. We probably need to call in our psychiatrist once again to explain why such excellent comics should be so shunned, but ignored they are, and even bound volumes of mint copies can be had from dealers for very little.

The other great area of neglect is that of the girls' comic. As we have noted above, ladies do not seem to have the same nostalgic urge as men, and in consequence old copies of *Mandy* and *Judy* and even the classic *Girl* (companion to *Eagle*) can be found for a few pence. More expensive are those comics for older girls dealing with once-current pop stars.

Buying and Selling Old Comics

Finding old comics is not as easy as it once was, nor is buying them as cheap. Gone are the days when every district had a second-hand bookshop with its pile of tattered old comics for sale at half the cover price; or almost gone, for there are still plenty of Oxfam shops, scout sales and village jumbles where piles of comics can go for a few pence. Incredible collectors' finds can still be made at such venues: recently a No 1 *Beano*, including the original free gift (the only copy of both known in the world), was bought by a boy for a few pence!

Dealers in old comics are fairly plentiful, and they are usually collectors who have turned their former hobby into a profitable part-time business. You will find many advertising in *Exchange and Mart* under the special heading of 'Comics' (a true sign of the times: this subheading recently replaced the former, 'Old Boys' Books'!). Dealers also advertise in several fan publications, or 'fanzines', although these are more likely to be oriented towards American comics. The same must be said of the dealers who rent tables at the several comic marts and 'comicons', or comics conventions, that are held in London and other major cities thoughout the year.

Selling old collections can be a problem, for while many collectors might be interested, few will actually want to buy a lot of old comics at any one time. Equally, if the value of an old comic is £1, it does not follow that a run of 50 or 100 comics will be worth £50 or £100. Buying comics in runs, or bulk, is always much cheaper than buying by the single copy. Again, if the comic is valued at £1, this is the price at which you will probably find a dealer offering it. It stands to reason, therefore, that a dealer is not going to buy the comic from you for £1 and then sell it for £1. A dealer is in business to make a profit. Therefore you can expect a dealer to offer you fifty per cent, perhaps more, perhaps less, of the value of your comic. However, as dealers are likely to be the only people who will buy your large collection or long run at a fell swoop, then selling to a dealer may be worth your while. But if you have only a small selection to dispose of, or perhaps to offer as exchanges for comics you require for your collection, then a small advertisement in *Exchange and Mart*, or one of the fanzines, is your best bet. Naturally, we recommend the advertisement columns of *Comic Cuts*, the publication of the Association of Comics Enthusiasts, details of which will be found at the end of the catalogue.

Condition of Comics

The ideal condition of an old comic is 'mint', which means as newly bought on the day of publication. American comic collectors and dealers have instituted a complex system of grading condition, with prices lessening a little with each degrading. One or two dealers in old British comics have similar systems, but these are mostly those whose business is conducted through the mails, and who wish to cover their liabilities with passing off poor-condition and tape-repaired comics. It is better to visit comic marts and shops where the comics can be examined before purchase. As explained elsewhere, this catalogue does not set out to be a graded price list, partly because old British comics are usually to be found in only two conditions: good (having been read by the owner and filed away) and not so good (having been read, swapped and generally handled around). Most comic collectors are so keen on their hobby that they will accept almost any condition of a comic if it is one they urgently need. Equally, all dealers will reduce prices on torn, tatty, and repaired comics, just as they will probably increase prices on pristine comics.

Caring for your Collection

Storage is one of the biggest problems for a comic collector, particularly if the collection is a large one. For a small, specialized collection (say of first editions), albums with transparent pockets can be obtained from art shops, the kind used by artists as display books. But these are expensive and hold perhaps just twenty-four or thirty-two comics. Similar ring-type binders with plastic sleeves can be used for comicbook collections, but again the costs soon mount up with a large collection. Runs can, of course, be bound by a local bookbinder, but the individual quality of each comic becomes lost. There are cardboard boxes which can be bought or taken away from a local supermarket, and box files of cardboard or rigid plastic. These stack nicely on shelves but are not normally to be found to fit the larger, older tabloid comics like *Eagle*. And no comic collector would willingly fold in half a previously unfolded comic! Comics are better laid flat than stood on end, particularly when unbound, but are liable to take up a lot of shelf room, as well as look untidy.

As to preservation, there are two schools of thought here. Some collectors believe in keeping the comic exactly 'as found', so if a second-hand comic comes their way, of any age, they carefully keep it exactly as it is. Others prefer to doctor the comic up as much as possible in order to restore it towards its original appearance. This means sellotape repairs to all tears, and trimming rough edges with a guillotine. Collectors have shied away from sellotape in the past because of the damage it does as it ages. However, today most tape manufacturers put out a special document-repairing tape guaranteed not to discolour or otherwise spoil the original. Comics which have been repaired with standard sellotape in the past can prove a great problem as the years go by, as the tape will eventually cause more damage than that which it originally repaired. Careful restoration will extend the life of an old comic, especially one already prone to tearing. Comics should also be stored away from sunlight. Modern comics are particularly prone to fading and yellowing, as today's paper is of poorer quality than that used prewar and in the fifties.

EARLY COLOURED COMICS

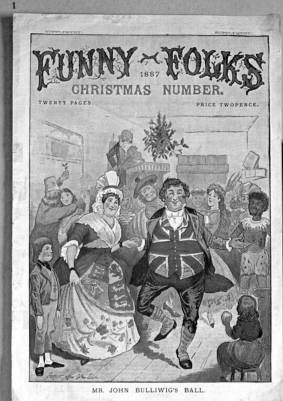

1 *Funny Folks Christmas Number*: December 1887 (Henderson)

2 *Comic Cuts Diamond Jubilee Number*: June 1897 (Harmsworth)

3 *Halfpenny Comic Guy Fawkes Number*: 5 November 1898 (Newnes)

4 *Big Budget Holiday Number*: 11 April 1903 (Pearson)

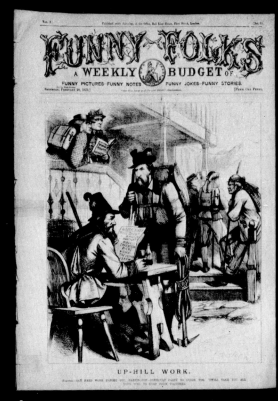

5

6

7

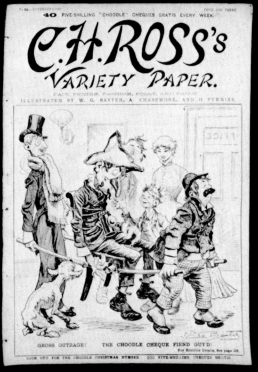

8

5   *Funny Folks* No. 11: 20 February 1875 (Henderson)

6   *Ally Sloper's Half-Holiday* No. 1: 3 May 1884 (Sinkins)

7   *'Arry's Budget* No. 1: 26 June 1886 (Rayner)

8   *C. H. Ross's Variety Paper* No. 15: 2 November 1887 (Ross)

9

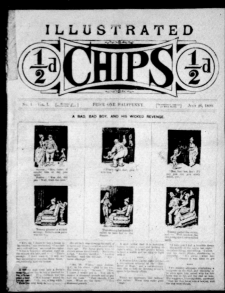

10

11

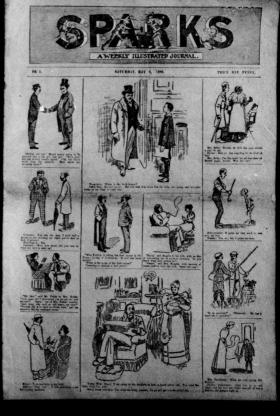

12

9 *Comic Cuts* No. 1: 17 May 1890 (Harmsworth)

10 *Illustrated Chips* No. 1: 26 July 1890 (Harmsworth)

11 *Funny Wonder* No. 1 New Series: 4 February 1893 (Harmsworth)

12 *Sparks* No. 1: 2 May 1896 (publisher unknown)

13

13 *Coloured Comic* No. 38 : 4 February 1899 (Trapps
Holmes)

14 *Puck* No. 1 : 30 July 1904 (Amalgamated Press)

15

15 *Lot-O'-Fun* No. 1 : 17 March 1906 (Henderson)

16 *Comic Life* No. 588 : 25 September 1909 : first coloured
issue (Henderson)

COLOURED COMICS: NUMBER ONES

17

17 *Chuckles* No. 1: 10 January 1914 (Amalgamated Press)
18 *Jungle Jinks* No. 1: 8 December 1923 (Amalgamated Press)

18

19
19 *Rainbow* No. 1: 14 February 1914 (Amalgamated Press)
20 *Tiger Tim's Weekly* No. 1 New Series: 19 November 1921 (Amalgamated Press)

20

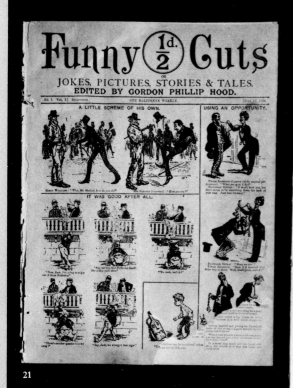

21

22

23

24

21 *Funny Cuts* No. 1: 17 July 1890 (Trapps Holmes)

22 *World's Comic Whitsun Number*: 24 May 1893 (Trapps Holmes)

23 *Best Budget* final issue: No. 12: 31 May 1902 (Trapps Holmes)

24 *Picture Fun* No. 168: 30 April 1912 (Trapps Holmes)

25

26

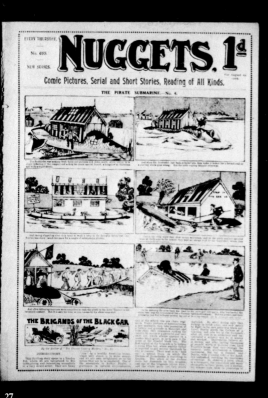

27

28

25 *Champion Comic* Vol 3 No. 10: 9 March 1895 (Joker)

26 *Comic Bits* No..6: 26 March 1898 (Unity)

27 *Nuggets New Series* No. 695: 19 August 1905 (Henderson)

28 *Sparks* No. 17: 11 July 1914 (Henderson)

29

29 *Chicks Own* No. 1: 25 September 1920 (Amalgamated Press)
30 *Sunday Fairy* No. 1: 10 May 1919 (Amalgamated Press)

30

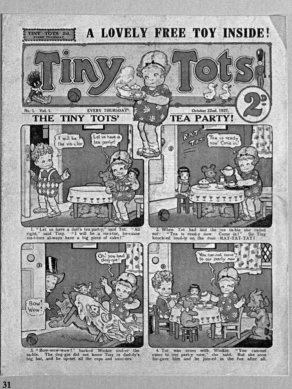

31

31 *Tiny Tots* No. 1: 22 October 1927 (Amalgamated Press)
32 *Playbox* No. 1: 14 February 1925 (Amalgamated Press)

32

33 *Sparks* No. 278: 10 May 1919 (Henderson)

34 *Little Sparks* New Series No. 22: 16 October 1920
(Amalgamated Press)

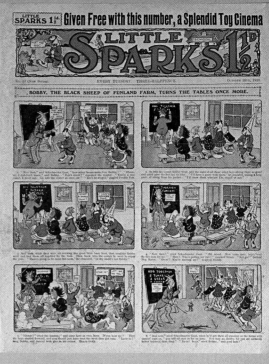

35 *Merry Moments* No. 1: 12 April 1919 (Newnes)

36 *My Favourite* No. 1: 28 January 1928 (Amalgamated
Press)

36

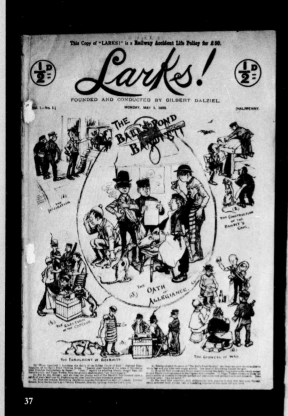

37

38

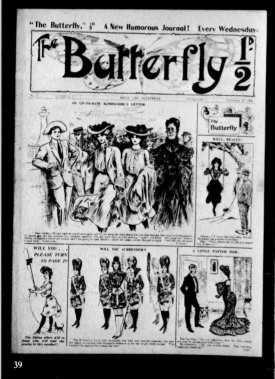

39

40

37 *Larks!* No. 1: 1 May 1893 (Dalziel)

38 *Larks!* New Series No. 1: 7 June 1902 (Trapps Holmes)

39 *Butterfly* No. 1: 17 September 1904 (Amalgamated Press)

40 *Butterfly & Firefly* New Series No. 1: 7 April 1917 (Amalgamated Press)

THE THOMSON INFLUENCE

51

52

53

54
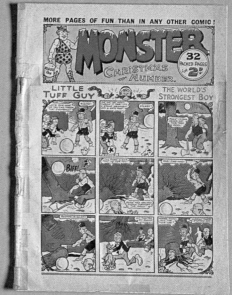

55

56

51 *Radio Fun* No. 1: 15 October 1938 (Amalgamated Press)

52 *Knockout Comic* No. 1: 4 March, 1939 (Amalgamated Press)

53 *Crackers Christmas Number*: No. 604: 28 December 1940 (Amalgamated Press)

54 *Monster Christmas Number*: No. 2: November 1939 (Pearson)

55 *Whizzer & Chips* No. 1: 18 October 1969 (IPC)

56 *Cor!!* No. 1: 6 June 1970 (IPC)

57   *Joker* Vol. 4 No. 3: 28 January 1893 (Joker)

58   *Comic Home Journal* No. 97: 13 March 1897
(Harmsworth)

59   *My Funnybone* No. 31: 1 April 1912 (Belvedere)

60   *Merry & Bright* No. 67: 27 January 1912

62

61

64

63

61 *Big Comic* No. 3: 31 January 1914 (Henderson)

62 *Monster Comic* No. 2: 30 September 1922 (United)

63 *Golden Penny Comic* No. 84: 17 May 1924 (Fleetway Press)

64 *Joker* No. 26: 28 April 1928 (Fleetway Press)

65

65 *Sparkler* No. 1: 20 October 1934 (Amalgamated Press)
66 *Okay Comics Weekly* No. 1: 16 October 1937
(Boardman)

66

67

67 *Mickey Mouse Weekly* No. 1: 8 February 1936
(Odhams/Willbank)
68 *Happy Days* No. 1: 8 October 1938 (Amalgamated
Press)

68

69 *Eagle* No. 1: 14 April 1950 (Hulton)
70 *Rocket* No. 1: 21 April 1956 (News of the World)

69

71

78

79

80

79 *Sports Fun* No. 1: 11 February 1922 (Amalgamated Press)
80 *Film Picture Stories*: No. 11: 6 October 1934 (Amalgamated Press)

81

81 *Topper* No. 1 : 7 February 1953 (D. C. Thomson)
82 *Beezer* No. 1 : 21 January 1956 (D. C. Thomson)

83

83 *Buzz* No. 1 : 20 January 1973 (D. C. Thomson)
84 *Buster* No. 1 : 28 May 1960 (Fleetway)

84

85 *Tarzan* No. 1: 15 September 1951 (Westworld)

86 *Zip* No. 1: 4 January 1958 (Odhams)

87/88 *Harold Hare's Own Paper* No. 1: 14 November 1959 (Fleetway)

89/90 *Jag* No. 1: 4 May 1968 (Fleetway)

91 *Sparkler* No. 1: 10 September 1931 (Provincial)

92 *Merry Midget* No. 1: 12 September 1931 (Provincial)

93 *Rattler* No. 1: 19 August 1933 (Target)

94 *Dazzler* No. 1: 19 August 1933 (Target)

95

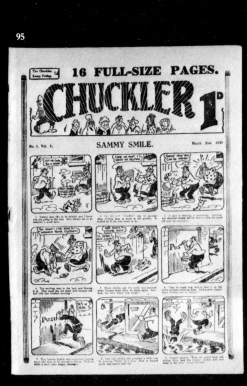

96

97

98

95   *Chuckler* No. 1: 31 March 1934 (Target)

96   *Target* No. 1: 15 June 1935 (Target)

97   *Rocket* No. 1: 26 October 1935 (Target)

98   *Sunshine* No. 1: 16 July 1938 (Target)

99

99   *Dandy-Beano Summer Special* No. 1: 1963
100   *Beano Summer Special* No. 2: 1965

100

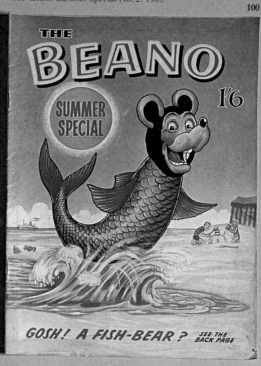

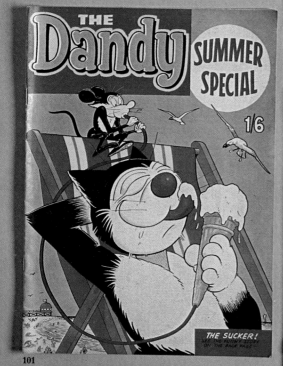

101

101   *Dandy Summer Special* No. 2: 1965
102   *Beezer Summer Special* No. 1: 1973

102

103 *Topper Summer Special* No. 1: 1983
104 *Bunty Summer Special* No. 1: 1969

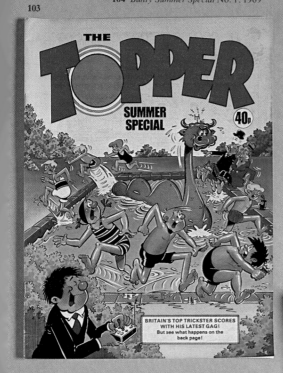

105 *Warlord Summer Special* No. 1: 1975
106 *Victor Summer Special* No. 1: 1967

107

108

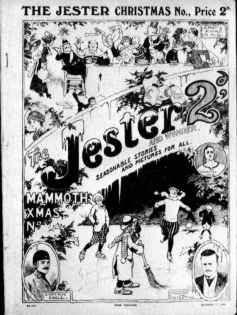

109

110

107 *Butterfly Grand Christmas Double Number* No. 482:
6 December 1913 (Amalgamated Press)

108 *Favorite Comic Grand Christmas Double Number*
No. 100: 14 December 1912 (Amalgamated Press)

109 *Jester & Wonder Mammoth Christmas Number* No. 476:
17 December 1910 (Amalgamated Press)

110 *Merry & Bright Grand Christmas Double Number*
No. 114: 21 December 1912 (Amalgamated Press)

112

111

114

113

111 *Firefly Grand Christmas Double Number* No. 40:
20 November 1915 (Amalgamated Press)

112 *Comic Home Journal Grand Christmas Number* No. 398:
20 December 1902 (Harmsworth)

113 *Funny Wonder Jubilee Christmas Double Number*
No. 1132: 7 December 1935 (Amalgamated Press)

114 *Chips Grand Xmas Double Number* No. 2519:
17 December 1938 (Amalgamated Press)

115

115 *Comic Life Grand Christmas Double Number* No. 652: 17 December 1910 (Henderson)

116 *Lot-O'-Fun Grand Christmas Double Number* No. 198: 25 December 1909 (Henderson)

117

117 *Puck Xmas Double Number* No. 125: 15 December 1906 (Amalgamated Press)

118 *Bo-Peep & Little Boy Blue Christmas Number* No. 63: 27 December 1930 (Amalgamated Press)

CHRISTMAS NUMBERS

119 *Jingles Christmas Number* No. 454: 30 December 1944 (Amalgamated Press)

120 *Playbox Christmas Number* No. 1151: 27 December 1952 (Amalgamated Press)

119

120

121

122

121 *Eagle Christmas Number* No. 37: 22 December 1950 (Hulton)

122 *Happy Days Christmas Number* No. 13: 31 December 1938 (Amalgamated Press)

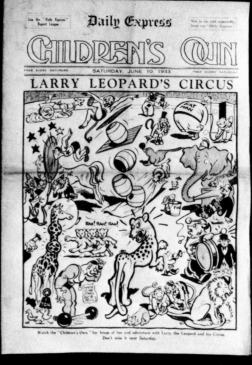

123 *Pip and Squeak* No. 1: 15 October 1921 (Daily Mirror)

124 *Boys and Girls Daily Mail* No. 1: 8 April 1933

125 *Scottish Daily Express Children's Own* No. 1: 8 April 1933

126 *Daily Express Children's Own*: 10 June 1933

COMIC SUPPLEMENTS IN NEWSPAPERS

127

128

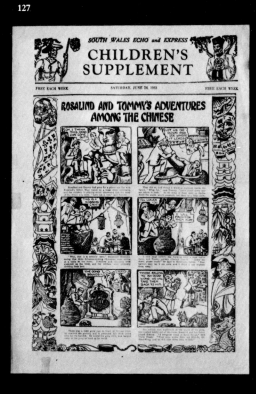

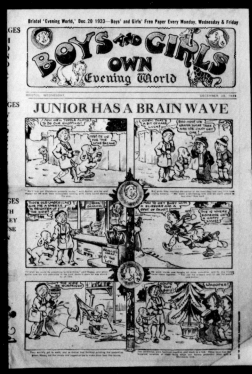

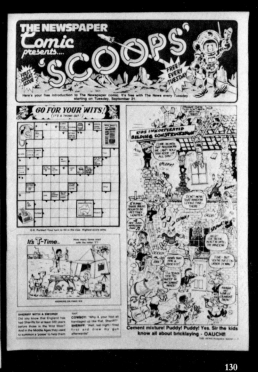

129

130

127 *South Wales Echo and Express Children's Supplement*:
24 June 1933

128 *Jolly Jack's Weekly* No. 1: 20 August 1933 (Sunday
Dispatch)

129 *Boys and Girls Own Evening World*: 20 December 1933

130 *Newspaper Comic Presents Scoops* No. 1: 10 September
1982 (Portsmouth News)

NURSERY COMICS: NUMBER ONES

131 *Robin* No. 1: 28 March 1953 (Hulton)

132 *Swift* No. 1: 20 March 1954 (Hulton)

133 *Jack and Jill* No. 1: 27 February 1954 (Amalgamated Press)

134 *Playhour Pictures* No. 1: 16 October 1954 (Amalgamated Press)

135 *Bimbo* No. 1: 18 March 1961 (D. C. Thomson)

136 *Playland* No. 1: 13 January 1968 (TV Publications)

229

230

231

232

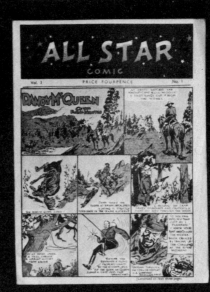

233

234

229 *Comic Adventures* Vol. 7 No. 1: 1949 (Soloway)

230 *Comic Capers* Vol. 7 No. 1: 1949 (Soloway)

231 *All Fun* Vol. 3 No. 1: 1943 (Soloway)

232 *All Star Comic* Vol. 3 No. 1: 1943 (Soloway)

233 *Bumper Comic Book* No. 1: 1946 (Barrett)

234 *Flash* No. 1: July 1948 (Amex)

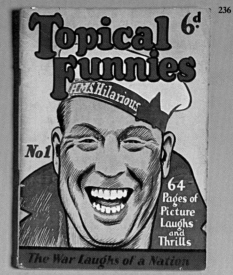

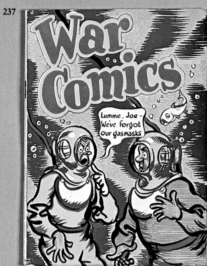

235 *New Funnies*: February 1940

236 *Topical Funnies*: April 1940

237 *War Comics*: April 1940

238 *Thrill Comics*: April 1940

239 *Fresh Fun*: April 1940

240 *Extra Fun*: August 1940

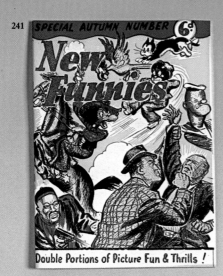

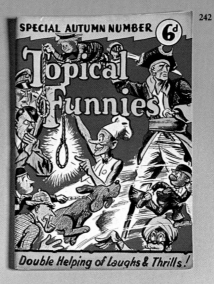

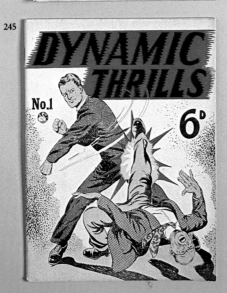

241 *New Funnies Special Autumn Number*: 1941
242 *Topical Funnies Special Autumn Number*: 1941
243 *Thrill Comics Special Spring Number*: 1942
244 *Slick Fun Special Spring Number*: 1942
245 *Dynamic Thrills* No. 1: January 1951
246 *Picture Epics* No. 1: October 1952

GERALD G. SWAN COMICS IN TRADITIONAL STYLE

247 *Coloured Slick Fun* No. 1 (No. 20): 1945
248 *Cute Fun* No. 1: June 1946
249 *Kiddyfun* No. 1: 1945
250 *Comicolour* No. 1: 1946
251 *Extra Fun New Series* No. 2: 1952
252 *Western War Comic* No. 1: June 1949

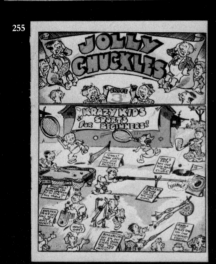

253 *Funny Features*: 1944
254 *Jolly Adventures*: 1946
255 *Jolly Chuckles*: 1946

256 *Merry Maker*: 1946
257 *Super Adventures*: 1946
258 *Jolly Western*: 1947

ONE-SHOTS AND SHORT RUN COMICS

259

260

261

262

263

264

259 *Surefire Comic*: 1949 (Philmar)

260 *Jolly Jack in the Box Comic*: 1949 (P.M.)

261 *Fido the Pup*: 1954 (Hotspur)

262 *Jumbo Comics*: 1949 (Hotspur)

263 *Jimmy Brindle*: 1948 (Brindle)

264 *Nimble Norman*: 1948 (Norman)

NURSERY ONE-SHOTS AND SHORT RUN COMICS

265

266
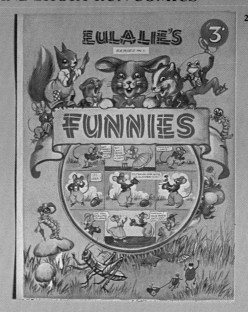

267

268

269

270

265 *Panda Comics*: 1949 (Birn)

266 *Eulalie's Funnies* No. 1: December 1949 (Apollo)

267 *Tom Puss Comics*: 1949 (Birn)

268 *Wide World Comics* No. 1: December 1949 (Apollo)

269 *Curly's Comic*: 1950 (Birn)

270 *Woodland Comics* No. 1: December 1949 (Apollo)

271 *Super Comics*: December 1943

272 *Radiant Comics*: December 1943

273 *Comical Comic*: 1945

274 *Crazy Comic*: 1945

275 *Funny Comic*: 1948

276 *Swell Comic*: 1948

PHILIPP MARX SMALL SIZE ONE-SHOT COMICS

277 *Miniature Comic*: August 1944

278 *Midget Comics*: 1944

279 *Pigmy Comic*: 1944

280 *Silver King*: 1946

281 *Sunny Comic*: 1945

282 *Silver Star*: 1946

283 *Glee Comic*: 1948

284 *Fun Fair Comic*: 1948

285 *Bang On Comic*: 1948

286 *Jolly Comic*: 1946

287 *Joker Comic*: 1946

288 *Danger Trail*: 1946

BOARDMAN COMICS: NUMBER ONES

289

290

291

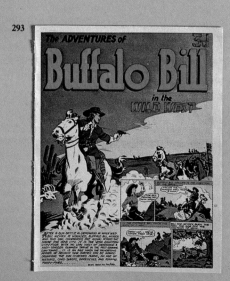

292

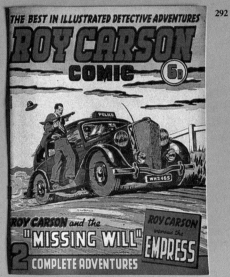

293

294

289 *Swift Morgan*: 1948
290 *Swift Morgan Space Comic*: March 1953
291 *Roy Carson*: 1948

292 *Roy Carson Comic*: 1953
293 *Buffalo Bill*: October 1948
294 *Buffalo Bill Comic*: January 1953

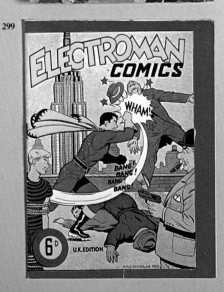

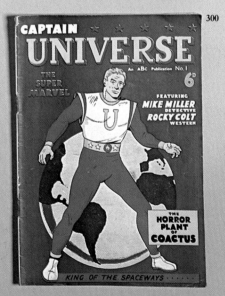

295 *Marvelman* (No. 25): 3 February 1954 (Miller)

296 *Young Marvelman* (No. 25): 3 February 1954 (Miller)

297 *Marvelman Family*: October 1956 (Miller)

298 *Masterman*: November 1952 (Streamline)

299 *Electroman Comics*: 1951 (Scion)

300 *Captain Universe*: 1954 (Arnold)

SMALL SIZE ONE-SHOT COMICS

301 *Midget Comic*: 1946 (Locker)

302 *Little Marvel Comic*: 1946 (Locker)

303 *Penny Comic*: 1944 (P.M.)

304 *Gay Comic*: 1944 (P.M.)

305 *A.1. Comic*: 1945 (P.M.)

306 *Tiny Comic*: 1946 (P.M.)

307 *Circus Comic*: 1945 (P.M.)

308 *Big Little Comic*: 1945 (P.M.)

309 *Hookey's Hoard*: 1943 (Miller)

310 *Weeny Comic*: 1944 (—)

311 *Egbert the Explorer*: 1944 (Miller)

SMALL SIZE STRIP BOOKS

312   *Noddy Strip Book* No. 1: 1952 (Sampson Low)

313   *Tumpy Strip Book* No. 3: 1952 (Sampson Low)

314   *Clicky* No. 2: 1957 (Brockhampton)

315   *Mary Mouse* No. 1: 1942 (Brockhampton)

316   *Toby Twirl Strip Book* No. 1: 1953 (Sampson Low)

317   *Nicholas Thomas Strip Book* No. 1: 1953 (Sampson Low)

318   *Honk* No. 5: 1950 (Brockhampton)

319   *Good Dog Caesar*: 1953 (Brockhampton)

320   *Henry* No. 3: 1964 (Brockhampton)

321   *Twins* No. 3: 1950 (Brockhampton)

322   *T.V. Mini-Book* No. 1: 1955 (News of the World)

323   *T.V. Mini-Book* No. 9: 1955 (News of the World)

324

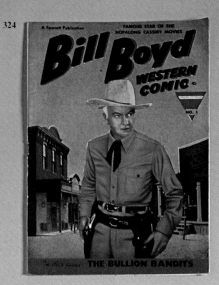

325

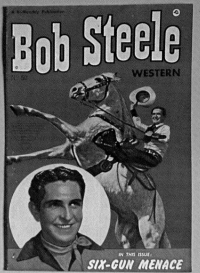

326

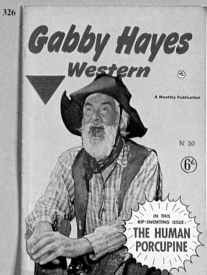

327

328

329

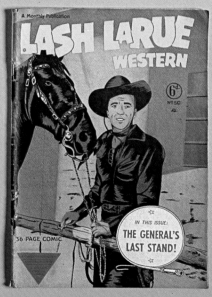

324 *Bill Boyd Western*: 1950

325 *Bob Steele Western* No. 50: 1951

326 *Gabby Hayes Western* No. 50: 1950

327 *Hopalong Cassidy Comic* No. 50: 1950

328 *Ken Maynard Western*: 1951

329 *Lash La Rue Western* No. 50: 1950

330

331

332
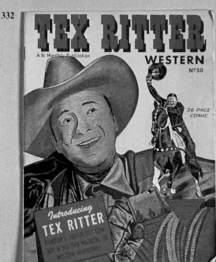

333
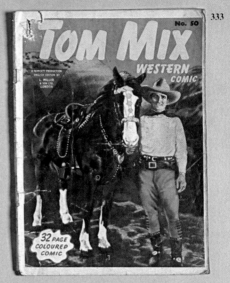

334

335

330 *Monte Hale Western* (No. 50): 1951
331 *Rod Cameron Western*: 1950
332 *Tex Ritter Western* (No. 50): 1951
333 *Tom Mix Western* (No. 50): 1951
334 *Six-Gun Heroes* (No. 50): 1951
335 *Motion Picture Comics*: 1951

336 *Tip Top Comics* No. 1: 1940

337 *Comics On Parade* No. 1: (No. 3): 1941

338 *Comics On Parade Series* No. 1: 1944

339 *Funny Animals*: 1949

340 *Family Favourites Comic Weekly* No. 1: 24 February 1954

341 *King Comic* No. 1: 5 May 1954

342

343

344

345

346

347

342 *Captain Marvel Adventures*: 1949

343 *Whiz Comics* No. 72: 1953

344 *Captain Marvel Jr* No. 66 (No. 100): 1952

345 *Master Comics* No. 83: 1953

346 *Marvel Family* No. 77: 1953

347 *Captain Midnight* No. 43: 1947

348

349

350

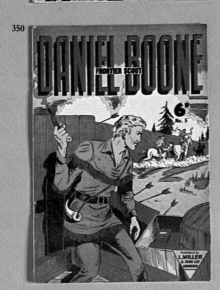

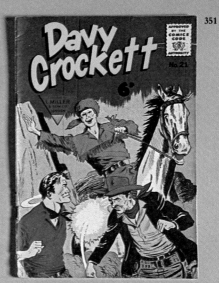

351

352

353

348 *Buffalo Bill Cody* No. 1
349 *Colorado Kid* No. 1: May 1954
350 *Daniel Boone* No. 5: 1957

351 *Davy Crockett* No. 21: 1958
352 *Jim Bowie* No. 7: 1957
353 *Kid Dynamite* No. 1: 1954

BRITISH WESTERNS

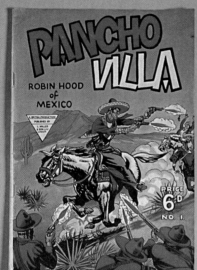

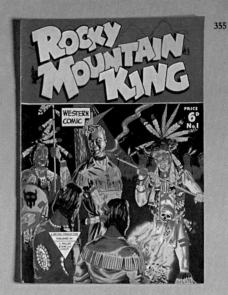

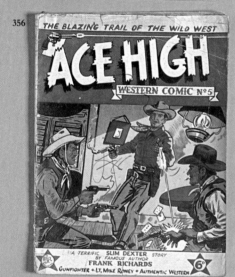

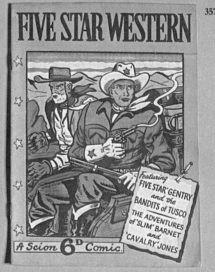

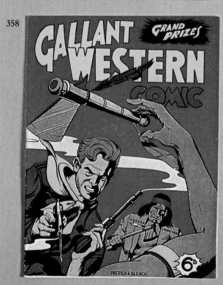

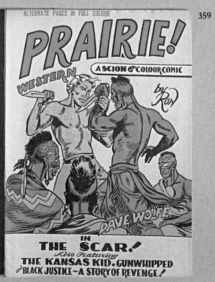

354 *Pancho Villa* No. 1: 1954 (Miller)

355 *Rocky Mountain King* No. 1: 1955

356 *Ace High Western Comics* No. 5: 1953 (Gould-Light)

357 *Five Star Western* No. 1: 1951 (Scion)

358 *Gallant Western Comic* No. 1: 1953 (Scion)

359 *Prairie Western* No. 1: 1952 (Scion)

360 *Crasher Comic*: 1946 (Kayebon)

361 *Smasher Comics*: 1947 (Tongard)

362 *Fizz*: 1949 (Modern Fiction)

363 *Merry Maker Comic*: 1946 (Algar)

364 *Merry-Go-Round*: 1949 (Allen)

365 *Comic Shots*: 1946 (Fisher)

366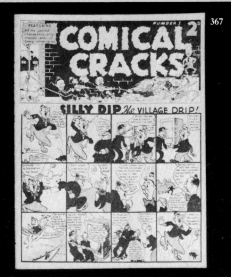

367

368

369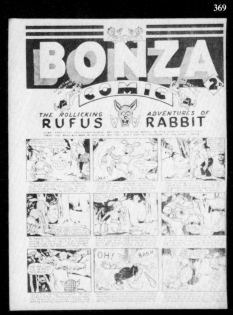

370

371

366 *Comical Pranks*: 1947

367 *Comical Cracks*: 1947

368 *Zip-Bang Comic*: 1946

369 *Bonza Comic*: 1947

370 *King Comic*: 1947

371 *Ensign Comic*: 1947

372

373

374

375

376

377

372 *Ace Malloy* No. 1: August 1952 (Arnold)

373 *Front-Line Combat* No. 1: 1959 (Miller)

374 *Bulldog Brittain Commando* No. 1: 1952 (Miller)

375 *Robin Hood* No. 1: 1957 (Miller)

376 *Speed Kings Comic* No. 13: 1953 (Man's World)

377 *True Life Adventures* No. 1 (No. 12): 1953 (Man's World)

378
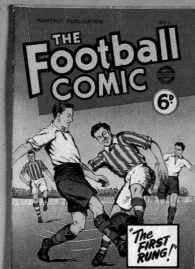

379

380

381

382

383

378 *Football Comic* No. 1: January 1953

379 *Dick Hercules* No. 1: December 1952

380 *Steve Samson* No. 1: January 1953

381 *Captain Vigour* No. 1: December 1952

382 *British Heroes* No. 8: 1954

383 *Thrilling Hero* No. 1 (No. 16): November 1953

384

385

386

387

388

389

384 *A.1. Comic*: 1946 (Burnside)

385 *Dazzle Comic* No. 2: 1946 (International)

386 *Okay Comic*: 1947 (International)

387 *Ripping Comic*: 1948 (JT)

388 *Sunny Comic*: 1945 (International)

389 *Winner Comic* No. 1: 1947 (Jeffrey)

390  391

392 393

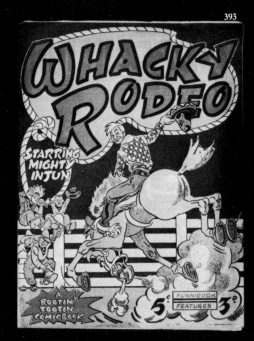

394 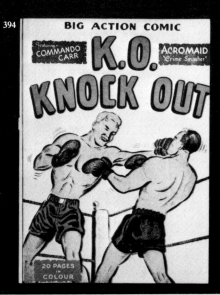  395

390 *Super Duper Comics* No. 7: 1948

391 *Zipper-Ripper Comic*: 1946

392 *Hubba-Hubba Comic Book*: 1947

393 *Whacky Rodeo* No. 2: 1947

394 *K. O. Knock Out*: 1947

395 *Zippy Comics*: 1947

SCIENCE-FICTION COMICBOOKS OF THE FIFTIES

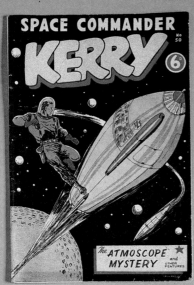

394a

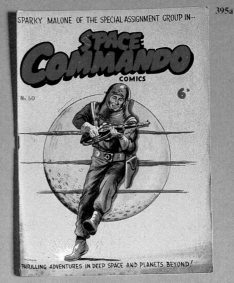

395a

396

397

398

399

394a *Space Commander Kerry* No. 1 (No. 50): 1953 (Miller)

395a *Space Commando Comics* No. 1 (No. 50): 1953 (Miller)

396 *Captain Valiant/Space Comics* No. 1 (No. 50): 1953 (Arnold)

397 *Pete Mangan* No. 2 (No. 51): 1953 (Miller)

398 *Spaceman* No. 7: 1953 (Gould-Light)

399 *Jet Comic*: 1953 (Hamilton)

SCIENCE-FICTION COMICBOOKS

400

401

402

403

404

405

400 *Strange Worlds* No. 2 (No. 13): 1953 (Man's World)
401 *Super-Sonic* No. 2 (No. 13): 1954 (Man's World)
402 *Star-Rocket* No. 1: 1953 (Comyns)
403 *Gallant Science Comic* No. 2: 1953 (Scion)
404 *Space Patrol* No. 1: 1964 (Young World)
405 *World of Space* (PR)

406

407

408

409

410

411

406 *Big Atlantis Comic*: 1948   409 *Big Flame Wonder Comic*: 1948

407 *Big Castle Comic*: 1948   410 *Big Game Comic*: 1948

408 *Big Chuckle Comic*: 1948   411 *Big Jungle Comic*: 1948

412

413

414

415

416

417

412 *Big Pirate Comic*: 1948

413 *Big Ranch Comic*: 1949

414 *Big Sahara Comic*: 1949

415 *Big Scoop Comic*: 1949

416 *Big Time Comic*: 1947

417 *Big Win Comic*: 1948

MARVEL U.K. AMERICAN REPRINTS: NUMBER ONES

418

419

420

421

422

423

418 *Mighty World of Marvel*: 7 October 1972

419 *Spider-Man Comics Weekly*: 17 February 1973

420 *Captain America*: 25 February 1981

421 *Captain Britain*: 13 October 1976

422 *Rampage*: 19 October 1977

423 *Hulk Comic*: 7 March 1979

MARVEL U.K.: NUMBER ONES

424 *Avengers*: 22 September 1973

425 *Savage Sword of Conan*: 8 March 1975

426 *Star Wars Weekly*: 8 February 1978

427 *Blakes 7*: October 1981

428 *Doctor Who Weekly*: 17 October 1979

429 *Worzel Gummidge Weekly*: 9 March 1983

430

431

432

433

434

435

430 *Adventure Hero*: 1951   433 *Sea Hero*: 1951
431 *Daring Hero*: 1951   434 *Sky Hero Comic*: 1952
432. *Detective Hero Comic*: 1951   435 *Space Hero*: 1951

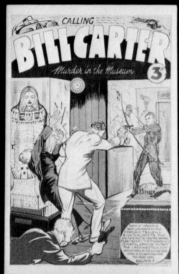

436 *Secret Service Series* No. 1: 1948 (Hotspur)

437 *Oh Boy! Comics* No. 3: 1948 (Paget)

438 *Bill Carter* No. 1: 1947 (Foldes)

439 *Modern Comics*: 1949 (Modern Fiction)

440 *Ray Regan*: 1949 (Modern Fiction)

441 *Wonderman* No. 17: 1949 (Paget)

CLASSIC COMICS

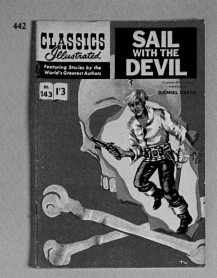

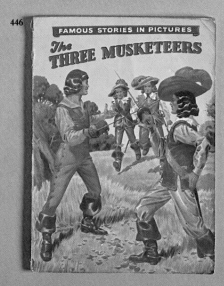

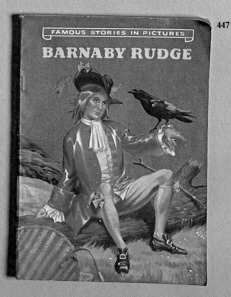

442 *Classics Illustrated* No. 143 (Thorpe & Porter)

443 *Classics Illustrated* No. 157 (Thorpe & Porter)

444 *A Classic in Pictures* No. 1 (Amex)

445 *A Classic in Pictures* No. 7 (Amex)

446 *Famous Stories in Pictures* (Bairns)

447 *Famous Stories in Pictures* (Bairns)

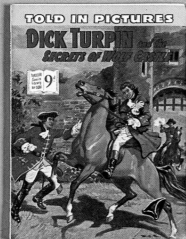

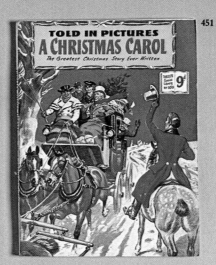

448 *Thriller Comics* No. 3: 1951

449 *Thriller Picture Library* No. 185

450 *Thriller Picture Library* No. 101

451 *Thriller Picture Library* No. 109

452 *Thriller Comics* No. 16: 1952

453 *Super Detective Library* No. 13: 1953

454

455

456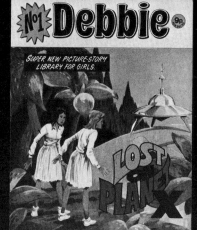

457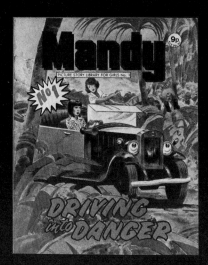

458

459

454 *Princess Picture Library*: July 1961 (Fleetway)

455 *Schoolgirls Picture Library*: July 1957 (Amalgamated Press)

456 *Debbie Picture Story Library*: April 1978 (D. C. Thomson)

457 *Mandy Picture Story Library*: April 1978 (D. C. Thomson)

458 *Beano Comic Library*: April 1982 (D. C. Thomson)

459 *Buster Comic Library*: August 1984 (IPC)

T.V. PICTURE STORIES: NUMBER ONES: PEARSON

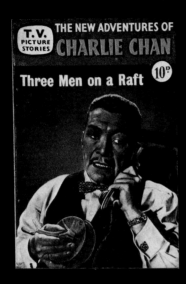

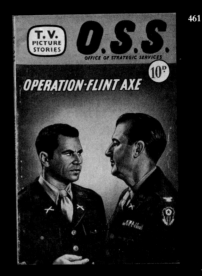

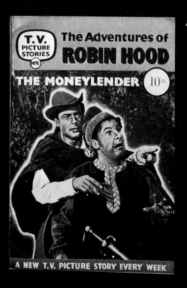

460 *New Adventures of Charlie Chan*: June 1958
461 *O.S.S.*: June 1958
462 *Hawkeye and the Last of the Mohicans*: June 1958

463 *Sword of Freedom*: February 1959
464 *William Tell*: February 1959
465 *Adventures of Robin Hood*: April 1959

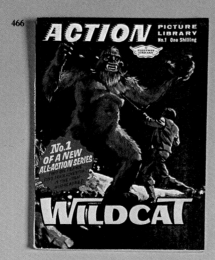

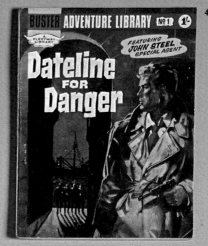

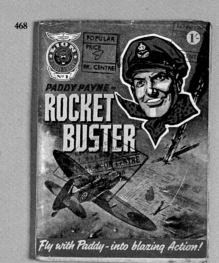

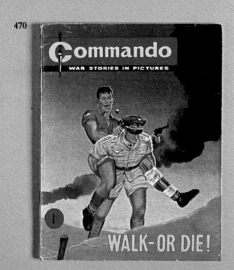

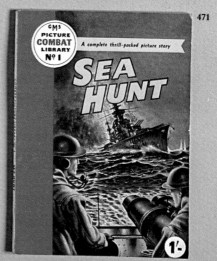

466 *Action Picture Library*: August 1969 (IPC)

467 *Buster Adventure Library*: July 1966 (Fleetway)

468 *Lion Picture Library*: October 1963 (Fleetway)

469 *Air Ace Picture Library*: January 1960 (Fleetway)

470 *Commando*: July 1961 (D. C. Thomson)

471 *Combat Picture Library*: August 1959 (Micron)

COMIC LIBRARIES: NUMBER ONES

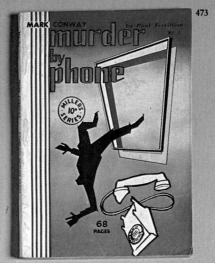

472 *Super Detective Library*: March 1953 (Amalgamated Press)

473 *Mark Conway*: 1959 (Miller)

474 *Tit-Bits Wild West Comics*: 1953 (Pearson)

475 *Lone Rider Picture Library*: July 1961 (Fleetway)

476 *Starblazer*: April 1979 (D. C. Thomson)

477 *Tit-Bits Science Fiction Comics*: 1953 (Pearson)

ADVERTISING COMICS

478 *Fun Fare*: 1934 (Lancs & Yorks Dairies)

479 *Gummy* No. 11: 1954 (Maynards)

480 *Wonder Weekly* No. 1: 5 July 1968 (Esso)

481 *Fizzer Christmas Number*: 1979 (Corona)

482 *Jif Junior* No. 1: 1973 (Reckitt & Colman)

483 *Muncher* No. 1: 1978 (Wimpy)

484

485
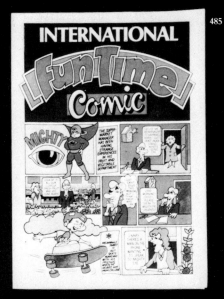

486

487
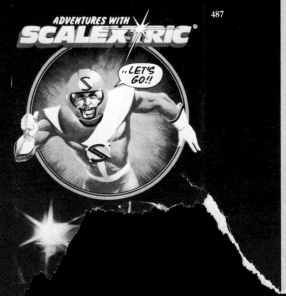

488

484 7
485
486

490

491

492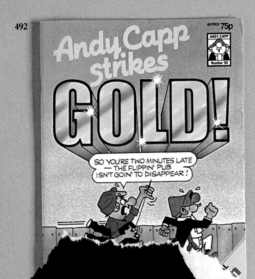

493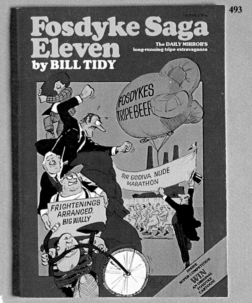

495

ress)

COMIC MAGAZINES AND MONTHLIES: NUMBER ONES

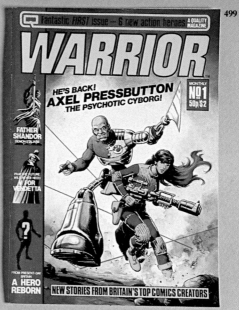

496 *Red Dagger*: October 1979 (D. C. Thomson)

497 *2000 A.D. Summer Special Supercomic*: June 1977 (IPC)

498 *Super D.C.*: June 1969 (Top Sellers)

499 *Warrior*: March 1982 (Quality)

500 *10-4 Action*: November 1981 (CB News)

501a *Pssst*: January 1982 (Never)

501

502

503

504

505

506
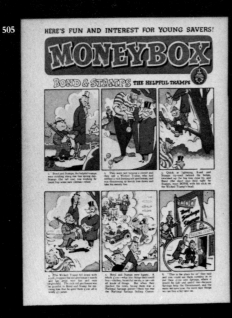

501 *Safety Light*: 1939 (ROSPA)
502 *Safety Fun*: 1946 (Cambridge)
503 *Traffic Light*: 1946 (ROSPA)

504 *Rospa Rocket*: 1951 (ROSPA)
505 *Moneybox* No. 1: 1945 (National Savings)
506 *Money Fun* No. 1: 1981 (National Savings)

507 *Form*: 1959 (Conservative)

508 *Superman* No. 1: February 1981 (Health Education)

509 *Young Warrior* No. 135: July 1954 (WEC)

510 *Playtime* No. 11: March 1951 (Roman Catholic)

511 *Man of Steel*: 1979 (British Steel)

512 *Commander Earth*: 1980 (Gulf Oil)

513 *Spring Comic*: No. 1 (1932)
514 *Summer Comic*: No. 4 (1938)

513

515 *Holiday Comic*: No. 6 (1938)
516 *Christmas Comic*: No. 5 (1935)

515

PART THREE

How to Use the Catalogue

This catalogue lists every known comic publication issued in the British Isles (including England, Scotland, Wales and Ireland) from the earliest known use of the comic format in 1825 to the end of December 1984. All types of comic publications are included: weeklies, monthlies, irregulars, one-shots, reprints, supplements, giveaways, newspaper strip compilations, etc.

Arrangement
Publications are alphabetically arranged by title.

Title
Titles are given without the article: *Beano* not *The Beano*.

Alternative titles (aka)
The abbreviation 'aka' means 'also known as' and is used where a comic has appeared under an alternative title during part of its run: *Diana* aka: *New Diana*; or where more than one title appears on the cover and can cause confusion: *Space Comics* aka: *Captain Valiant*.

Publication Dates
Given as day/month/year of first issue to day/month/year of last issue, for weekly comics. Less frequent comics have publication dates as month/year, where known, or year. Many publications are completely undated, so deduced years are given as either 1983(?) or 198–.

Run
The total number of published issues is given in brackets following the publication dates: (1), (12), (123), etc. This number does not necessarily equate with the final number as printed on the final issue of the comic (see 'First Issue' below).

Publisher
The name of the original publisher is given without 'Ltd', 'Co', etc. The following publishers are abbreviated: AP (Amalgamated Press); IPC (International Publishing Corporation); ITV (Independent Television Publications). The several Philipp Marx companies (Amex, PM Productions, Philmar, Bairns Books) are identified by the name Marx in brackets. The several Martin and Reid companies (John Matthew, Rayburn) are similarly identified.

Alternative Publisher
Where another publisher has taken over a publication, the second publisher's name is given following a stroke: Henderson/AP.

American Publisher
The original American publisher of a comic reprinted by a British publisher is given in brackets following the name of the British publisher: Streamline (Fox). Detective Comics Inc (National Periodical Publications) is abbreviated to DC.

Amalgamations and Combinations
Where a comic has another comic combined with it, leading to a temporary change in title, this information is given following the use of an ampersand (&) together with the date of the first combined edition: & *Cracker*: 18 Sep 1976.

Cessation with Amalgamation
When a comic ceases publication, it is usually combined with another comic issued by the same publisher. This information is given following the word 'to': to: *Beezer*. Thus for further details of the comic, the reader should turn to the entry for the title given.

New Series
When a comic is revived, or revitalized, with a 'New Series' (usually beginning a new sequence of numbering from 1), a separate entry is made following the original title, with a cross-reference following the word 'to' as for 'Cessation with Amalgamation' (above): to: *New Series*.

First Issue
Number one of each comic is given as the numeral 1, with the remainder of the run following (usually from 2) in the next line. This is because the first issue of every comic is usually the most collectable and commands a higher value. Where a bracketed numeral follows 1, this is the number of the first issue as it appears on the comic: 1(50). There are several reasons for this apparent contradiction. Many comics published by L. Miller and Son (Miller) commenced with No 50, in an attempt to deceive prospective readers into thinking the comic was a well-established title. Another reason for a higher number than 1 on a first issue is where a new series (see above) commences without renumbering from 1:

1(123). A third reason is where a comic has had a previous existence as a non-comic publication, usually a juvenile story-paper, and is changed into a comic from a certain number.

Last Issue

The issue number of the final edition of a comic is given, and may differ from the total run (see 'Run' above) for reasons explained above.

Format

The basic format of British comics today is the Eurosize A4, give or take an inch here and there according to the age of their printers. *2000 AD* is more square, for instance, than *Beano*. All comics listed may be presumed to be of this standard size, except where noted. The earlier basic format of the comic was tabloid (approximately the page size of today's *Daily Mirror*), or half broadsheet newspaper (approximately the page size of *The Times*). This size held from the early *Funny Folks* (1874) to 1940, when wartime paper shortage began to reduce comics to *Beano* proportions. This early format is indicated by the word 'tabloid'. The other modern format, in the tradition of the American comicbook, may be described as 'comicbook' but is not separately identified in this catalogue. It is quite obvious from the entry itself.

Page Count

The number of pages in comics is fairly standardized: 8 and 12 in the early years, 24, 28, 32 later, and 48, 52, 64, etc in comicbook formats. The page count of each comic is given in brackets following the number 1, with the abbreviation 'p' for 'pages': (16p).

Colour

British comics are rarely printed in full colour throughout. The older comics often had full colour on the front page only, with a two-colour (red/black) centre spread and back page. Comicbook formats are usually black-and-white pages set in a four-colour cover, unlike their American originals. Where a rare full-colour interior occurs, the abbreviation (4C) is used. Occasionally a two-colour interior (usually red/black) is identified as (2C). These are aids to identification of specific issues within a series, as is the occasional notation of the use of coloured paper.

Unnumbered Issues

Many comicbook reprints do not carry a number. When this happens, the abbreviation (nn) for 'no number' follows the numeral 1, indicating that the first issue is not numbered.

Artists

Artists of interest or collectability are noted in many of the entries, or are given as an aid to identification of the comic. It is regretted that complete lists of all artists cannot be given for each comic due to lack of space.

Subtitles: Libraries

The library comic (see below) usually features a different story in each issue. The title of the first of each library is given.

Subtitles: Series

A number of comics, mainly American reprints, were grouped into series: *Action Series*, etc. Full titles of each issue within the series are given: *Action Series 1: Ghost Riders*.

Libraries

The library format (known in the USA as the 'digest format') is pocket-size and is a comic adaptation of the older story libraries such as *The Sexton Blake Library*. The page count is usually sixty-eight, including covers. Libraries differ from weekly comics in that they are normally published once a month (often in batches of two or four), and contain one single, complete story in pictures. The library size of comic is indicated by the word 'small' in brackets.

Giveaways

Comics which are produced as promotions for a product, or for a purpose (eg road safety), and are given away rather than sold, are distinguished as 'Giveaways'.

Supplements

These are comics issued as free supplements to other publications, such as pull-outs in comics or story-papers, newspaper supplements, children's sections in adult magazines, etc.

Story-papers

The story-paper, which grew out of the notorious Penny Dreadfuls of the last century and lasted to the final issue of *Rover* (13 January 1973), is not included in this catalogue of comics, despite the fact that colloquially they were bracketed with comics by newsagents and children from the forties. By universally accepted definition, a comic must be primarily a strip-cartoon publication, not a textual one.

Annuals and Albums
Most regular comics have an allied annual published for the Christmas period. These are normally hardback books, and are not included in this catalogue. Albums are also normally hardback collections, often reprints, of strips, and are only included in this catalogue where the format is softback or otherwise close to regular comic format.
Specials
The special (holiday, summer, Christmas, etc) is the fastest growing format and although larger in page size and count than the regular weekly comic to which it is normally allied, it will be found in this catalogue. Where a comic's specials have undergone several title changes, they will be found listed chronologically under a single heading: *Donald and Mickey Specials.*
Facsimiles
There have been a number of facsimile reproductions of old comics issued in recent times (*Beano* No 1, etc). These are listed with their current values, which are much lower than those of the original editions, but may be higher than the selling price when first published due to the limited edition of such facsimiles.
Values
Values for each comic are given as a span of low/high. This is not neccessarily a key to condition of comics (*ie* bad/good), but is a reflection of prices which dealers are currently asking. Prices can be both lower than the low figure, and higher than the high figure, if condition is very poor or absolutely mint. Values are per single copy, and would generally be lower if a run or large quantity is offered.

Abbreviations

ACG	American Comics Group
AP	Amalgamated Press
BB	Birn Brothers
DC	Detective Comics Inc
EC	Entertaining Comics Inc
GB	Great Britain
IPC	International Publishing Corporation
ITV	Independent Television Publications
ME	Magazine Enterprises
NEL	New English Library
nn	no number
p	pages
promo	promotional comic
ROSPA	Royal Society for the Prevention of Accidents
supp	supplement
tab	tabloid
UG	underground comic
US	United States of America
2C, 3C, 4C	two colours, three colours, four colours

A.1. COMIC
1946 (3)
Burnside/International
1 (nn) (16p) J. R. Turner   50p–£1.50
2 (nn) (16p) J. R. Turner   50p–£1.50
3 (nn) (20p) J. R. Turner   50p–£1.50

A.1. COMICS
1945 (1)
PM (Marx)
1 (nn) (folded card) D. Gifford   50p–£1.00

ABBOTT AND COSTELLO COMICS
1950 (2)
Streamline/United Anglo-American (St John)
1 (nn) (28p) (4C)   £1.00–£1.50
2 (nn) (28p) (2C)   50p–£1.00

ABRAHAM FOUNDER OF A NATION
1979 (1)
Lion/Fleurus
1 (nn) (52p) (4C) French reprint   50p–95p

ACE
Sep 1947 (1)
Hamilton
1 (nn) (16p) Bob Wilkin   50p–£1.00

ACE COMIC
1948 (1)
Valentine (Mallard Features)
1 (nn) (16p) Nat Brand   £1.00–£1.50

ACE HIGH WESTERN COMIC
1953 (5)
Gould-Light
1 (24p) Ron Embleton   50p–£1.50
2–5 Norman Light   50p–£1.00

ACE HIGH WESTERN COMICS
Jun 1946 (1)
International
1 (nn) (8p) Denis Gifford   £1.00–£2.00

ACE MALLOY
Aug 1952–1954 (16)
Arnold
1 (nn) (24p) Mick Anglo   £1.00–£1.50
51–65 Dudley Page   50p–75p

ACE OF COMICS
Oct 1947 (1)
Foster
1 (nn) (8p) Bob Wilkin   50p–£1.00

ACE OF FUN COMIC
Nov-Dec 1947 (2)
Estuary Supply
1 (nn) (blue) Bob Wilkin   50p–£1.00
2 Bob Wilkin   50p–£1.00

ACOMIC BOMBSHELL
1947 (1)
Cartoon Art
1 (16p) Dennis Reader   75p–£1.50

ACTION
Sep 1948 (1)
Pictorial Art
1 (nn) (8p) 'MMM' (Mazure?)   50p–£1.00

ACTION
14 Feb 1976–16 Oct 1976 (36)
IPC
to: Action New Series
1 (32p)   50p–£1.00
2–36   35p–75p
37 (23 Oct) not distributed   50p–£1.00

ACTION (NEW SERIES)
4 Dec 1976–12 Nov 1977 (50)
IPC
to: Battle Action
1 (32p)   15p–30p
2–50   10p–15p

ACTION COMICS
1958 (2)
Miller (Magazine Enterprises)
1–2 (68p) US reprint   35p–75p

ACTION FORCE MINI-COMIC
16 Jul 1983–10 Sep 1983 (5)
IPC/CPG Products (toy promo)
giveaway in Battle, Eagle, Tiger
1 (8p) (4C) (small) R. Turner   10p–15p
2–5   5p–10p

ACTION GIRL SPECIAL
see: Girl Specials

ACTION PICTURE LIBRARY
Aug 1969–
IPC
to: War Picture Library
1: (60p) Wildcat   35p–75p
2–   25p–50p

ACTION SERIES
1958 (12)
Miller (ME/Fawcett)
1 (68p) Ghost Riders   35p–75p
2 Prairie Guns   25p–75p
3 B-Bar-B Riders   25p–75p
4 Red Mask   25p–75p
5 Thunda   £1.00–£2.00
6; 8 Cave Girl   35p–£1.00
9 Lone Vigilante   25p–75p
10 Kid Cowboy   25p–75p
11; 12 Dan Adams (Autry)   25p–75p

ACTION SERIES
Jul–Sep 1964 (12)
Young World (King Features)
1 (80p); 8 Secret Agent X9   25p–50p
2 Big Ben Bolt   25p–50p
3; 10 Flash Gordon   35p–75p
4 Tim Tyler   25p–50p
5; 12 Brick Bradford   25p–50p
6 Mandrake   25p–50p
7; 11 Ripcord   25p–50p

ACTION SPECIALS
May 1976–May 1980 (5)
IPC
1: Summer Special 1976 (64p)   25p–50p
4: Holiday Special 1979   25p–50p
5: Holiday Special 1980 Don Lawrence   25p–50p

ACTION STREAMLINE COMICS
195– (1)
Streamline
1 (nn) (68p) US reprints   £1.00–£2.00

ACTION WAR PICTURE LIBRARY
1965
1–   15p–25p

ADAM THE GARDENER
1946–1984 (3)
Express Books (Sunday Express reprints)
1 (1946) (148p) Cyril Cowell (oblong)   £1.00–£2.00
2 (1978)   25p–50p
3 (1984)   20p–35p

ADVENTURE HERO
1951 (1)
Scion
1 (24p) King-Ganteaume   25p–£1.00

116

ADVENTURE KNOWLEDGE
1979 (4)
Macdonald/Sackett
1: *Lost in the Amazon* (36p) (4C)
   Gerry Embleton   50p–75p
2: *Mystery of the Pharaoh*   50p–75p
3: *Death in the Arctic*   50p–75p
4: *Danger on the Red Planet*   50p–75p

ADVENTURE STORIES OF WORLD FAMOUS
EXPLORERS
19— (2)
Elders & Fyffes (Mather & Crowther)
1–2 (44p) (oblong) (4C) Tony Weare
   (promo)   £1.00–£2.00

ADVENTURE STORY COMICS
Nov 1951 (1)
Odhams
1 (nn) (52p)   £1.00–£1.75

ADVENTURE STREAMLINE COMICS
195– (1)
Streamline
1 (nn) (68p) US reprint   £1.00–£2.00

ADVENTURES IN 3.D.
1953 (2)
Streamline/United Anglo-American (Harvey)
1–2 (36p) (with glasses) US reprint   £1.00–£2.00

ADVENTURES IN WONDERLAND
1955 (2)
Miller (Gleason)
1–2 (36p) US reprint   25p–50p

ADVENTURES INTO THE UNKNOWN
1950–
Arnold/Thorpe & Porter (ACG)
1 (68p) US reprint   £1.00–£2.50
2–   75p–£1.50

ADVENTURES INTO WEIRD WORLDS
1952–
Thorpe & Porter (Marvel)
1 (68p) US reprint   £1.00–£2.00
2–   75p–£1.50

ADVENTURES OF BIGGLES
195– (9)
Strato (Action)
1 (68p) Australian reprint   50p–£1.00
2–9   35p–75p

ADVENTURES OF BLONDIE AND DAGWOOD
1956 (1)
Associated Newspapers (King Features)
1 (nn) (84p) US reprint   £1.00–£2.50

ADVENTURES OF CHARLIE CHICK
1946 (1)
no imprint
1 (8p) (yellow) Fred Robinson   75p–£1.50

ADVENTURES OF DINKIE AND DOO
1946 (3)
Walthamstow Guardian
1 (nn) (folder) Fred Robinson   £1.00–£2.00
2 (1) (8p)   75p–£1.00
3 (2) (8p)   50p–£1.00

ADVENTURES OF ELMO
1942 (1)
Kingsbury
to: *Further Adventures of Elmo*
1 (20p) Charles Cole   50p–£1.50

ADVENTURES OF FAT FREDDY'S CAT
1978–1979 (5)
Hassle Free Press
1–5 (52p) (adult) US reprint (small)   50p–75p

ADVENTURES OF GOOD DEED DANNY
1943? (1)
W. H. Allen
1 (16p) Ern Shaw   50p–£1.00

ADVENTURES OF JASPER
1944? (1)
Hawks (*The Dog Owner* strips)
1 (28p) Walkden Fisher   £1.00–£2.00

ADVENTURES OF LAZARUS LAMB
1981 (1)
Knockabout Comics
1 Ralph Edney (adult)   £2.00–£2.90

ADVENTURES OF P. C. FRANK
1969 (2)
Heavy Tripp Rock'n'Roll Kartoon Korp
1–2 (sheet) Dave Webster   £1.00–£3.00

ADVENTURES OF ROBIN HOOD
Apr–Aug 1959 (3)
Pearson (*TV Picture Stories*)
1 (TVP 8) *The Moneylender*   25p–£1.00
2 (TVP 13) *Friar Tuck*   25p–75p
3 (TVP 24) *Husband for Marion*   25p–75p

ADVENTURES OF SIM
1953 (1)
Brockhampton
1 (nn) W. Tymym (small)   25p–£1.00

ADVENTURES OF STEVE
1947 (1)
PJ Press (*Sunday Dispatch* strips)
1 (nn) (48p) Roland Davies (oblong) £1.00–£2.00

ADVENTURES OF TINTIN
1972–
Methuen (Casterman)
1: *Black Island* (64p) (4C) reprints 50p–£1.00
2–   50p–75p

ADVENTURES WITH SCALEXTRIC
1981 (1)
Hornby Hobbies/Studio System
1 (nn) (40p) (4C) (toy catalogue)
   Ian Kennedy   50p–£1.00

AIR ACE PICTURE LIBRARY
Jan 1960–
Fleetway
to: *War Picture Library*
1 (68p) *Target Top Secret*   50p–75p
2–   25p–50p

AIR ACE PICTURE LIBRARY
HOLIDAY SPECIAL
Jun 1969–
Fleetway
1 (224p) reprints   50p–75p
2– (192p)   25p–75p

AIR FIGHTS OF FLYER HART
27 Jan 1962 (1)
Thomson
giveaway: *New Hotspur* 119   50p–£1.50

AIR WAR PICTURE STORIES
Feb 1961–Apr 1962 (38)
Pearson
1 (68p) *Mission of No Return*   25p–75p
2–38 (small)   25p–50p

AIRBOY COMICS
1951 (2)
Streamline/United Anglo-American (Hillman)
1 (nn) (4C) (28p)   50p–£1.00
2 (nn) (36p) US reprint   35p–75p

AIRBOY COMICS
1953 (1)
Thorpe & Porter (Hillman)
1 (68p) US reprint   50p–£1.00

ALEC
1984 (1)
Escape
1 (40p) Eddie Campbell   £1.00–£2.00

ALICE IN WONDERLAND
Nov 1941 (1)
Miller (United Features)
1 (nn) (20p) (small) US reprint   £1.00–£2.00

ALL ACTION COMIC
1954 (1)
Moring
1 (nn) (68p) McLoughlin reprints   £1.00–£2.00

ALL FUN COMIC
1940–1949 (27)
Soloway
V1/1 (8p) (tabloid)   £2.00–£3.00
V1/2–5 (tabloid)   £1.50–£2.00
V2/1–4 (16p) Nat Brand   £1.00–£1.75
V3/1–4 Denis Gifford   £1.00–£1.75
V4/1–4 Alan Fraser   £1.00–£1.75
V5/1–4 Bob Monkhouse   50p–£1.00
V6/1–4 Mick Anglo   50p–£1.00
V7/1–2 (4C) Louis Diamond   50p–£1.00

ALL PICTURE COMIC
12 Mar 1921–25 Jun 1921 (16)
Sphinx
1 (8pp)   £2.50–£5.00
2–16   £1.00–£2.00

ALL SORTS COMIC
1948 (1)
Scion
1 (nn) R. Plummer   50p–£1.00

ALL STAR COMIC
1940–1949 (27)
Soloway
V1/1 (tabloid) (8p)   £2.00–£3.00
V1/2–5 (tabloid) Nat Brand   £1.50–£2.00
V2/1–4 (16p) Alan Fraser   £1.00–£1.75
V3/1–4 Louis Diamond   £1.00–£1.75
V4/1–4 Bob Monkhouse   £1.00–£1.75
V5/1–4 Alf Farningham   50p–£1.00
V6/1–4 Edward Lowe   50p–£1.00
V7/1–2 (4C) Glyn Protheroe   50p–£1.00

ALL STAR WESTERN
see: Giant Comic

ALL TOP COMICS
1949 (1)
Streamline/United Anglo-American (Fox)
1 (nn) (28p) US reprint   50p–£1.50

ALL-WAR MONTHLY
Feb 1981–Mar 1982 (13)
Byblos
1 (52p) foreign reprints   25p–40p
2–13   15p–25p

ALL-WAR SPECIALS
May 1980–
Byblos
1: Holiday Special 1980 (52p) (foreign reprints)   20p–40p
2: Autumn Special 1980   20p–40p
3: Summer 1981   20p–40p
4: Winter 1981   20p–40p

ALLY SLOPER (New Series)
6 Jun 1914–9 Sep 1916 (109)
Sloperies
to: London Society

1 (1571) W. F. Thomas   £3.00–£5.00
2–109 James Brown   75p–£1.25

ALLY SLOPER
1948 (1)
McKenzie
1 (8p) (2C) T. Reid   50p–£1.00

ALLY SLOPER
Oct 1976–Jan 1977 (4)
Class/Creative Comics
1 (36p) Frank Bellamy   20p–50p
2 Harry Bishop   20p–35p
3 Frank Hampson   20p–35p
4 John Richardson   20p–30p

ALLY SLOPER BOOKS
Judy
1873 A.S.A. Moral Lesson C. H. Ross   £5.00–£15.00
1877 A.S. Book of Beauty   £2.50–£5.00
1878 Eastern Question Tackled   £2.50–£5.00
1878 A.S. Guide to Paris Exhibition   £2.50–£5.00
1880 Contra-Dictory of London   £2.50–£5.00
1882 Ups and Downs of A.S.   £2.50–£5.00
1883 A.S. Comic Crackers   £2.50–£5.00
188? True Story of A.S. and Paint Pot
      (20p) (4C) (Art Litho Co)   £5.00–£10.00

ALLY SLOPER'S CHRISTMAS HOLIDAYS
Dec 1884–Dec 1913 (30)
Sinkins/Dalziel/Sloperies
1 (16p) W. G. Baxter   £3.50–£10.00
2–30 W. F. Thomas   £2.00–£5.00

ALLY SLOPER'S COMIC KALENDAR
Dec 1875–Dec 1887 (13)
Judy
1 (nn) Charles Ross   £3.50–£10.00
2–13 Marie Duval   £2.00–£5.00

ALLY SLOPER'S COMIC VOLUME
1913(?)–
Sloperies
(remainders rebound)   £2.50–£5.00

ALLY SLOPER'S HALF-HOLIDAY
3 May 1884–30 May 1914 (1570)
Sinkins/Dalziel/Sloperies
to: Ally Sloper (new series)
1 (8p) (tabloid)   £5.00–£20.00
2– W. G. Baxter   50p–£2.00
1903: (12p) W. F. Thomas   50p–£1.50
1907: (16p) (magazine)   50p–£1.25

ALLY SLOPER'S HALF-HOLIDAY
5 Nov 1922–14 Apr 1923 (23)
Sloperies
to: Half-Holiday
1 (16p) (magazine)   £2.00–£5.00
2–23 W. F. Thomas   £1.00–£2.00

ALLY SLOPER'S HALF-HOLIDAY
May 1949 (1)
Ally Sloper
1 (8p)   £1.00–£1.50

ALLY SLOPER'S HA'PORTH
23 Jan 1899–21 Mar 1899 (10)
Dalziel
1 (8p) (tabloid)   £3.00–£10.00
2–10 Ernest Wilkinson   £2.50–£3.00

ALLY SLOPER'S QUARTERLY
Dalziel
(12 weekly issues rebound)   £2.50–£5.00

ALLY SLOPER'S SUMMER NUMBER
1880–1887 (8)
Judy
1 Charles Ross   £3.50–£10.00
2–8 Marie Duval   £2.00–£5.00

AMAZING ADVENTURES OF CAPTAIN
KRUNCH
1977 (1)
KP Foods (giveaway)
1 (nn) (20p) (4C) Alf Saporito   50p–£1.00

AMAZING COMICS
Oct 1949 (1)
Modern Fiction
1 (nn) (8p) Denis Gifford   75p–£1.50

AMAZING STORIES
196–
Class (ACG)
1 (68p) US reprints   25p–£1.00
2–   25p–75p

AMAZING EXPLOITS OF JEREMY BEAR
1971 (1)
Golden Press/Quaker Oats (giveaway)
1 (nn) (20p) (4C) (3D) Sugar Puffs   £1.00–£3.00
  (worth less without 3D specs)

AMAZING SPIDER-MAN POSTER MAGAZINE
1977 (1)
Marvel
1 (16p) (4C) (poster) US reprint   20p–35p

AMERICAN COMIC ANNUAL
1943 (1)
Miller (NEA)
1 (nn) (68p) (gravure) US reprints   £2.00–£5.00

ANDY CAPP
1958–
Daily Mirror
1: The AC Book (1958) Reg Smythe
    reprints   £2.00–£5.00
2: AC's Spring Tonic (1959)   £1.50–£3.00
3: Life With AC (1959)   £1.00–£2.00
4: AC Spring Collection (1960)   £1.00–£2.00
5: Best of AC (1960) (oblong)   £1.00–£2.00
6: Laugh With AC (1961)   £1.00–£2.00
7: World of AC (1961)   £1.00–£2.00
8: More AC (1962)   £1.00–£2.00
9: AC, I Must be Dreaming (1962)   £1.00–£2.00
10: AC Picks His Favourites (1963)   £1.00–£2.00
11: Happy Days With AC (1963)   £1.00–£2.00
12: Laugh at Life With AC (1964)   £1.00–£2.00
13: AC and Florrie (1964)   £1.00–£2.00
14: All the Best From AC (1965)   £1.00–£2.00
15–44 (numbered)   £1.00–£1.50
45– (comicbook format)   50p–£1.00
50 (special)   75p–£1.25
Xmas issues: World of AC (oblong) (192p) 50p–£1.00
see: Laugh Again With AC

ANDY DEVINE
1950–
Miller (Fawcett)
50 (1) (28p) US reprint   75p–£1.00
51–   50p–£1.00

ANDY PANDY HOLIDAY SPECIAL
May 1980 (1)
Polystyle
1 (nn) (48p) (reprints)   25p–40p

ANIMAL WEIRDNESS
Oct 1974 (1)
H. Bunch/Cosmic Comics
1 (36p) (adult) Malcolm Poynter   35p–75p

ANNIE
Jul 1982 (1)
Seymour
1 (nn) (68p) US reprint (film)   75p–£1.50

ANNIE OAKLEY
Jun 1957–1958 (17)

Miller (Gower Studios)
1 (28p) Arthur Baker   50p–£1.00
2–17 Denis Gifford   25p–75p

ANNIE OAKLEY AND TAGG
1955–1956 (10)
World (Dell)
1 (28p) US reprint   50p–£1.00
2–10   25p–75p

APACHE KID
1951 (2)
Streamline (Atlas)
1 (nn) (28p) US reprint   25p–75p
2   25p–50p

ARCHIE
1950–1953
Swan (Archie)
1 (68p) US reprint   50p–£1.00
2–   25p–50p

ARCHIE COMICS
1953–
Thorpe & Porter (Archie)
1– US reprint   25p–50p

ARIZONA KID
1952 (1)
Streamline/United Anglo-American (Marvel)
1 (28p) US reprint   50p–£1.00

ARROWHEAD
1954 (2)
Streamline (Atlas)
1 (28p) US reprint   50p–£1.00
2   50p–75p

ARRY'S BUDGET
26 Jun 1886–6 Nov 1886 (21)
Rayner
to: Arry's Illustrated Budget
1 (8p) (tabloid)   £5.00–£10.00
2–21   £2.50–£3.50

ARRY'S ILLUSTRATED BUDGET
13 Nov 1886–
Rayner
1 (8p) (tabloid)   £3.50–£7.00
2–   £2.00–£3.00

ASTERIX
1969–1983 (28)
Brockhampton/Hodder
1 (52p) (4C) Asterix the Gaul   50p–£1.00
2–28 foreign reprints   45p–£1.00

ASTERIX PRESENTS KRYPTIX PUZZLE
MAGAZINE
Nov 1982–Feb 1984 (16)
London Editions
1 (52p) foreign reprints   15p–25p
2–16   10p–20p

ASTONISHING STORIES
196–
Class (Atlas)
1 (68p) US reprints   25p–£1.00
2–   25p–75p

ASTOUNDING STORIES
Feb 1966–
Class (Charlton)
1 (68p) US reprints   25p–£1.00
2–   25p–75p

ATOM
1947 (1)
Buchanan
1 (nn) (12p) Rex Hart   50p–£1.50

ATOMIC AGE COMIC
1947 (1)
Burn/Algar
1 (nn) (36p) Walter Booth   £1.50–£2.50

ATOMIC COMIC
Sep 1947 (1)
Fudge
1 (nn) (8p) Bob Wilkin   50p–£1.00

ATOMIC MOUSE
1953 (4)
Miller (Charlton)
1 (28p) US reprint   25p–75p
2–4   25p–50p

ATOMIC SPY RING
1949 (1)
Hotspur (*Secret Service Series* 6)
1 (6) (8p) Bob Wilkin (gravure)   50p–£1.00

ATTACK
Famepress/Award/White
1962–
1 (68p) (4C) (small)   50p–£1.00
2– Italian reprints   25p–75p

ATTACK PICTURE LIBRARY HOLIDAY
SPECIAL
May 1982–May 1984 (3)
IPC
1 (nn) (196p) reprints (small)   25p–50p
2–3   20p–25p

AUGUSTA
1977–1978 (2)
Barrie & Jenkins (*Evening Standard* reprints)
1: *Augusta the Great* (76p)   50p–£1.00
2: *I, Augusta* Domenic Poelsma   50p–75p

AUTHENTIC POLICE CASES
1949 (1)
Locker (St John)
1 (36p) (nn) US reprints   £1.00–£1.75

AVENGERS
1966 (1)
Thorpe & Porter
1 (68p) Mick Anglo   £1.00–£3.00

AVENGERS
22 Sep 1973–14 Jul 1976 (147)
Marvel
to: *Marvel*
1 (36p) US reprints   50p–£1.50
2–147   25p–50p

AVENGERS TREASURY
1982 (1)
Marvel
1 (nn) (56p) (4C) US reprint   50p–£1.00

AVENGERS WINTER SPECIAL
Nov 1982 (1)
Marvel
1 (US reprint)   50p–80p

BADTIME BEDTIME STORYBOOK
14 Jun 1975–
IPC
supplement to *Monster Fun*
1: *Jack the Nipper* (8p) (small)   10p–25p
2– Leo Baxendale   10p–20p

BAIRNS COMIC
1948 (2)
P.M. (Marx)
1 (8p) Bob Wilkin   50p–£1.00
2 Walter Bell   50p–£1.00

BALLOON
1949 (1)
Paget
1 (nn) (12p) Harry Banger   50p–£1.00

BANANAMAN SUMMER SPECIAL
May 1984 (1)
Thomson
1   20p–40p

BANG ON COMIC
1947 (1)
Fudge
1 (8p) David Williams   50p–£1.00

BANG ON COMIC
1948 (1)
Philmar (Marx)
1 (8p) W. Robertson   50p–£1.00

BANTAM COMICS
1944 (1)
P.M. (Marx)
1 (nn) (card) Glyn Protheroe   50p–£1.00

BARBARA CARTLAND PICTURE ROMANCES
1982 (1)
Macmillan (United Features)
1 (132p) (oblong) (US reprints)   50p–£1.95

BARKER
1949 (1)
Locker (Quality)
1 (36p) (4C) US reprint   £1.00–£2.00

BARNARDO STORY
1980 (1)
Barnardo
1 (20p) (4C) children's home promo   25p–50p

BARRY McKENZIE
1968–1972 (2)
MacDonald/*Private Eye*
1 *Wonderful World of B.M.* (reprints)   £1.00–£1.50
2 *Bazza Pulls It Off*   £1.00–£1.50

BASIL BRUSH SPECIALS
May 1977–May 1981 (4)
Polystyle
1: *Holiday Special 1977* (48p) reprints   25p–40p
2: *Winter Special 1978*   25p–35p
3: *Holiday Special 1980*   20p–30p
4: *Summer Special 1981*   20p–30p

BASSETT'S FUN BOOK
1966 (1)
Bassetts/Odhams (giveaway)
1 (nn) (16p) (small) puzzles   25p–50p

BAT MAGAZINE
1952 (2)
Cartoon Art
1 (68p)   £1.50–£3.00
2   £1.00–£1.50

BATMAN POCKETBOOK
Nov 1978–1979
Egmont/Methuen (DC)
1 (100p) (small) (4C) US reprint   20p–35p
2–   15p–25p

BATTLE
Nov 1960–Jul 1961 (9)
Anglo/Atlas
1 (28p) Roy Castle   50p–£1.00
2–9   25p–50p

BATTLE ACTION/BATTLE
19 Nov 1977–1 Oct 1983 (307)
IPC
to: *Battle Action Force*

1 (32p) Carlos Ezquerra 15p–25p
2–307 John Cooper 10p–15p
see: *Best of Battle*

BATTLE ACTION COMIC
1952 (1)
Cartoon Art (Fiction House)
1 (nn) (28p) US reprint 75p–£1.00

BATTLE ACTION FORCE
8 Oct 1983–
IPC
1 (32p) Joe Colquhoun 15p–20p
2– Geoff Campion 5p–10p

BATTLE ACTION FORCE HOLIDAY SPECIAL
Apr 1984 (1)
IPC
1 25p–50p

BATTLE ACTION IN PICTURES
1959 (3)
Miller
1 (68p) US reprint (small) 25p–75p
2–3 25p–50p

BATTLE ATTACK
1953 (1)
Streamline/Anglo-American (Stanmor)
1 (nn) (28p) US reprint 25p–50p

BATTLE CRY
1953 (2)
Streamline/United Anglo-American (Stanmor)
1 (nn) (28p) US reprint 25p–50p
2 (nn) (68p) 25p–50p

BATTLE FIRE
1955 (1)
Streamline (Stanmor)
1 (nn) (28p) US reprint 50p–75p

BATTLE GROUND
1955 (1)
Streamline/Anglo-American (Atlas)
1 (28p) (nn) US reprint 25p–50p

BATTLE GROUND
1960–1961 (11)
Miller (Fawcett)
1 (68p) US reprint 25p–50p
2–11 25p–35p

BATTLE OF THE PLANETS HOLIDAY SPECIAL
28 Jul 1983–18 May 1984 (2)
Polystyle
1 (48p) US reprints 25p–50p
2 20p–30p

BATTLE PICTURE LIBRARY
Jan 1961–Dec 1984 (1706)
Fleetway/IPC
1 (68p) *Rats of Tobruk* 25p–£1.00
2–1706 25p–50p

BATTLE PICTURE LIBRARY HOLIDAY SPECIAL
May 1969–
IPC
1 (224p) reprints 50p–75p
2– (192p) 25p–50p

BATTLE PICTURE WEEKLY
8 Mar 1975–12 Nov 1977 (140)
IPC
& *Valiant*: 23 Oct 1976
to: *Battle Action*
1 (32p) 25p–50p
2–140 Geoff Campion 10p–15p

BATTLE SPECIALS
May 1975–May 1984 (10)
IPC
1: *Summer Special 1975* (80p) 30p–50p
2: *Summer Special 1976* (64p) 25p–35p
3: *Summer Special 1977* 20p–30p
4: *Summer Special 1978* 15p–25p
5: *Holiday Special 1979* 15p–25p
6: *Holiday Special 1980* 15p–25p
7: *Holiday Special 1981* 15p–25p
8: *Summer Special 1982* 15p–25p
9: *Holiday Special 1983* 15p–25p
10: *Holiday Special 1984* 15p–20p

BATTLE SQUADRON
1956 (2)
Streamline/United Anglo-American (Stanmor)
1 (nn) (28p) US reprint 25p–50p
2 (nn) (68p) 25p–50p

BATTLE STORIES
1952–1953 (9)
Miller (Fawcett)
1 (28p) US reprint 50p–£1.00
2–9 (68p) 50p–75p

BATTLECRY PICTURE LIBRARY
Jan 1966–
Famepress
1 (68p) (small) reprints 25p–75p
2– 25p–50p

BATTLEFIELD
1962–
Brugeditor/Holding
1 (68p) foreign reprints (small) 25p–50p
2– 20p–35p

BATTLEGROUND
1965–
Famepress/White
1 (68p) (small) reprints 25p–50p
2– 20p–35p

BATTLER BRITTON PICTURE LIBRARY HOLIDAY SPECIAL
May 1977–
IPC
1 (nn) (196p) (small) reprints 30p–50p
2– 20p–30p

BAZOOKA JOE AND HIS GANG
196–
Bazooka
small strips inserted with bubblegum 1p–5p

BEANO COMIC
30 Jul 1938–
Thomson
1 (28p) Dudley Watkins £20.00–£50.00
1938–1939 Hugh McNeill £2.50–£10.00
1940–1944 Allan Morley £2.00–£4.00
1945–1949 Basil Blackaller £2.00–£3.00
1950–1955 David Law £1.00–£1.50
1955–1959 Ken Reid £1.00–£1.25
1960–1969 Leo Baxendale 50p–£1.00
1970–1979 Ron Spence 10p–50p
1980– Bill Ritchie 10p–20p
Beano No 1 facsimile £1.00–£2.00

BEANO COMIC LIBRARY
13 Apr 1982–
Thomson
1: *King Dennis the Menace* (64p) 15p–25p
2– 10p–20p

BEANO SUMMER SPECIAL
1964–
Thomson
1 (nn) (32p) (tabloid) (4C) £1.00–£5.00
2– 50p–£2.00

BEAU PEEP
1980–1984 (5)
Express Books (*Daily Star* reprints)
1 (68p) Andrew Christine   50p–£1.00
2–5   50p–75p

BEEZER
21 Jan 1956–
Thomson
& *Cracker*: 18 Sep 1976
& *Plug*: 3 Mar 1979
1 (12p) (tabloid) Dudley Watkins   £1.00–£3.50
1956–1959 Allan Morley   50p–£1.00
1960–1969 David Law   25p–50p
1970–1979 Bill Ritchie   10p–25p
1980– 21 Mar 81 (last tabloid)   10p–15p
28 Mar 1981 – (small)   5p–10p

BEEZER COMIC
1947 (1)
Scoop
1 (nn) (8p folder)   £1.00–£2.00

BEEZER SUMMER SPECIAL
Jun 1973–
Thomson
1 (32p) (4C) (tabloid)   50p–£1.00
2–   25p–50p

THE BELCHERS
1983 (1)
Blandford
1 (nn) (52p) (oblong) *Vole* reprints   50p–95p

BELINDA
1945–1948 (2)
Daily Mirror reprints
1 B & the Bomb Alley Boys Dunlop (32p)   £1.00–£2.00
2 B in Shooting Star Mirror Features (36p) £1.00–£2.00

BEN BOWIE AND HIS MOUNTAIN MEN
1955–
World (Dell)
1 (28p) US reprint   35p–75p
2–   25p–75p

BENJY ALL COLOUR PAPERBACK
1973 (1)
Top Sellers
1 (132p) (4C) reprints   10p–50p

BENJY AND HIS FRIENDS
1971–1972
Top Sellers
1– (36p) (4C) reprints   10p–25p

BEST OF ALL COMICS
Oct 1948 (1)
Cartoon Art
1 (20p) Dennis Reader   £1.00–£2.00

BEST OF BATTLE
1983
Titan (IPC)
1: *Charley's War* (68p) reprints   £3.95

BEST OF DONALD DUCK
1978 (2)
Purnell/Egmont (Disney)
1 (52p) (4C) reprints   50p–85p
2   35p–50p

BEST OF ELMER T. HACK
1979 (1)
BSFA/Hack Press (*Vector* reprints)
1 (nn) (60p) Jim Barker   40p–80p

BEST OF KRAZY
Jun 1978 (1)
IPC
1 (64p) reprints   25p–35p

BEST OF MY GUY MONTHLY
Apr 1984–Jul 1984 (4)
IPC
to: *My Guy Monthly*
1 (68p) (reprints)   10p–20p
2–4   10p–15p

BEST OF MY GUY SPECIAL
Jun 1982–Jun 1984 (3)
IPC
1 (68p) reprints   15p–25p
2–3   10p–25p

BEST OF OUR KID
1981 (1)
Sandwell *Evening Mail*
1 (100p) strips by Rali   50p–85p

BEST OF THE WEST
1951 (3)
Cartoon Art (Magazine Enterprises)
1 (32p) (4C) US reprints   50p–£1.00
2–3 (68p)   50p–£1.00

BEST OF 2000 AD
1982–
Titan (IPC)
1: *Robo-Hunter Book 1* (68p) reprints   £2.95–£3.50
2: *Robo-Hunter Book 2*   £2.95–£3.50
3: *ABC Warriors Book 1*   £3.50–£3.95
4: *ABC Warriors Book 2*   £3.50–£3.95
5: *Nemesis*   £3.95
6: *Robusters Book 1*   £3.95
7: *Robusters Book 2*   £3.95

BEST OF WHIZZER AND CHIPS MONTHLY
Nov 1984–
IPC
1 (68p) (reprints)   15p–25p
2–   10p–15p

BIBLE ILLUSTRATED
1947–1948 (8)
Bible Pictures/Thorpe & Porter
1 (52p) (4C) US reprint   50p–75p
2–8   25p–50p

BIBLE STORY
7 Mar 1964–
Fleetway
1 (28p) (4C) Peter Jackson   35p–50p
2–   25p–35p

BIBLE TALES FOR YOUNG PEOPLE
1954 (5)
Miller (Atlas)
to: *Ilustrated Bible Tales*
1 (28p) US reprint   35p–50p
2–5   25p–35p

BIFF: THE EARLY YEARS
1984 (1)
Biff Products
1 (24p) (collage comic) (small)   35p–50p

BIG BEN
28 Mar 1984–19 Jul 1984 (18)
Marvel
to: *Spiderman*
1 US reprints   20p–25p
2–18   10p–20p

BIG BEN SUMMER SPECIAL
Jun 1984 (1)
Marvel
1 US reprints   50p–75p

BIG BOY COMIC
1948 (1)
Scion
1 (nn) (8p) Ron Embleton   50p–£1.00

BIG BUDGET
19 Jun 1897–20 Mar 1909 (614)
Pearson
& Boys Leader: 18 Aug 1905
to: The Comet
1 (24p) (tabloid) Tom Browne   £5.00–£10.00
2–614 Ralph Hodgson   £1.00–£2.00
Xmas Double Numbers   £2.00–£3.00
Special Colour Numbers   £2.00–£4.00

BIG BUDGET HOLIDAY SUPPLEMENT
28 May 1898 (1)
Pearson
supplement to Big Budget
1 (50) (8p) (tabloid) 'Yorick'   £1.00–£2.50

BIG CASTLE COMIC
1948 (1)
Scion
1 (nn) (8p) A. Philpott   50p–£1.00

BIG CHEER COMIC
1948 (1)
Scion
1 (nn) (8p) Frank Minnitt   50p–£1.00

BIG CHIEF COMIC
1948 (1)
Scion
1 (nn) (8p) R. Plummer   50p–£1.00

BIG CHUCKLE COMIC
1948 (1)
Scion
1 (nn) (8p) Frank Minnitt   50p–£1.00

BIG COMBAT COMIC
1949 (1)
Scion
1 (nn) (8p) R. Turner   50p–£1.00

BIG COMIC
17 Jan 1914–28 Sep 1918 (246)
Henderson
& Sparks: 5 Jan 1918
to: Sparks & Big Comic
1 (12p) H. O'Neill   £5.00–£10.00
2–208 G. M. Payne   £1.00–£2.00
209–246 Walter Booth   £1.50–£2.00

BIG COWBOY COMIC
1948 (1)
Scion
1 (nn) (8p) Ron Embleton   50p–£1.00

BIG DIP COMIC
1948 (1)
Scion
1 (nn) (8p) R. Plummer   50p–£1.00

BIG DYNAMO COMIC
1948 (1)
Scion
1 (nn) (8p) Serge Drigin   50p–£1.00

BIG EAGLE COMIC
1948 (1)
Scion
1 (nn) (8p) Ron Embleton   50p–£1.00

BIG FLAME WONDER COMIC
1948 (1)
Scion
1 (nn) (8p) Ron Embleton   50p–£1.00

BIG GAME COMIC
1948 (2)
Scion
1 (nn) (8p) R. Plummer   50p–£1.00
2 (nn) (8p) 'Maskman'   50p–£1.00

BIG HIT COMIC
1949 (1)
Scion
1 (nn) (8p) Ron Embleton   50p–£1.00

BIG IDEA COMIC
1948 (1)
Scion
1 (nn) (8p) Ron Embleton   50p–£1.00

BIG INDIAN COMIC
1948 (1)
Scion
1 (nn) (8p) Ron Embleton   50p–£1.00

BIG JUNGLE COMIC
1948 (1)
Scion
1 (nn) (8p) Ron Embleton   50p–£1.00

BIG LAUGH COMIC
1949 (1)
Scion
1 (nn) (8p) Bob Wilkin   50p–£1.00

BIG LITTLE COMIC
1945 (1)
PM (Marx)
1 (nn) (folded card) D. Gifford   50p–£1.00

BIG MOUNTY COMIC
1949 (1)
Scion
1 (nn) (8p) R. Turner   50p–£1.00

BIG NOISE WONDER COMIC
1948 (1)
Scion
1 (nn) (8p) Ron Embleton   50p–£1.00

BIG ONE
17 Oct 1964–20 Feb 1965 (19)
Fleetway
to: Buster
1 (12p) (outsize) (reprints)   50p–£1.00
2–19 Roy Wilson   25p–50p

BIG PARADE COMIC
1947 (1)
Grant Hughes
1 (nn) (16p) Bob Wilkin   50p–£1.00

BIG PIRATE COMIC
1948 (1)
Scion
1 (nn) (8p) Ron Embleton   50p–£1.00

BIG RACER COMIC
1948 (1)
Scion
1 (nn) (8p) Serge Drigin   50p–£1.00

BIG RANCH COMIC
1949 (1)
Scion
1 (nn) (8p) R. Turner   50p–£1.00

BIG SAHARA COMIC
1949 (1)
Scion
1 (nn) (8p) R. Plummer   50p–£1.00

BIG SCOOP COMIC
1949 (1)
Scion
1 (nn) (8p) R. Turner   50p–£1.00

BIG SHOT
1949 (2)
Streamline/United Anglo-American (Columbia)
1 (nn) (36p) (4C) US reprint   £1.00–£2.00
2 (nn) (28p)   50p–£1.00

BIG SHOT COMIC
1949 (1)
Scion
1 (nn) (8p) R. Plummer   50p–£1.00

BIG SHOW COMIC
1949 (1)
Scion
1 (nn) (8p) R. Plummer   50p–£1.00

BIG SLIDE COMIC
1948 (1)
Scion
1 (nn) (8p) Ron Embleton   50p–£1.00

BIG STAR COMIC
1948 (1)
Scion
1 (nn) (8p) Serge Drigin   50p–£1.00

BIG SURPRISE COMIC
1950 (3)
Tower
1–3 (with transfers) W. Robertson   50p–£1.50

BIG THRILL COMIC
1948 (1)
Scion
1 (nn) (8p) Serge Drigin   50p–£1.00

BIG TIME COMIC
1947 (1)
Scion
1 (nn) (8p) R. Plummer   50p–£1.00

BIG TONG COMIC
1948 (1)
Scion
1 (nn) (8p) Ron Embleton   50p–£1.00

BIG TOP
1948 (1)
Scion
1 (nn) (8p) Bob Wilkin   50p–£1.00

BIG TOP COMIC
1949 (1)
Martin & Reid
1 (nn) (8p) Harry Banger   50p–£1.00

BIG TRAIL COMIC
1949 (1)
Scion
1 (nn) (8p) Frank Minnitt   50p–£1.00

BIG TRAIN COMIC
1948 (1)
Scion
1 (nn) (8p) Walter Booth   50p–£1.00

BIG TREAT COMIC
1948 (1)
Scion
1 (nn) (8p) R. Plummer   50p–£1.00

BIG WIN COMIC
1948 (1)
Scion
1 (nn) (8p) Ron Embleton   50p–£1.00

BIGGLES
Sep 1952 (2)
Brockhampton
1: *B Breaks the Silence* (52p) (small)   50p–£1.00
2: *B Hunts Big Game*   50p–£1.00

BIGGLES
1977–1981
Hodder & Stoughton (Bonnier)
1: *B & the Sargasso Triangle* (52p) (4C)   50p–95p
2: *B & the Golden Bird*   25p–50p
3: *B & the Tiger*   25p–50p
4: *B & the Menace from Space*   25p–50p
see: *Adventures of Biggles*

BIJOU FUNNIES
Mar 1974 (1)
H. Bunch/Cozmic Comix (Krupp)
1 (36p) US reprint   25p–50p

BILL BOYD WESTERN
1950–1955 (78)
Miller (Fawcett)
1 (24p) US reprint   £1.00–£1.25
2–78   50p–£1.00

BILL CARTER (Calling . . .)
1947–1948 (3)
Foldes
1–3 (12p) Rex Hart   50p–£1.00

BILLY BUCKSKIN WESTERN
1956 (2)
Miller (Atlas)
1–2 (28p) US reprint   25p–50p

BILLY THE KID
1956–1957
Miller (Charlton)
1 (50) (28p) US reprint   25p–75p
51–   25p–50p

BILLY THE KID ADVENTURE MAGAZINE
1953–1959 (76)
World (Toby)
1 (28p) US reprint   50p–£1.00
2–78 (68p)   50p–75p

BIMBO
18 Mar 1961–22 Jan 1972 (567)
Thomson
inc: *Little Star*
1 (20p) Dudley Watkins   25p–75p
2–567 Bob Dewar   20p–50p

BIMBO GOES TO THE MOON
Mar 1946 (1)
Locker
1 (nn) (20p) Bob Monkhouse   50p–£1.00

BIRTHDAY NOVELTIES PAINTING BOOKS
1960 (2)
Melody Cards/Mick Anglo
1: *Happy Birthday* (Young Joey reprints)   50p–£1.00
2: *Happy Birthday* (Flip & Flop reprints) 50p–£1.00

BLACK CAT WESTERN
1950 (1)
Streamline/United Anglo-American (Harvey)
1 (28p) US reprint   50p–£1.00

BLACK DIAMOND WESTERN
1951–1954 (33)
Pemberton/World (Gleason)
1 (36p) US reprint   50p–£1.00
2–33 (28p)   50p–75p
see: *Giant Comic*

BLACK FURY
Jan 1955–1956 (8)
World (Charlton)

1 (28p) US reprint   50p–£1.00
2–8   50p–75p

BLACK FURY
1957–1958 (12)
Miller (Charlton)
1 (50) (28p) US reprint   50p–£1.00
51–61   50p–75p

BLACK HOLE
Jan 1980 (1)
IPC
1 (48p) US reprint (Disney film)   25p–40p

BLACK JACK (Rocky Lane's)
1956–1957 (11)
Miller (Charlton)
1 (28p) US reprint   50p–£1.00
2–11   50p–75p

BLACK KNIGHT
1953 (5)
Miller (Atlas)
1 (28p) US reprint   50p–£1.00
2–5   50p–75p

BLACK MAGIC
1952–1953 (16)
Arnold (Prize)
1 (68p) US reprint   £2.00–£3.50
2–16   £1.00–£2.00

BLACK RIDER
1955 (4)
Miller (Atlas)
1 (28p) US reprint   50p–£1.00
2–4   50p–75p

BLACK STALLION CARTOON BOOKS
1983 (2)
Hodder & Stoughton (Hachette)
1: *Black Stallion* (52p) (French reprints)   £1.00–£1.95
2: *BS & Satan* (4C)   £1.00–£1.95

BLACKHAWK
1949–1953 (15)
Boardman/Popular (Quality)
1 (11) (12p) (gravure) US reprint   £1.00–£2.50
15–61   £1.00–£1.50
numbered: 11; 15; 18; 20; 21; 25; 27; 28;
32; 40; 42; 48; 57; 59; 61

BLACKHAWK
1956–1958 (36)
Strato (Quality)
1 (68p) US reprint   75p–£1.00
2–36   50p–75p

BLAKE THE TRAPPER
1955 (2)
Miller
1–2 (28p) foreign reprint   25p–50p

BLAKES 7
Oct 1981–Aug 1983 (23)
Marvel
1 (36p) (TV series) Ian Kennedy   40p–50p
2–22 David Lloyd   25p–40p
23 (double number)   75p–£1.20

BLAKES 7 SPECIALS
May 1981–Nov 1982 (3)
Marvel
1: *Summer Special 1981* (48p)   40p–60p
2: *Summer Special 1982*   40p–60p
3: *Winter Special 1982*   40p–60p

BLAZER COMIC
1949 (1)
Philmar (Marx)
1 (nn) (16p) Reg Parlett   75p–£1.25

BLAZING TRAILS
196– (1)
Class (Charlton)
1 (nn) (68p) US reprint   35p–50p

BLAZING WEST
1951 (1)
Streamline/United Anglo-American (ACG)
1 (nn) (28p) US reprint   50p–£1.00

BLAZING WEST/BOYS RANCH
1951 (1)
Streamline/United Anglo-American (ACG/Harvey)
1 (nn) (68p) US reprint   75p–£1.00

BLISS
4 Mar 1961–
City
1   50p–£1.00
2–   20p–30p

BLOCKBUSTER
Jun 1981–Feb 1982 (9)
Marvel
to: *Rampage*
1 (52p) US reprints   30p–45p
2–9   25p–40p

BLOCKBUSTER WINTER SPECIAL
27 Nov 1980 (1)
Marvel
1 (52p) US reprints   25p–40p

BLOOPER
1984
Planet Gaff
1– (24p)   20p–30p

BLUE BEETLE
1950 (2)
Streamline/United Anglo-American (Fox)
1–2 (nn) (28p) US reprint   50p–£1.00

BLUE BEETLE
195– (3)
Miller (Fox)
1 (28p) US reprint   50p–£1.00
2–3   50p–75p

BLUE BOLT ADVENTURES
1951 (2)
Miller (Novelty)
1–2 (28p) US reprint   50p–£1.00
see: *Blue Bolt Series*

BLUE BOLT SERIES
Aug 1952–May 1954 (22)
Swan (Novelty)
1 (36p) *Indian Warriors*   50p–£1.00
2 *White Rider*   50p–75p
3 *Young King Cole*   50p–75p
4 *Blue Bolt* –1   50p–£1.00
5 *Super Horse*   50p–75p
6 *Indian Warhawks*   50p–75p
7 *Spacehawks*   75p–£1.50
8 *Dick Cole* –1   50p–£1.00
9 *Blue Bolt* –2   50p–75p
10 *Dick Cole* –2   50p–75p
11 *Target* –1   50p–£1.00
12 *Outlaws* –1   50p–75p
13 *Blue Bolt* –3   50p–75p
14 *Target* –2   50p–75p
15 *Blue Bolt* –4   50p–75p
16 *Outlaws* –2   50p–75p
17 *Blue Bolt* –5   50p–75p
18 *Blue Bolt* –6   50p–75p
19 *Blue Bolt* –7   50p–75p
20 *Blue Bolt* –8 (some GB strips)   50p–75p
21 *Blue Bolt* –9 (some GB strips)   50p–75p
22 *Blue Bolt* –10 (some GB strips)   50p–75p

BLUE CIRCLE
1953 (1)
Streamline (Fox)
1 (28p) US reprint   75p–£1.00

BLUE JEANS
22 Jan 1977–
Thomson
1 (32p)   15p–25p
2–   10p–15p

BLUE JEANS PHOTO NOVEL
10 Jun 1980–
Thomson
1 (68p) (small)   15p–20p
2–   10p–15p

BLUE JEANS SPECIALS
1979–
Thomson
1: *Summer Special 1979* (48p)   25p–30p
2: *Summer Special 1980*   20p–25p
3: *Supergirl Special 1981*   20p–25p
4: *Summer Special 1981*   20p–25p
5: *Spring Special 1982*   20p–25p
6: *Summer Special 1982*   20p–25p
7: *Summer Special 1983*   20p–25p
8: *Spring Special 1984*   20p–25p
9: *Summer Special 1984*   20p–25p

BLUE PETER HOLIDAY SPECIAL
1976 (1)
IPC/BBC
1 (40p) TV series   25p–35p

BO-PEEP AND LITTLE BOY BLUE
19 Oct 1929–14 Apr 1934 (245)
AP
to: *Chicks Own*
1 (12p) Walter Bell (tabloid)   £5.00–£10.00
2–245 Stanley White   £1.25–£2.00

BOB COLT
1951–1952 (9)
Miller (Fawcett)
1 (50) (36p) US reprint   50p–£1.00
51–58 (24p)   50p–75p

BOB COMIC BOOK
1949 (1)
PM (Marx)
1 (nn) (28p) Colin Merritt   50p–£1.50

BOB STEELE WESTERN
Oct 1951–1952 (7)
Miller (Fawcett)
1 (50) (24p) US reprint   50p–£1.00
51–56   50p–75p

BOB SWIFT BOY SPORTSMAN
1951–1952 (4)
Miller (Fawcett)
1 (36p) US reprint   50p–£1.00
2–4 (24p)   50p–75p

BOBBY BEAR
1920–1930 (10)
Daily Herald
1: *Daily Herald Bobby Bear Book* (1920)   £2.50–£5.00
2: *Bobby Bear Annual* (1922)   £2.00–£3.00
3: *Bobby Bear Annual* (1923)   £2.00–£3.00
4: *Bobby Bear's Annual* (1924)   £2.00–£3.00
5: *Bobby Bear's Annual* (1925)   £2.00–£3.00
6: *Bobby Bear's Annual* (1926)   £2.00–£3.00
7: *Bobby Bear's Annual 1928* (1927)   £2.00–£3.00
8: *Bobby Bear's Annual 1929* (1928)   £2.00–£3.00
9: *Bobby Bear's Annual 1930* (1929)   £2.00–£3.00
10: *Bobby Bear's Annual 1931* (1930)   £2.00–£3.00
(becomes hardback; not catalogued)

BOBBY BENSON'S B-BAR-B RIDERS
1950–1951 (12)
World (Parkway)
1 (36p) US reprint   50p–£1.00
2–10   50p–75p
see: *Action Series*

BOBO BUNNY
22 Mar 1969–27 Jan 1973 (201)
IPC
& *Esmeralda*: 5 Feb 1972
to: *Hey Diddle Diddle*
1 (16p) (gravure)   25p–50p
2–201   20p–25p

BOGEY
1975 (1)
Ghura
1 (36p) (adult) Antonio Ghura   50p–£1.00

BOLTON EVENING NEWS CARTOONS
8 Mar 1983–
supplement to *Bolton Evening News*
1 (4p) (2C) (tabloid) US reprints   15p–25p
2–   5p–10p

BOM
1959–1963 (4)
Brockhampton
1: *Hello Bom & Wuffy Dog* (oblong)   75p–£1.50
2: *Here Comes Bom*   50p–£1.00
3: *Bom Goes To The Circus*   50p–£1.00
4: *Here's To Little Bom*   50p–£1.00

BONANZA
1970–1971
Top Sellers (Dell)
1 (36p) (4C) US reprint   10p–25p
2–   10p–25p
see: *Western Classics*

BONANZA WORLD ADVENTURE LIBRARY
Jun 1967–Aug 1967 (3)
World (Dell)
1: *Ponderosa Ranch* (68p)   15p–35p
2–3 US reprint   10p–25p

BONGO COMIC
Apr 1963 (1?)
Wolfe/Tonibell
1 (16p) (4C) sold on ice cream vans   £1.00–£2.00

BONNIE
16 Mar 1974–10 May 1975 (61)
IPC
inc: *Playhour*
1 (16p) Hugh McNeill   10p–25p
2–61 Gordon Hutchings   5p–15p

BONNIE'S HOLIDAY SPECIAL
May 1974–Mar 1975 (2)
IPC
1–2 (48p)   15p–25p

BONZA COMIC
1947–1948 (4)
Forshaw (1) Ensign (2–4)
1 (nn) (8p) (brown) W. Forshaw   75p–£1.50
2 (nn) (8p) (blue) Bryan Berry   75p–£1.50
3 (nn) (8p) (gravure) W. Forshaw   75p–£1.50
4 (nn) (8p) (gravure) F. Minnitt   75p–£1.50

BOO-BOO AND JUBILEE
1938? (1)
Hutchinson
1 (nn) (132p) (oblong) strip reprint   £2.00–£3.00

BOOKWORMS
1953 (1)
Brockhampton
1 (68p) (oblong)   50p–£1.00

126

BOOMERANG COMIC
1948 (1)
Scion
1 (nn) (8p) Bob Wilkin   50p–£1.00

BORE DA
1967–
Cwmni Urdd Gobaith Cymru
1 (20p) Welsh Language   50p–75p
2–   20p–30p

BOUNCER COMIC
1931 (?)–14 Nov 1931
(publisher unknown)
1   £3.00–£6.00
2–   £2.00–£4.00

BOUNCER COMIC
11 Feb 1939–8 Apr 1939 (9)
Target
1 (16p) Harry Banger (tabloid)   £2.50–£8.00
2–9 Bert Hill   £1.50–£2.50

BOUNCER COMIC
1949 (1)
PM (Marx)
1 (nn) (8p) (gravure) Reg Parlett   £1.00–£1.50

BOURNEMOUTH COMIC CAPERS
1979 (1)
Bournemouth Tourism Dept
1 (nn) (6p) (3C) (giveaway)   10p–25p

BOY COMICS
1950–1951 (8)
Miller (Gleason)
1–8 (28p) US reprint   50p–£1.00

BOY DETECTIVE COMICS
1952 (1)
Hermitage/Thorpe & Porter (Avon)
1 (68p) US reprint   50p–£1.00

BOYFRIEND
16 May 1959–12 Mar 1966 (351)
City
to: Trend & Boyfriend
1   25p–50p
2–351   15p–25p

BOYFRIEND AND TREND
14 May 1966–2 Sep 1967 (69)
City
to: Petticoat (magazine)
1 (360)   25p–50p
361–428   15p–25p

BOYS AND GIRLS DAILY MAIL
8 Apr 1933–9 Oct 1937
Associated Newspapers
supplement to Daily Mail newspaper
1 (8p) (yellow paper) (tabloid)   £2.00–£5.00
2–8 Harry Folkard   £1.50–£2.00
9 (8p) (first 2C)   £2.00–£3.00
10– Herbert Foxwell   £1.50–£2.00
26 Jul 1933–(twice weekly)   £1.50–£2.00
12 Sep 1933–(thrice weekly)   £1.50–£2.00
16 Nov 1933 (magic ink)   £2.00–£3.00
29 Nov 1933–(twice weekly)   £1.50–£2.00
14 Mar 1934–(weekly)   £1.50–£2.00
14 Sep 1935–(outsize) (4p)   £1.50–£2.50
4 Jan 1936–(tabloid) (4p)   £1.00–£1.50
(NB: numbered same as newspaper)

BOYS AND GIRLS OWN EVENING WORLD
31 May 1933–17 Jan 1936 (478)
Western Newspapers
supplement to Bristol Evening World
1 (8p) (tabloid) (green paper) Cyril Price   £2.00–£5.00
2–20 Dec 1933 (thrice weekly)   £1.50–£2.00
22 Dec 1933 (first 3C) John Turner   £2.00–£3.00

27 Dec 1933–16 Feb 1934 (8p) (3C)   £1.50–£3.00
19 Feb 1934–2 Aug 1935 (5 weekly) (4p)   £1.50–£2.00
5 Aug 1935–17 Jan 1936 (3 weekly) (4p)   £1.50–£2.00

BOYS AND GIRLS OWN SOUTH WALES
ECHO . . .
see: South Wales Echo & Express

BOYS AND GIRLS OWN YORKSHIRE
EVENING NEWS
21 Nov 1933–11 Sep 1935 (95)
Provincial Newspapers
supplement to Yorkshire Evening News
to: Auntie Muriel's Fun Shop (mag. supp.)
1 (4p) (tabloid) (yellow paper) A. Fraser   £2.00–£3.50
2–23 May 1934 Reg Perrott   £1.00–£2.00
30 May 1934–11 Sep 1935 (white)   £1.00–£1.50

BOYS DUX
1948 (1)
Cartoon Art
1 (8p) Dennis Reader   50p–£1.00

BOYS OF ENGLAND COMIC SHEET
FOR CHRISTMAS
Dec 1876 (1)
Brett
1 (nn) (broadside)   £5.00–£10.00

BOYS RANCH
1951 (1)
Streamline/United Anglo-American (Harvey)
1 (nn) US reprint   50p–£1.00

BOYS WORLD
26 Jan 1963–3 Oct 1964 (89)
Longacre
to: Eagle
1 Ron Embleton   £1.00–£2.00
2–89 Frank Bellamy   50p–£1.00

BRAINSTORM COMIX
1975–1976 (6)
Alchemy Publications
1 (36p) (adult) Bryan Talbot   50p–£1.00
2–3   50p–75p
4: Mixed Bunch Chris Welch   50p–75p
5: Brainstorm Fantasy Comix   50p–75p
6: Amazing Rock & Roll Adventures   50p–75p

BRASSIE
195– (2)
Northern Press
1–2 (64p) Doug Smith strips reprint   £1.00–£1.50

BREEZY COMIC
1946 (1)
PM (Marx)
1 (nn) Reg Carter (reprints)   50p–£1.00

BREEZY COMIC
1947 (1)
G & C
1 (nn) (tabloid) A. Farningham   £1.50–£2.00

BRICK BRADFORD
1959 (6)
World (King Features)
1 (68p) US reprints   50p–£1.00
2–6   50p–75p
see: Action Series

BRIGHT AND BEEEZY
1948 (1)
PM (Marx)
1 (nn) (8p) George Parlett   50p–£1.00

BRING ON THE BIG YIN
1977 (1)
Collins/Sunday Mail reprints
1 (nn) (68p) (4C) Malcolm McCormick   £1.00–£1.75

BRISTOW
1970–1982 (8)
Alison & Busby/Abelard Schuman/Barrie & Jenkins
1: *Bristow!*	£1.00–£2.00
2: *Bristow*	£1.00–£1.25
3: *More Bristow*	£1.00–£1.25
4: *Bristow Extra*	£1.00–£1.25
5: *Bristow Latest*	£1.00–£1.25
6: *Bristow v Chester Perry*	50p–85p
7: *Bristow's Guide to Living*	£2.00–£2.95
8: *The Penguin Bristow*	£1.00–£1.50

BRITISH HEROES
Jun 1953–1954 (8)
Sports Cartoons (Miller)
1 (28p)	50p–£1.00
2–8	50p–75p

BRONC SADDLER
1959 (2)
Miller
1–2 (68p) US reprint (small)	50p–75p

BRONCHO BILL COMIC
1950 (1)
Peters (Miller) (United Features)
1 (23) (36p) US reprint	50p–£1.00

BRONCHO BILL WESTERN COMIC
1951 (10)
Peters (Miller) (United Features)
1– (28p) US reprint	50p–£1.00
2–10	50p–75p

BRONCO WEST INDIAN SCOUT
1960 (1)
Miller
1 (28p)	25p–75p

BROONS SUMMER FUN SPECIAL
Jun 1982 (1)
Thomson
1 (36p)	25p–35p

BROTHER GOOSE COMIC
1981 (1)
Big Flame
1 (nn) (20p) political (reprints)	25p–50p

BRUIN SERIES
1957–1959 (3)
Brockhampton
1: *Bruin Sets Sail* (oblong)	£1.00–£1.25
2: *Bruin Is Shipwrecked*	75p–£1.00
3: *Bruin the Deep Sea Diver*	75p–£1.00

BRUCE THE BARBARIAN
1973 (1)
Quartet
1 (nn) (132p) reprints: Murray Ball	£1.00–£1.25

BRUSH-OFF
Nov 1982 (1)
Health Education Council
1 (8p) (2C) dental hygiene	1p–5p

BUBBLES & THE CHILDREN'S FAIRY
16 Apr 1921–24 May 1941 (1024)
AP
to: *Chicks Own*
1 (12p) H. Foxwell (tabloid)	£7.00–£10.00
1921–1929 issues	£1.00–£2.00
1930–1939 issues	£1.00–£2.50
1940–1941 issues	£1.00–£2.00

BUCCANEERS
May 1951–
Popular (Boardman) (Quality)
1 (4) (36p) (4C) US reprints	50p–£1.50
2–	50p–£1.00

BUCCANEERS
Feb 1959–Apr 1959 (2)
Pearson (TV Picture Stories)
1 *The Wasp* (small)	50p–£1.00
2 (TVP 6) *Gunpowder Plot*	25p–75p

BUCK JONES
1953–1954 (11)
World (Dell)
1 (36p) US reprint	50p–£1.00
2–11	50p–75p
see: *Cowboy Comics*; *Cowboy Picture Library*

BUCK RYAN
1946 (1)
Mirror Features
1 (nn) *Case of the Broken Thistle* (oblong)	£2.00–£3.50

BUDDY
14 Feb 1980–6 Aug 1983 (130)
Thomson
to: *Victor*
1 (32p)	12p–20p
2–130	10p–15p

BUFFALO BILL
Oct 1948–1951 (15)
Boardman/Popular
to: Buffalo Bill Comic
1 (nn) (12p) (gravure)	£1.00–£2.50
10; 14; 19; 22; 24; 26; 29; 31; 33; 35; 37; 39; 41; 43	£1.00–£2.00

BUFFALO BILL
1952 (2)
Streamline/United Anglo-American (Youthful)
1 (nn) (28p) US reprint	50p–75p
2 (nn) (68p)	50p–75p

BUFFALO BILL CODY
195– (19)
Miller
1 (28p) Colin Andrew	50p–£1.00
2–19 George Bunting	25p–50p

BUFFALO BILL COMIC
1952–1953 (3)
Popular (Boardman); Moring
1 (28p) (45) 2 (49) D. McLoughlin	£1.00–£1.50
Moring reprint (68p)	50p–£1.00

BUGS BUNNY
1953
Thorpe & Porter (Dell)
1– (28p) US reprint	50p–£1.00

BUGS BUNNY
1972–1973
Top Sellers (Dell)
1– (36p) (4C) US reprint	25p–50p

BUGS BUNNY SPECIALS
May 1973–Jul 1983 (10)
World/IPC/Polystyle
1: *Summer Special 1973* (32p)	25p–50p
2: *Summer Special 1974*	20p–45p
3: *Christmas Special 1977* (48p)	25p–40p
4: *Holiday Special 1978*	25p–30p
5: *Holiday Special 1979*	25p–30p
6: *Winter Special 1979*	25p–30p
7: *Holiday Special 1980*	25p–30p
8: *Summer Special 1981*	25p–30p
9: *Holiday Special 1982*	25p–30p
10: *Summer Special 1983*	25p–30p

BULLDOG BRITTAIN COMMANDO
1952 (6)
Miller (King-Ganteaume)
1 (28p) Colin Andrew	50p–£1.00
2–6	50p–£1.00

BULLET
14 Feb 1976–2 Dec 1978 (147)
Thomson
to: *Warlord*
1 (36p)   15p–25p
2–147 (32p)   10p–15p

BULLET SPORTS SPECIAL
2 Apr 1977 (1)
Thomson
1 (32p) (gravure)   20p–30p

BULLETMAN
1951 (1)
Arnold (Miller) (Fawcett)
1 (10) (24p) US reprint   75p–£1.50

BUMPER COMIC ADVENTURES
Jan 1949 (1)
Soloway
1 (nn) reprints   £1.50–£2.00

BUMPER COMIC BOOK
1946–1949 (16)
Barrett
1 (8p) A. W. Browne   £1.00–£2.00
2–8 (12p)   75p–£1.00
9–16 (tabloid) H. Banger   75p–£1.25

BUMPER COMIC CAPERS
Jan 1949 (1)
Soloway
1 (nn) reprints   £1.50–£2.00

BUMPER NEW FUNNIES
Jan 1950 (1)
Swan
1 (nn) (36p)   £1.50–£2.00

BUMPER SUPER MAG
Jun 1964 (1)
Young World (Disney)
1 (80p) (4C) US reprint   50p–75p

BUNDLE BEAR SERIES
1975 (2)
Collins/Carlsen
1: *Bundle Bear's Boat* (36p) (4C)   25p–35p
2: *Bundle & the Whale* Danish reprint   25p–35p

BUNNIES LITTLE BOOK OF COMICS
194– (1)
Buck & Harding
1 (nn) (6p) (folder) Fred Robinson   £1.00–£3.00

BUNTY
18 Jan 1958–
Thomson
1 (28p)   50p–£1.00
2–   20p–40p

BUNTY FOR GIRLS SUMMER SPECIAL
1969–1973 (5)
Thomson
1 (32p) (gravure) (tabloid)   50p–75p
2–5   35p–50p

BUNTY JUDY BUMPER LIBRARY
1977 (1)
Thomson
1 (nn) (196p) reprints   20p–35p

BUNTY JUDY SUMMER SPECIAL
1974–
Thomson
1– (32p) (gravure) (tabloid)   35p–50p
2– (smaller format 1977–)   25p–35p

BUNTY PICTURE STORY LIBRARY FOR GIRLS
1963–
Thomson
1– (68p)   25p–35p
2–   15p–20p

BUSTER
28 May 1960–
Fleetway/IPC
& *Radio Fun*: 26 Feb 1961
& *Film Fun*: 15 Sep 1962
& *Big One*: 27 Feb 1965
& *Giggle*: 20 Jan 1968
& *Cor!!!*: 27 Jun 1974
& *Monster Fun*: 6 Nov 1976
& *Jet*: 2 Oct 1971
& *Jackpot*: 6 Feb 1982
& *School Fun*: 2 Jun 1984
1 (16p) (tabloid) Eric Parker   75p–£1.50
2– Hugh McNeill   25p–50p
5 Jun 1965 (smaller format) Reg Parlett   25p–75p
30 Oct 1965 (standard format) Roy Wilson   25p–50p
1966–Leo Baxendale   20p–35p

BUSTER ADVENTURE LIBRARY
Jul 1966–Dec 1967 (36)
Fleetway
1: *Dateline for Danger*   25p–50p
2–36   20p–35p

BUSTER AND MONSTER FUN HOLIDAY
SPECIAL
Apr 1977–
IPC
1 (nn) (64p) reprints   50p–75p
2–   35p–50p

BUSTER COMIC
1947 (1)
Marx
1 (nn) (8p) Glyn Protheroe   35p–75p

BUSTER COMIC LIBRARY
Aug 1984–
IPC
1 (68p) reprints   15p–25p
2–   10p–15p

BUSTER COMICS
1947 (1)
Cartoon Art
1 (nn) (16p) Dennis Reader   75p–£1.25

BUSTER HOLIDAY (FUN) SPECIAL
1969–
IPC
1 (nn) (96p) Reg Parlett   75p–£1.25
2–5 Jack Pamby   35p–75p
6–7 (80p) Ken Reid   35p–50p
8– (64p) Arthur Martin   35p–40p

BUSTER PUZZLE (BOOK) (SPECIAL)
Apr 1975–
IPC
1 (nn) (80p) Roy Wilson   25p–50p
2–4 (64p) Geoff Campion   20p–35p
5– (36p) Les Barton   15p–20p

BUSTER'S COR-MIC
22 Jun 1974–10 Aug 1974 (4)
IPC
1–4 (supplement to *Buster*)   25p–50p

BUSY HANDS
1974
New English Library
1 (52p) puzzles   15p–25p
2–   10p–20p

BUTTERFLY
17 Sep 1904–31 Mar 1917 (656)

AP
to: *Butterfly & Firefly*
1 (8p) (tabloid) H. O'Neill	£5.00–£10.00
2–656 G. M. Payne	£1.25–£2.00
Xmas double numbers	£2.00–£3.00

BUTTERFLY
24 Oct 1925–18 May 1940 (760)
AP
& Merry & Bright: 26 Jan 1935
to: *Tip Top*
1 (447)–1186 (tabloid) G. Wakefield	£1.00–£1.50
1187–1206 (4C) T. Wakefield	£1.50–£2.00

BUTTERFLY AND FIREFLY
7 Apr 1917–17 Oct 1925 (446)
AP
to: *Butterfly*
1 (12p) (tabloid) J. B. Yeats	£5.00–£7.50
2–446 Bertie Brown	£1.25–£1.75

BUTTERFLY AND JOLLY COMIC
19 Jan 1935–28 Oct 1939 (250)
AP
Overseas edition: two comics	£2.00–£3.00

BUTTONS
3 Oct 1981–
Polystyle
1 (0) promo issue: free in *Mother & Baby*	25p–50p
1 (20p) TV characters	10p–20p
2–	5p–10p

BUTTONS HOLIDAY SPECIAL
Jun 1982–
Polystyle
1 (48p) TV characters	20p–30p
2–	15p–25p

BUZBY HOLIDAY SPECIAL
May 1979 (1)
Polystyle
1 (nn) (48p) Bill Mevin	25p–35p

BUZZ
20 Jan 1973–4 Jan 1975 (103)
Thomson
to: *Topper*
1 (16p) (tabloid) Brian White	50p–£1.00
2–103 George Martin	25p–50p

C. H. ROSS'S VARIETY PAPER
27 Jul 1887–14 Mar 1888 (34)
Ross
1 (8p) (tabloid) W. Baxter	£5.00–£10.00
2–34	£2.00–£3.00

CAIN'S HUNDRED
1962 (1)
Top Sellers (Dell)
1 (68p) US reprint	25p–75p

CALIMERO
1973–1974
Top Sellers
1 (36p) (4C) Italian reprint	25p–35p
2–	20p–25p

CALLING MATT HARDY
1947 (1)
Foldes/Overend
1 (nn) (12p) Rex Hart	50p–£1.00

CAMBERWICK GREEN HOLIDAY SPECIAL
May 1981 (1)
Polystyle
1 (nn) (48p) reprints (TV series)	35p–50p

CANDIDA THE MARCHESA
1974 (3)
Top Sellers
1–3 (128p) (small) foreign reprint (adult)	25p–50p

CANDY
21 Jan 1967–27 Dec 1969 (154)
City
to: *Jack & Jill*
1 (20p) (oblong)	50p–75p
2–154	25p–50p

CANDY COMIC
Sep 1947–Oct 1948 (2)
Philmar (Marx)
1 (8p) (red/blue) T. Gilson	50p–£1.00
2 (8p) (red/green) Ern Shaw	50p–£1.00

CAPTAIN
1948 (1)
Alexander Hamilton
1 (16p) A. Philpott	£1.00–£2.00

CAPTAIN AMERICA
1954
Miller (Marvel)
1 (28p) US reprint	50p–£1.00
2–	35p–75p

CAPTAIN AMERICA
25 Feb 1981–3 Apr 1982 (59)
Marvel
& Marvel Action: 15 Jul 1981
& Marvel Super Adventure: 29 Oct 1981
1 (32p) US reprints	15p–20p
2–36	10p–15p
37 (first 4C issue)	20p–25p
38–59	15p–20p

CAPTAIN AMERICA SUMMER SPECIAL
28 May 1981 (1)
Marvel
1 (nn) (52p) US reprints	40p–50p

CAPTAIN AND THE KIDS
1942 (1)
Miller (United Features)
1 (nn) (12p) (oblong) US reprint	£1.00–£2.00

CAPTAIN BRITAIN (WEEKLY)
13 Oct 1976–6 Jul 1977 (39)
Marvel
to: *Super Spiderman*
1	25p–50p
2–39	15p–25p

CAPTAIN BRITAIN (MONTHLY)
Dec 1984–
Marvel
1 (36p) Steve Parkhouse	20p–25p
2– David Lloyd	15p–20p

CAPTAIN BRITAIN SUMMER SPECIAL
Jun 1980–Jun 1981 (2)
Marvel
1 (nn) (52p) reprints	40p–50p
2	35p–45p

CAPTAIN FIGHT
1950 (1)
Cartoon Art (Fiction House)
1 (28p) (4C) US reprint	£1.00–£1.25

CAPTAIN FLASH
1954 (2)
Miller (Sterling)
1–2 (28p) US reprint	50p–£1.00

CAPTAIN GALLANT
1956 (4)
Miller (Charlton)
1–4 (28p) US reprint	50p–75p

CAPTAIN KREMMEN AND THE KRELLS
1977 (1)

Corgi/Transworld
1 (nn) (68p) (4C) Roger Walker   £1.00–£1.50

CAPTAIN MAGNET
1947–1948 (2)
Cartoon Art
1 (8p)   £1.00–£1.50
2 (16p)   £1.00–£1.50

CAPTAIN MARVEL
Dec 1944 (1)
Miller (Fawcett)
1 (nn) (68p) (gravure) (Xmas) US reprint   £2.00–£3.00

CAPTAIN MARVEL ADVENTURES
1946–27 Jan 1954
Miller (Fawcett)
to: *Marvelman*
1 (54) (16p) (gravure) US reprint   75p–£1.25
55–58 (16p) (gravure)   50p–£1.00
P747–(non-gravure)   50p–£1.00
(outsize) (gravure)   75p–£1.25
50 (Apr 1950)–84 (28p)   75p–£1.00
V1 N1 (19 Aug 1953)   £1.00–£1.25
V1 N2–24 (–27 Jan 1954)   75p–£1.00

CAPTAIN MARVEL COLORING BOOK
1948 (1)
Miller (Fawcett)
1 (nn) (24p) US reprint   £1.00–£2.00

CAPTAIN MARVEL JR
1945–27 Jan 1954
Miller (Fawcett)
to: *Young Marvelman*
1 (nn) (16p) (gravure) US reprint   75p–£1.25
33; 37; 50 (etc?) (16p) (gravure)   50p–£1.00
(outsize) (gravure)   75p–£1.25
50 (May 1950)–83 (24p)   75p–£1.00
V1 N1 (19 Aug 1953) (28p)   £1.00–£1.25
V1 N2–N24 (27 Jan 54)   75p–£1.00

CAPTAIN MIDNIGHT
1946–1963 (54?)
Miller (Fawcett)
1 (42) (16p) (gravure) US reprint   75p–£1.00
43 (52p) (gravure)   £2.00–£3.00
100–139 (28p)   75p–£1.00
1 (Aug 1962)–12 (Jul 1963)   50p–£1.00

CAPTAIN MIRACLE
Oct 1960–Jun 1961 (9)
Anglo (Atlas)
1 (28p) (Marvelman reprints)   50p–£1.00
2–9 Don Lawrence   50p–75p
(*NB*: 6 entitled *Invincible*)

CAPTAIN SCIENCE
1951 (1)
Cartoon Art (Youthful)
1 (nn) (28p) US reprint   50p–£1.00

CAPTAIN STARLIGHT: ROBBERY UNDER ARMS
1957 (1)
Miller
1 (28p) King Studio   50p–£1.00

CAPTAIN 3.D.
1954 (1)
Streamline/United Anglo-American (Harvey)
1 (nn) (36p) (with specs)   £1.00–£2.00

CAPTAIN TORNADO
Feb 1952–1953 (38)
SNPI/Mundial (Miller)
1 (50) (28p) foreign reprint   50p–£1.00
51–87   35p–50p

CAPTAIN UNIVERSE
1954 (2)

Arnold (Gower)
1–2 (28p) Mick Anglo   £1.00–£1.50

CAPTAIN VALIANT
see: *Space Comics*

CAPTAIN VIDEO
Apr 1951–1952 (5)
Miller (Fawcett)
1 (36p) US reprint   75p–£1.25
2–5   50p–£1.00

CAPTAIN VIGOUR
Dec 1952–Apr 1954 (17)
Sports Cartoons (Miller)
to: *Steve Samson*
1 (28p) Philip Mendoza   50p–£1.00
2–17   35p–£50p

CAPTAIN ZENITH COMIC
1950 (1)
Martin & Reid (Gower) (Mascot)
1 (8p) Mick Anglo   50p–£1.00

CAREFUL NIPPERS
1948–1950 (2)
White (road safety promo)
1 (20p) (oblong) (small) Brian White   £1.00–£2.00
2 (4p) (tabloid)   £2.00–£2.50

CARNIVAL COMIC
1949 (1)
Martin & Reid (Gower)
1 (8p) (tabloid) F. Minnitt   75p–£1.25

CARTOON CAPERS COMIC
1949 (1)
Martin & Reid (Gower)
1 (8p) (tabloid) H. Banger   75p–£1.25

CARTOONS AND SKETCHES
13 Jul 1901–26 Apr 1902 (42)
Henderson
(club edition of *Snap-Shots*)
1 (571)   £1.00–£2.00
572–612   £1.00–£1.50

CARY COLT
1954 (8)
Miller
1–8 (28p) foreign reprint   35p–50p

CASEY RUGGLES COMIC
1951–1955 (47)
Peters (Miller)
1 (36p) US reprint   £1.00–£2.00
2–47 (28p)   £1.00–£1.50

CASPER THE FRIENDLY GHOST
1953 (1)
Streamline/United Anglo-American (Harvey)
1 (28p) US reprint   50p–£1.00

CASPER THE FRIENDLY GHOST
1973–1974
Top Sellers
1– (36p) (4C) US reprint   35p–50p

CASTLE OF HORROR
Sep 1978–
Portman (Marvel)
1 (68p) US reprints   20p–50p
2–   15p–25p

CAVE GIRL
see: *Action Series*

CHALLENGER COMIC
1948 (2)
PM (Marx)

1 (8p) Frank Minnitt	75p–£1.25
2 Reg Parlett	50p–£1.00

CHALLENGERS OF THE UNKNOWN
1960 (4)
Strato (National)

1 (68p) US reprint	£1.00–£1.50
2–4	75p–£1.00

CHAMP
25 Feb 1984–
Thomson
& *Spike*: 5 May 1984

1 (28p)	10p–20p
2–	10p–15p

CHAMPION
26 Feb 1966–4 Jun 1966 (15)
Fleetway
to: *Lion*

1 (40p)	25p–50p
2–15	15p–25p

CHAMPION COMIC
9 Jan 1894–11 Jan 1896 (106)
Joker
to: *Joker New Series*

1 (8p) (tabloid)	£5.00–£10.00
2–106	£1.50–£2.00

CHANNEL 33⅓ SUMMER SPECIAL
May 1983 (1)
Marvel

1 (nn) (48p) Dicky Howett reprints	25p–50p

CHARLES RAND
1966 (1)
Thorpe & Porter

1 (68p) Mick Anglo	50p–75p

CHARLIE CHAN
1950 (1)
Streamline/United Anglo-American (Prize)

1 (28p) US reprint	50p–£1.00

CHARLIE CHAN
1955 (2)
Miller (Charlton)

1–2 (28p) US reprint	50p–£1.00

CHARLIE CHAPLIN
Dec 1973–1974
Top Sellers

1– (36p) (4C)	50p £1.00

CHARLIE CHAPLIN FUN BOOK
1915 (1)
AP

1 (nn) (44p) *Funny Wonder* reprints	£10.00–£20.00

CHARLIE CHICK'S PAPER
Feb 1934 (1)
Woolworth

1 (8p) Alan Fraser	£2.00–£5.00

CHEEKY SPECIAL
Jun 1978–May 1982 (5)
IPC

1: *Summer Special 1978* (64p)	25p–40p
2: *Summer Special 1979*	20p–30p
3: *Holiday Special 1980*	20p–30p
4: *Summer Special 1981*	20p–30p
5: *Summer Special 1982*	20p–30p

CHEEKY WEEKLY
22 Oct 1977–2 Feb 1980 (120)
IPC
to: *Whoopee*

1 (32p) Frank McDiarmid	15p–30p
2–120 Reg Parlett	10p–15p

CHEERFUL COMIC
17 Sep 1928–20 Apr 1929 (28)
Ransom

1 (8p) *Monster Comic* reprints	£3.00–£5.00
2–28 Reg Carter	£1.50–£2.00

CHEERIE COMIC
1946 (1)
McCrickrick

1 (8p) John Turner	£1.00–£1.25

CHEERY CHICKS CHUMMY COMIC
Jun 1947–Jun 1948 (12)
Reubens

1: *Cheery Chicks Comic* (8p)	£1.50–£2.00
2–12 (8p) Dennis Childs	£1.00–£1.25

CHEERY COMIC
Aug 1944 (1)
PM (Marx)

1 (nn) (16p) Reg Carter	£1.00–£1.25

CHEERY TIME COMIC
1948 (1)
Philmar (Marx)

1 (nn) (8p) (tabloid) Wally Robertson	75p–£1.00

CHERIE
1 Oct 1960–19 Oct 1963 (160)
Thomson
to: *Romeo*

1 (20p) (tabloid)	35p–50p
2–160	25p–35p

CHEYENNE KID
1957–1958 (18)
Miller (Charlton)

1 (28p) US reprint	75p–£1.00
2–18	35p–75p

CHICKS OWN
25 Sep 1920–9 Mar 1957 (1605)
AP
& *Bo-Peep*: 21 Apr 1934
& *Happy Days*: 12 Aug 1939
& *Bubbles*: 31 May 1941
to: *Playhour*

1 (12p) (tabloid) Arthur White	£7.50–£10.00
1920–1929 H. O'Neill	£1.25–£1.50
1930–1939 Walter Holt	£1.50–£1.75
1940–1949 Fred Crompton	£1.00–£1.50
1950–1957 Vera Bowyer	50p–75p

CHILDREN'S FAIRY
1 Nov 1919–9 Apr 1921 (76)
AP
to: *Bubbles*

1 (12p) Julius Baker	£2.00–£5.00
2–76 Herbert Foxwell	£1.75–£2.50

CHILDREN'S HOLIDAY FUN
May 1937–May 1940 (4)
Leng

1–4 (84p) (oblong) George Jones	£2.00–£5.00

CHILDREN'S OWN FAVOURITE
15 Oct 1938–10 Dec 1938 (9)
World Service

1 (8p) (supp. to *Favourite Weekly*)	£1.00–£3.00
2–9 Norman Ward	£1.00–£1.50

CHILDREN'S OWN SUNDAY PICTORIAL
6 Aug 1933–4 Feb 1934 (27)
Sunday Pictorial

1 (4p) (supplement) A. B. Payne	£2.00–£3.00
2–27 Steve Dowling	£1.50–£2.00
(single sheet thereafter)	

CHILDREN'S ROCKET BOOK
1949 (1)
Allen

1 (12p) Harry Banger (gravure)	£1.00–£1.50

CHILDREN'S SOUTH WALES ECHO & EXPRESS
see: *South Wales Echo & Express*

CHILDREN'S SUNDAY FAIRY
11 Oct 1919–25 Oct 1919 (3)
AP
to: *Children's Fairy*
1 (23–25) Harry Neilson .... £1.75–£2.50

CHILDSPLAY
1980
Atlas (Dell)
1 (36p) US reprints 10p–40p
2– 10p–20p

CHILLER POCKET BOOK
Mar 1980–Jul 1982 (28)
Marvel
1 (52p) (small) US reprints 15p–25p
2–28 .... 10p–15p
9; 20 Xmas double numbers (100p) 20p–30p

CHILLING TALES OF HORROR
1979–1980 (4)
Portman (Stanley)
1 (52p) US reprints 15p–35p
2–4 .... 10p–15p

CHIPPER HOLIDAY SPECIAL
7 July 1980 (1)
Birmingham Evening Mail
1 (nn) (20p) (tabloid) Jack Bell 10p–25p

CHIPS
see: *Chips Comic*
     Illustrated Chips
     Whizzer & Chips

CHIPS COMIC
12 Mar 1983–30 Jul 1983 (21)
IPC
to: *Playhour*
1 (16p) (TV series) 10p–20p
2–21 .... 5p–10p

CHIPS COMIC BOOK
Oct 1984 (1)
IPC
1 (with sound cassette) .... £1.00–£2.00

CHRISTMAS COMIC
1899–1906 (8)
Trapps Holmes
1–8 (annual double issue of *Halfpenny*
     Comic) .... £2.00–£4.00

CHRISTMAS COMIC
8 Dec 1931–22 Nov 1935 (5)
Pearson
to: *Christmas Holiday Comic*
1 (8 Dec 31) Walter Bell .... £2.50–£5.00
2 (3 Dec 32) Walter Bell .... £2.00–£3.50
3 (24 Nov 33) Walter Bell .... £2.00–£3.50
4 (16 Nov 34) *Jolly Jumbo's CC* .... £2.50–£3.50
5 (22 Nov 35) Ray Bailey .... £2.00–£3.50

CHRISTMAS HOLIDAY COMIC
22 Nov 1936–17 Nov 1939 (4)
Pearson
1 (22 Nov 36) Ray Bailey .... £2.50–£3.50
2 (19 Nov 37) Ray Bailey .... £2.00–£3.00
3 (18 Nov 38) Norman Ward .... £2.00–£3.00
4 (17 Nov 39) Walter Bell .... £2.00–£3.00

CHRISTMAS STORYTELLER
Nov 1983–Nov 1984 (2)
Marshall Cavendish
1–2 (nn) (64p) (4C) with cassette .... £2.50–£3.50

CHRONICLES OF JUDGE DREDD
1981–

Titan (IPC)
1: *Judge Dredd* (68p) reprints .... £2.95–£3.50
2: *Judge Dredd Book 2* .... £2.95–£3.50
3: *Cursed Earth Part 1* .... £2.95–£3.50
4: *Cursed Earth Part 2* .... £2.95–£3.50
5: *Judge Caligua Book 1* £3.50
6: *Judge Caligua Book 2* £3.50
7: *Judge Death* £3.50
8: *Judge Child Book 1* £3.95
9: *Judge Child Book 2* £3.95
see: *Judge Dredd Colour Series*

CHUCKLER
31 Mar 1934–15 Oct 1938 (238)
Target
to: *Rattler & Chuckler*
1 (16p) (tabloid) Harry Banger .... £5.00–£7.50
2–29 (12p) Bert Hill .... £2.00–£3.00
30–238 (8p) Louis Diamond .... £2.00–£2.50

CHUCKLES
10 Jan 1914–1 Dec 1923 (517)
AP
to: *Jungle Jinks*
1 (8p) Tom Wilkinson (tabloid) .... £5.00–£10.00
2– H.O'Neill .... £2.00–£2.50
21 Apr 17: (2C) .... £1.50–£2.00
22 Sep 17: (4C) .... £2.00–£2.50
31 May 19: 1st 'nursery' edition .... £1.75–£2.00
30 Sep 22: (12p) .... £2.00–£2.25

CHUMMY COMIC
Aug 1944 (1)
PM (Marx)
1 (nn) (16p) Reg Carter .... £1.00–£1.25

CHUMMY COMIC
1948 (1)
Jeffrey
1 (8p) J. R. Turner .... £1.00–£2.00

CIRCUS COMIC
1945 (1)
PM (Marx)
1 (nn) (folded strip) Reg Carter .... 50p–£1.00

CIRCUS COMICS
1949 (1)
Hotspur
1 (8p) (gravure) Denis Gifford .... £1.00–£1.50

CISCO KID
1952–1955 (51)
World (Dell)
1 (36p) US reprint .... 75p–£1.00
2–48 .... 50p–£1.00
49–51 (68p) 35p–75p

CLASH OF THE TITANS
Jul 1981 (1)
ITV/*Look-In* Special
1 (nn) (64p) (4C) US reprint .... 75p–£1.25

CLASS WAR COMIX: NEW TIMES
Jul 1974 (1)
Epic
1 (36p) (adult) Clifford Harper .... 50p–£1.00

CLASSIC IN PICTURES
1949 (12)
Amex (Marx)
1: *Oliver Twist* (52p) .... £1.00–£1.75
2: *Ivanhoe* A. Philpott .... 50p–£1.00
3: *Macbeth* Colin Merritt .... 50p–£1.00
4: *Westward Ho* Colin Merritt .... 50p–£1.00
5: *Treasure Island* .... 50p–£1.00
6: *Tale of Two Cities* .... 50p–£1.00
7: *Three Musketeers* .... 50p–£1.00
8: *Lorna Doone* .... 50p–£1.00
9: *Henry V* A. Philpott .... 50p–£1.00
10: *Barnaby Rudge* .... 50p–£1.00
11: *Mutiny on the Bounty* .... 50p–£1.00

12: *Julius Caesar*   50p–£1.00
see: *Famous Stories in Pictures* (reprints)

CLASSICS ILLUSTRATED
Oct 1951–
Thorpe & Porter (Gilberton)

(a) shilling series
1: *Huckleberry Finn* (52p) (4C)   50p–£1.25
2– US reprints   35p–£1.00
(b) Popular classics 1s 3d series
1: *Alice in Wonderland* (52p) (4C)   35p–£1.00
2– US reprints   35p–£1.00
(c) Special Edition series
1: (96p) (4C) US reprints   50p–£1.00
2–8   35p–£1.00
(d) Super classics 1s 6d series
1: *Dr Jekyll & Mr Hyde* (52p) (4C)   50p–£1.00
2– US reprints   35p–£1.00
(e) Giant Classics 2s series
1: *Ivanhoe* (64p) (4C)   50p–£1.00
2– US reprints   35p–£1.00
(f) De Luxe Library Edition 2s 6d
1: *Uncle Tom's Cabin* (4C)   75p–£1.25
2– US reprints   50p–£1.00

CLASSICS ILLUSTRATED (BRITISH ORIGINALS)
1960 (13)
Thorpe & Porter
  84: *Gold Bug* (36p) (4C)   50p–£1.00
143: *Sail With The Devil*   50p–£1.00
146: *Baron Munchausen*   50p–£1.00
147: *Through the Looking Glass*   50p–£1.00
148: *Nights of Terror*   50p–£1.00
149: *Gorilla Hunters*   50p–£1.00
150: *Canterville Ghost*   50p–£1.00
156: *Dog Crusoe*   50p–£1.00
157: *Queen of Spades*   50p–£1.00
159: *Master and Man*   50p–£1.00
161: *The Aeneid*   50p–£1.00
162: *Saga of the North*   50p–£1.00
163: *Argonauts*   50p–£1.00

CLASSICS ILLUSTRATED JUNIOR
1953–1954 (16)
Thorpe & Porter (Gilberton)
1 (501) *Snow White* (36p) (4C) US reprints   35p–75p
502–516   35p–50p

CLICKY SERIES
1957–1961 (6)
Brockhampton (Enid Blyton)
1: *Clicky the Clockwork Clown*   £1.00–£1.50
2: *Clicky and Tiptoe*   75p–£1.00
3: *Clicky & Flying Horse*   75p–£1.00
4: *Clicky Gets Into Trouble*   75p–£1.00
5: *Happy Holiday Clicky*   75p–£1.00

CLIVE SERIES
1968–1971 (3)
Michael Joseph (1) W. H. Allen (2, 3)
1 (84p) *Evening Standard* strip reprints   50p–£1.00
2: *Clive in Love* Domenic Poelsma   50p–75p
3: *Clive & Augusta*   50p–75p

THE CLOGGIES SERIES
1969 (2)
André Deutsch/Private Eye
1: *The Cloggies* (68p) (oblong) Bill Tidy   50p–£1.00
2: *The Cloggies Dance Again* reprints   50p–75p

CLUB LIBRARY: SECRET SERVICE
1976–
Med/NEL
1: *Shadow Strikes* (68p) (small)   10p–25p
2– Spanish reprints   10p–15p

CLUB LIBRARY: WAR
1976–
Med/NEL
1: (68p) (small)   10p–25p
2– Spanish reprints   10p–15p

CLUB LIBRARY: WESTERN
1976–
Med/NEL
1: *Fugitive* (68p) (small)   10p–25p
2– Spanish reprints   10p–15p

CLUMSY BOY CRUSOE (Surprising Adventures of)
1877 (1)
Griffith & Farran
1 (16p) (4C) Charles Ross (oblong)   £15.00–£25.00

COLLECTED ADVENTURES OF FAT FREDDY'S CAT
1975 (1)
(no imprint)
1 (36p) US/UG reprint (small)   30p–50p

COLONEL PEWTER
1957–1979 (4)
Pall Mall/Penguin
1: *CP in Ironicus* (68p) Arthur Horner   £1.50–£2.50
2: *Sirius Dog Star* (94p)   £1.50–£2.00
3: *Penguin CP* (148p)   £2.00–£2.50
4: *Book of Uriel* (150p)   £2.00–£2.50

COLORADO KID
1 May 1954–1959 (84)
Miller (King-Ganteaume)
1 (28p) John Wheeler   75p–£1.00
2–84 Colin Andrew   35p–75p

COLOURED COMIC
21 May 1898–28 Apr 1906 (415)
Trapps Holmes
to: *Smiles*
1 (8p) (tabloid) Oliver Veal   £5.00–£10.00
2–72 (last coloured) Charles Genge   £2.00–£2.50
73–403 Alfred Gray   £1.25–£1.50
404–415 (16p)   £1.50–£2.00

COLOURED COMICS
1935–1939
USA Sunday sections stapled in specially-drawn cover for market sales, etc
(nn)   £1.50–£5.00

COLOURED SLICK FUN
1945–Jan 1951 (69)
Swan
1 (20) (16p) John McCail   £1.00–£2.00
21–45 Harry Banger   75p–£1.00
46–51 (monthly: Mar-Aug 1949)   75p–£1.00
52–65 (fortnightly)   50p–£1.00
66–73 (weekly)   50p–75p
74–86 (fortnightly)   50p–75p
87–88 (monthly)   50p–75p
NB: full colour issues: 35–67 only

COLOURED SLICK FUN BUDGET
1950–1952 (3)
Swan
rebound remainders in new covers (H. Banger)
1 (1950)   £1.00–£3.00
2 (1951) 44, 53, 67, 74, 48, 65, 46, 63   £1.00–£2.50
3 (1952) 87, 77, 85, 68, 82, 84, 80, &
Scramble 50   £1.00–£2.00

COMBAT PICTURE LIBRARY
Aug 1959–
Micron/Smith
1– *Sea Hunt*   35p–50p
2–   20p–25p

COMET
27 Mar 1909–26 Jun 1909 (14)
Pearson
1– (16p)   £2.00–£3.00
6–14 (32p)   £1.50–£2.00

COMET
20 Sep 1946–17 Oct 1959 (587)
Allen (1 70); AP

aka: *Comet Comic/Comet Adventure Weekly/Comet Weekly*
to: *Tiger*

1 (8p) (tabloid) Alan Fraser	£1.50–£2.00
15 (8p) (gravure) R. Beaumont	£1.50–£2.00
193 (16p) (comicbook format)R. Parlett	75p–£1.00
519 (20p) (letterpress) Geoff Campion	25p–50p

COMIC ADVENTURES
1940–1949 (27)
Soloway

V1/1 (tabloid) (8p)	£2.00–£3.00
V1/2–5 Harry Banger	£1.50–£2.00
V2/1–4 (16p) Louis Diamond	£1.00–£1.75
V3/1–4 John Turner	£1.00–£1.75
V4/1–4 Alf Farningham	£1.00–£1.75
V5/1–4 Denis Gifford	50p–£1.00
V6/1–4 Alan Fraser	50p–£1.00
V7/1–2 (4C) R. Beaumont	50p–£1.00

COMIC ALBUM OF FOLLY AND FASHION
1870 (1)
Judy Office

1 (nn) (48p) CH Ross strip reprints	£5.00–£7.50

COMIC ALMANAC
1878– (1?)
Fortey

1 (1879) (16p) cartoons	£8.00–£10.00

COMIC BITS
19 Feb 1898–12 Apr 1898 (10)
Unity

1 (tabloid) (12p)	£5.00–£10.00
7–10 (8p)	£1.75–£2.50

COMIC CAPERS
1940–1949 (27)
Soloway

V1/1 (tabloid) (8p)	£2.00–£3.00
V1/2–5 Nat Brand	£1.50–£2.00
V2/1–4 (16p) Louis Diamond	£1.00–£1.75
V3/1–4 Denis Gifford	£1.00–£1.75
V4/1–4 Glyn Protheroe	£1.00–£1.75
V5/1–4 Bob Monkhouse	50p–£1.00
V6/1–4 Mick Anglo	50p–£1.00
V7/1–2 (4C) Edward Lowe	50p–£1.00

COMIC CHUCKLES
1944 (1)
Martin & Reid

1 (nn) (16p) H. E. Pease	75p–£1.25

COMIC COMPANION
1854–1860 (7)
Goode

1 (1855) (16p) cartoons	£7.50–£10.00
1856–1861	£7.50–£10.00

COMIC COMPANION
3 Oct 1908–13 Feb 1909 (20)
Odhams
supplement to *You and I* magazine

1 (4p) G. W. Wakefield	£1.50–£2.50
2–20	£1.00–£1.50

COMIC CUTS
17 May 1890–12 Sep 1953 (3006)
Harmsworth/AP
& *Golden Penny*: 4 Feb 1928
& *Jolly Comic*: 4 Nov 1939
& *Larks*: 25 May 1940
to: *Knockout*

1 (8p) (tabloid)	£5.00–£10.00
331 (Sep 1896) (4C)	£5.00–£8.00
4-colour editions	£3.50–£5.00
Xmas & Double Numbers	£2.50–£4.50
1890–1899 Tom Browne	£1.25–£1.75
1900–1929 Percy Cocking	£1.25–£1.75
1930–1939 Frank Minnitt	£1.25–£1.75
4 Nov 1939–(2C)	£1.00–£1.75
1940–1949 Albert Pease	75p–£1.25
1950–1953 Ron Embleton	50p–£1.00

COMIC CUTS
14 Sep 1983–
Crawley News supplement

1 (4p) (4C) US reprints	10p–25p
2–	5p–10p

COMIC CUTS AND CHIPS
AP

Overseas edition: two comics	£2.00–£3.00

COMIC FLICKS FLICKER BOOK
1943 (1)
Philmar (Marx)

1 (oblong) Reg Parlett	50p–£1.00

COMIC FUN
1948 (1)
Martin & Reid

1 (nn) (8p) Bob Monkhouse	75p–£1.00

COMIC HOLIDAY ANNUAL
Aug 1877 (1)
Ward Lock

1 (132p) C. H. Ross strip reprints	£5.00–£10.00

COMIC HOME JOURNAL
11 May 1895–10 Sep 1904 (488)
Harmsworth
to: *Butterfly*

1 (8p) (tabloid) J. B. Yeats	£5.00–£10.00
2–488 Tom Browne	£1.25–£2.00

COMIC LEDGER
1949 (1)
Martin & Reid (Gower)

1 (tabloid) Percy Cocking	50p–£1.00

COMIC LIFE
30 Dec 1899–21 Jan 1928 (1465)
Henderson/AP
to: *My Favourite*

1 (79) (8p) (tabloid)	£5.00–£10.00
25 Sep 1909: (4C issues)	£2.00–£2.50
1916 (smaller wartime issues)	£1.50–£2.00
13 Mar 1920 (first AP issue)	£1.50–£2.00
30 Sep 1922 (12p issues)	£2.00–£2.25

COMIC MOVIES FLICKER BOOKS
1949 (10)
Books & Pictures

1: *Bimbo Catches Big Bad Bear* (oblong)	50p–£1.00
2: *Red Riding Hood & Wicked Wolf*	50p–£1.00
3: *Cowboy Joe & Bandit*	50p–£1.00
4: *Flick & Slip the Circus Clowns*	50p–£1.00
5: *Jokey Jumpy the Winner*	50p–£1.00
6: *Blacky & Whity the Boxers* Walter Booth	50p–£1.00
7: *Punch & Judy* E. Williams	50p–£1.00
8: *Brumas* W. Mevin	50p–£1.50
9: *Jack & Jill* E. Williams	50p–£1.00
10: *Cinderella* Walter Booth	50p–£1.00

COMIC MUPPET BOOK
1979 (1)
Fontana/Collins

1 (nn) (36p) (4C) Graham Thompson	50p–£1.00

COMIC PICTORIAL NUGGETS
7 May 1892–19 Nov 1892 (29)
Henderson
to: *Nuggets*

1 (16p) Julius Stafford Baker	£5.00–£10.00
2–29	£2.00–£2.50

COMIC PICTORIAL SHEET
29 Sep 1891–28 Sep 1904 (1601)
Henderson
to: *Snap-Shots*

1–1601 (broadsheet)	£2.00–£5.00
(*NB*: produced for copyright reasons only)	

COMIC REVUE
13 Sep 1941 (1)
Listed in *National Newsagent* as 'new comic price 4d',
but no copy known.   £2.00–£5.00

COMIC SHOTS
May–Aug 1946 (4)
Fisher
1 (nn) (12p) (red/green) Forshaw   £1.00–£2.00
2 (nn) (12p) (blue)   £1.00–£1.50
3 (nn) (16p) (brown)   £1.00–£1.75
4 (nn) (16p) (brown)   £1.00–£1.75

COMIC WONDER
1948–1949 (8)
Paget
1 (8p) Alan Fraser   50p–£1.00
2–7 Mick Anglo   50p–75p
8 (No 1) (larger size) W. Robertson   75p–£1.00

COMICAL COMIC
1945 (1)
Marx
1 (nn) (16p) Reg Carter   50p–£1.00

COMICAL CRACKS
1947 (4)
Ensign
1–4 (8p) W. Forshaw   75p–£1.00

COMICAL PRANKS
1947 (3)
Ensign
1–3 (8p) W. Forshaw   75p–£1.00

COMICAL SNIPS
1947 (1)
Modern fiction
1 (nn) (16p) Dick Brook   75p–£1.00

COMICOLOUR
1946–1949 (11)
Swan
1 (8p) Harry Banger   £1.00–£2.00
2, 3, 4, 6, 7, 8 John McCail   75p–£1.00
5, 9, 10 (gravure) H. Pease   £1.00–£1.25
11 (12p) (gravure) D. Newhouse   £1.00–£1.50

COMICOLOUR (NEW SERIES)
1953 (3)
Swan
1–3 (28p)   £1.00–£2.00

COMICS ON PARADE
Feb 1941–1943 (11)
Miller (United Features)
1 (3) (32p) (gravure) US reprints   £2.00–£3.00
4–13   £1.00–£1.50

COMICS ON PARADE
1950 (2)
Peters (Miller) (United Features)
to: *Spark Man*
1 (17), 2 (18) US reprint (16p)   75p–£1.00

COMICS ON PARADE
1952 (1)
Compix (United Features)
1 (28p) US reprint   50p–£1.00

COMICS ON PARADE SERIES
1944 (4)
Miller (United Features)
1 (nn) *Iron Vic* (16p) (gravure) US reprint £1.00–£1.50
2 (nn) *Captain & the Kids*   £1.00–£1.50
3 (nn) *Cynical Susie*   £1.00–£1.50
4 (nn) *Joe Jinks*, (etc)   £1.00–£1.50

COMICS 101
1976 (1)

Gifford
1 (80p) (small) convention souvenir   50p–£1.50

COMICS TO HOLD YOU SPELLBOUND
Mar 1953–
Thorpe & Porter (Marvel)
1 (68p) US reprint   £1.50–£2.00
2–   £1.00–£1.25

COMICUTE BUDGET
1951–1952 (2)
Swan
rebound remainders in new cover (McCail)
1: *Cute Fun* 34, 35, 37, 39, 38, 26
   Comicolour 8, 6
   Kiddyfun 3, 9, 4   £1.00–£3.00
2: *Cute Fun* 34, 35, 36, 37, 39, 38
   Comicolour 8, 7
   Kiddyfun 3, 9, 4   £1.00–£3.00

COMMANDER BATTLE
AND THE ATOMIC SUB
Streamline/United Anglo-American (ACG)
1955 (3)
1–3 (28p) US reprint   50p–£1.00

COMMANDER COMIC
1947 (2)
Pearce/Ensign
1 (8p) (nn) (gravure: red/blue)   75p–£1.00
2 (8p) (nn) (gravure: green/orange)   75p–£1.00

COMMANDER EARTH
1980 (1)
Gulf Oil/CB Marketing
1 (nn) (4p) (2C) Geoff Jones   5p–15p

COMMANDO
Jul 1961–
Thomson
1 (68p) *Walk or Die* (small)   75p–£1.00
2–   25p–50p

COMMANDO CRAIG
Jun 1950–Aug 1950 (3)
Scion
1 (16p) Norman Light   50p–£1.00
2–3   50p–75p

COMMITTED COMIX
1977 (1)
Birmingham Arts Lab
1 (nn) (28p) (adult) Chris Welch   50p–75p

COMPLETE COMICS
1944 (1)
Newton Wickman
1 (nn) (8p) John Turner   75p–£1.25

COMPLETE FANTASTIC FOUR
28 Sep 1977–8 Jun 1978 (53)
Marvel
to: *Mighty World of Marvel*
1 (36p) US reprints   15p–25p
2–53   10p–15p

CONAN POCKET BOOK
11 Sep 1980–12 Nov 1981 (13)
Marvel
1 (52p) (small) US reprint   15p–25p
2   15p–20p
3 (100p)   25p–30p
4–13   15p–20p

CONAN WINTER SPECIAL
Nov 1982 (1)
Marvel
1 US reprint   60p–£1.00

CONFESSIONS LIBRARY
Feb 1959–Dec 1960 (44)

AP
to: *Romantic Confessions Picture Library*
1: *Men Could Not Resist Me* (68p)　　25p–50p
2–44　　　　　　　　　　　　　　　　10p–25p

CONFESSIONS OF LOVE
1954–1955 (14)
Swan (Star)
1 (68p) US reprint　　　　　　　　　25p–50p
2–14　　　　　　　　　　　　　　　　20p–25p

CONFIDENTIAL ROMANCES
1957 (9)
Miller
1 (68p) US reprint　　　　　　　　　25p–50p
2–9　　　　　　　　　　　　　　　　10p–20p

CONFIDENTIAL STORIES
1957–1959 (33)
Miller
1–33 (68p) US reprint　　　　　　　10p–25p

CONFLICT PICTURE LIBRARY
1959–1963
Brown Watson
1– (68p) foreign reprint　　　　　　25p–50p

CONQUEROR
Aug 1984–
Harrier
1– (32p) Brian Bolland　　　　　　　25p–50p

CONQUEROR COMIC
1951 (1)
Scion (King-Ganteaume)
1 (nn) (20p)　　　　　　　　　　　　75p–£1.00

CONTINENTAL FILM PHOTO STORIES
Jan 1960–
Pearson
1: *Harbour of Desire* (36p)　　　　　25p–50p
2– foreign reprints　　　　　　　　　25p–45p

COOPER KIDS
1944 (1)
Pendock
1 (nn) (20p) *Sunday Pictorial* strips　　75p–£1.50

COR!!!
6 Jun 1970–15 Jun 1974 (210)
IPC
to: *Buster*
1 (32p) Reg Parlett　　　　　　　　25p–50p
2–210 Brian Lewis　　　　　　　　　15p–20p

COR!!! SUMMER SPECIAL
1971–1976 (6)
IPC
1 (98p)　　　　　　　　　　　　　　25p–50p
2–5 (80p)　　　　　　　　　　　　　20p–25p
6 (64p)　　　　　　　　　　　　　　20p–25p

CORKER COMIC
Jul 1946 (1)
International
1 (nn) (8p) Denis Gifford　　　　　　£1.00–£2.00

CORKER COMIC
1949 (1)
Philmar (Marx)
1 (nn) (16p) Walter Bell　　　　　　75p–£1.00

CORONATION SPECIAL
1953 (1)
Sports Cartoons (Miller)
1 (nn) (20p) (with map)　　　　　　50p–£1.00

COUNTDOWN
20 Feb 1971–24 Mar 1972 (58)
Polystyle

to: *T.V. Action*
1 (24p) (gravure) H. Lindfield　　£1.00–£2.00
2–58 John Burns　　　　　　　　　25p–50p

COUNTDOWN HOLIDAY SPECIAL
1971 (1)
Polystyle
1 (nn) (48p) (gravure)　　　　　　50p–£1.00

COUNTDOWN WITH T.V. ACTION HOLIDAY
SPECIAL
Mar 1972 (1)
Polystyle
1 (nn) (48p)　　　　　　　　　　　50p–£1.00

COUPLES
1972 (1)
Workshop/Calman
1 (nn) (oblong) *Sunday Times* strip　　35p–50p

COWBOY ACTION
1956–1957 (18)
Miller (Atlas)
1 (28p) US reprint　　　　　　　　　25p–75p
2–18　　　　　　　　　　　　　　　25p–50p

COWBOY ADVENTURE LIBRARY
1964–
Micron
1– (68p) foreign reprint　　　　　　25p–50p

COWBOY COMICS/PICTURE LIBRARY
6 May 1950–Sep 1962 (468)
AP
1 (68p) *Buck Jones* G. Campion　　£1.00–£2.00
2 *Kit Carson* D. Eyles　　　　　　50p–75p
9 *Tim Holt* US reprint　　　　　　35p–50p
　Davy Crockett　　　　　　　　　50p–75p
　Kansas Kid　　　　　　　　　　50p–75p

COWBOY WESTERN COMICS
1953 (6)
Miller (Charlton)
1 (28p) US reprint　　　　　　　　　50p–£1.00
2–6　　　　　　　　　　　　　　　　25p–75p

COZMIC COMICS
May 1972–Mar 1974 (6)
H. Bunch
1 (52p) US/UG reprints (adult)　　50p–£1.00
2 US reprints　　　　　　　　　　25p–50p
3: *The Firm* M. Weller　　　　　　50p–75p
4–5 Rod Beddall　　　　　　　　　50p–75p
6 Brian Bolland　　　　　　　　　50p–£1.00

CRACK ACTION
1953 (5)
Archer/Award/*King Series*
1–5 (68p) US reprints　　　　　　　35p–75p

CRACK COMICS
1950 (1)
Locker (Quality)
1 (36p) (4C) US reprint　　　　　　£1.00–£2.00

CRACK SHOTS
Jul–Sep 1946 (2)
Fisher
1 (16p) W. Forshaw　　　　　　　£1.00–£1.25
2 Denis Gifford　　　　　　　　　£1.00–£1.25

CRACK WESTERN
Mar 1951–1952 (4)
Popular (Boardman) (Quality)
1 (36p) (4C) US reprint　　　　　　50p–£1.25
3; 47; 51　　　　　　　　　　　　50p–£1.00

CRACKER
18 Jan 1975–11 Sep 1976 (87)
Thomson
to: *Beezer*

1 (32p) Bill Ritchie 15p–25p
2–87 (28p) Phil Millar 10p–15p

CRACKER JACK COMIC
1947 (1)
Philmar (Marx)
1 (16p) Frank Jupo 75p–£1.25

CRACKER JACK COMIC
1948 (1)
Rayburn (Martin & Reid)
1 (8p) Bob Wilkin 75p–£1.00

CRACKERS
22 Feb 1929–31 May 1941 (615)
AP
& Sparkler: 12 Aug 1939
to: Jingles
1 (12p) (tabloid) W. Robertson £5.00–£7.00
2– Walter Bell £1.25–£2.00
178 layout change Sid Pride £1.25–£2.00
3 Feb 40: first small format £2.00–£2.50
–615 Hilda Boswell £1.50–£2.00

CRASH!! COMIC BOOK
1975 (1)
Children of God
1 (16p) (small) religious sect promo 10p–25p

CRASH COMICS
1948 (1)
Rayburn (Martin & Reid)
1 (16p) Bob Monkhouse £2.00–£2.50

CRASHER COMIC
1946–1947 (10)
Kayebon
1 (8p) (2C) £1.00–£1.50
2–10 75p–£1.00

CRASHO COMIC
1947 (1)
Daly
1 (28p) Crewe Davies £1.00–£1.50

CRAZY COMIC
1945 (1)
Philmar
1 (nn) (16p) Reg Carter 50p–£1.00

CREEPY WORLDS
Aug 1962–
Class (Atlas, ACG, etc)
1 (64p) US reprints 25p–£1.00
2– 25p–75p

CRIME AND PUNISHMENT
1951 (3)
Pemberton/World (Gleason)
1 (36p) US reprint £1.50–£2.00
2–3 75p–£1.50

CRIME DETECTIVE COMICS
1951 (3)
Streamline/ United Anglo-American (Hillman)
1 (28p) US reprint £1.00–£1.10
2–3 75p–£1.00

CRIME DOES NOT PAY
1951 (6)
Pemberton/World (Gleason)
1 (36p) US reprint £1.00–£1.50
2–6 75p–£1.00

CRIME DOES NOT PAY
1950 (2)
Arnold (Gleason)
1 (12p) (gravure) US reprint £1.00–£1.50
2 (36p) £1.00–£1.25

CRIME FILES
1962 (1)
Cartoon Art
1 US reprint 50p–£1.00

CRIME PATROL
1953 (5)
Archer/Award/King Series (Quality)
1–5 (68p) US reprint 35p–75p

CRIME REPORTER
1954 (1)
Streamline/United Anglo-American (Fox)
1 (28p) US reprint 75p–£1.25

CRIME SYNDICATE
1948 (1)
Hotspur/Secret Service Series 3
1 (3) (8p) (gravure) B. Wilkin 50p–£1.00

CRIMEBUSTER
1959 (6)
World (?)
1– (68p) (Johnny Hazard) US reprint 35p–75p
2–6 35p–50p

CRIMEFIGHTER COMICS
1951 (1)
Scion (King-Ganteaume)
1 (24p) 50p–£1.00

CRUNCH
20 Jan 1979–26 Jan 1980 (54)
Thomson
to: Hotspur
1 (32p) Denis McLoughlin 15p–35p
2–54 10p–15p

CUBA FOR BEGINNERS
1975 (1)
Writers Cooperative
1 (76p) (oblong) Rius reprint £1.00–£2.00

CUBBY AND THE CHRISTMAS STAR
1946 (1)
Locker
1 (nn) (20p) Bob Monkhouse 50p–£1.00

CURLY KAYOE COMIC
1950 (2)
Peters (Miller) (United Features)
1 (nn) (12p) (gravure) US reprint 75p–£1.25
2 (22) (20p) 50p–£1.00

CURLY'S COMIC
1950 (1)
B.B
1 (702) (16p) (gravure) (4C) £1.00–£2.00

CUTE COMIC
1945 (1)
Philmar (Marx)
1 (nn) (16p) Reg Carter 50p–£1.00

CUTE FUN
Jun 1946–Sep 1951 (43)
Swan
1 (8p) (folder) Harry Banger £1.00–£2.00
2–29 William Ward 50p–£1.00
30–43 (2C) H. Pease 75p–£1.00

CYCLONE ILLUSTRATED COMIC
Jan 1946 (1)
Locker
1 (16p) R. Beaumont 75p–£1.25

CYCLOPS
Jul 1970–Oct 1970 (4)
Innocence & Experience

1 (tabloid) (adult)	£1.00–£1.50		
2–4	50p–£1.00		

CYMRAEG
Sep 1955–
Cwmni Urdd Gobaith Cymru
1 (36p) (small) Welsh Language	50p–£1.00
2–	20p–35p

DAD'S ARMY
1973 (1)
Pan/Piccolo (*TV Comic* reprints)
1 (100p) Bill Titcombe (small)	20p–50p

DAFFY DUCK
1972
Top Sellers (Dell)
1– (36p) (4C) US reprint	20p–25p

DAILY DEEDS OF SAMMY THE SCOUT
1946 (3)
Readers Library
1–3 (20p) (gravure) Ern Shaw	£1.00–£1.50

DAILY EXPRESS CHILDREN'S OWN
13 May 1933–15 Jul 1933 (10)
London Express Newspapers
Supplement to *Daily Express* newspaper
1 (8p) (2C) (tabloid) George Parlett	£2.50–£5.00
2–10 Walter Bell	£1.50–£2.00

(*NB*: numbered same as newspaper)
see: *Scottish Daily Express Children's Own*

DAILY MIRROR BOOK OF GARTH
see: *Garth Series*

DAILY MIRROR REFLECTIONS
1908–1935 (28)
Pictorial Newspaper/Mirror
1 (112p) W. Haselden reprints	£2.00–£5.00
2–28	£2.00–£3.50

DALE EVANS QUEEN OF THE WEST
1955 (12)
World (Dell)
1–12 (28p) US reprint	75p–£1.00

DAN ADAMS
see: *Action Series*

DAN DARE: THE MAN FROM NOWHERE
1979 (1)
Dragons Dream (IPC)
1 (118p) (4C) *Eagle* reprints	£2.50–£4.25

DAN DARE PILOT OF THE FUTURE
1981 (1)
Hamlyn
1 (100p) (4C) *Eagle Annual* reprints	£1.00–£2.00

DAN DARE POSTER MAGAZINE
1977 (1)
IPC
1 (16p) (4C) Dave Gibbons	30p–50p

DAN LENO'S COMIC JOURNAL
26 Feb 1898–2 Dec 1899 (93)
Pearson
1 (8p) (tabloid) Tom Browne	£7.50–£10.00
2–93 Frank Holland	£2.00–£2.75

DANDY COMIC
4 Dec 1937–
Thomson
1 (28p) Dudley Watkins	£5.00–£25.00
1938–1939 Allan Morley	£2.50–£7.00
1940–1944 Sam Fair	£2.00–£3.50
1945–1949 Eric Roberts	£2.00–£2.75
1950–1955 Paddy Brennan	£1.00–£1.50
1956–1959 Ken Reid	£1.00–£1.25
1960–1969 David Law	50p–75p
1970–1979 Bill Holroyd	10p–35p
1980– George Martin	10p–20p
Dandy No 1 facsimile	£1.00–£1.50

DANDY–BEANO SUMMER SPECIAL
1963 (1)
Thomson
1 (nn) (36p) (gravure)	£2.50–£5.00

DANDY COMIC LIBRARY
Apr 1983–
Thomson
1 (64p) *Desperate Dan*	10p–25p
2–	10p–15p

DANDY SUMMER SPECIAL
1964–
Thomson
1 (nn) (32p) (gravure)	£1.00–£3.00
2–	50p–£2.00

DANGER AND ADVENTURE
1955 (3)
Miller (Charlton)
1–3 (28p) US reprint	50p–£1.00

DANGER MAN
1966 (1)
Thorpe & Porter
1 (68p) Mick Anglo	50p–£2.00

DANGER TRAIL
1946 (1)
Bairns (Marx)
1 (nn) (16p) Ern Shaw	50p–£1.00

DANIEL BOONE
Feb 1957–1959 (35)
Miller (Gower)
1 (28p) F. Castells	50p–£1.00
2–35 Don Lawrence	35p–£1.00

DAN'L BOONE
1955 (7)
World (Magazine Enterprises)
1–7 (28p) US reprint	50p–75p

DAREDEVIL
1951–1952 (7)
Pemberton (World) (Gleason)
1 (36p) US reprint	75p–£1.25
2–7	50p–£1.00

DAREDEVIL
1953 (3)
Miller (Gleason)
1–3 (28p) US reprint	50p–£1.00

DAREDEVIL WESTERN COMICS
1949 (1)
Cartoon Art (Fiction House)
1 (28p) US reprint	50p–£1.00

DAREDEVIL WINTER SPECIAL
Nov 1982 (1)
Marvel
1 (52p) US reprints	30p–50p

DAREDEVILS
Jan 1983–Nov 1983 (11)
Marvel
& *Marvel Superheroes*: Jun 1983
to: *Mighty World of Marvel*
1 (56p) US reprints	30p–60p
2–11 Alan Davis	25p–50p

DARING HERO COMIC
July 1951–1953 (5)
Scion (King-Ganteaume)

1 (24p) (4C) 75p–£1.00
2–5 50p–£1.00

DARK STAR HEROES
1984 (1)
Anti-Matter
1 (20p) Dave Harwood 25p–50p

DARLING ROMANCE
1950
Swan (Closeup)
1– (36p) US reprint 20p–50p

DAVID THE SOLDIER KING
1979 (1)
Lion/Fleurus
1 (52p) (4C) French reprint 50p–95p

DAVY CROCKETT
Oct 1956–Jan 1960 (50)
Miller (Gower)
1–12 (28p) US reprints 50p–75p
13–50 Don Lawrence 50p–£1.00

DAZZLE COMIC
1946–1948 (5)
International
1 (nn) (8p) (tabloid) J. R. Turner £1.00–£1.75
2–4 (20p) Bob Monkhouse £1.00–£1.25
5 (4p) (tabloid) J. R. Turner £1.00–£1.25

DAZZLER
19 Aug 1933–8 Apr 1939 (294)
Target
to: *Golden*
1 (12p) (tabloid) Bert Hill £5.00–£7.50
2–60 (12p) Harry Banger £2.00–£3.00
61–84 (8p) L. Diamond £2.00–£2.50
85–87 (12p) G. Larkman £2.00–£2.50
88–270 (8p) S. Perkins £2.00–£2.50
271–294 (12p) £1.75–£2.00

DE LUXE ALBUM SERIES
May 1973–Apr 1974 (12)
Williams/Top Sellers
1 *Tarzan of the Apes* (52p) (4C) 25p–50p
2 *Buffalo Bill* 15p–25p
3 *Casper the Ghost* 15p–25p
4 *Richie Rich & Gang* 15p–25p
5 *Boom-Boom the Dolphin* 15p–25p
6 *Laurel & Hardy* 20p–30p
7 *Dastardly & Muttley* 15p–25p
8 *Motormouse & Autocat* 15p–25p
9 *Calimero* 15p–25p
10 *Mr Sandman* 15p 25p
11 *Doctor Dolittle* 15p–25p
12 *Boom-Boom the Dolphin* 10p–20p

DEAD-EYE WESTERN
1950–1951 (7)
Streamline/United Anglo-American (Hillman)
1–6 (nn) (36–28p) US reprint 50p–75p
7 (4C) 50p–75p

DEADEYE WESTERN COMIC
Feb 1953–
Thorpe & Porter
1– (68p) US reprint 50p–£1.00

DEADSHOT DICK WESTERN COMIC
1947 (1)
Foldes/Gaywood
1 (nn) (12p) Rex Hart 50p–£1.00

DEBBIE
17 Feb 1973–15 Jan 1983 (518)
Thomson
& *Spellbound*: 21 Jan 1978
to: *Mandy*
1 (28p) 35p–75p
2–518 20p–35p

DEBBIE PICTURE STORY LIBRARY
1 Apr 1978–
Thomson
1 *Lost on Planet X* 20p–30p
2– 15p–20p

DEEPSEA
1952 (1)
Scion
1 (nn) (20p) Terry Patrick 50p–£1.00

DEMON
1978
Portman (Marvel)
1 (68p) US reprints 20p–50p
2– 15p–25p

DEPUTY DAWG PICTURE BOOK
1973 (1)
PBS/Total (Western)
1 (36p) (4C) US reprint (promo) 50p–75p

DERYN
Sep 1979–
Cwmni Urdd Gobaith Cymru
1 (20p) Welsh language 25p–50p
2– 15p–20p

DETECTIVE COMIC
1959 (8)
Miller (ACG/Fawcett)
1–8 (68p) US reprint 50p–75p

DETECTIVE COMICS
Feb 1947 (1)
Kosmos
1 (nn) (16p) Piet Van Elk 50p–£1.00

DETECTIVE HERO COMIC
1951 (1)
Scion (King-Ganteaume)
1 (24p) 50p–£1.00

DIAMOND ADVENTURE COMIC
Jul 1960–1963 (31)
Atlas (Fiction House)
1 (28p) US reprint 50p–£1.00
2–31 50p–75p

DIANA
23 Feb 1963–4 Dec 1976 (720)
Thomson
aka: *New Diana*
& *Romeo*: 21 Sep 1974
to: *Jackie*
1 (24p) (tabloid) (gravure) 35p–75p
2–720 25p–50p

DICK BOSS
1947 (2)
Literary Press
1: *Adventures of DB* (small) A. Mazure £1.00–£2.50
2: *DB in Texas* £1.00–£2.25

DICK COLE
see: *Blue Bolt Series*

DICK HERCULES OF ST. MARKHAM'S
Dec 1952–Jan 1954 (17)
Sports Cartoons (Miller)
to: Steve Samson
1 (28p) Sydney Jordan 75p–£1.25
2–17 James Holdaway 50p–£1.00

DICK TRACY
1953
Streamline/United Anglo-American
1– (28p) US reprint 50p–£1.00

DICKORY DOCK
1 Mar 1980–20 Sep 1980 (30)

IPC
to: *Jack & Jill*
1 (16p) Peter Woolcock   15p–25p
2–30   5p–15p

DICKORY DOCK SUMMER SPECIAL
Jul 1980 (1)
IPC
1 (nn) (40p) Peter Woolcock   25p–40p

DINGBATS COMIC
1948 (1)
Philmar (Marx)
1 (nn) (8p) (gravure) Ern Shaw   50p–£1.00

DINGDONGS COMIC
1948 (1)
Philmar (Marx)
1 (8p) (gravure) Ern Shaw   50p–£1.00

DISNEY MAGAZINE
1978 (4?)
House of Grolier (Disney)
1 (32p) (4C) US reprints (giveaway)   25p–50p
2–4   20p–30p

DISNEY MAGAZINE
Feb 1982–
London Editions
1 (32p) (4C) foreign reprints   10p–25p
2–12 (provincial release)   10p–15p
1 (Mar 1983) (national release)   10p–25p
2–   10p–15p

DISNEY PUZZLE
Apr 1983–
London Editions
1 (48p) reprints   20p–35p
2–   15p–20p

DISNEY TIME
29 Jan 1977–18 Jun 1977 (21)
IPC
to: *Mickey Mouse*
1 (16p) Peter Woolcock   15p–25p
2–21   10p–15p

DISNEY TIME SPECIALS
May 1977–Aug 1977 (3)
IPC
1: *Funtime Special* (40p)   15p–25p
2: *Holiday Special*   15p–25p
3: *Summer Special*   15p–25p

DISNEYLAND
27 Feb 1971–13 Nov 1976 (298)
IPC
aka: *Disneyland Magazine*
& Sunny Stories: 26 Jun 1971
& Once Upon a Time: 29 Apr 1972
& Now I Know: 20 Oct 1973
to: *Mickey Mouse*
1 (20p) (4C) Basil Reynolds   50p–75p
2–298 Hugh McNeill   15p–35p

DISNEYLAND SPECIALS
1971–1980 (41)
IPC
1: *Fun Time Special 1971* (48p) (4C)   25p–50p
2: *Christmas Special 1971*   35p–50p
3: *Springtime Special 1972*   25p–40p
4: *Fun Time Special 1972*   20p–35p
5: *Holiday Special 1972*   35p–50p
6: *Summer Special 1972*   35p–50p
7: *Christmas Special 1972*   35p–50p
8: *Springtime Special 1973*   25p–40p
9: *Fun Time Special 1973*   20p–35p
10: *Holiday Special 1973*   35p–40p
11: *Summer Special 1973*   35p–50p
12: *Autumn Special 1973*   35p–50p
13: *Christmas Special 1973*   35p–50p
14: *Springtime Special 1974*   25p–40p
15: *Fun Time Special 1974*   20p–35p

16: *Holiday Special 1974*   35p–40p
17: *Summer Special 1974*   35p–40p
18: *Christmas Special 1974*   35p–50p
19: *Springtime Special 1975*   25p–35p
20: *Fun Time Special 1975*   20p–35p
21: *Holiday Special 1975*   35p–40p
22: *Summer Special 1975*   35p–40p
23: *Christmas Special 1975*   35p–50p
24: *Springtime Special 1976*   25p–35p
25: *Fun Time Special 1976*   20p–35p
26: *Holiday Special 1976*   35p–40p
27: *Summer Special 1976*   35p–40p
28: *Christmas Special 1976*   35p–50p
29: *Springtime Special 1977*   25p–35p
30: *Fun Time Special 1977*   20p–35p
31: *Holiday Special 1977*   35p–40p
32: *Summer Special 1977*   35p–40p
33: *Springtime Special 1978*   25p–35p
34: *Fun Time Special 1978*   20p–30p
35: *Holiday Special 1978*   35p–40p
36: *Summer Special 1978*   35p–40p
37: *Fun Time Spring Special 1979*   25p–35p
38: *Holiday Special 1979*   35p–40p
39: *Summer Special 1979*   35p–40p
40: *Holiday Special 1980*   35p–40p
41: *Summer Special 1980*   35p–40p

DIXIE COMIC
1947 (1)
Ensign
1 (8p) (gravure) W. Forshaw   50p–£1.00

DIXIE DUGAN
1950–1951 (2)
Streamline/United Anglo-American (Columbia)
1 (nn) (36p) (4C) US reprint   £1.00–£1.50
2   50p–£1.00

DIXON OF DOCK GREEN
Nov 1959–Mar 1960 (6)
Pearson (TV Picture Stories)
1 (TVP 27) *Whiff of Garlic*   35p–75p
2 (TVP 30) *Bracelets for Groom*   25p–50p
3 (TVP 32) *The Heel*   25p–50p
4 (TVP 34) *Gentleman from Siberia*   25p–50p
5 (TVP 35) *Little Bit of French*   25p–50p
6 (TVP 36) *Case of Mrs X*   25p–50p

DIZZLING COMIC
Sep 1947 (1)
Co-ordination
1 (20p) Piet Van Elk   50p–£1.00

DOC CHAOS
1984 (2)
Hydra/Escape
1 (12p) Phil Elliott   20p–30p
2 (44p)   75p–£1.00

DOCTOR DOLITTLE
1973–1974
Top Sellers
1 (36p) (4C)   25p–50p
2–   20p–35p

DOCTOR SNUGGLES HOLIDAY SPECIAL
May 1981–May 1982 (2)
Polystyle
1 (48p) (TV series) reprints   35p–50p
2   20p–35p

DOCTOR WHO COMIC
see: *Mighty Midget*

DOCTOR WHO SPECIALS
May 1974–
Polystyle/Marvel
1: *Holiday Special 1974* (48p)   75p–£1.50
2: *Winter Special 1977*   50p–£1.00
3: *Summer Special 1980* (52p)   40p–75p
4: *Very Best of Doctor Who*   40p–60p
5: *Winter Special 1981*   40p–60p
6: *Summer Special 1982*   40p–60p

7: *Winter Special 1982*	40p–60p
8: *Summer Special 1983*	40p–60p
9: *Winter Special 1983*	35p–60p
10: *Summer Special 1984*	30p–60p
11: *Winter Special 1984*	30p–60p

DOCTOR WHO WEEKLY
17 Oct 1979–6 Aug 1980 (43)
Marvel
to: *Doctor Who (Monthly)*

1 (28p) Dave Gibbons	50p–£1.00
2–43	30p–50p

DOCTOR WHO (MONTHLY)
Sep 1980–
Marvel

1 (44) (36p) Dave Gibbons	50p–60p
45–	30p–50p

DOLL MAN
Aug 1949
Locker (Quality)

1 (nn) (36p) (4C) US reprint	£1.00–£1.50

DOLL MAN
Sep 1951 (1)
Popular (Boardman) (Quality)

1 (No 6) (36p) (4C) US reprint	£1.00–£1.50

DON WINSLOW OF THE NAVY
1948–1953 (63)
Miller (Fawcett)

1 (nn) (12p) (gravure)	75p–£1.25
50–61 (24p) US reprint	50p–£1.00
100–149 (28p)	50p–£1.00

DONALD AND MICKEY
4 Mar 1972–29 Aug 1975 (182)
IPC (Disney)
& *Goofy*: 18 May 1974
to: *Mickey & Donald*

1 (24p) US reprints	15p–25p
2–182	10p–15p

DONALD AND MICKEY SPECIALS
June 1972–Jun 1975 (11)
IPC (Disney)

1: *Holiday Special 1972* (48p)	30p–50p
2: *Fun Time Extra 1972*	30p–50p
3: *Christmas Special 1972*	30p–50p
4: *Fun Time Extra 1973*	30p–50p
5: *Holiday Special 1973*	30p–50p
6: *Christmas Special 1973*	30p–50p
7: *Fun Time Extra 1974*	25p–45p
8: *Holiday Special 1974*	25p–45p
9: *Christmas Holiday Special 1974*	25p–45p
10: *Fun Time Extra 1975*	20p–40p
11: *Holiday Special 1975*	20p–40p

DONALD DUCK
27 Sep 1975–24 Jan 1976 (18)
IPC (Disney)
to: *Mickey Mouse*

1 (32p) (4C) US reprints	15p–25p
2–18	10p–20p

DONALD DUCK CHRISTMAS SPECIAL
Nov 1975 (1)
IPC (Disney)

1 (48p) US reprints	25p–35p

DONALD DUCK FUN LIBRARY
Apr 1978–
Egmont/Purnell (Disney)

1 (100p) (4C) (small) foreign reprints	25p–50p
2–	20p–25p

DON'T RUSH ME
Mar 1975 (1)
Wandsworth Council

1 (nn) (4p) race relations promo	10p–25p

DOPE FIEND FUNNIES
Sep 1974 (1)
H. Bunch/Cozmic Comics

1 (36p) (adult) Chris Welch	50p–£1.00

DOT AND CARRIE SERIES
1923–1925 (3)
Daily News strip reprints

1: *Dot & Carrie* (68p) (oblong)	£5.00–£7.50
2: *D & C & Adolphus*	£2.50–£5.00
3: *D & C Not Forgetting Adolphus*	£2.50–£5.00

DOUBLE DUO
1976
Williams

1 (68p) *Brigands/Voyages* (foreign reprint)	15p–25p
2–	10p–20p

DOUBLE TROUBLE
1950 (1)
Star

1 (nn) (68p) US strip reprint (oblong)	50p–£1.00

DOWN WITH CRIME
1952 (7)
Arnold (Fawcett)

1 (50) (28p) US reprint	50p–£1.00
51–56	50p–£1.00

DRACULA
1962 (1)
Top Sellers (Dell)

1 (nn) (68p) US reprint	50p–£1.00

DRACULA
30 Sep 1972–24 Feb 1973 (12)
New English Library (Buru Lan)

1 (24p) (4C) (Spanish reprint)	50p–75p
2–12	35p–50p

DRACULA COMICS SPECIAL
Apr 1984 (1)
Quality

1 (52p) reprints	50p–75p

DRACULA LIVES
26 Oct 1974–16 June 1976 (87)
Marvel
to: *Planet of the Apes*

1 (36p) US reprint	25p–50p
2–87	20p–25p

DRACULA LIVES SPECIAL EDITION
1976 (1)
World (Marvel)

1 (68p) US reprints	50p–£1.00

DRACULA SUMMER SPECIAL
May 1982 (1)
Marvel

1 (48p) US reprints	35p–50p

DRAGONSLAYER
1982 (1)
Marvel

1 (52p) (4C) US reprint (Disney film)	50p–75p

DREAMER
19 Sep 1981–15 May 1982 (35)
IPC
to: *Girl*

1 (32p) (photos)	15p–25p
2–35	10p–15p

DUCK SOUP
1979 (3)
Duck Soup

1 (24p) Tom Johnston (adult)	30p–50p
2–3 Steve Bell	25p–35p

DUMMY
6 Dec 1975 (1)
supplement to *New Musical Express* magazine
1 (nn) (4p) (tabloid) Tony Benyon   25p–50p

DURANGO KID
1952–1953 (20)
Compix/Cartoon Art (Magazine Enterprises)
1 (20p) (4C) US reprint   75p–£1.50
2–20   50p–£1.00

DURANGO KID
1951
Streamline (Magazine Enterprises)
1 (28p)   75p–£1.25
2–   50p–£1.00

DUSTY BEAR MONTHLY
1975
New English Library
1 (24p) (4C)   10p–25p
2–   10p–15p

DUSTY BEAR SUMMER FUN BOOK
1976 (1)
New English Library
1 (48p)   20p–30p

DYNAMIC
Feb 1949 (1)
Paget
1 (nn) (16p) Mick Anglo   50p–£1.00

DYNAMIC COMICS
1945 (1)
International
1 (nn) (8p) Denis Gifford   £1.00–£2.00

DYNAMIC THRILLS
Jan 1951–1952 (10)
Swan
1 (36p) John McCail   £1.50–£2.00
2–10 Ron Embleton   £1.00–£1.50

DYNAMITE DUNN
1944 (1)
Miller (United Features)
1 (nn) (16p) (gravure) US reprint   75p–£1.25

EAGLE
14 Apr 1950–26 Apr 1969 (991)
Hulton/Longacre/Odhams/IPC
& *Swift*: 9 Mar 1963
& *Boys World*: 10 Oct 1964
to: *Lion*
1 (tabloid) (gravure) Frank Hampson   £2.50–£5.00
2 John Worsley   £1.50–£3.50
1950 issues Jack Daniel   75p–£1.25
1951–1959 Peter Jackson   35p–£1.00
1960–1967 Frank Bellamy   25p–75p
1968–1969 IPC editions   15p–20p

EAGLE
27 Mar 1982–
IPC
& *Scream*: 1 Sep 1984
1 (32p) Gerry Embleton   20p–40p
2–   10p–20p

EAGLE EXTRA
11 Sep 1953–13 Nov 1953 (10)
Hulton
1–10 (4p) (supplement) P. Nevin   25p–50p

EAGLE HOLIDAY SPECIAL
Apr 1983–
IPC
1 (64p)   35p–50p
2–   30p–45p

EAGLE SPECIALS
Odhams
1962: *Eagle Holiday Extra* (48p)   £1.50–£2.00
1966: *Eagle Summer Special* (48p)   £1.25–£2.00

EARLY LIFE OF WINSTON CHURCHILL
194– (1)
Burrow (newspaper strip reprints)
1 (nn) (60p) (oblong) Philip Mendoza   £1.50–£3.00

ECHO CHILDREN'S CHRISTMAS
SUPPLEMENT
20 Dec 1957 (1)
Liverpool Echo
supplement to *Liverpool Echo*
1 (nn) (4p) (large) R. Clibborn   50p–£1.00

EDWARD'S HEAVE COMICS
Apr 1973 (1)
H. Bunch/Cozmic Comics
1 (nn) (35p) (adult) Edward Barker   50p–£1.00

EERIE
1972 (4)
Gold Star (Warren)
1–4 (52p) US reprint   50p–£1.00

EERIE COMICS
Oct 1951–
Thorpe & Porter (Avon)
1 (68p) US reprint   £1.00–£2.00
2–   £1.00–£1.50

EERIE TALES
1962–
Alan Class
1– (68p) US reprints   35p–50p

87th PRECINCT
1962 (1)
Top Sellers (Dell)
1 (68p) US reprint   25p–50p

ELECTRIC COMPANY BOOK
1975 (1)
BBC/School Broadcasting Council
1 (44p) Malcolm Harrison   25p–50p

ELECTROMAN COMICS
1951–1952 (6)
Scion (King-Ganteaume)
1 (24p) (nn)   50p–£1.00
2–6 (3, 4 only numbered)   50p–£1.00

ELLA CINDERS
1942 (1)
Miller (United Features)
1 (nn) (12p) (small) US reprint   £1.00–£2.00

ELMO'S OWN
1946(?)–1949
Chascol
to: *Sheriff & Elmo's Own*
1 Charles Cole   75p–£1.50
2–V3 N9(?) (12p)   50p–£1.00

EMERGENCY WARD 10
Jun 1958–May 1960 (21)
Pearson
1: *Calling Nurse Roberts*   25p–50p
2: *Calling Nurse Young*   20p–35p
3: *Date for Carole*   20p–30p
4: *O'Meara Makes Amends*   20p–30p
5: *Cocktail Party*   20p–30p
6: *Trouble for Simon*   20p–30p
7: *Coming Sister*   20p–30p
8: *Night Duty*   20p–30p
9: *Casting Vote*   20p–30p
10: *Daily Round*   20p–30p
11: *Rivals*   20p–30p
12: *Checkmate*   20p–30p

13: *Contract* 20p–30p
14: 20p–30p
15: *Night Falls on Oxbridge* 20p–30p
16: *Carole's Dilemma* 20p–30p
17: 20p–30p
18: *Very Special Baby* 20p–30p
19: *Nurse Roberts Evening Out* 20p–30p
20: 20p–30p
21: *Two Lives in His Hands* 20p–30p

EMMA
25 Feb 1978–8 Sep 1979 (81)
Thomson
to: *Judy*
1 (32p) 15p–25p
2–81 5p–10p

ENID BLYTON TINY STRIP BOOKS
see: *Clicky Series*
    Gobo Strip Books
    Mandy Mops and Cubby Strip Books
    Mary Mouse Series
    Noddy Strip Books
    Tumpy Strip Books

ENID BLYTON'S NODDY AND HIS FRIENDS
see: *Noddy and His Friends*

ENSIGN COMIC
1947 (4)
Ensign
1 (8p) (gravure) W. Forshaw £1.00–£1.75
2–3 (8p) (gravure) F. Minnitt 75p–£1.00
4 (8p) Bryan Berry 50p–£1.00

EPIC
see: *Lion Summer Spectacular Epic*

ERIC AND ERNIE'S T.V. FUNBOOK
Oct 1978 (1)
ITV Books
1 (nn) (128p) Terry Wakefield 50p–65p

ESMERALDA
12 Jun 1971–29 Jan 1972 (33)
Gresham/IPC
to: *Bobo Bunny*
1 (16p) (gravure) 25p–35p
2–33 10p–25p

ESPIONAGE
1967 (8)
Brugeditor (Holding)
1–8 (68p) (small) foreign reprint 25p–35p

EULALIE'S FUNNIES
Dec 1949–Jan 1950 (2)
Apollo
1–2 (8p) Eulalie 75p–£1.00

EVENING GAZETTE FAMILY CARTOONS
21 Mar 1982–
Colchester Evening Gazette
supplement to *Evening Gazette*
1 (4p) (2C) (tabloid) US reprints 15p–25p
2– 5p–10p

EVERY BODY'S ALBUM AND CARICATURE MAGAZINE
1 Jan 1834–27 Jul 1835 (37)
Kendrick
1 (1p) (tabloid) C. J. Grant £10.00–£15.00
2–37 £5.00–£10.00

EVERYDAY NOVELS AND COMICS
1940 (1)
Popular Fiction
1 (nn) (8p) (tabloid) J. Greenall £1.50–£3.00

EVIL EYE THRILLER
1947 (2)
Kaye/Art Publicity

1 (nn) (8p) Les Barton 50p–£1.00
2 (nn) (smaller size) 50p–£1.00

EXCITING ROMANCES
1952 (2)
World (Fawcett)
1–2 (36p) US reprint 35p–50p

EXCITING WAR
1962 (1)
Cartoon Art
1 US reprint 50p–£1.00

EXPRESS (SUPER COLOUR) (WEEKLY)
18 Feb 1956–16 Apr 1960 (212)
Beaverbrook
& *Rocket*: 1 Dec 1956
to: *T.V. Express*
1 (74) (20p) (tabloid) (gravure) H. Bishop £1.00–£1.25
75–285 Ron Embleton 50p–75p

EXPRESS THRILLER COMIC
Jul 1946 (1)
Foster
1 (nn) (16p) Bob Wilkin 50p–£1.00

EXTRA FUN
Aug 1940–Nov 1940 (4)
Swan
1 (36p) John McCail £2.00–£3.00
2–4 Harry Banger £1.50–£2.00

EXTRA FUN (NEW SERIES)
1952 (2)
Swan
1–2 (36p) John McCail £1.00–£1.50

FABULOUS FURRY FREAK BROTHERS
1976 (4)
Hassle Free Press
1–4 (44p) US/UG reprints 35p–50p

FAIRY FUN COMIC
1948 (1)
PM (Marx)
1 (nn) (8p) (gravure) Walter Bell 50p–£1.00

FAIRY TIME COMIC
1948 (1)
Jones
1 (nn) (8p) 50p–£1.00

FALCON COMICS
1979–1980 (3)
Hutchinson
1: *Tram Fury* 25p–50p
2: *Rollin' Through* 25p–50p
3: *Adventures of Moven Marven* 25p–50p

FALLING IN LOVE
1955 (8)
Trent (DC)
1–8 (68p) US reprint 25p–35p

FAMILY CARTOONS
SEE: *Evening Gazette Family Cartoons*

FAMILY FAVOURITES COMIC WEEKLY
24 Feb 1954–1954 (34)
Miller (Chicago Tribune)
1 (28p) US reprints 75p–£1.50
2–34 50p–75p

FAMILY FUN
1953 (1)
Pentland
1 (nn) (8p) (giveaway) D. Gifford 50p–£1.00

FAMOUS CRIMES
1951 (2)
Streamline (Fox)
1–2 (28p) US reprint   £1.00–£1.50

FAMOUS FIVE CARTOON BOOKS
1983 (2)
Hodder & Stoughton (Hachette)
1: *FF & the Golden Galleon* French reprint £1.00–£1.95
2: *FF & the Inca God* (52p)   £1.00–£1.95

FAMOUS ROMANCE LIBRARY
Jan 1958–
AP
1– (68p)   25p–35p

FAMOUS STORIES IN PICTURES
1955? (12)
Bairns (Marx)
(reprints of *Classic in Pictures*)
1–12 (52p)   50p–75p

FANCY FREE
1948 (1)
Scion
1 (nn) (8p) R. Plummer   50p–£1.00

FANTASIA POSTER MAGAZINE
1979 (1)
IPC (Disney)
1 (4C) (poster)   45p–50p

FANTASTIC
10 Feb 1967–2 Nov 1968 (91)
Odhams (Marvel)
& *Terrific*: 10 Feb 1968
to: *Smash*
1 (40p) US reprints   50p–£1.00
2–91   35p–50p

FANTASTIC FOUR
6 Oct 1982–14 Mar 1983 (23)
Marvel
to: *Spiderman*
1 (24p) US reprints   20p–25p
2–23   15p–20p

FANTASTIC FOUR POCKET BOOK
Mar 1980–Jul 1982 (28)
Marvel
1 (52p) (small) US reprints   15p–25p
2–28   10p–20p
20 (Xmas double number)   25p–40p

FANTASTIC FOUR SPECIALS
Oct 1981–Oct 1983 (3)
Marvel
1: *Winter Special 1981* (52p) US reprints   30p–50p
2: *Summer Special 1982*   30p–50p
3: *Winter Special 1983*   25p–50p

FANTASTIC SERIES
16 Jan 1967 (2)
Fleetway
to: *Stupendous Series*
1 (132p) *Steel Claw*   35p–50p
2   30p–40p

FANTASTIC SUMMER SPECIAL
1968 (1)
Odhams (Marvel)
1 (nn) (56p) US reprints   50p–£1.00

FANTASTIC TALES
1963 (20)
Top Sellers (National)
1–20 (68p) US reprints   50p–75p

FANTASTIC WORLDS
1962 (1)
Cartoon Art
1 US reprints   50p–£1.00

FANTASY STORIES
196– (6)
Spencer
1–6 (52p) Mick Anglo   25p–75p

FAREWELL TO JANE
see: *Jane Series*

FARGO KID
1959
Strato (Prize)
1– (68p) US reprint   50p–75p

FAST ACTION WESTERN COMIC
see: *Giant Comic*

FAT CAT
1979 (1)
Express Books (*Sunday Express* reprints)
1 (nn) (100p) (oblong) (4C) Mike Atkinson   50p–£1.00

FAT FREDDY'S COMICS AND STORIES
1984 (1)
Knockabout (Rip Off)
1 (36p) US/UG reprint   50p–£1.00

FATHER CHRISTMAS
1975 (1)
Puffin/Hamish Hamilton
1 (nn) (36p) (4C) Raymond Briggs   35p–50p

FATMAN
1978 (1)
Rochdale Alternative Paper
1 (nn) (76p) (oblong) Tony Smart (reprints)   25p–50p

FAVOURITE COMIC
21 Jan 1911–31 Mar 1917 (324)
AP
to: *Merry & Bright*
1 (8p) (tabloid) G. M. Payne   £5.00–£10.00
2–324 George Wakefield   £1.75–£2.00

FAWCETT MOVIE COMIC
1951–1952 (13)
Miller (Fawcett)
1 (50): *The Old Frontier* US reprint   £1.00–£2.00
51–62   £1.00–£1.25

FAWCETT'S FUNNY ANIMALS
see: *Funny Animals*

F.B.I. COMIC
1951 (2)
Streamline/United Anglo-American (Fox)
1–2 (28p) US reprint   50p–£1.00

FEATURE COMICS
1940–1941 (5)
Boardman (Quality
1 (29) (36p) (4C) US reprint   £2.00–£3.50
30–33 (20p)   £1.50–£2.00

FEATURE STORIES MAGAZINE
1951 (1)
Streamline/United Anglo-American (Fox)
1 (28p) US reprint   75p–£1.00

FEELINGS
Aug 1984–
Atlas
1 (photos)   15p–25p
2–   10p–15p

FELIX THE CAT SERIES
May–Dec 1949 (5)
Bruce (King)
1: *Felix the Cat* (8p) (gravure)US reprint   £1.00–£2.00
2–4: *Felix Funnies*   £1.00–£1.50
5: *Felix Christmas Book*   £1.00–£1.50

FELIX THE CAT
1953 (9)
Paladin (Toby)
1 (28p) US reprint   50p–£1.00
2–9   50p–75p

FELIX THE CAT LITTLE PICTURE BOOKS
1948 (6)
Bruce (Dell)
1–6 (28p) (small) US reprint   £1.00–£1.50

FFANTOM OF THE OPERA
Nov 1984 (1)
Welsh National Opera
1 (8p) (4C) (promo) Arthur Ranson   10p–20p

FIDO SERIES
Jan–Apr 1954 (4)
Hotspur
1: *Fido the Pup* (8p) (gravure) Denis Gifford 75p–£1.00
2: *Fido's Fun* Harry Banger   50p–£1.00
3: *Fido at Fair* Bob Wilkin   50p–£1.00
4: *Fido at Seaside*   50p–£1.00

FIGHT COMICS
1950 (1)
Cartoon Art (Fiction House)
1 (36p) (4C) US reprint   75p–£1.50

FIGHT COMICS
1949 (1)
Streamline/United Anglo-American (Fiction House)
1 (36p) (4C) US reprint   75p–£1.50

FIGHT COMICS
1960 (2)
Trent (Fiction House)
1–2 (68p) US reprint   50p–£1.00

FIGHT COMICS–ATTACK
1951 (1)
Cartoon Art
1 (68p) US reprint   75p–£1.00

FIGHTIN' AIR FORCE
1956 (3)
Miller (Charlton)
1–3 (28p) US reprint   50p–75p

FIGHTIN' NAVY
1956 (3)
Miller (Charlton)
1–3 (28p) US reprint   50p–75p

FIGHTING BRIT
1948 (1)
Cartoon Art
1 (nn) (broadside)   £1.00–£2.50

FILM FUN
17 Jan 1920–8 Sep 1962 (2225)
AP
& *Picture Fun*: 31 Jul 1920
& *Kinema Comic*: 22 Oct 1932
& *Film Picture Stories*: 23 Feb 1935
& *Chips*: 19 Sep 1953
& *Top Spot*: 23 Jan 1960

aka: *Film Fun and Thrills*: 13 Jan 1959
to: *Buster*
1 (24p) George Wakefield   £5.00–£10.00
1920–1929 Tom Radford   £2.00–£2.50
1930–1939 Jos Walker   £2.00–£3.00
1940–1949 Norman Ward   £2.00–£2.50
1950–1962 Terry Wakefield   50p–£1.00

FILM PICTURE LIBRARY
Jul 1959–Nov 1959 (3)
Pearson
1 (68p): *Warlock* T. Aspin   50p–£1.00
2–3   35p–50p

FILM PICTURE STORIES
28 Jul 1934–16 Feb 1935 (30)
AP
to: *Film Fun*
1 (24p) George Wakefield   £5.00–£10.00
2–30 Jos Walker   £2.50–£3.00

FILM SHOTS
Oct 1948 (1)
McKenzie
1 (nn) (8p) (photos)   50p–£1.00

FIREFLY
28 Feb 1914–13 Feb 1915 (51)
AP
to: *New Series*
1 (20p) (small) G. Wakefield   £5.00–£7.50
2–51 Fred Crompton   £1.75–£2.50

FIREFLY NEW SERIES
20 Feb 1915–31 Mar 1917 (111)
AP
to: *Butterfly*
1 (8p) (tabloid) G. M. Payne   £5.00–£10.00
2–111 Harry Parlett   £1.75–£2.00

FIREHAIR COMICS
1950 (1)
Streamline/United Anglo-American (Fiction)
1 (28p) US reprint   75p–£1.25

FIRST
1981 (1)
Interstellar Rat
1 (40p) (adult)   25p–50p

FIRST LOVE
1959– (18)
Strato (Harvey)
1–18 (68p) US reprint   25p–35p

FITNESS AND SUN
see: *Sun*

FITS
1946 (1?)
Morris (Dublin)
1 (nn) (8p)   £2.00–£3.00

FIVE STAR WESTERN
1951–1952 (8)
Scion
1 (24p) Norman Light   75p–£1.25
2–8 Ron Embleton   50p–£1.00

FIZZ
Apr 1949 (1)
Modern Fiction
1 (16p) (gravure) Arthur Martin   £1.50–£2.00

FIZZER (Corona Fizzer)
1978–1981 (5)
Corona Soft Drinks/TJR (giveaway)
1 (8p) (4C)   50p–£1.00
2   25p–50p
3 (nn) Holiday 1979   25p–50p

4 (nn) Christmas 1979   25p–50p
5 (nn) Spring 1981   15p–25p

FLAG COMIC
1946 (1)
Reynand/Atlas
1 (nn) (8p) Tom Cottrell   50p–£1.00

FLASH
Jul 1948–Dec 1949 (11)
Amex (Marx)
1–3 (8p) (small) Colin Merritt   £1.00–£1.50
4–9 (tabloid) (gravure) Reg Parlett £1.50–£1.75
10–11 (tabloid) (4C)George Parlett £1.50–£2.00

FLASH
1962 (5)
Top Sellers (DC)
1–5 (52p) US reprint   50p–75p

FLASH-BANG COMICS ADVENTURE
1948 (1)
Cartoon Art
1 (36p) Dennis Reader   £1.00–£2.00

FLASH COMICS
1940–1941 (16)
Camden
1 (32p)   £2.00–£5.00
2–16   £2.00–£3.50

FLASH FEARLESS
1975
Chrysalis (*New Musical Express* supplement)
1 (12p) (4C) Paul Sample (record promo) 50p–75p

FLASH FILSTRUP
1981 (1)
Arrow/Hutchinson
1 (nn) (100p) (oblong) US reprint   50p–75p

FLASH GORDON
1953 (3)
World (King Features)
1 (36p) US reprint   75p–£1.25
2–3   75p–£1.00

FLASH GORDON
1959 (6)
World (King Features)
1–6 (68p) US reprint   75p–£1.00

FLASH GORDON
1962 (5)
Miller (King Features)
1 (68p) US reprint   75p–£1.00
2–5   50p–75p

FLASH GORDON WORLD ADVENTURE LIBRARY
Jan 1967–Aug 1967 (8)
World (King Features)
1 (68p) US reprint   35p–50p
2–8   30p–40p

FLASH STREAMLINE COMICS
195– (1)
Streamline/United Anglo-Amercan
1 (nn) (68p) US reprints   £1.00–£2.00

FLASHER GORDON
1978 (1)
Tabor
1 (32p) (small) (adult)   25p–40p

FLICKER FUN
1948 (1)
Philmar (Marx)
1 (nn) (8p) Arthur Martin   50p–£1.00

FLINTSTONES MINI-COMIC
6 Mar 1965 (1)
City
1 (16p) (supplement to *Huckleberry Hound*) 10p–25p

FLOOK SERIES
1949–1975 (5)
Associated Newspapers (strip reprints)
1 (1949) *Amazing Adventures of Rufus & Flook* £3.00–£7.00
2 (1950) *Rufus & Flook v Moses Maggot* £2.00–£5.00
3 (1951) *Rufus & Flook at School* £2.00–£5.00
4 (1970) *Flook* £1.00–£3.00
5 (1975) *Flook & Peasants Revolt* 25p–50p

FLYING A'S RANGE RIDER
1954–1955 (16)
World (Dell)
1 (28p) US reprint   50p–£1.00
2–16   50p–75p

FLYING ACES
1956 (2)
Streamline/United Anglo-American (Key)
1 (nn) (28p) US reprint   35p–50p
2 (nn) (68p)   35p–75p

FOCUS ON FACT SERIES
1977–1978 (7)
Allen/Star (*Daily Mail* reprints)
1: *World of Invention* (132p) (oblong) 25p–50p
2: *Story of Sport*   20p–35p
3: *Psychic World*   20p–35p
4: *Story of Christmas*   20p–35p
5: *Unsolved Mysteries*   20p–35p
6: *Story of Flight*   20p–35p
7: *Story of Travel*   20p–35p

FOLDOUT POSTER MAGAZINE
1974–1975 (2)
Poster Magazines/NEL
to: *T.V. Poster Magazine*
1 (16p) (4C) *Noddy Sunshine Special* 20p–30p
2 (nn) *Noddy Special*   20p–30p

FOLD-OUT POSTER MAGAZINE CARTOON STRIP SERIES
May–Jul 1974 (2)
Poster Magazine/NEL
1: *Pink Panther* (4C)   25p–35p
2: *Scooby Doo*   25p–35p

FOOD FIRST
1980 (1)
Third World/New Internationalist
1 (nn) (24p) US reprint; promo 25p–50p

FOOTBALL COMIC
Jan 1953–Nov 1953 (11)
Sports Cartoons (Miller)
to: *Supersonic*
1 (28p)   50p–£1.00
2–11 James Holdaway   50p–£1.00

FOOTBALL FUN BOOK
3 Nov 1934 (1)
Thomson (*Skipper* giveaway)
1 (nn) (32p) Dudley Watkins £1.50–£3.00

FOR YOUR EYES ONLY/JAMES BOND
Jul 1981 (1)
Marvel
1 (nn) (64p) US reprint   50p–75p

FORBIDDEN WORLDS
195–196– (145)
Strato
1 (68p) US reprint   75p–£1.25
2–145   75p–£1.00

FORCES IN COMBAT
15 May 1980–21 Jan 1981 (37)
Marvel
to: *Future Tense*
1 (32p) US reprint   15p–25p
2–37   10p–15p

FOREIGN INTRIGUES
1956 (2)
Miller (Charlton)
1–2 (28p) US reprint   50p–75p

FORGERS
1948 (1)
Hotspur: *Secret Service Series* 4
1 (4) (gravure) (8p) Bob Wilkin   50p–£1.00

FORM
1959? (1)
Conservative & Unionist
1 (nn) (12p) (4C) political   50p–£1.00

FOSDYKE SAGA
1972–
Wolfe/Mirror
1 (196p) Bill Tidy strip reprint   £1.00–£2.00
2–   75p–£1.00

FOTOSTRIP
1970? (3)
Top Sellers
1–3 (68p) photos; adult   50p–75p

FOUR ACES
1945 (1)
Newton Wickham
1 (nn) (8p) Glyn Protheroe   50p–£1.00

FOUR ACES COMIC
1954 (6)
Miller (King Features)
1–6 (28p) US reprint   50p–£1.00

FOUR DEUCES COMIC
Nov 1947 (1)
Transatlantic (Cartoon Art)
1 (8p) Dennis Reader   50p–£1.00

FOUR JOLLY MILLER COMIC STRIPS
1943 (1)
Miller (4 folders in banded pack)
1: *Hookey's Hoard* (reprints)   50p–75p
2: *Egbert the Explorer*   50p–75p
3: *Pampas Pete*   50p–75p
4: *Frolicsome Flossie*   50p–75p

FOX AND CROW
1970
Top Sellers (DC)
1– (36p) (4C) US reprint   25p–35p

FOX AND THE HOUND
Nov 1981 (1)
London Editions (Disney)
1 (nn) (68p) (4C) US reprint   50p–95p

FOX AND THE HOUND POSTER MAGAZINE
1981 (1)
London Editions (Disney)
1 (nn) (4C)   25p–50p

FRANK BUCK
1950 (1)
Streamline/United Anglo-American (Fox)
1 (28p) US reprint   75p–£1.00

FRANKENSTEIN
1963 (1)
Top Sellers (Dell)
1 (68p) US reprint   75p–£1.00

FRANKENSTEIN COMICS
1951 (5)
Arnold (Prize)
1 (68p) US reprint   £1.50–£2.50
2–5   £1.00–£2.00

FRANKIE STEIN'S MINI-MONSTER COMIC BOOK
9 Mar 1974–30 Mar 1974 (1)
IPC
1 (32p) supplements to *Shiver & Shake*   25p–50p

FRANTIC
Mar 1980–Jul 1981 (18)
Marvel
to: *Marvel Madhouse*
1 (36p) US reprints   25p–35p
2–18   20p–30p

FRANTIC SUMMER SPECIAL
May 1979 (1)
Marvel
1 (52p) US reprints   25p–50p

FRANTIC WINTER SPECIAL
Oct 1979 (1)
Marvel
1 (52p) US reprints   25p–50p

FREAKY FABLES
1979 (1)
Sphere
1 (nn) (68p) (oblong) J. Handelsman   50p–£1.00
   Punch strip reprints

FRED BASSET
1966–
Associated Newspapers/Harmsworth
1 Alex Graham strip reprints   £1.00–£2.50
2–35 (oblong)   75p–£1.00
36 (80p) (first 4C)   50p–90p

FRED LESLIE'S JOURNAL COMIC BUDGET
8 Jul 1902–30 Aug 1902 (7)
Strong
1 (8p) (2C) supplement to story-paper   £2.50–£4.00
2–7   £1.00–£2.00

FRESH FUN
Apr 1940–Jan 1951 (35)
Swan
to: *Laughitoff* (1943)
to: *Scramble* (1947)
1 (36p) William Ward   £2.50–£5.00
2–10 (36p) Harry Banger   £1.50–£2.00
11–12 (28p) Glyn Protheroe   £1.00–£1.50
13–18 (20p) John McCail   £1.00–£1.25
19–22 (16p) John Turner   75p–£1.00
23–30 (16p) (format change)   50p–75p
31–32 (20p) Ron Embleton   50p–75p

FRIENDLY BEACON
1951 (1)
ROSPA (giveaway)
1 (nn) (8p) Bob Wilkin   £1.00–£1.50

FRITZ AND WIZBY
1982 (1)
Image Arts
1 (nn) (4C) folded broadside poster   10p–20p

FRITZ THE CAT
1972–1973 (2)
Heavy Duty Comics
1 (28p) US/UG reprint   25p–50p
2 (32p)   20p–45p

FRIZZ & FRIENDS
1977
Egmont/Methuen (DeSousa)

1 (small) (100p) (4C) Brazil reprint   25p–35p
2–   20p–25p

FROGMAN COMICS
1952 (4)
Thorpe & Porter (Hillman)
1 (68p) US reprint   50p–£1.00
2–4   50p–75p

FROLICOMIC
May–Dec 1949 (4)
Martin & Reid (Gower)
1 (8p) (gravure) Frank Minnitt   £1.00–£2.00
2–4 Wally Robertson   75p–£1.00

FROLIX
Aug 1928–9 May 1930 (46)
Barton
1 (16p) Murdock Stimpson   £2.50–£5.00
2–14 (monthly) Reg Carter   £1.00–£2.00
15–46 (weekly) Louis Diamond   £1.00–£2.00

FRONT LINE COMBAT
1959 (4)
Miller
1 (28p) Alan Willow   75p–£1.25
2–4   75p–£1.00

FRONTIER TRAIL
1958
Miller (Ajax)
1 (50)–(28p) US reprint   50p–75p

FRONTIER WESTERN
1956 (12)
Miller (Atlas)
1–12 (28p) US reprint   50p–75p

FUDGE
1981 (2)
Savoy/NEL
1: *Fudge and the Dragon* (140p) K. Reid   £2.00–£3.50
2: *Fudge in Bubbleville*   £2.00–£3.50
    Manchester Evening News reprints

FUDGE COMIC
1946 (1)
Fudge
1 (nn) (8p) David Williams   50p–£1.00

FULL O' FUN
1949 (3)
Philmar/PM (Marx)
1–2 (8p) Arthur Martin   50p–£1.00
3 (8p) (tabloid) Reg Parlett   50p–£1.25

FUN AND FICTION
14 Oct 1911–21 Feb 1914 (124)
AP
to: *Firefly*
1   £5.00–£7.50
2–124   £1.50–£2.00

FUN AND FROLIC
1945 (1)
International
1 (nn) (8p) John Turner   75p–£1.00

FUN FAIR
May–Oct 1929 (6)
Britannia & Eve
supplement to *Britannia & Eve* magazine
1 (8p) (3C) Jacques Browne   £2.00–£4.00
2–6 Alan D'Egville   £2.00–£3.00

FUN FAIR COMIC
1948 (1)
Philmar (Marx)
1 (nn) (8p) Wally Robertson   50p–£1.00

FUN FARE
1934 (1)
Lancs & Yorks Dairies (giveaway)
1 (nn) (8p) Basil Reynolds   £2.00–£5.00

FUN FARE
1946 (1)
Martin & Reid
1 (nn) (8p) H. E. Pease   50p–£1.00

FUN FOR THE FAMILY
21 Jul 1940–6 Apr 1941 (38)
Sunday Mail (supplement)
1–38 (2p) (4C) Ern Shaw   £1.00–£2.00

FUN–IN
1973–1974 (26)
Williams
1 (36p) Doug Woodall   25p–35p
2–26   20p–25p

FUN 'N' GAMES
25 Oct–Nov 1969 (3)
Tesco
1–3 (24p) (4C) supermarket promo   25p–50p

FUN PARADE
1949 (1)
Hotspur
1 (nn) (8p) (gravure) D. Gifford   50p–£1.00

FUN TIME
3 Nov 1972–23 Mar 1973 (22)
Williams
1 (16p) (4C)   15p–25p
2–22   10p–20p

FUN TO DO
14 Oct 1978–6 Mar 1982 (178)
IPC
& *Fun To Know*: 12 Jul 1980
to: *Playhour*
1 (16p) John Donnelly   10p–25p
2–178   5p–10p

FUN TO DO SPECIALS
Jun 1979–Jun 1981 (3)
IPC
1: *Summer Special 1979* (40p)   20p–35p
2: *Holiday Special 1980*   20p–35p
3: *Holiday Special 1981*   20p–30p

FUN TO KNOW
15 Sep 1979–5 Jul 1980 (43)
IPC
to: *Fun To Do*
1 (16p) John Donnelly   15p–20p
2–43   10p–15p

FUN TO KNOW HOLIDAY SPECIAL
Apr 1980 (1)
IPC
1 (nn) (40p)   20p–40p

FUN'S FUNNY SCRAPS
Aug–Sep 1892 (2)
Fun
1–2 (68p) J. F. Sullivan   £3.00–£5.00

FUNBEAM
1949 (1)
PM (Marx)
1 (nn) (8p) Reg Parlett   50p–£1.00

FUNDAY MERCURY
3 Sep 1978–
Birmingham Sunday Mercury
supplement to *Sunday Mercury* newspaper
1 (4p) (tabloid) Roger Hargreaves   10p–25p
2– Chas Grigg   5p–10p

FUNDERGROUND COMIC
Aug 1984 (1)
London Transport (promo)
1 (8p) (4C) Ron Tiner   25p–50p

FUNFAIR
1947 (1)
McKenzie Vincent
1 (nn) (12p)   50p–£1.00

FUNFAIR
1949 (1)
Hotspur
1 (8p) (gravure) D. Gifford   50p–£1.00

FUNFAIR COMIC
1947 (1)
Marx
1 (8p) (reprints) G. Protheroe   75p–£1.00

FUNFARE COMIC
1949 (1)
Martin & Reid (Gower)
1 (8p) (tabloid) Walter Booth   75p–£1.00

FUNNIES BUDGET
Jun 1950 (1)
Swan
1 (132p) (remaindered *New Funnies*)   £2.00–£3.00

FUNNY ANIMALS (FAWCETT'S)
Dec 1945–1952
Miller (Fawcett)
1 (nn) (68p) (gravure) US reprints   £2.00–£3.00
28; 39; etc (12/16p) (gravure)   75p–£1.00
P448 (16p) (letterpress)   50p–£1.00
large format (gravure)   75p–£1.00
1951: 50–56 (28p)   50p–75p

FUNNY COMIC
1948–1949 (2)
PM (Marx)
1–2 (8p) Reg Parlett   50p–£1.00

FUNNY COMICS
1948 (1)
Halle
1 (nn) (8p) (Soloway reprints)   50p–75p

FUNNY CUTS
see: *Paget's Funny Cuts*

FUNNY CUTS
12 Jul 1890–10 Nov 1908 (958)
Trapps Holmes
& *Halfpenny Comic*: 5 Jan 1906
& *World's Comic*: 17 Oct 1908
& *Smiles*: 17 Nov 1908
to: *Funny Cuts the Boys Companion*
1 (8p) (tabloid)   £5.00–£10.00
2–958   £1.75–£2.00
Xmas coloured number (1898)   £2.50–£4.00

FUNNY CUTS THE BOYS COMPANION
17 Nov 1908–3 Jul 1920 (608)
Trapps Holmes
to: *Funny Wonder*
1 (16p) Charles Genge   £3.00–£4.50
23 Sep 1913: colour strips   £2.00–£2.25
3 Feb 1914: 8p issues   £1.00–£1.50

FUNNY FEATURES
1944 (1)
Martin & Reid
1 (16p) H. E. Pease   £1.50–£2.00

FUNNY FOLK
1947 (1)
Hamilton
1 (nn) (8p) Alan Fraser   50p–£1.00

FUNNY FOLKS
12 Dec 1874–28 Apr 1894 (1614)
Henderson
1 (supplement to *Weekly Budget*)   £5.00–£10.00
2– (8p) tabloid   £1.50–£2.50
(magazine format issues) (16p)   £1.25–£1.50

FUNNY FOLKS MONTHLY SCRAPBOOK
Jan 1893–Jun 1893 (6)
Henderson
1 (7) (64p) reprints   £2.00–£3.50
8–12   £1.50–£2.00

FUNNY PIPS
12 Sep 1903–26 Dec 1903 (16)
Pearson
1 (4p) (supplement to *Boys Leader*)   £2.50–£5.00
2–16 G. E. Studdy   £1.00–£2.00

FUNNY STUFF
1947 (1)
Holland
1 (nn) (8p) H. C. Milburn   50p–£1.00

FUNNY 3.D
1954 (1)
Streamline/United Anglo-American (Harvey)
1 (36p) (with glasses)   £1.50–£2.00

FUNNY TUPPENNY
1947 (4)
Matthew (Martin & Reid)
1 (8p) H. E. Pease   50p–£1.00
2–4 Bob Monkhouse   50p–£1.00

FUNNY WONDER
4 Feb 1893–22 Apr 1899 (325)
Harmsworth
to: *New Series*
1 (8p) (tabloid) F. Wilkinson   £5.00–£10.00
2–325 Jack B. Yeats   £1.50–£2.00
203: 4-colour Xmas number   £2.00–£3.00

FUNNY WONDER NEW SERIES
29 Apr 1899–25 May 1901 (109)
Harmsworth
to: *The Wonder*
1 (8p) (tabloid) Tom Browne   £5.00–£10.00
2–109 J. B. Yeats   £1.50–£2.00

FUNNY WONDER
26 Dec 1914–16 May 1942 (1404)
AP
& *Funny Cuts*: 10 Jul 1920
& *Jester*: 1 Jun 1940
to: *Wonder*
1 (40) (tabloid) Bertie Brown   £3.00–£4.00
1915–1929 Don Newhouse   £1.00–£1.50
1930–1939 Roy Wilson   £1.00–£1.75
1940–1942 George Heath   75p–£1.25
26 Apr 1941: 2C   75p–£1.50

FUNNY WONDER AND THE JESTER
193–1940
AP
Overseas edition: two comics in one   £1.75–£2.50

FUNNYLAND COMICS
1948 (1)
Martin & Reid
1 (8p) H. E. Pease   50p–£1.00

FUNSTAR COMIC
1949 (1)
Martin & Reid (Gower)
1 (8p) (tabloid) Walter Booth   75p–£1.50

FUNTIME
Mar 1979–Jul 1980 (17)
Byblos
1 (36p) (puzzles)   10p 30p
2–17   10p–15p

FUNTIME SPECIALS
May 1979–May 1982 (7)
Byblos
1: *Summer Special* (52p)	15p–30p
2: *Winter Special 1979*	15p–30p
3: *Summer Special 1980*	15p–30p
4: *Winter Special 1980*	15p–30p
5: *Summer Special 1981*	15p–30p
6: *Winter Special 1982*	15p–25p
7: *Spring Special 1982*	15p–25p

FUNTOWN
Dec 1949 (1)
Modern Fiction
1 (8p) Bob Monkhouse	50p–£1.00

FURTHER ADVENTURES OF ELMO
1943 (1)
Kingsbury
1 (nn) (16p) Charles Cole	50p–£1.50

FURTHER ADVENTURES OF ROBINSON CRUSOE
1971 (1)
Grosvenor (Pictorial Media)
1 (nn) (16p) (promotional)	50p–£1.00

FURY
16 Mar 1977–31 Aug 1977 (25)
Marvel
to: *Mighty World of Marvel*
1 (32p) US reprints	10p–25p
2–25	5p–10p

FUTURE TENSE (WEEKLY)
5 Nov 1980–1 Jul 1981 (35)
Marvel
& *Forces in Combat*: 28 Jan 1981
& *Valour*: 18 Mar 1981
to: *Future Tense Monthly*
1 (32p) US reprints	15p–25p
2–35	10p–15p

FUTURE TENSE MONTHLY
Aug 1981–Jan 1982 (6)
Marvel
1 (36) US reprints	35p–45p
37–41	25p–40p

G-BOY COMICS
Nov 1947 (1)
Funnibook (Cartoon Art)
1 (nn) (20p) Dennis Reader	75p–£1.25

GABBY HAYES WESTERN
1951–1955 (71)
Miller (Fawcett)
1 (50) (28p) US reprint	75p–£1.00
51–111	50p–75p

GAG!
Dec 1984
Gag
1 (8p) Eddie Campbell	15p–20p

GAG-MAG
1946 (1)
Cartoon Art
1 (nn) (8p)	50p–£1.00

GALLANT ADVENTURE COMIC
1952 (4)
Scion
1 (nn) (24p) Ron Embleton	50p–£1.00
2–3 Ron Embleton	50p–£1.00
4 (nn) James Bleach	35p–75p

GALLANT DETECTIVE COMIC
1952 (2)
Scion

1 (nn) (24p) James Holdaway	75p–£1.00
2 (nn) Ron Embleton	50p–£1.00

GALLANT SCIENCE COMIC
1953 (2)
Scion
1 (24p) Ron Embleton	75p–£1.00
2 Ron Embleton	50p–£1.00

GALLANT WESTERN COMIC
1953 (3)
Scion
1 (24p) Terry Patrick	50p–£1.00
2–3 Ron Embleton	75p–£1.00

GALLERY OF COMICALITIES
24 Jun 1831–1841 (8)
Goodyer
1 (4p) (broadsheet)	£5.00–£10.00
2–8 (reprints: *Bell's Life in London*)	£5.00–£7.00

GAMBOLS
1952–
Daily Express/Beaverbrook
1 (nn) Barry Appleby strip reprints	£1.00–£2.50
2–	50p–75p

GANNETS
1981 (1)
Boyle/Southwark Development
1 (nn) (12p) Francis Boyle	10p–25p

GARLAND
1 Aug 1896–29 Jul 1900 (209)
Henderson
to: *Nuggets*
1 (32p) (magazine) Julius Baker	£2.50–£5.00
2–209	£1.25–£2.00

GARTH SERIES
1946–1976 (4)
Daily Mirror (strip reprints)
1: *Garth Man of Mystery* (Dowling)	£2.00–£5.00
2: *Garth/Romeo Brown* (Dowling)	£1.50–£2.50
3: *Daily Mirror Book of Garth* (Bellamy)	£1.00–£1.50
4: *Daily Mirror Book 1976* (Bellamy)	£1.00–£1.50

GAY COMIC
Nov 1944 (1)
PM (Marx)
1 (nn) (folded strip)	50p–£1.00

GEE WHIZ COMIC
1947 (1)
International
1 (nn) (20p) John Turner	50p–£1.25

GEMINI 2000 PICTURE LIBRARY
1966– (8)
Famepress
1 (68p) *Hell on Astra 6* (foreign reprint)	20p–35p
2–8	20p–25p

GENE AUTRY AND CHAMPION
1956–1958 (34)
World (Dell)
1–29 (28p) US reprint	50p–£1.00
30–34 (68p)	50p–75p

GENE AUTRY COMICS
1950–1952 (19)
Cartoon Art (Dell)
1 (28p) US reprint	75p–£1.00
2–19	50p–75p

GENE AUTRY COMICS
1952
Strato (Dell)
1 (68p) US reprint	75p–£1.00
2–	50p–75p

GENE AUTRY COMICS
Apr 1953–1954 (14)
Thorpe & Porter (Dell)
| 1 (68p) US reprint | 75p–£1.00 |
| 2–14 | 50p–75p |

GERRY ANDERSON'S THUNDERBIRDS
1971 (1)
Polystyle
| 1 (nn) (48p) reprints | £1.00–£2.50 |

GHOST RIDER
1952 (3)
Compix/Cartoon Art (Magazine Enterprises)
| 1 (28p) US reprint | 75p–£1.25 |
| 2–3 | 50p–£1.00 |

GHOST RIDERS
see: *Action Series*

GHOST SQUADRON COMICS
1950 (1)
Streamline/United Anglo-American (Fiction House)
| 1 (nn) (28p) US reprint | 50p–£1.00 |

GHOSTLY WEIRD STORIES
1953 (1)
Arnold (Star)
| 1 (68p) US reprint | £1.00–£2.00 |

GHOUL TALES
1979–1980 (5)
Portman (Stanley)
| 1 (52p) US reprints | 15p–35p |
| 2–5 | 10p–15p |

GIANT CLASSICS ILLUSTRATED
see: *Classics Illustrated*

GIANT COMIC
1956–1957 (20)
World (US reprints)
1: *Black Diamond Western* (68p)	50p–£1.00
2: *All Star Western*	50p–£1.00
3: *Turok Son of Stone*	£1.00–£2.00
4: *Fast Action Western*	50p–£1.00
5: *Black Diamond Western*	50p–£1.00
6: *All Star Western*	50p–£1.00
7: *Turok Son of Stone*	£1.00–£2.00
8: *Fast Action Western*	50p–£1.00
9: *Turok Son of Stone*	£1.00–£2.00
10: *All Star Western*	50p–£1.00
11: *Turok Son of Stone*	£1.00–£2.00
12: *Fast Action Western*	50p–£1.00
13: *Black Diamond*	50p–£1.00
14: *All Star Western*	50p–£1.00
15: *Turok Son of Stone*	£1.00–£2.00
16: *Fast Action Western*	50p–£1.00
17: *Black Diamond*	50p–£1.00
18: *All Star Western*	50p–£1.00
19: *Turok Son of Stone*	£1.00–£2.00
20: *Fast Action Western*	50p–£1.00

GIANT SUPER MAG
Jun 1964–Sep 1964 (4)
Young World (Gold Key)
| 1 (80p) *Donald Duck & Friends* | 75p–£1.00 |
| 2–4 US reprints | 50p–£1.00 |

GIANT WAR PICTURE LIBRARY
Jun 1964–Dec 1965 (76)
Fleetway
| 1 (68p) (tall) *Red Devils* | 75p–£1.00 |
| 2–76 | 25p–50p |

GIDEON
1979 (4)
Knight Books/Hodder & Stoughton
1: *Gideon* (52p) (4C) French reprint	25p–60p
2: *Gideon & His Friends*	25p–60p
3: *Gideon's House*	25p–60p
4: *Gideon on the River Bank*	25p–60p

GIFT COMICS
1952–1953 (2)
Miller (Fawcett)
coverless remainders rebound in card covers
1: 6 comics	£2.50–£3.00
2: *Captain Marvel* 62, 63	£2.00–£3.00
Captain Marvel Jr 63	
Master Comics 62, 63	
Bob Colt 52	

GIGGLE
29 Apr 1967–13 Jan 1968 (38)
Fleetway
to: *Buster*
| 1 (28p) Hugh McNeill | 35p–50p |
| 2–38 Reg Parlett | 25p–35p |
16 Sep 1967: size reduction

GIGGLES
1948 (1)
(no imprint)
| 1 (nn) (8p) | 75p–£1.50 |

GIRL
2 Nov 1951–3 Oct 1964 (664)
Hulton/Longacre/IPC
to: *Princess*
1 (16p) (tabloid) (gravure)	£1.00–£2.50
2–12 Mar 1960 Ray Bailey	35p–50p
19 Mar 1960: first Longacre	25p–40p
9 Feb 1963: reduced size	20p–30p
4 Apr 1964: magazine format	15p–25p

GIRL
14 Feb 1981–
IPC
& *Dreamer*: 22 May 1982
& *Tammy*: 25 Aug 1984
| 1 (32p) photos | 10p–20p |
| 2– | 5p–10p |

GIRL OF THE ISLANDS
4 Oct 1958 (1)
Thomson
| 1 (nn) (28p) given with *Bunty* | 50p–£1.00 |

GIRL PICTURE LIBRARY
Aug 1984–
IPC
| 1 (68p) *Patty's World* | 10p–15p |
| 2– reprints | 10p–15p |

GIRL SPECIALS
Jun 1982–
IPC
1: *Girl Summer Special 1982* (48p)	15p–25p
2: *Action Girl Special 1983*	15p–25p
3: *Girl Summer Special 1983*	15p–25p
4: *Action Girl Special 1984*	15p–25p
5: *Girl Holiday Special 1984*	15p–25p

GIRLS CRYSTAL
21 Mar 1953–18 May 1963 (529)
AP
to: *School Friend*
| 1 R. McGillivray | £1.00–£1.50 |
| 2–529 Cecil Orr | 25p–50p |

GIRLS DIARY
1964–1965 (22)
Famepress
| 1–22 (68p) reprints (small) | 10p–25p |

GIRLS DUX
1948 (1)
Cartoon Art
| 1 (8p) Dennis Reader | 50p–£1.00 |

GLAMOUR
see: *New Glamour*

GLASGOW LOOKING GLASS
11 Jun 1825–Aug 1825 (5)
John Watson
to: *Northern Looking Glass*

1: 11 Jun 1825 (3p) (tabloid) first comic	£10.00–£25.00
2: 25 Jun 1825 (3p)	£5.00–£10.00
3: 9 Jul 1825 (4p)	£5.00–£10.00
4: 23 Jul 1825 (4p) first strip: part 1	£5.00–£10.00
5: Aug 1825 (4p) strip: part 2	£5.00–£10.00

NB: facsimile (reduced) editions 1906 (D. Bryce)

GLEAM
3 Aug 1901–21 May 1904 (147)
Shaw/Bedford/Brett

1 (16p) Frank Holland	£3.00–£5.00
2–20 Tom Browne	£1.50–£2.00
21 (24p) (story paper)	£1.50–£2.00
22–147 (magazine)	£1.25–£1.50

GLEE COMIC
1948 (1)
Philmar (Marx)

1 (nn) (small) Harry Parlett	50p–£1.00

GLEE CUB COMIC
1946 (1)
Globe (Cartoon Art)

1 (nn) (8p)	50p–£1.00

GLOOPS SERIES
1928–1957 (35)
W. Leng/Sheffield Telegraph/Star
(newspaper strip reprints)

1928 *The Book of Gloops*	£5.00–£10.00
1929 *Gloops Club First Anniversary*	£2.00–£5.00
1930 *Gloops Club Second Anniversary*	£2.00–£5.00
1930 *Christmas Book of Gloops*	£2.00–£5.00
1931 *Gloops Club Third Birthday Number*	£2.00–£5.00
1931 *Second Gloopers Annual*	£2.00–£5.00
1932 *Fourth Birthday Book of Gloops*	£2.00–£5.00
1932 *Gloops Christmas Annual*	£2.00–£5.00
1933 *Fifth Birthday Book of Gloops*	£2.00–£5.00
1933 *Gloops Children's Comic Xmas Annual*	£2.00–£5.00
1934 *Gloops the Laughter Cat Birthday Number*	£2.00–£5.00
1934 *Gloops the Laughter Cat Xmas Annual*	£2.00–£5.00
1935 *Gloops the Comic Cat Jubilee Number*	£2.00–£5.00
1935 *Gloops Comic Cat Xmas Annual*	£2.00–£5.00
1936 *Gloops Comic Cat Birthday Number*	£2.00–£5.00
1936 *Gloops Comic Cat Xmas Annual*	£2.00–£5.00
1937 *Gloops Childrens Comic Birthday Number*	£2.00–£5.00
1937 *Gloops Comic Cat Xmas Annual*	£2.00–£5.00
1938 *Gloops Childrens Comic Birthday Number*	£2.00–£5.00
1938 *Gloops Childrens Comic Xmas Annual*	£2.00–£5.00
1939 *Gloops Childrens Comic Birthday Number*	£2.00–£5.00
1939 *Gloops Christmas Annual*	£2.00–£5.00
1940 *Gloops Childrens Comic Birthday Number*	£2.00–£5.00
1940 *Gloops Christmas Annual Childrens Comic*	£2.00–£5.00

sixpenny series:

1949 *Gloops Christmas Number*	£2.00–£3.00
1950 *Gloops Birthday Number*	£1.50–£2.00
1950 *Gloops Christmas Number*	£1.00–£1.50
195₁ *Gloops Summer Number*	50p–£1.00
1951 *Gloops Christmas Number*	50p–£1.00
1952 *The Star Gloops Christmas Number*	50p–£1.00
1953–1957 *Star Gloops Christmas Number*	50p–£1.00

GO GIRL
13 Jan 1968–10 Aug 1968 (31)
City

1	35p–50p
2–31	20p–35p

GOBO STRIP BOOKS
1953 (2)
Sampson Low Marston (Enid Blyton)

1: *Gobo & Mr Fierce*	£1.00–£1.50
2: *Gobo in Land of Dreams*	50p–£1.00

GOLDEN
23 Oct 1937–18 May 1940 (135)
AP
to: *Jingles*

1 (8p) (tabloid) Roy Wilson	£5.00–£7.50
2–115 Reg Perrott	£1.50–£2.00
116–135: colour issues	£2.00–£2.50

GOLDEN AND BUTTERFLY
4 Nov 1939–18 May 1940
AP

Overseas edition: two comics together	£2.00–£3.00

GOLDEN ARROW WESTERN
1951 (4)
Miller/Arnold (Fawcett)

1 (10) (Arnold) (24p) US reprint	50p–75p
2–4 (Miller) (28p)	50p–75p

GOLDEN HEART LOVE STORIES
196–
Thomson

1: *No Other Man* (small) (68p)	25p–35p
2–	10p–25p

GOLDEN HOURS
Jan–Dec 1972 (31)
Shelbourne/Williams
to: *Sleepytime Stories*

1–31	25p–50p

GOLDEN PENNY COMIC
14 Oct 1922–28 Jan 1928 (276)
United/Fleetway/AP
to: *Comic Cuts*

1 (8p) (tabloid) Reg Carter	£5.00–£7.50
2– Walter Bell	£1.50–£2.00
21 Jan 1928: first AP issue	£1.50–£1.75

GOLLIWOG COMIC
1948 (1)
Philmar (Marx)

1 (nn) (8p) Walter Bell	50p–£1.00

GOOD DOG CAESAR
1953 (1)
Brockhampton

1 (nn) (68p) (oblong) W. Tymym	£1.00–£2.00

GOOD HEALTH
Jul 1982 (1)
Health Education Council

1 (8p) don't drink and drive	2p–5p

GOODIES FUN BOOK
1977 (1)
Cadbury/IPC

1 (52p) (4C) (reprints) (promo)	50p–£1.00

GOOFY
20 Oct 1973–11 May 1974 (29)
IPC
to: *Donald & Mickey*

1 (24p) US reprints	25p–35p
2–29	20p–25p

GRAND ADVENTURE COMIC
1946 (1)
Martin & Reid

1 (nn) (16p) R. Beaumont	50p–£1.00

GRANDSTAND COMIC
1949 (1)
Martin & Reid (Gower)
1 (nn) (8p) (tabloid) F. Minnitt   50p–£1.25

GRANGE HILL MAGAZINE
1980–1981 (2)
IPC
1 (48p) (TV series)   35p–50p
2   25p–40p

GRAPHIXUS
Feb 1978–Mar 1979 (6)
Graphic Eye
1 (36p) (adult) Garry Leach   50p–75p
2–5 Hunt Emerson   50p–75p
6 (5B) (32p) J. Szostek   15p–25p

GREAT FUN COMIC
1950 (1)
Paget
1 (nn) (16p) Harry Banger   50p–£1.00

GREMLINS
Nov 1984 (1)
Marvel
1 (nn) (68p) (4C) (film) US reprint   £1.00–£1.25

GROW FLOWERS
195 (1)
Mirror
1 (nn) Jack Dunkley *Mr Digwell* strips   35p–50p

GUILTY
see: *Justice Traps the Guilty*

GUMMY
1954 (12)
Maynards
1–12 (8p) (giveaway)   50p–£1.00

GUNFLASH WESTERN
Aug–Oct 1951 (2)
Scion
1 (24p) Ron Embleton   75p–£1.00
2 Ron Embleton   50p–£1.00

GUNHAWK
1951 (2)
Streamline (Marvel)
1 (28p) US reprint   75p–£1.25
2   50p–£1.00

GUNHAWKS WESTERN
Oct 1960–Jun 1961 (10)
Anglo (Atlas)
1 (28p) (reprints) Don Lawrence   50p–£1.00
2–10 Denis Gifford   50p–75p

GUNS OF FACT AND FICTION
1950 (1)
Streamline/United Anglo-American (ME)
1 (nn) (36p) (4C) US reprint   75p–£1.50

GUNSMOKE
1970–1971
Top Sellers (Dell)
1– (36p) (4C) US reprint   25p–35p
see: *Western Classics*

GUNSMOKE TRAIL
1957 (4)
Miller (Farrell)
1 (28p) US reprint   50p–£1.00
2–4   50p–75p

GUNSMOKE WESTERN
1955–1956 (23)
Miller (Atlas)
1 (28p) US reprint   75p–£1.00
2–23   50p–75p

HAGAR THE HORRIBLE
1977 (2)
Egmont/Methuen (King Features)
1: *H the Horrible* (52p) (4C) US reprint   50p–75p
2: *H & the Basilisk*   35p–50p

HAGAR THE HORRIBLE WINTER SPECIAL
1976 (1)
Polystyle (King Features)
1 (48p) US reprints   25p–50p

HALCON COMICS
1949 (1)
Halle (Soloway reprints)
1 (nn) (8p) Nat Brand   50p–£1.00

HALF ASSED FUNNIES
1973 (1)
H. Bunch/Cozmic Comics
1 (36p) Edward Barker (adult)   25p–50p

HALF-HOLIDAY
21 Apr 1923–29 Sep 1923 (24)
Sloperies (Milford)
to: *London Life*
1 (24) (16p)   £1.00–£2.00
25–47   £1.00–£1.50

HALFPENNY COMIC
22 Jan 1898–29 Dec 1906 (467)
Newnes/Trapps Holmes
to: *Funny Cuts*
1 (12p) (tabloid) Tom Browne   £5.00–£10.00
2–26 J. B. Yeats   £2.00–£3.00
27– (8p) Frank Holland   £1.75–£2.00
coloured numbers: 10 Sep 1898,
                   5 Nov 1898   £2.00–£3.00
4 Feb 1899: Trapps Holmes   £1.75–£2.00
1900–1906   £1.50–£2.00
Xmas double numbers   £2.00–£2.50

HALFPENNY WONDER
28 Mar 1914–19 Dec 1914 (39)
AP
to: *Funny Wonder*
1 (8p) Bertie Brown   £5.00–£10.00
2–39 Percy Cocking   £2.00–£2.50

HALLS OF HORROR WINTER SPECIAL
Oct 1982 (1)
Quality
1 (nn) Brian Lewis reprints   25p–50p

HANS KRESSE SERIES
1975 (4)
Methuen (Casterman)
1: *Masters of Thunder* (52p) (4C)   50p–£1.00
2: *Riders of the Wind* foreign reprints 25p–50p
3: *Sons of the Chief*   25p–50p
4: *Song of the Coyote*   25p–50p

HAPPIJACK
1945 (1)
Scottish Book Distributors
1 (nn) (16p) (small) Frank Jupo   75p–£1.25

HAPPY COMIC
17 Sep 1928–20 Apr 1929 (28)
Ransom
1 (8p) reprints *Golden Penny*   £3.00–£5.00
2–28 Reg Carter   £1.50–£2.00

HAPPY DAYS
8 Oct 1938–5 Aug 1939 (45)
AP
to: *Chicks Own*
1 (12p) (gravure) Roy Wilson   £5.00–£10.00
2–45 Reg Perrott   £2.00–£3.00

HAPPY FAMILIES
1938–1939 (4)

Birds Custard (giveaway)
1 (8p) (2C) (tab) Ben Somers   £2.00–£4.00
2 (nn) (8p) (2C)   £1.50–£3.00
3(nn) (4C) Xmas   £2.00–£4.00
4 (nn) (4C) Easter H. Foxwell   £2.00–£4.00

HAPPY GANG
1947 (1)
Children's Press
1 (nn) (12p) Hugh McNeill   £1.50–£2.00

HAPPY HIGHWAY
1947 (1)
ROSPA (giveaway)
1 (nn) (8p) Bob Wilkin   £1.00–£1.50

HAPPY MOMENTS
1946 (1)
John Matthew (Martin & Reid)
1 (8p) Mick Anglo   50p–£1.00

HAPPY TIMES FAMILY COMIC
1946–1947 (5)
Algar
1 (16p) Walter Booth   75p–£1.25
2–5 Stanley White   50p–£1.00

HAPPY TUPPENNY
1947 (2)
Rayburn (Martin & Reid)
1–2 (8p) H. E. Pease   50p–£1.00

HAPPY WORLD
1949 (1)
Martin & Reid (Gower)
1 (nn) (8p) (tabloid) Frank Minnitt   75p–£1.25

HAPPY YANK
1947–1948 (4)
Rayburn (Martin & Reid)
1–4 (8p) Mick Anglo   50p–£1.00

HAROLD HARE'S OWN PAPER
14 Nov 1959–4 Apr 1964 (230)
Fleetway
& Walt Disney's Weekly: 29 Apr 1961
to: Playhour
1 (16p) (tabloid) Hugh McNeill   50p–£1.00
2–   25p–50p
  (smaller format)   20p–25p

HAUNT OF FEAR
1954 (1)
Arnold (EC)
1 (68p) US reprint   £1.50–£2.50

HAWKEYE AND THE LAST OF THE MOHICANS
Jun 1958–May 1959 (6)
Pearson (TV Picture Stories)
1: The Long Rifles (small) (68p)   25p–£1.00
2: The Renegade   25p–75p
3: La Salle's Treasure   25p–75p
4: Revenge   25p–75p
5 (TVP 2) The Wild One   25p–75p
6 (TVP 11) The Reckoning   25p–75p

HAYSEEDS
1971–1972 (2)
Macmillan
1–2 (68p) Hargreaves strip reprints   50p–75p

HEARTBEAT
3 Oct 1981–10 Apr 1982 (28)
IPC
to: My Guy
1 (32p) (photos)   15p–20p
2–28   5p–10p

HEAVY PERIODS
1980 (1)
Grass Roots
1 (nn) (36p) (oblong) (2C) Fanny Tribble   50p–£1.00

HELL-FIRE RAIDERS
1966 (1)
Class (Fawcett)
1 (68p) US reprint   50p–75p

HENRY SERIES
1961–1964 (3)
Brockhampton
1: Henry's Exciting Flight   75p–£1.00
2: Henry's Mountain Adventure   35p–75p
3: Henry Goes To Town   35p–75p

HERE COME THE PERISHERS
Jul 1979 (1)
Mirror (Daily Mirror reprints)
1 (nn) Dennis Collins   50p–65p

HERMAN AND HIS PALS
1970
Bazooka Joe/Graperoo
1–Bubble gum strips   1p–5p

HERO
1975 (1)
Premier
1 (4C)   25p–35p

HEROES OF THE WEST
1959 (9)
Miller (Fawcett)
1 (150) US reprint   75p–£1.00
151–158   50p–£1.00

HEROIC ADVENTURE LIBRARY
Apr 1964–
Pearson
1 (68p) The Gallant Crusaders   50p–75p
2–   25p–50p

HEROINE
1978 (1)
Birmingham Arts Lab
1 (36p) (adult) feminist   50p–£1.00

HEY DIDDLE DIDDLE
25 Mar 1972–15 Sep 1973 (78)
IPC
& Bobo Bunny: 3 Feb 1973
to: Playhour
1 (24p)   25p–35p
2–78   15p–25p

HEY DIDDLE DIDDLE HOLIDAY SPECIAL
Jun 1972–Jun 1973 (2)
IPC
1–2 (48p)   25p–35p

HI-YO SILVER
1953 (9)
World (Dell)
1 (28p) US reprint   75p–£1.00
2–9   50p–75p

HIGH COMMAND
1981 (1)
Dragons Dream (IPC)
1 (nn) (100p) (4C) Frank Bellamy reprints £2.00–£4.00

HIGH JINKS COMIC
1947 (1)
Hamilton
1 (nn) (8p)   50p–£1.00

HIGH SEAS COMIC
1952 (1)
Scion (King-Ganteaume)
1 (20p)   50p–£1.00

HIGH SPEED COMIC
1951 (1)
Scion (King-Ganteaume)
1 (24p)   50p–£1.00

HIGHWAY PATROL
Jun 1959–Jan 1960 (9)
Pearson (TV Picture Stories)
1 (TVP 15) *Double Cross* (small) (68p)   50p–£1.00
2 (TVP 19) *Bank Robbers*   25p–75p
3 (TVP 23) *Stolen Brain*   25p–75p
4 (TVP 25) *Man Who Drove Away*   25p–75p
5 (TVP 17) *Reckless Driver*   25p–75p
6 (TVP 28) *Larchmont Mystery*   25p–75p
7 (TVP 31) *Disappearing Casino*   25p–75p
8 (TVP 38) *Search Party*   25p–75p
9 (TVP 17a) *Reckless Driver*   25p–75p

HIP HIP HOORAY COMIC
1948 (1)
Philmar (Marx)
1 (8p) Wally Robertson   50p–£1.00

HITLER
1977 (2)
Morcrim (Mercocomic)
1: *Hitler's Last Days* (132p) (small)   25p–50p
2 Spanish reprint   20p–35p

HOLIDAY COMIC
27 Jun 1931–2 Jun 1939 (7)
Pearson
1 (27 June 31) Walter Bell   £2.50–£5.00
2 (24 June 33) Walter Bell   £2.00–£3.50
3 (14 Jun 34) Walter Bell   £2.00–£3.50
4 (28 May 36) Sidney Stanley   £2.00–£3.50
5 (4 Jun 37) G. Larkman   £2.00–£3.50
6 (3 Jun 38) Frank Minnitt   £2.00–£3.50
7 (2 Jun 39) Norman Ward   £2.00–£3.50

HOLLYWOOD ACES
1950 (1)
Cartoon Art (Fiction House)
1 (4C) US reprint   75p–£1.00

HOMER THE HAPPY GHOST
1955 (1?)
Miller (Atlas)
1– (28p) US reprint   50p–75p

HONEY MONSTER COMIC BOOKS
Oct 1984 (6)
Quaker Oats/Megaprint (Sugar Puffs promo)
1: *HM in Space* (12p) (small) (4C)   5p–15p
2: *HM & the Go-Cart*   5p–10p
3: *HM & the Ghost Train*   5p–10p
4: *HM & the Boating Lake*   5p–10p
5: *HM at the Seaside*   5p–10p
6: *HM at the Zoo*   5p–10p

HONK SERIES
1950–1960 (9)
Brockhampton
1: *Honk Runs Away* (oblong)   50p–75p
2: *Honk and Tonk*   30p–50p
3: *Happy Xmas Honk*   30p–50p
4: *Fun with Honk*   30p–50p
5: *Honk & the Donkey*   30p–50p
6: *Holiday for Honk*   30p–50p
7: *Honk for Sale*   30p–50p
8: *Happy Go Lucky Honk*   30p–50p
9: *Honk & Gypsy Rose*   30p–50p

HOODED HORSEMAN
1953 (1)
Streamline/United Anglo-American (ACG)

1 (28p) US reprint   50p–75p
2 (68p)   50p–75p

HOOKS DEVLIN
1950 (1)
Cartoon Art (Fiction House)
1 (16p) (4C) US reprint   75p–£1.00

HOORAY
Dec 1949 (1)
Modern Fiction
1 (8p) Arthur Martin   50p–£1.00

HOOT GIBSON
1950 (6)
Streamline/United Anglo-American (Fox)
1 (28p) US reprint   50p–£1.00
2–6   50p–75p

HOPALONG CASSIDY COMIC
Feb 1948–1958 (107)
Miller (Fawcett)
1 (5) (16p) (gravure) US reprint   £1.00–£1.50
2 (nn) (68p) (gravure)   £2.00–£2.50
50–153 (32/24p)   75p–£1.00

HORNET
14 Dec 1963–7 Feb 1976 (648)
Thomson
to: *Hotspur*
1 (32p)   50p–£1.00
2–648   10p–35p

HOSPITAL NURSE PICTURE LIBRARY
Feb 1964–
Pearson
1 (68p) *Nurse in Love* (foreign reprint) 20p–35p
2–   10p–15p

HOT NADS
1980 (1)
Ghura
1 Antonio Ghura (adult)   50p–75p

HOT ROD AND SPEEDWAY COMICS
Apr 1953 (1)
Streamline/United Anglo-American (Hillman)
1 (28p) US reprint   50p–75p

HOT ROD COMICS
1951 (4)
Arnold (Fawcett)
1–4 (28p) US reprint   35p–75p

HOT RODS AND RACING CARS
1953 (2)
Miller (Charlton)
1 (50)–51 (28p) US reprint   35p–75p

HOTCH-POTCH
18–(1)
Judy Office
1 (nn) James Brown strip reprints   £2.50–£5.00

HOTSHOT
1976–
Hope Press
1 (8p) (folder) (2C) temperance promo   50p–£1.00
2–   10p–25p

HOTSPUR
16 Feb 1963–24 Jan 1981 (944)
Thomson
& *Hornet*: 14 Feb 1976
& *Crunch*: 2 Feb 1980
to: *Victor*
1 (174)   35p–40p
175–1118   10p–35p

HOTSPUR CHRISTMAS SPECIAL
Dec 22 1963 (1)
Thomson
(8p supplement)   25p–35p

HOW T'MAKE IT AS A ROCKSTAR
1977 (1)
IPC/New Musical Express
1 (nn) (36p) Tony Benyon   40p–75p

HOW YOU PICK WINNERS
1971 (1)
Norfil
Harry Bishop strip reprint   25p–50p

HUBBA-HUBBA COMIC BOOK
1947 (1)
Transatlantic (Cartoon Art)
1 (8p) Dennis Reader   50p–£1.00

HUCKLEBERRY HOUND & YOGI BEAR
SUMMER EXTRA
1963 (1)
City
1 (48p) (gravure)   25p–35p

HUCKLEBERRY HOUND & YOGI BEAR
WINTER EXTRA
1963 (1)
City
1 (48p) (gravure)   25p–35p

HUCKLEBERRY HOUND MINI-COMIC
20 Feb 1965 (1)
City
1 (16p supplement to *H.H. Weekly*)   25p–30p

HUCKLEBERRY HOUND SUMMER EXTRA
1965 (1)
City
1 (40p) (gravure)   25p–35p

HUCKLEBERRY HOUND WEEKLY
7 Oct 1961–28 Aug 1967 (308)
City/Hayward
& *Yogi Bear's Own*: 4 Apr 1964
1 (16p) (tabloid) (gravure)   35p–50p
2–283   20p–25p
284–308 (Hayward issues)   10p–15p

HUCKLEBERRY HOUND WINTER EXTRA
1964 (1)
City
1 (48p) (gravure)   25p–35p

HULK COMIC
7 Mar 1979–15 May 1980 (63)
Marvel
to: *Spiderman*
1 (24p) US reprints   10p–25p
2–63   10p–15p

HULK POCKET BOOK
25 Sep 1980–12 Nov 1981 (13)
Marvel
1 (52p) (small) US reprint   15p–25p
2   15p–20p
3 (100p)   20p–30p
4–13   15p–20p

HUMAN SOUP COMICS
1981–1983 (3)
Szostek
1 (32p) (adult) J. H. Szostek   40p–60p
2–3 (36p) (small)   35p–50p

HUMPHREY
see: *Joe Palooka's Humphrey*

HUNDRED JACKLIN GOLFSTRIPS
1972 (1)
Beaverbrook
1 (88p) Horak strip reprints   25p–50p

HURRICANE
29 Feb 1964–8 May 1965 (63)
Fleetway
to: *Tiger*
1 (32p)   10p–25p
2–63   5p–10p

HURRICANE ADVENTURE COMIC
Jan 1946 (1)
Locker
1 (nn) (16p) R. Beaumont   50p–£1.00

HWYL
Jul 1949–
Evans/Owen
1 (monthly; Welsh language)   50p–£1.00
2–32 (4C issues)   25p–50p
33– (2C issues)   20p–25p

I LOVE LUCY
1954 (16)
World (Dell)
1 (28p) US reprint   75p–£1.00
2–16   35p–75p

I LOVE YOU
1955–1956 (23)
Miller (Charlton)
1–23 (68p) US reprint   10p–25p

IBIS THE INVINCIBLE
1950 (1)
Miller (Fawcett)
1 (nn) (16p) (gravure) US reprint   50p–£1.00

IDEAL ACTION COMIC
1979 (1)
Ideal Toys (giveaway)
1 (nn) (8p folder) (4C)   5p–10p

IF I CAN MANAGE SO CAN YOU
1979 (1)
Action Opportunities
1 (nn) (16p) (oblong) equality promo   10p–25p

IF SERIES
1983–1984 (2)
Methuen (*Guardian* strips)
1: *If Chronicles* (164p)   £2.00–£2.50
2: *If Only Again* Steve Bell reprints   £2.00–£2.50

ILLUSTRATED BIBLE TALES
1953 (8)
Miller (Gower)
1 (28p) Don Lawrence   50p–£1.00
2–8   50p–75p

ILLUSTRATED BITS
1 Nov 1884–10 Jan 1885 (11)
Davis & Marshall
to: *New Series*
1 (5) (16p) (magazine)   £2.50–£5.00
6–15   £1.00–£1.75

ILLUSTRATED BITS NEW SERIES
17 Jan 1885–8 Jun 1889 (229)
Davis & Marshall
to: *New Series*
1 (16p) (magazine)   £2.00–£3.50
2–229   £1.00–£1.75

ILLUSTRATED BITS NEW SERIES
15 Jun 1889–20 Nov 1909 (1064)
Roberts/Lucas
& *Pick-Me-Up*: 11 Jan 1909

1 (magazine) (16p) (230)　　　　　　£2.00–£3.50
231–1293　　　　　　　　　　　　£1.00–£1.75

ILLUSTRATED BITS NEW SERIES
4 Feb 1911–10 Feb 1917 (315)
IB (Milford)
to: *Bits of Fun*
1 (16p) (magazine)　　　　　　　£2.00–£3.50
2–315　　　　　　　　　　　　　£1.00–£1.75

ILLUSTRATED CHIPS
26 Jul 1890–30 Aug 1890 (6)
Harmsworth
to: *New Series*
1 (16p) (small)　　　　　　　　£5.00–£10.00
2–6　　　　　　　　　　　　　　£2.50–£3.00

ILLUSTRATED CHIPS NEW SERIES
6 Sep 1890–12 Sep 1953 (2997)
Harmsworth/AP
& *Joker*: 25 May 1940
to: *Film Fun*
1 (8p) (tabloid)　　　　　　　　£5.00–£10.00
1890–1899 Tom Browne　　　　　£1.00–£1.25
1900–1929 Julius Baker　　　　　£1.00–£1.50
1930–1939 Albert Pease　　　　　£1.00–£1.75
4 Nov 1939: 2C　　　　　　　　£1.00–£1.75
1940–1949 John Jukes　　　　　　75p–£1.25
11 Aug 1951: pink (12p)–1953　　50p–£1.00
Xmas and double numbers　　　　£2.00–£3.00

ILLUSTRATED ROMANCE LIBRARY
196–
World (ACG)
1– (68p) (small) US reprint　　　　15p–20p

ILLUSTRATED TID-BITS
4 Oct 1884–25 Oct 1884 (4)
Davis & Marshall
to: *Illustrated Bits*
1–4 (16p) (magazine)　　　　　　£2.00–£3.00

IMAGES
1984
Anti-Matter
1– (8p) Eddie Campbell　　　　　10p–20p

IMPRESSIONS OF PAPA AND SON
1923? (1)
Daily Sketch (strip reprints)
1 (32p) A. E. Morton　　　　　　£2.00–£3.00

INCREDIBLE HULK
31 Mar 1982–29 Sep 1982 (27)
Marvel
to: *Spiderman*
1 (32p) US reprints　　　　　　　15p–25p
2–27　　　　　　　　　　　　　10p–20p

INCREDIBLE HULK SPECIAL
May 1982–Oct 1982 (2)
Marvel
1: *Summer 1982* (52p) US reprints　40p–55p
2: *Winter Special 1982*　　　　　40p–50p

INDIAN CHIEF
1953–1954 (31)
World (Dell)
1 (36p) US reprint　　　　　　　75p–£1.00
2–31　　　　　　　　　　　　　50p–75p

INDIAN FIGHTER
1951 (2)
Streamline/United Anglo-American (Youthful)
1 (nn) (28p) US reprint　　　　　50p–75p
2 (nn) (68p)　　　　　　　　　　50p–£1.00

INDIAN WARHAWKS
see: *Blue Bolt Series*

INDIAN WARRIORS
1951 (1)
Streamline/United Anglo-American (Star)
1 (nn) (28p) US reprint　　　　　50p–75p
see: *Blue Bolt Series*

INDIAN WARRIORS SUPER-BUMPER STREAMLINE COMIC
195– (1)
Streamline/United Anglo-American (Star)
1 (nn) (132p) US reprints　　　　£1.00–£2.00

INDIANA JONES
Oct 1984–
Marvel
1 (52p) US reprints　　　　　　　25p–35p
2–　　　　　　　　　　　　　　20p–25p

INDIANA JONES WINTER SPECIAL
Nov 1984 (1)
Marvel
1 US reprints　　　　　　　　　50p–75p

INDIANS
1951 (1)
Cartoon Art (Fiction House)
1 (4C) (20p) US reprint　　　　　75p–£1.00

INDIANS
1953
Streamline (Fiction House)
1– (28p) US reprint　　　　　　　50p–75p

INDIANS ON THE WARPATH
see: *Warpath*

INSIDE WOODY ALLEN
1979 (1)
Coronet/Robson
1 (nn) (88p) US reprints　　　　　60p–£1.25

INTERNATIONAL COMICS
1936–1939
American Sunday supplements stapled into pictorial
paper cover, sold in markets
(nn)　　　　　　　　　　　　　£2.00–£3.00

INTERNATIONAL FUN TIME COMIC
1980 (1)
International (giveaway)
1 (nn) (8p) (4C) supermarket promo　10p–25p

INTIMATE LOVE
1953 (6)
World (Standard)
1–6 (28p) US reprint　　　　　　25p–50p

INTRODUCTION TO CHILE
1976 (1)
Bolivar
1 (nn) (100p) Chris Welch　　　　50p–£1.00

INVINCIBLE
Mar 1961 (1)
Anglo (Atlas)
1 (6) (28p) No 6 of *Captain Miracle*　50p–75p

ISOMETRICS (Complete book of . . .)
1978 (1)
Express Newspapers (*Daily Express* reprints)
1 (nn) (132p) (oblong) Enrique Romero　50p–£1.00

IT'S ALL LIES
Oct 1973–Dec 1973 (6)
Gemsanders
1 (16p) (adult) M. Freeth　　　　25p–50p
2–6 Steve Parkhouse　　　　　　25p–50p

IT'S ONLY ROCK & ROLL COMIX
1975 (1)

Petagno
1 (nn) (32p) (adult) Petagno   50p–£1.00

IT'S THE SMURFS POSTER MAGAZINE
SPECIAL
1980 (1)
IPC
1 (16p) (4C) (poster) foreign reprint   10p–20p

IVANHOE
196– (1)
Treasure Hour
1 (36p) (small)   25p–35p

IVOR THE ENGINE HOLIDAY SPECIAL
May 1983 (1)
Polystyle
1 (48p) (TV series) reprints   25p–40p

IVORY CASTLE ARROW
1963–1966 (11)
Gibbs/Longacre
1 (8p) (4C) (toothpaste promo)   £1.00–£2.00
2–11 John Ryan   50p–£1.00

IZNOGOUD
1977
Egmont/Methuen (Dargaud)
1: *I on Holiday* (48p) (4C) reprint   50p–85p
2: *I the Infamous*   25p–50p

J.J. IT'S ONLY MONEY
1972 (1)
Beaverbrook
1 (nn) (100p) Roy Dewar strip reprint   25p–50p

JACE PEARSON OF THE TEXAS RANGERS
1953–1954 (21)
World (Dell)
1 (36p) US reprint   75p–£1.00
2–21   50p–75p

JACK AND JILL
7 Mar 1885–7 May 1887 (114)
Long
to: *Jack's Journal*
1 (8p)(tabloid)   £5.00–£7.50
2–7   £1.50–£2.00
8–114 (adult)   £1.25–£2.00

JACK AND JILL
29 Jul 1909–17 Sep 1909 (3)
AP (free in *Wonder Box*)
1 (nn) (8p) (3C) (small)   £3.00–£5.00
2–3   £2.00–£3.50

JACK AND JILL
27 Feb 1954–
AP/Fleetway/IPC
& Playbox: 11 Jun 1955
& Candy: 3 Jan 1970
& Teddy Bear: 22 Sep 1973
& Toby: 7 Oct 1978
& Dickory Dock: 27 Sep 1980
& Teddy Bear's Playtime: 31 Oct 1981
& Playbox: 16 Oct 1982
1 (16p) (gravure) Hugh McNeill   50p–£1.00
2– Fred Robinson   20p–30p

JACK AND JILL AND BOBO BUNNY HOLIDAY
SPECIAL
Mar 1971–Mar 1972 (2)
IPC
1–2 (48p)   20p–30p

JACK AND JILL SUMMER SPECIAL
1961–1964 (4)
Fleetway/IPC
1 (48p)   25p–35p
2–4   20p–30p

JACK AND JILL'S HOLIDAY SPECIAL
1965–
Fleetway/IPC
1 (48p)   25p–35p
2–   20p–30p

JACK POT
Nov 1946 (1)
Swinnerton
1 (8p)   50p–£1.00

JACK'S JOURNAL
14 May 1887–25 Jun 1887 (7)
Long
1 (115) (8p) (tabloid)   £2.50–£3.00
116–121   £2.00–£2.50

JACKIE
11 Jan 1964–
Thomson
& Diana: 11 Dec 1976
1 (24p) (tabloid) (gravure)   50p–£1.00
2–   10p–20p

JACKIE PUZZLE SPECIAL
Mar 1982 (1)
Thomson
1 (32p) (gravure)   15p–25p

JACKIE SPRING SPECIAL
23 Mar 1979–
Thomson
1– (48p) (gravure)   15p–25p

JACKIE SUMMER SPECIAL
1976–
Thomson
1 (48p) (gravure)   20p–30p
2–   15p–25p

JACKPOT
5 May 1979–30 Jan 1982 (141)
IPC
to: *Buster*
1 (32p) Reg Parlett   10p–25p
2–141   5p–10p

JACK-POT COMIC
May 1947 (1)
Grant Hughes
1 (nn) (16p) Bob Wilkin   50p–£1.00

JACKPOT SUMMER SPECIAL
Jun 1979–Jun 1982 (4)
IPC
1 (nn) (64p)   20p–40p
2–4   20p–35p

JAG
4 May 1968–29 Mar 1969 (48)
Fleetway
to: *Tiger*
1 (16p) (outsize)   35p–50p
2–48 (small format from 43)   25p–30p

JANE
Norman Pett *Daily Mirror* strips
1944 *Jane's Journal* (68p) (Thomas)   £10.00–£15.00
1944 *Pett's Annual* (80p) (Thomas)   £5.00–£10.00
1945 *Another Jane's Journal* (Thomas)   £7.50–£10.00
1946 *Jane's Journal* (84p) (Rylee)   £7.50–£10.00
1946 *Jane's Summer Idle* (36p) (Mirror)   £5.00–£7.00
1947 *Jane on Sawdust Trail* (36p) (Mirror)   £5.00–£7.00
1948 *Another Journal* (68p) (Rylee)   £5.00–£7.00
1950 *Another Journal* (68p) (Rylee)   £5.00–£7.00
1960 *Farewell to Jane* (100p) (Mirror)   £2.00–£3.00
1976 *Jane At War* (386p) (Wolfe)   £1.50–£3.00
1983 *Jane* (oblong) (100p) (Pelham)   £1.00–£2.50

JAPHET BOOK
1924–1925 (2)

159

Daily News
1 (68p) (oblong) Horrabin strips   £3.50–£7.00
2   £3.00–£5.00

JAPHET HOLIDAY BOOK
Jul 1936–Jul 1940 (5)
News Chronicle
1 (68p) Horrabin strip reprints   £3.50–£5.00
2–5   £2.50–£4.00

JESSE JAMES COMICS
1952 (6)
Thorpe & Porter (Avon)
1 (68p) US reprint   75p–£1.00
2–6   50p–75p

JESTER
27 Jan 1912–18 Dec 1920 (465)
AP
to: *Jolly Jester*
1 (534) G. M. Payne (tabloid)   £1.25–£1.75
535–998 J. B. Yeats   £1.00–£1.25

JESTER
23 Feb 1924–18 May 1940 (847)
AP
to: *Funny Wonder*
1 (1164) Don Newhouse (tabloid)   £1.25–£1.75
1924–1929 Reg Parlett   £1.00–£1.25
1930–1939 George Parlett   £1.00–£1.75
1940 Roy Wilson   75p–£1.50

JESTER AND WONDER
24 May 1902–20 Jan 1912 (506)
Harmsworth/AP
to: *Jester*
1 (28) Tom Wilkinson (tabloid)   £1.50–£2.00
1902–1912 J. B. Yeats   £1.00–£1.50
colour: 14 Jun 1902; 29 Nov 1902   £2.50–£3.50

JET
1 May 1971–25 Sep 1971 (21)
IPC
to: *Buster*
1 (40p)   25p–35p
2–21   20p–30p

JET COMIC
1953 (1)
Hamilton
1 (nn) (28p) Ron Embleton   50p–£1.00

JET PLANE RAIDERS
1948 (1)
Hotspur/*Secret Service Series* No 1
1 (8p) (gravure) Bob Wilkin   50p–£1.00

JIF JUNIOR
1973 (1)
Reckitt & Colman
1 (6p) (giveaway)   25p–75p

JIM BOWIE
Mar 1957–1959 (24)
Miller (Gower)
aka: *Brave JB/Adventures of JB*
1–4 (Charlton reprints)   50p–75p
5–24 Denis Gifford   35p–75p

JIM BRIDGER MOUNTAIN MAN
see: *Western Picture Library*

JIMMY BRINDLE
1948 (1)
Brindle
1 (16p) (4C) B. Wilkin   50p–£1.00

JIMMY DURANTE COMICS
1950 (2)
Streamline/United Anglo-American (ME)

1 (nn) (36p) (4C) US reprint   50p–£1.00
2 (nn) (28p)   35p–75p

JIMMY SERIES
1948–1958 (9)
Brockhampton
1: *J & the Little Old Engine* (oblong)   50p–£1.00
2: *J at the Seaside*   35p–50p
3: *J Goes to a Party*   35p–50p
4: *J at the Fair*   35p–50p
5: *J Goes Sailing*   35p–50p
6: *J at the Zoo*   35p–50p
7: *J & the Redskins*   35p–50p
8: *J & the Space Ship*   35p–50p
9: *J & the Pirates*   35p–50p

JINGLE BELLS COMIC
Sep 1947 (1)
Philmar (Marx)
1 (nn) (8p) Walter Bell   50p–£1.00

JINGLES
13 Jan 1934–29 May 1954 (741)
AP
& *Golden*: 8 Jun 1940
& *Crackers*: 7 Jun 1941
to: *T.V. Fun*
1 (8p) (tabloid) Roy Wilson   £5.00–£7.50
2– Reg Parlett   £1.50–£2.00
6 Jan 1940: colour issues   £2.00–£2.25
1940–1949 Bertie Brown   £1.25–£1.50
1950–1954 George Heath   75p–£1.00

JINGLES AND TIP-TOP
Overseas edition:
one comic inside the other   £2.00–£3.00

JINGO COMIC
1946–1947 (4)
Forshaw/Ensign
1 (nn) (green) W. Forshaw   50p–£1.00
2 (nn) (blue)   50p–£1.00
3 (brown)   50p–£1.00
4 (nn) (gravure) Frank Minnitt   75p–£1.25

JINTY
11 May 1974–21 Nov 1981 (393)
IPC
& *Lindy*: 8 Nov 1975
& *Penny*: 12 Apr 1980
to: *Tammy*
1 (40p)   25p–45p
2–393   10p–20p

JINTY SUMMER SPECIAL
May 1974–May 1983 (10)
IPC
1 (80p)   35p–45p
2–10   20p–25p

JOE LOUIS COMICS
Nov 1950–Jan 1951 (2)
Miller (Fawcett)
1–2 (28p) US reprint   50p–£1.00

JOE 90
18 Jan 1969–6 Sep 1969 (34)
City
to: *TV 21 & Joe 90*
1 (20p) (gravure) (tabloid)   £2.00–£3.00
2–34   £1.00–£1.50

JOE PALOOKA
Mar 1953–
Streamline/United Anglo-American (Harvey)
1 (28p) (4C) US reprint   50p–£1.00
2–   35p–75p

JOE PALOOKA'S HUMPHREY
1950–1951 (13)
Streamline/United Anglo-American (Harvey)
1 (28p) US reprint   50p–£1.00
2–13   35p–75p

JOE YANK
1962 (1)
Cartoon Art
1 US reprint   50p–£1.00

JOHN CARTER OF MARS
1953 (2)
World (Dell)
1–2 (28p) US reprint   75p–£1.25

JOHN WAYNE ADVENTURE COMICS
Aug 1952–1958 (82)
Pemberton/World (Toby)
1 (28p) US reprint   £1.50–£2.00
2–77 (28p)   75p–£1.00
78–82 (68p)   75p–£1.00

JOHN WESLEY
16 May 1953
AP
1 (nn) *Sunday Companion* reprints   50p–£1.00

JOHNNY HAZARD
1954 (1)
Miller
1 (28p) US reprint   35p–75p

JOHNNY LAW SKY RANGER ADVENTURES
1955 (2)
World (Gleason)
1 (28p) US reprint   50p–£1.00
2   50p–75p

JOHNNY MACK BROWN
1954–1955 (21)
World (Dell)
1 (28p) US reprint   75p–£1.00
2–21   50p–75p

JOJO CONGO KING
1950 (1)
Streamline/United Anglo-American (Fox)
1 (28p) US reprint   75p–£1.25

JOKER
18 Jul 1891–16 Jan 1896 (237)
Ford
to: *New Series*
1 (16p)   £5.00–£7.50
2–237   £1.50–£2.00

JOKER
5 Nov 1927–18 May 1940 (655)
Fleetway/AP
& *Monster Comic*: 1 Feb 1930
to: *Illustrated Chips*
1 (8p) (tabloid) S. K. Perkins   £5.00–£7.50
1927–1929 Albert Pease   £2.00–£2.50
21 Jan 1928: first AP issue   £2.00–£2.75
1930–1939 Percy Cocking   £1.50–£2.00
1940 J. L. Jukes   £1.75–£2.00

JOKER COMIC
1946 (1)
Bairns (Marx)
1 (nn) (12p) (card) (reprints)   50p–75p

JOKER NEW SERIES
23 Jan 1896–28 Oct 1897 (93)
Greyfriars
inc: *The New Joker*
1 (238)   £2.00–£3.00
239–330   £1.50–£2.00

JOKES
20 Jan 1898–16 Jun 1898 (22)
Greyfriars/Marshall (10–22)
1 (12p)   £5.00–£7.50
2–22   £2.00–£2.50

JOLIDAY COMIC
1948 (2)
McKenzie
1–2 (8p) Mack Earl   35p–75p

JOLLY ADVENTURES
1946–1949 (9)
Martin & Reid
1 (8p) H. E. Pease   50p–£1.00
2–9 Louis Diamond   50p–£1.00

JOLLY ARROW
1948 (2)
Matthew (Martin & Reid)
1–2 (16p) Bob Monkhouse   50p–£1.25

JOLLY BITS FROM JOLLY BOOKS
8 Aug 1892–17 Sep 1892 (6)
Fox
1 (8p)   £2.00–£5.00
2–6   £1.75–£2.00

JOLLY CHUCKLES
1946–1949 (11)
Martin & Reid
1 (8p) H. E. Pease   50p–£1.00
2–11 R. Beaumont   50p–£1.00

JOLLY COMIC
19 Jan 1935–28 Oct 1939 (250)
AP
to: *Comic Cuts*
1 (8p) (tabloid) Roy Wilson   £5.00–£7.50
25 May 1935: yellow paper   £2.00–£2.50
19 Oct 1935: pink paper   £2.00–£2.50
18 Mar 1939: red/black   £2.00–£2.50
1935–1939   £1.50–£2.00

JOLLY COMIC
1946 (1)
PM (Marx)
1 (nn) (folded card) (reprint)   50p–75p

JOLLY COWBOY
1948 (1)
Martin & Reid
1 (8p) Bob Monkhouse   50p–£1.00

JOLLY FUN
1946 (2)
Martin & Reid
1–2 (8p) H. E. Pease   50p–£1.00

JOLLY FUN-RAY COMIC
Sep 1947 (1)
Philmar (Marx)
1 (8p) Stanley White   50p–£1.00

JOLLY GIANT COMIC
1946 (1)
Philmar (Marx)
1 (8p) Tony Speer   50p–£1.00

JOLLY JACK IN THE BOX COMIC
1949 (1)
PM (Marx)
1 (8p) (gravure) Frank Minnitt   50p–£1.00

JOLLY JACK'S WEEKLY
20 Aug 1933–16 Dec 1934 (70)
Associated Newspapers
supplement to *Sunday Dispatch* newspaper
1 (8p) (tabloid) Stanley White   £3.00–£5.00
27 Aug 1933–22 Jul 1934 (2C)   £2.00–£2.50
29 Jul 1934–16 Dec 1934 (4p) (2C)   £1.00–£1.50
(*NB*: numbered same as newspaper)

JOLLY JESTER
25 Dec 1920–15 Feb 1924 (165)
AP

to: *Jester*
1 (999) (8p) (tabloid) P. Cocking   £1.25–£1.75
1000 Roy Wilson   £1.50–£2.50
1001–1163 Bertie Brown   £1.00–£1.25

JOLLY JESTER COMIC
1948 (2)
Philmar/PM (Marx)
1–2 (8p) Harry Parlett   50p–£1.00

JOLLY JINKS
Dec 1938 (1)
Leng
1 (nn) (84p) *Fairyland Tales Xmas*   £2.50–£5.00

JOLLY JINKS COMIC
1944 (1)
Martin & Reid
1 (nn) (8p) H. E. Pease   50p–£1.00

JOLLY JUMBO'S CHRISTMAS HOLIDAY
COMIC
16 Nov 1934 (1)
Pearson
1 (nn) (12p) (tabloid) A. W. Browne   £2.50–£3.50

JOLLY MILLER CHILDREN'S BOOK
1944 (1)
Miller (United Features)
1 (nn) (12p) US reprints   50p–£1.25

JOLLY ROGER
24 Apr 1963–
Purnell
1– (16p) (4-colour)   50p–75p

JOLLY TIMES
May–Sep 1920 (5)
AP
supplement to *London Magazine*
1 (115) (8p) (2C) Phil Swinnerton   £1.50–£2.50
116–119 Leonard Shields   £1.00–£1.50
(*NB*: numbers as for magazine)

JOLLY TIMES
Aug 1947 (1)
Burn (Algar)
1 (16p) Walter Booth   50p–£1.00

JOLLY WESTERN
1947–1949 (9)
Martin & Reid
to: *Rangeland Western*
1 (8p) Norman Light   £1.00–£1.25
2–5 Louis Diamond   50p–£1.00
6–9 (gravure) John McCail   £1.00–£1.50

JOLLYBOYS AND GIRLS COMIC
1949 (1)
Philmar (Marx)
1 (8p) Arthur Martin (gravure)   50p–£1.00

JONES FAMILY
1982 (1)
Gibbs/Mentadent (giveaway)
1 (nn) (28p) (4C) Italian reprint (promo)   10p–25p

JOURNEY INTO DANGER
1957 (8)
Class (Atlas)
1–8 (68p) US reprint   50p–75p

JOURNEY INTO NIGHTMARE
1978
Portman (Marvel)
1 (68p) US reprints   20p–50p
2–   15p–25p

JOY WHEEL
1947 (1)

Children's Press
1 (nn) (12p) Serge Drigin   75p–£1.25

JOYRIDE COMIC
1946 (5)
Foster
1 (nn) (8p) Bob Wilkin   50p–£1.00
2–5   50p–£1.00

JU JITSU COMIC
1947 (1)
Buchanan
(sequel to *Atom*; advertised but not traced) £1.00–£2.00

JUDGE DREDD COLOUR SERIES
1982 (1)
Titan (IPC)
1: *JD Streets of Mega City* (52p) (reprint)   £1.95–£2.95
see: *Chronicles of Judge Dredd*

JUDY
16 Jan 1960–
Thomson
& *Emma*: 15 Sep 1979
& *Tracy*: 26 Jan 1985
1 (32p)   35p–50p
2–   10p–15p

JUDY PICTURE STORY LIBRARY
May 1963–
Thomson
1 (68p) *Dixie of Dude Ranch*   35p–45p
2–   10p–25p

JUDY'S COMICAL PENNYWORTHS
Nov 1881–20 Feb 1882 (7)
Judy Office
1 (24p) (small) C. H. Ross   £2.50–£5.00
2–7 A. Chasemore   £2.00–£3.50

JUGHEAD
195–
Thorpe & Porter (Archie)
1– (28p) US reprint   25p–50p

JULIETTE PICTURE LIBRARY
Jan 1966–
Famepress
1: *One Starlit Night* (68p) (small)   10p–25p
2– foreign reprint   10p–15p

JUMBO COMICS
1949 (1)
Hotspur
1 (8p) Denis Gifford   50p–£1.00

JUMBO COMICS
1950 (2)
Cartoon Art (Fiction House)
1 (nn) (4C) US reprint   £1.00–£1.50
2 (68p)   50p–£1.00

JUMBO COMICS
1951
Locker (Fiction House)
1– (36p) (4C) US reprint   £1.00–£1.50

JUMBO COMICS
1952
Thorpe & Porter (Fiction House)
1– (28p) US reprint   75p–£1.00

JUMPIN' JACK FLASH
1972 (1)
no imprint
1 (36p) US reprint   25p–50p

JUNE
18 Mar 1961–15 Jun 1974 (690)
Fleetway/IPC

& *Poppet*: 18 Jul 1964
& *School Friend*: 30 Jan 1965
& *Pixie*: 20 Jan 1973
to: *Tammy*

1 (32p)	25p–50p
2–690	10p–20p

JUNE AND PIXIE HOLIDAY SPECIAL
1973–1976 (4)
IPC

1–4 (80p)	15p–25p

JUNE AND SANDIE HOLIDAY SPECIAL
Aug 1972 (1)
IPC

1 (96p)	15p–25p

JUNE AND SCHOOL FRIEND HOLIDAY
SPECIAL
1966–1971; 1977–1980 (10)
IPC

1–6 (96p)	15p–25p
7–10 (64p)	15p–25p

JUNE & SCHOOL FRIEND AND PRINCESS
PICTURE LIBRARY
Jul 1966–
Fleetway

1– (68p)	10p–20p

JUNE AND SCHOOL FRIEND PICTURE
LIBRARY
Oct 1965–Jun 1966
Fleetway

1 (328)–	10p–20p

JUNE AND SCHOOL FRIEND PICTURE
LIBRARY HOLIDAY SPECIAL
1966–1970 (5)
Fleetway

1–5 (228p)	25p–45p

JUNE AND SCHOOL FRIEND SPECIAL EXTRA
1965–1966 (2)
Fleetway

1–2 (96p)	15p–25p

JUNE PICTURE LIBRARY HOLIDAY SPECIAL
1971–
IPC

1– (228p)	25p–40p

JUNGLE
1950 (1)
Streamline (Fox)

1 (nn) (28p) (gravure) US reprint	50p–£1.00

JUNGLE COMICS
1949–1950 (4)
Streamline (Fiction House)

1 (nn) (36p) (4C) US reprint	£1.00–£1.50
2–4	50p–£1.00

JUNGLE COMICS
1952
Thorpe & Porter (Fiction House)

1– (28p) US reprint	75p–£1.00

JUNGLE HERO
1951 (1)
Scion (King-Ganteaume)

1 (nn) (24p)	50p–£1.00

JUNGLE JIM
1955 (10)
World (Dell)

1 (28p) US reprint	75p–£1.00
2–10	50p–£1.00

JUNGLE JINKS
8 Dec 1923–7 Feb 1925 (62)
AP
to: *Playbox*

1 (12p) (tabloid) Tom Wilkinson	£5.00–£7.50
2–62 William Radford	£2.00–£2.50

JUNGLE LIL
1951 (1)
Streamline/United Anglo-American (Fox)

1 (nn) (28p) US reprint	50p–£1.00

JUNGLE THRILLS
1952 (1)
Streamline/United Anglo-American (Fox)

1 (nn) (28p) US reprint	50p–£1.00

JUNGLE TRAILS
Jul 1951 (3)
Scion (King-Ganteaume)

1–3 (24p) Ron Embleton	50p–£1.00

JUNGLIES CHRISTMAS SPECIAL
1977 (1)
IPC

1 (40p)	15p–30p

JUNIOR EXPRESS
4 Sep 1954–11 Jun 1955 (38)
Beaverbrook
to: *Junior Express Weekly*

1 (tabloid)	50p–£1.00
2–38	25p–50p

JUNIOR EXPRESS WEEKLY
18 Jun 1955–11 Feb 1956 (35)
Beaverbrook
to: *Express*

1 (39) (16p) Harry Bishop	50p–£1.00
40–73 Desmond Walduck	35p–50p

JUNIOR FORD EXPRESS
1967? (1?)
Ford Motors (giveaway)

1 (nn)–(4p) (4C)	25p–50p

JUNIOR GUIDE TO FRENCH
1979 (1)
Usborne

1 (nn) (68p) (4C) (small)	75p–£1.25

JUNIOR MIRROR
1 Sep 1954–29 Feb 1956 (75)
Daily Mirror

1 (tabloid)	50p–£1.00
2–75	35p–50p

JUNIOR NEWS AND MAIL
26 Jul 1977–
Aldershot News
supplement to *Aldershot News & Mail*

1 (8p) (tabloid) (magazine)	10p–25p
2–4	5p–10p
5–(2C) (increased comic content)	15p–25p

JUNIOR PUZZLES
Jun 1978–Jun 1982 (5)
IPC

1 (nn) (36p)	10p–20p
2–5	10p–15p

JUNIOR QUIZZER
1975–1976 (10)
Byblos
to: *Quizzer Monthly*

1 (36p) R. Turner	20p–30p
2–10 Ian Kennedy	15p–25p

JUNIOR SPIDERMAN SUMMER SPECIAL
May 1983 (1)

Marvel
1 (nn) (48p) US reprints   25p–50p

JUNIORS MAGAZINE
1947 (1)
Pearce
1 (8p) (gravure) W. Forshaw   50p–£1.50

JUPITER ADVENTURE COMIC
1947 (1)
Scoop Books
1 (8p) George Blow   50p–£1.00

JUST DENNIS
1965 (1)
Class (Hallden)
1 (68p) US reprint   35p–50p

JUSTICE TRAPS THE GUILTY
1949 (1)
Streamline/United Anglo-American (Prize)
1 (28p) (4C) US reprint   75p–£1.50

JUSTICE TRAPS THE GUILTY
1951–1954 (43)
Arnold/Thorpe & Porter (Prize)
1 (68p) US reprint   75p–£1.00
2–28 (Arnold)   50p–75p
29–43 (T & P)   50p–75p

K.O. KNOCKOUT
1947 (1)
Cartoon Art
1 (nn) (20p) Crewe Davies   75p–£1.25

KAANGA
1952
Thorpe & Porter (Fiction House)
1– (28p) US reprint   50p–£1.00

KANG THE MIGHTY
1950 (1)
Scion
1 (nn) (16p) Frank Minnitt   50p–£1.00

KAYO KIRBY
1950 (1)
Cartoon Art (Fiction House)
1 (16p) US reprint   35p–75p

KELTIK KOMIX
1979–1982 (2)
Aberdeen People's Press
1 (28p) (adult)   40p–65p
2 (36p)   75p–£1.00

KEN MAYNARD WESTERN
1950–1959
Miller (Fawcett)
1950: large format (gravure)   75p–£1.50
1951: 1–8 (28p) US reprint   50p–£1.00
1959: 1–3 (68p)   35p–75p

KENNEDY
1977 (2)
Morcrim (Mercocomic)
1: *President Must Die* (132p) (small) 25p–50p
2 Spanish reprint   20p–35p

KEVIN KEEGAN SOCCER SPECIAL
Aug 1980 (1)
IPC
1 (nn) (64p)   45p–60p

KICK-OFF FOOTBALL WEEKLY
16 Aug 1975–
Soccerfile
1– (20p)   10p–15p

KID COLT OUTLAW
1951 (3)
Miller (Atlas)
1 (50) (28p) US reprint   75p–£1.00
51–52   50p–75p

KID COLT OUTLAW
1954 (58)
Strato/Top Sellers
1 (68p) US reprint   50p–£1.00
2–58   35p–75p

KID COLT WESTERN COMICS
1952 (7)
Thorpe & Porter (Atlas)
1 (68p) US reprint   50p–£1.00
2–7   35p–75p

KID COWBOY
see: *Action Series*

KID DYNAMITE WESTERN COMIC
1954–1960 (65)
Miller
1 (28p) John Wheeler   50p–£1.00
2–65 Tom Barling   35p–75p

KID ETERNITY
1950 (3)
Locker (Quality)
1 (36p) (4C) US reprint   £1.00–£1.50
2–3   75p–£1.00

KID MONTANA
1959 (5)
Miller (Charlton)
1 (50) (28p) US reprint   75p–£1.00
51–54   50p–75p

KID SLADE GUNFIGHTER
1957 (7)
Strato/Top Sellers (Atlas)
1 (68p) US reprint   75p–£1.00
2–7   50p–75p

KIDDIES COMIC
see: *Lilley & Skinner's Kiddies Comic*

KIDDYFUN
1945–1951 (12)
Swan
to: *Girls Fun*
1 (8p) (4C) William Ward   £2.00–£3.00
2–12 Harry Banger   £1.00–£1.25

KIM
24 Apr 1982–2 Jun 1983 (59)
Marvel
1 (32p) (photos)   15p–25p
2–59   10p–15p

KIM WINTER SPECIAL
Nov 1982 (1)
Marvel
1 (nn) (photos)   15p–25p

KINEMA COMIC
24 Apr 1920–15 Oct 1932 (651)
AP
to: *Film Fun*
1 (24p) G. W. Wakefield   £5.00–£7.50
2–651 Reg Carter   £1.75–£2.00

KING COMIC
1947 (4)
Ensign/Pearce
1 (8p) (nn) (gravure) W. Forshaw   50p–£1.00
2–4 Frank Minnitt   50p–£1.00

KING COMIC
5 May 1954–7 Aug 1954 (14)

Miller (King Features)
1–8 (28p) (gravure) US reprints 50p–£1.00
9–14 35p–75p

KING COMIC SERIES
see: *Crack Action*
Crime Patrol
Police Comic
T-Man

KING KONG
1970 (1)
Top Sellers (Dell)
1 (68p) (4C) US reprint 50p–£1.00

KING OF THE ROYAL MOUNTED
1953 (21)
World (Dell)
1 (28p) US reprint 75p–£1.00
2–21 50p–75p

KING OF THE ROYAL MOUNTED
1962–1963 (15)
Miller (King Features)
1 (68p) US reprint 50p–75p
2–15 35p–50p

KING ROLLO SERIES
1982–
Sparrow/Arrow
1 *Adventures of KR* 50p–£1.00
2 *Further Adventures of KR* 50p–£1.00
3 *KR's Playroom* 50p–£1.00

KING SMURF
Aug 1978 (1)
Hodder & Stoughton
1 (50p) (4C) foreign reprint 50p–95p

KIT CARSON COMICS
1952 (1)
Thorpe & Porter (Avon)
1 (68p) US reprint 50p–£1.00

KIT COWBOY
Jun 1957–1958 (10)
Miller
1 (28p) foreign reprint 50p–75p
2–10 35p–50p

KIT MARAIN
1949 (1)
Martin & Reid (Gower)
1 (nn) (8p) (tabloid) Mick Anglo 75p–£1.25

KLONDIKE PETE SERIES
1971–1973 (7)
Nabisco (IPC) (cereal giveaways)
Klondike Pete 1–3 25p–35p
Klondike Pete's Comic 1–3 25p–35p
Klondike Pete's Comic Story Book 25p–35p

KNOCKABOUT COMICS
1981–
Knockabout
1 (36p) (adult) Hunt Emerson 50p–75p
2– 50p–75p

KNOCKOUT
12 Jun 1971–23 Jun 1973 (106)
IPC
to: *Whizzer & Chips*
1 (20p) Mike Lacey 15p–25p
2–106 Reg Parlett 5p–10p

KNOCKOUT COMIC
4 Mar 1939–16 Feb 1963 (1251)
AP/Feetway
& *Magnet*: 1 Jun 1940
& *Comic Cuts*: 19 Sep 1953
aka: *Billy Bunter's Knockout*: 10 Jun 61

to: *Valiant*
1 (28p) Hugh McNeill £5.00–£15.00
1939 issues Frank Minnitt £2.50–£3.00
1940–1945 Fred Robinson £2.00–£2.50
1946–1949 Eric Parker £1.75–£2.00
1950–1959 Reg Wootton 50p–£1.00
1960–1963 Tony Weare 35p–50p

KNOCKOUT HOLIDAY SPECIAL
Jun 1972–Jun 1973 (2)
IPC
1–2 (48p) 15p–25p

KNOCKOUTS (SERIES)
1980 (5)
Longman
1: *Cave Rescue* (16p) (4C) 25p–50p
2: *Undersea Adventure* 20p–35p
3: *Maiden Flight* 20p–35p
4: *Haunted Castle* 20p–35p
5: *Danger at Sea* 20p–35p

KNOWLEDGE
9 Jan 1961 (black) 1962 (yellow) 1963 (blue)–1964
Purnell/Fratelli Fabbri
1 (4C magazine) 15p–35p
2– 15p–20p

KOMIC FUN
1948 (1)
Reynard
1 (nn) (8p) Alan Fraser 50p–75p

KOMIC KRACKERS
1949 (1)
Hamilton
1 (nn) (8p) 50p–£1.00

KORAK SON OF TARZAN
1971–1973
Williams (Dell)
1– (36p) (4C) reprint 20p–30p

KORAK SON OF TARZAN BUMPER ALBUM
1973 (1)
Top Sellers (DC)
1 (nn) (52p) (4C) reprint 20p–30p

KRACKER COMIC
1947 (6)
Reynard
1 (16p) Tom Cottrell 50p–£1.25
2–6 (8p) 50p–£1.00

KRAZY
16 Oct 1976–15 Apr 1978 (79)
IPC
to: *Whizzer & Chips*
1 (32p) Reg Parlett 10p–25p
2–79 Robert Nixon 10p–15p
see: *Best of Krazy*

KRAZY HOLIDAY SPECIAL
May 1977–Jun 1983 (7)
IPC
1 (64p) Reg Parlett 25p–35p
2–7 Robert Nixon 20p–30p

LADY PENELOPE
22 Jan 1966–18 May 1968 (122)
City
aka: *Lady P.*: 27–52
aka: *The New Lady Penelope*: 53–122
to: *Penelope*
1 (20p) (gravure) Ron Embleton £1.00–£2.50
2–122 John Burns 50p–£1.00

LAMBCHOP WEEKLY
see: *Shari Lewis, Lambchop Weekly*

165

LANCE O'CASEY
1951 (1)
Arnold (Fawcett)
1 (10) (24p) US reprint ... 50p–75p

LAREDO CROCKETT RANGER
1953–1955 (44)
Peters (Miller)
to: *Ranger Western Comic*
1 (28p) US reprint ... £1.50–£2.00
2–44 ... £1.00–£1.50

LARIAT
Jul 1950 (1)
Martin & Reid (Gower)
1 (nn) (16p) Mick Anglo ... 50p–£1.00

LARKS
1 May 1893–3 Mar 1902 (462)
Dalziel/Trapps Holmes
to: *Best Budget*
1 (8p) Gordon Fraser ... £5.00–£10.00
2–136 J. F. Sullivan ... £1.50–£2.00
137–462 (Trapps Holmes issues) ... £1.00–£1.75

LARKS
7 Jun 1902–29 Dec 1906 (239)
Trapps Holmes
to: *World's Comic*
1 (8p) Oliver Veal ... £3.00–£5.00
2–239 Frank Holland ... £1.50–£2.00

LARKS
29 Oct 1927–18 May 1940 (656)
AP
to: *Comic Cuts*
1 (8p) (tabloid) Bertie Brown ... £5.00–£7.50
1927–1930 issues Roy Wilson ... £1.50–£2.00
1931–1940 issues Reg Parlett ... £1.25–£1.75

LASH LARUE WESTERN
Sep 1950–1959 (76)
Miller (Fawcett)
1 (50) (36p) US reprints ... 75p–£1.25
51–125 (28p) ... 35p–75p

LASSIE
Oct 1952–1953 (18)
World (Dell)
1 (52p) (4C) US reprints ... £1.00–£1.25
2–18 (36/28p) ... 35p–50p

LAST OF THE SUMMER WINE
Dec 1983 (1)
Daily Star strip reprints
1 (nn) (128p) Roger Mahoney ... 75p–£1.25

LAUGH AGAIN WITH ANDY CAPP
1968–
Hamlyn
1 (reprints from *Andy Capp Series*) ... 75p–£1.00
2– ... 50p–75p

LAUGH FUN BOOK
Sep 1947 (1)
PM (Marx)
1 (nn) (16p) Denis Gifford ... 75p–£1.50

LAUGH WITH MURRAY BALL
1974 (1)
Leader
1 (nn) reprints of 'Stanley' (strip) ... 25p–50p

LAUGHTER
15 Feb 1890–28 Jun 1890 (20)
Woodford Fawcett
1 (16p) (small) ... £5.00–£7.50
2–20 ... £1.75–£2.25

LAUGHTER
7 Oct 1933–27 Nov 1937; 14 Jan 1939–26 Feb 1939

Odhams
(supplement to *Passing Show*)
1 (4p) Will Owen ... £1.00–£2.00
1933 issues G. E. Studdy ... £1.00–£1.50
1934 issues Bruce Bairnsfather ... 75p–£1.00
1935 issues A. Barrett ... 50p–75p
1936 issues Harry Dodd ... 35p–50p
1937 issues Alfred Mazure ... 25p–35p
1939 issues ... 25p–35p

LAUGHTER
4 Mar 1939–29 Apr 1939 (9)
Odhams
(supplement to *Illustrated*)
1 (8p) Lawson Wood ... £1.00–£1.50
2–4 (8p) 5 (7p) 6 (6p) 7 (5p) 9 (3p) ... 25p–50p

LAUREL AND HARDY
Mar 1969–
Top Sellers/Williams
1 (36p) (4C) ... 25p–50p
2– ... 15p–25p

LAUREL AND HARDY
Mar 1979–1980
Byblos
1 (52p) foreign reprints ... 25p–40p
2– ... 20p–25p

LAUREL AND HARDY (MONTHLY)
Mar 1981–Mar 1982 (13)
Byblos
1 (52p) foreign reprints ... 25p–40p
2–13 ... 20p–30p

LAUREL AND HARDY EXTRA
1969–1972 (8)
Top Sellers
1 (36p) (4C) foreign reprints ... 25p–45p
2–8 (52p) (4C) ... 15p–25p

LAUREL AND HARDY HOLIDAY SPECIAL
Jul 1983 (1)
Polystyle
1 (nn) (48p) John McLusky reprints ... 25p–50p

LAUREL AND HARDY SPECIAL
Aug 1979–Nov 1981 (9)
Byblos
1: *Summer Special 1979* (52p) reprints ... 25p–40p
2: *Autumn Special 1979* ... 25p–35p
3: *Winter Special 1979* ... 25p–35p
4: *Spring Special 1980* ... 25p–35p
5: *Summer Special 1980* ... 25p–35p
6: *Autumn Special 1980* ... 25p–35p
7: *Winter Special 1980* ... 25p–35p
8: *Summer Special 1981* ... 25p–35p
9: *Winter Special 1981* ... 25p–35p

LAZARUS LAMB IN THE RIDDLE OF THE SPHINCTER
1983 (1)
Pluto Press
1 (nn) (96p) Ralph Edney (adult) ... £2.00–£2.95

LEARN THROUGH STRIPS SERIES
1975 (8)
Chancerel/WHS
1: *Fresh Water Angling* George Stokes ... 30p–50p
2: *Sea Fishing* ... 25p–35p
3: *Plain Sailing: Dinghy* Gary Keane ... 25p–30p
4: *Plain Sailing: Cruising* ... 25p–30p
5: *Plain Sailing: Power Boat* ... 25p–30p
6: *Bridge* Larry Horak ... 25p–30p
7: *Football* ... 25p–30p
8: *Come Riding* George Stokes ... 25p–30p
strip reprints from *Evening News, Daily Express*, etc

LEGEND HORROR CLASSICS
1975–Jan 1976 (9)
Legend
1 (20p) (4C) (poster) Kevin O'Neill ... 25p–50p
2–9 (continues as film magazine) ... 20p–35p

LET'S PLAY GAMES
1980
Walton Press
1 (52p) (puzzles)   10p–20p
2–   10p–15p

LIEUTENANT BLUEBERRY
1977
Egmont/Methuen (Dargaud)
1: *Fort Navajo* (52p) (4C) reprints   50p–85p
2: *Thunder in the West*   25p–50p

LIFE AND TIMES OF THE SHMOO
1949 (1)
Convoy (United Features)
1 (100p) US reprint (Al Capp)   £1.50–£3.50

LIFE IS ONE BIG BED OF NAILS
1968 (1)
Papas (*Guardian* reprints)
1 (nn) (84p) (oblong) Bill Papas   50p–£1.00

LIFE OF CHRIST
1977 (1)
Darton Longman & Todd (1)
1 (100p) (oblong) Eric Fraser   £1.00–£2.00

LIFE STORY
1959 (24)
Miller (Fawcett)
1 (68p) US reprints   10p–25p
2–24   10p–20p

LIFE WITH THE LARKS
Sep 1978 (1)
Mirror Books (*Daily Mirror* reprints)
1 (nn) (100p) Jack Dunkley   50p–75p

LIFE'S PICTORIAL COMEDY
Jul 1908–Dec 1908 (6)
Henderson
1 (112) US reprints   £1.00–£2.00
113–117   £1.00–£2.00

LIGHTNING COMICS
1946 (1)
Kangaroo
1 (nn) (8p) Denis McLoughlin   £1.00–£1.50

LI'L ABNER
1945 (1)
Miller (United Features)
1 (nn) (16p) (gravure) US reprint   50p–£1.50

LILLEY & SKINNER'S KIDDIES COMIC
Sep 1937–1938
Lilley & Skinner (giveaway)
1 (8p) G. Larkman   £3.50–£5.00
2–   £2.50–£3.00

LINDY
21 Jun 1975–1 Nov 1975 (20)
IPC
to: *Jinty*
1–20   10p–15p

LINUS
May 1970 (1)
Milano Libri (UK)
1 (86p) US/foreign reprints   75p–£1.00

LION
23 Feb 1952–18 May 1974 (1156)
AP/Fleetway/IPC
& *Sun*: 24 Oct 1959
& *Champion*: 11 Jun 1966
& *Eagle*: 3 May 1969
& *Thunder*: 20 Mar 1971
to: *Valiant*
1 (24p) Ron Forbes   £1.00–£3.00

1952–1959 A. Philpott   25p–50p
1960–1969 Don Lawrence   20p–40p
1970–1974 Geoff Campion   10p–15p

LION AND LAMB COMICS
Aug 1975 (1)
Satyuga Novelties
1 (36p) (adult) M. Livingstone   50p–75p

LION AND VALIANT SPECIAL EXTRA
1970 (1)
IPC
1 (96p) (reprints)   35p–50p

LION PICTURE LIBRARY
Oct 1963–May 1969 (136)
Fleetway
1 (60p) *Paddy Payne Rocket Buster*   25p–50p
2–136   20p–35p

LION SPECIALS
1967–1980 (14)
Fleetway/IPC
1: *Summer Spectacular Epic 1967* (96p)   50p–£1.00
2: *Summer Special 1968*   25p–50p
3: *Summer Special 1969*   25p–50p
4: *Summer Special 1970*   25p–50p
5: *Summer Special 1971*   25p–50p
6: *Summer Special 1972*   25p–50p
7: *Summer Special 1973*   25p–50p
8: *Holiday Special 1974* (80p)   25p–50p
9: *Holiday Special 1975*   25p–50p
10–14: *Holiday Special 1976–1980* (64p)   25p–35p

LITTLE ASPIRIN
1950 (1)
Streamline/United Anglo-American (Atlas)
1 (28p) US reprint   25p–50p

LITTLE LENNY
1950 (1)
Streamline/United Anglo-American (Atlas)
1 (28p) US reprint   25p–50p

LITTLE LULU
1955 (3)
World (Dell)
1 (28p) US reprint   50p–£1.00
2–3   50p–75p

LITTLE MARVEL COMIC
Jan 1946 (1)
Locker
1 (nn) (folded strip) R. Beaumont   50p–£1.00

LITTLE MAX COMICS
1953 (4)
Streamline/United Anglo-American (Harvey)
1 (28p) US reprint   50p–£1.00
2–4   50p–75p

LITTLE SHERIFF WESTERN COMIC
Jul 1951–1958 (96)
Peters/Westworld
V1N1 (36p) foreign reprint   75p–£1.00
V1N2–V7N12 (32/20p)   50p–75p

LITTLE SPARKS
24 Apr 1920–15 May 1920 (4)
AP
1 (328) (tabloid)   £2.00–£3.50
329–331   £2.00–£3.00

LITTLE SPARKS NEW SERIES
22 May 1920–30 Sep 1922 (124)
AP
to: *Sunbeam*
1 (12p) (tabloid) S. J. Cash   £5.00–£7.50
2–124 Walter Booth   £1.75–£2.00

167

LITTLE STAR
29 Jan 1972–24 Jan 1976 (209)
Thomson
to: *Twinkle*
1 (20p) Bob Dewar   35p–50p
2–209   20p–35p

LITTLE WONDER COMIC
Jan 1946 (1)
Locker
1 (nn) (folded strip) R. Beaumont   50p–£1.00

LOAD RUNNER
23 Jun 1983–8 Dec 1983 (13)
ECC Publications
1 (40p) Peter Dennis   30p–40p
2–13 (32p) John Canning   25p–30p

LOBEY DOSSER
1953(?) (2)
Evening Times
1: *Secret of Hickory Hollow* (oblong)   £2.50–£5.00
2: *His Life Story* (36p) Bud Neil reprints   £2.00–£5.00

LOLLIPOPS COMIC
1947–1949 (3)
Philmar (Marx)
1–3 (8p) Ern Shaw   50p–£1.00

LONDON EXPLORER
1952 (1)
Associated Newspapers/Evening News
1 (68p) Peter Jackson reprints   £1.00–£2.00

LONDON IS STRANGER THAN FICTION
1951 (1)
Associated Newspapers/Evening News
1 (84p) Peter Jackson reprints   £1.00–£2.00

LONE EAGLE
1956
Miller (Farrell)
1– (28p) US reprint   50p–75p

LONE GROOVER EXPRESS
1976 (1)
Benyon
1 (nn) (24p) (tabloid) (adult)   50p–75p

LONE GROOVER'S LITTLE READ BOOK
1981 (1)
Eel Pie
1 (100p) (small) Tony Benyon   50p–75p

LONE RANGER
Jan 1953–Jun 1958 (66)
World (Dell)
1 (36p) US reprints   50p–£1.00
2–61 (36p)   50p–75p
62–66 (68p)   50p–75p

LONE RANGER
1970–
Top Sellers (Dell)
1 (36p) (4C) US reprints   20p–25p
2–   10p–20p

LONE RANGER
1977 (2)
Egmont-Methuen (Dell)
1 (100p) (small) (4C) US reprints   25p–35p
2   20p–25p

LONE RIDER
1951 (3)
Pemberton/World (Farrell)
1 (36p) US reprint   50p–£1.00
2–3 (28p)   35p–75p

LONE RIDER PICTURE LIBRARY
Jul 1961–Feb 1962 (16)
Fleetway
1 (68p) *The Payoff* (small)   15p–35p
2–16   15p–25p

LONE STAR MAGAZINE
Nov 1952–Apr 1963
DCMT/Atlas (Vol 3–9)
V1N1 (24p)   £1.00–£1.50
V1N2–34 (Dec 1955) R. Embleton   50p–£1.00
V2N1–12 (1956) Colin Andrew   35p–75p
V3N1–12 (1957) Terry Patrick   35p–75p
V4N1–12 (1958) Ron Turner   35p–75p
V5N1–12 (1959) Brian Lewis   35p–75p
V6N1–12 (1960) Kingshott   35p–75p
V7N1–12 (1961) Aldoma   25p–50p
V8 85–97 (1962) Spanish art   25p–50p
V9 98–99 (1963) Spanish art   20p–45p

LONE VIGILANTE
see: *Action Series*

LONG BOW
Sep 1960–1964 (31)
Atlas (Fiction House)
1 (28p) US reprint   50p–75p
2–31   35p–50p

LONG JOHN SILVER
1956 (2)
Miller (Charlton)
1–2 (28p) US reprint   50p–75p

LONGMAN THINKSTRIPS
1977 (3)
Longman
1: *It's Your Round* (4p)   10p–25p
2: *It's Only Fair* (4p)   10p–25p
3: *It'll Never Be the Same* (4p)   10p–25p

LOOK AND LAUGH
Sep 1947–1948 (2)
Philmar (Marx)
1 (nn) (16p) Ern Shaw   50p–£1.25
2 Arthur Martin   50p–£1.00

LOOK AND LEARN
20 Jan 1962–17 Apr 1982 (1049)
Fleetway/IPC
& *Childrens Newspaper*: 8 May 1965
& *Ranger*: 25 Jun 1966
& *Speed & Power*: 29 Nov 1975
& *World of Knowledge*: 10 Jan 1981
1 (24p) (4C) Peter Jackson   50p–£1.00
2–72   25p–50p
73 (32p) enlarged   25p–50p
74–1049   20p–25p

LOOK AND LEARN HOLIDAY SPECIAL
Apr 1976 (1)
IPC
1 (52p)   20p–35p

LOOK-IN
9 Jan 1971–
ITV
1 (24p) Mike Noble   25p–50p
2– Harry North   15p–20p

LOOK-IN DANGER MOUSE SPECIAL
Nov 1982 (1)
ITV
1 (nn) TV series   25p–40p

LOOK-IN FOLLYFOOT SPECIAL
1973 (1)
1 (64p) Mike Noble   20p–35p

LOOK-IN MADABOUT SPECIAL
Feb 1984 (1)

ITV
1 (48p) TV series — 50p–75p

LOOK-IN SUMMER EXTRA
1974–
ITV
1 (64p) — 20p–35p
2– — 15p–25p

LOOKING GLASS
1 Jan 1830–1 Dec 1832 (36)
Thos McLean (plain or hand-coloured editions)
1 (4p) (tabloid) William Heath — £10.00–£25.00
2–7 — £7.50–£15.00
8: first by R. Seymour — £10.00–£20.00
9–12 — £7.50–£15.00
13 (1 Jan 1831) title changed to:
McLean's Monthly Sheet of Caricatures or The Looking Glass
13–36 — £7.50–£15.00

LOONEY TUNES
1953
World (Dell)
1– (28p) US reprint — 50p–75p

LORNA THE JUNGLE GIRL
1952 (9)
Miller (Atlas)
1 (28p) US reprint — 75p–£1.00
2–9 — 50p–75p

LOST WORLD COMICS
1950 (1)
Cartoon Art (Fiction House)
1 (84p) (4C) US reprint — 75p–£1.50

LOT-O'-FUN
17 Mar 1906–16 Feb 1929 (1196)
Henderson/AP
to:*Crackers*
1 (8p) (tabloid) Geo Davey — £5.00–£10.00
1906–1920 — £1.50–£2.00
13 Mar 1920: first AP — £1.50–£2.00
1922: 12-page issues — £1.75–£2.00
7 Feb 1925: 4C back pages — £1.75–£2.00
1925–1929 Walter Booth — £1.50–£2.00

LOT O' FUN PICTORIAL SCRAPBOOK
Jul 1892–Dec 1892 (6)
Henderson
to:*Funny Folks Monthly Scrapbook*
1 (64p) US reprints — £2.50–£5.00
2–6 — £2.00–£3.50

LOVE AFFAIR
195– (3)
Miller (Fawcett?)
1–3 (68p) US reprint — 20p–35p

LOVE AND LIFE LIBRARY
196–
Thomson
1 (68p) — 20p–35p
2– — 10p–20p

LOVE ROMANCE
May 1950 (2)
AP
1–2 (28p) — 35p–50p

LOVE ROMANCES
1956
Miller (Atlas)
1– (28p) US reprint — 20p–30p

LOVE STORY OF CHARLES AND DIANA
Jul 1982 (1)
IPC
1 (nn) (40p) royalty — 50p–£1.00

LOVE STORY PICTURE LIBRARY
Aug 1952–
AP/Fleetway/IPC
1 (68p): *Dancing Heart* — 25p–50p
2– — 15p–25p

LOVE STORY PICTURE LIBRARY HOLIDAY SPECIAL
1972–
IPC
1 (224p) — 20p–30p
2 (192p) — 15p–25p

LOVERS
1956 (12)
Miller (Marvel)
1 (28p) US reprint — 35p–50p
2–12 — 25p–35p

LUCKY CHARM
Oct 1979–Jun 1984 (30)
Thomson
1 (68p) *Valda* (reprints) — 25p–35p
2–30 — 15p–25p

LUCKY COMIC
1948 (1)
Martin & Reid (Gower)
1 (nn) (8p) Harry Banger — 50p–£1.00

LUCKY DICE COMIC
1946 (1)
Funnibook (Cartoon Art)
1 (8p) Dennis Reader — 50p–£1.00

LUCKY DIP
1947 (1)
Childrens Press
1 (nn) (12p) C. Montford — 50p–£1.25

LUCKY DIP COMIC
1948 (1)
Philmar (Marx)
1 (nn) (8p) (small) Jack Pamby — 50p–75p

LUCKY LUKE SERIES
1970–
Nicolas/Brockhampton
1 (52p) (4C) *Jesse James* — 25p–75p
2– French reprints — 25p–50p

LUCKY TUB
1921–1923
New Picture Press
1 — £3.00–£5.00
2– — £2.50–£3.00

MACABRE STORIES
196– (6)
Spencer
1–6 (52p) — 25p–75p

MAGGIE'S FARM
1981–1982 (2)
Penguin
1: *Maggie's Farm* (96p) (oblong) — £1.50–£2.50
2: *Further Down on MF* — £1.00–£2.00
Steve Bell *Time Out* strip reprints

MAGIC
31 Jan 1976–24 Feb 1979 (161)
Thomson
to: *Twinkle*
1 (24p) Bob Dewar — 35p–50p
2–161 Bill Ritchie — 25p–35p

MAGIC COMIC
22 Jul 1939–25 Jan 1941 (80)
Thomson
1 (24p) Dudley Watkins — £7.50–£20.00

2–80 Allan Morley   £3.00–£5.00
Magic No 1 facsimile   £1.00–£1.50

MAGIC COMIC
1948 (1)
Martin & Reid (Gower)
1 (nn) (8p) Reg Parlett   50p–£1.00

MAGIC FRUIT
1944? (1)
Guardian Press
1 (nn) (22p) (oblong)   75p–£1.00

MAGIC ROUNDABOUT HOLIDAY SPECIAL
1975–1976 (2)
IPC
1 (48p) TV characters   20p–45p
2 (40p)   15p–25p

MAGIC WHEEL
1949 (1)
ROSPA
1 (nn) (4C) Bob Wilkin   50p–£1.00

MAGNO COMIC
1946 (1)
International
1 (nn) (20p) Paddy Brennan   50p–£1.00

MAIL ON SUNDAY CARTOONS
17 Oct 1982–
Associated Newspapers
supplement to *Mail on Sunday* newspaper
1 (nn) (12p) (4C) promotional issue   25p–50p
1 (24 Oct) Alex Graham   10p–25p
2–34 Paul Sellers   5p–10p
35– (small format) (16p)   5p–10p

MAKE YOUR OWN COMIC STRIPS
1973 (1)
Geminiscan (Geminikits)
Boxed kit with booklet   50p–£1.00

MAN FROM UNCLE WORLD ADVENTURE LIBRARY
1966 (14)
World
1–4 (68p) US reprints (small)   25p–35p
5–14 Mick Anglo   30p–45p

MAN OF STEEL
1979 (1)
British Steel Corporation (giveaway)
1 (8p) (4C) steel promo   25p–50p

MAN'S WORLD COMIC LIBRARY
see: *Speed Kings*; *Strange Worlds*; *Thrilling Hero*; *True Life Adventures*

MANDRAKE THE MAGICIAN
1961–1962 (24)
Miller (King Features)
1 (68p) US reprint   75p–£1.00
2–24   50p–75p
see: *Action Series*

MANDRAKE THE MAGICIAN WORLD ADVENTURE LIBRARY
Jan–Aug 1967 (8)
World (King Features)
1 (68p) US reprint (small)   35p–50p
2–8   30p–40p

MANDY
21 Jan 1967–
Thomson
& Debbie: 22 Jan 1983
1 (32p)   25p–50p
2–   10p–20p

MANDY MOPS AND CUBBY STRIP BOOKS
1952–1953 (4)
Sampson Low Marston (Enid Blyton)
1: *Mandy Mops & Cubby Find a House*   £1.00–£2.00
2: *Mandy Mops & Cubby Again*   50p–£1.00
3: *Mandy Makes Cubby a Hat*   50p–£1.00
4: *Mandy Mops & Cubby & Whitewash*   50p–£1.00

MANDY PICTURE STORY LIBRARY
1 Apr 1978–
Thomson
1–*Driving into Danger*   20p–30p
2–   15p–20p

MANHUNT
1951 (4)
Streamline/United Anglo-American (Fox)
1 (36p) US reprint   50p–£1.00
2–4 (28p)   50p–75p

MANHUNT
1959 (6)
World (King Features)
1 (68p) (Secret Agent X9) US reprint   75p–£1.00
2–6   50p–75p

MANHUNTER
195– (1)
Miller
1 (50) (28p) US reprint   50p–75p

MARILYN
19 Mar 1955–18 Sep 1965 (547)
AP
to: *Valentine*
1 (20p)   35p–50p
2–547   25p–30p

MARINES IN ACTION
1955 (1)
Streamline/United Anglo-American (Atlas)
1 (28p) US reprint   50p–75p

MARINES IN BATTLE
1955 (1)
Streamline/United Anglo-American (Atlas)
1 (28p) US reprint   50p–75p

MARK CONWAY
1959 (1)
Miller
1 (68p) *Murder by Phone* (small)   50p–£1.00

MARK TYME
196– (2)
Spencer
1–2 (48p) Michael Jay   50p–75p

MARKED FOR MURDER
196– (2)
Top Sellers
1 (52p) *One Body Too Many*   25p–35p
2   20p–30p

MARMADUKE
1962–1964 (2)
Brockhampton
1: *Marmaduke's Great Day* (oblong)   50p–75p
2: *A Week with Marmaduke*   35p–50p

MARRIED BLISS
1946 (1)
Martin & Reid
1 (12p) Styx   50p–£1.50

MARS COMICS
1950 (1)
Streamline (Fiction House)
1 (nn) (28p) US reprint   50p–£1.00

MARSMAN COMICS
1948 (1)
Cartoon Art
1 (20p) Dennis M. Reader   75p–£1.25

MARTIAL AWE
1946 (1)
Fisher
1 (nn) (16p) W. Forshaw   £1.00–£2.00

MARTY
23 Jan 1960–23 Feb 1963 (162)
Pearson
& Silver Star: 29 Oct 1960
to: Mirabelle
1 (28p) (photostrips)   50p–£1.00
2–162   35p–75p

MARVEL ACTION
1 Apr 1981–8 Jul 1981 (15)
Marvel
to:Captain America
1 (32p) US reprints   15p–20p
2–15   10p–15p

MARVEL CLASSICS COMICS
Oct 1981–Mar 1982 (12)
Marvel
1 (52p) US reprints (small)   20p–30p
2–12   15p–20p

MARVEL COMIC
24 Jan 1979–25 Jul 1979 (23)
Marvel
to: Spiderman; Marvel Super Heroes
1 (330) (24p) US reprints   10p–25p
331–352   10p–15p

MARVEL FAMILY
1949–1953 (43)
Miller (Fawcett)
1–3 (nn) (gravure)   £1.00–£1.50
50–70 (gravure)   75p–£1.00
71–89 (28p)   50p–£1.00

MARVEL MADHOUSE
Jun 1981–Oct 1982 (17)
Marvel
& Frantic: Aug 1981
1 (36p) US reprints   30p–40p
2–17 Dicky Howett   25p–35p

MARVEL SUPER ADVENTURE
6 May 1981–28 Oct 1981 (26)
Marvel
to: Captain America
1 (32p) US reprints   15p–20p
2–26   10p–15p

MARVEL SUPER ADVENTURE WINTER
SPECIAL
Dec 1980 (1)
Marvel
1 (52p) US reprints   25p–40p

MARVEL SUPER HEROES
Sep 1979–May 1983 (45)
Marvel
& Savage Action: Feb 1982
& Rampage: Jan 1983
to: Daredevils
1 (353) (52p) US reprints   35p–50p
354–397   25p–35p

MARVEL SUPER HEROFS AND THE OCCULT
Nov 1980 (1)
Marvel
1 (64p) US reprints   25p–50p

MARVEL SUPER HEROES SUMMER SPECIAL
May 1979 (1)

Marvel
1 (nn) (52p) US reprints   25p–50p

MARVEL TALES
1959 (2?)
Miller (Atlas)
1–(68p) US reprints (small)   50p–75p

MARVEL TEAM-UP
11 Sep 1980–4 Mar 1981 (25)
Marvel
to: Spiderman
1 (32p) US reprints   15p–25p
2–25   10p–15p

MARVEL TEAM-UP WINTER SPECIAL
20 Nov 1980 (1)
Marvel
1 (52p) US reprints   25p–40p

MARVELMAN
3 Feb 1954–Feb 1963 (346)
Miller
1 (25) (28p) R. Parker   £2.00–£3.00
26–370 Don Lawrence   50p–£1.00

MARVELMAN FAMILY
Oct 1956–Nov 1959 (30)
Miller (Gower)
1 (28p) Don Lawrence   £1.00–£2.00
2–30 Leo Rawlings   50p–£1.00

MARVELMAN HOLIDAY SPECIAL
May 1984 (1)
Quality
1 reprints   50p–70p

MARY MARVEL
1947?
Miller (Fawcett)
1 (nn) (16p) (gravure) US reprint   £1.00–£1.75
(numbers vary)   75p–£1.00

MARY MOUSE SERIES
1942–1964 (22)
Brockhampton (Enid Blyton)
1: Mary Mouse & the Dolls House   £1.00–£2.00
2–22 (36p) (oblong)   50p–£1.00

MARY POPPINS TRAVELLING FUN BOOK
1964 (1)
Young World/Shell-Mex BP
1 (nn) (36p) (4C) sold in garages   50p–£1.00

MASKED RAIDER
1955 (4)
World (Charlton)
1 (28p) US reprint   50p–£1.00
2–4   50p–75p

MASKED RAIDER
1957–1958 (17)
Miller (Charlton)
1 (50) (28p) US reprint   50p–£1.00
51–66   50p–75p

MASKED RIDERS OF THE RANGE
1952 (1)
Cartoon Art (Magazine Enterprises)
1 (nn) (20p) US reprint   50p–£1.00

MASTER BUNNY SERIES
1951–1954 (3)
Brockhampton
1: Master Bunny the Bakers Boy (oblong)   50p–£1.00
2: Master Bunny at the Seaside   50p–75p
3: Master Bunny has a Birthday   50p–75p

MASTER COMICS
1945–1958 (95)

Miller (Fawcett)
1945: nn; nn; 49; 55 (gravure)   £1.00–£1.75
1946: (gravure) (outsize)   75p–£1.50
1950: 50–140 (28p)   50p–£1.00

MASTERMAN COMIC
Nov 1952–Aug 1953 (10)
Streamline (King-Ganteaume)
1 Joe Colquhoun   75p–£1.00
2–10   50p–75p

MATES
8 Feb 1975–29 Aug 1981 (342)
IPC
& *Pink*: 21 Jun 1980
to: *Oh Boy*
1 (40p)   20p–45p
2–342   10p–15p

MATES SUMMER SPECIAL
May 1977–May 1984 (8)
IPC
1 (56p) (photos)   15p–25p
2–8   15p–20p

MATT SLADE GUNFIGHTER
1957 (5)
Strato (Atlas)
1 (68p) US reprint   35p–75p
2–5   35p–50p

MAVERICK MARSHAL
1959 (3)
Miller (Charlton)
1 (50) (28p) US reprint   50p–75p
51–52   25p–50p

McLEAN'S MONTHLY SHEET OF CARICATURES
see: *Looking Glass*

THE MENU
1978
Rock Garden
1 (8p) (4C) restaurant menu in comic format 50p–£1.00
1 (2nd edition; differences)   50p–75p
2–   50p–75p

MERE QUACKS ALBUM
1976 (1)
Diss Express
1 (64p) Michael Webb strip reprint   50p–75p

MERLIN AND EXCALIBUR QUEST OF THE KING
Jul 1981 (1)
Marvel
1 (nn) US reprint   25p–50p

MERRIDAY COMIC
1948 (1)
McKenzie
1 (nn) (8p)   50p–£1.00

MERRY AND BRIGHT
22 Oct 1910–31 Mar 1917 (337)
AP
to: *Merry & Bright the Favorite Comic*
1 (8p) (tabloid) G. M. Payne   £5.00–£7.50
2–337 G. W. Wakefield   £1.50–£2.00

MERRY AND BRIGHT THE FAVORITE COMIC
7 Apr 1917–19 Jan 1935 (928)
AP
to: *Butterfly*
1 (12p) (tabloid) G. W. Wakefield   £5.00–£7.50
1917–1919 Fred Crompton   £1.50–£2.00
1920–1929 Reg Parlett   £1.25–£1.75
1930–1935 Roy Wilson   £1.25–£1.75

MERRY COMIC
1947 (1)

Hamilton
1 (nn) (16p) Bob Wilkin   50p–£1.00

MERRY COMICS
1944 (1)
PM (Marx)
1 (nn) (16p) Glyn Protheroe   50p–£1.00

MERRY-GO-ROUND
1946–1949 (14)
Martin & Reid
1 (8p) H. E. Pease   50p–£1.00
2–13 R. Beaumont   50p–£1.00
14 (tabloid) Frank Minnitt   75p–£1.25

MERRY-GO-ROUND
Nov 1946 (1)
Swinnerton
1 (8p)   50p–75p

MERRY-GO-ROUND
27 Sep–18 Oct 1949 (4)
Allen
to: *Eagle*
1–4 (12p) Bill Holroyd   50p–£1.00

MERRY-GO-ROUND COMIC
1947 (1)
Foldes
1 (nn) (12p) Bob Wilkin   50p–£1.00

MERRY MADCAP COMIC
1947 (1)
Philmar (Marx)
1 (nn) (8p) Ern Shaw   50p–£1.00

MERRY MAKER
1946–1948 (10)
Matthew (Martin & Reid)
1–10 (8p) H. E. Pease   50p–£1.00

MERRY MAKER COMIC
1946–1947 (11)
Algar/Burn
1 (8p) Walter Booth   75p–£1.00
2–11 Basil Reynolds   50p–£1.00

MERRY MARVEL COMIC
Sep 1947 (1)
Philmar (Marx)
1 (nn) (8p) Tony Speer   50p–£1.00

MERRY MASCOT
1947 (2)
Matthew (Martin & Reid)
1–2 (8p) H. E. Pease   50p–£1.00

MERRY MAYPOLE COMIC
1949 (1)
PM (Marx)
1 (nn) (8p) Walter Bell   50p–£1.00

MERRY MIDGET
12 Sep 1931–23 Jan 1932 (20)
Provincial
1 (8p) (tabloid) Bert Hill   £5.00–£7.50
2–20 Louis Diamond   £2.00–£2.50

MERRY MINIATURES
1937–1939
Home Publicity (giveaway booklets)
(a) 12p booklets (4C)   75p–£2.00
(b) 8p folders (3C)   75p–£1.50
(c) larger format (2C)   75p–£2.00
series: *Bruin Boys* H. Foxwell
         Arkubs J. Horrabin
         Nipper Brian White
         Popeye E. Segar (US)
         Pip Squeak & Wilfred A. Payne
         Golly (anon)

MERRY MIRTHQUAKE COMIC
1949 (1)
Philmar (Marx)
1 (nn) (8p) (tabloid) F. Minnitt   50p–£1.25

MERRY MOMENTS
12 Apr 1919–23 Dec 1922 (194)
Newnes
1 (8p) (tabloid)   £5.00–£10.00
2–194 Walter Bell   £2.00–£3.00
18 Feb 1922: 10p issues   £2.00–£2.50
16 Dec 1922: 8p issues   £2.00–£2.25

MERRY MOMENTS
17 Sep 1928–20 Apr 1929 (28)
Ransom (reprints *Golden Penny Comic*)
1 (8p) (tabloid) Jack Walker   £3.00–£5.00
2–28 Reg Carter   £1.50–£2.00

MERRY MOMENTS
Feb 1946–1948 (5)
Martin & Reid
1 (nn) (8p) H. E. Pease   50p–£1.00
1–4 (8p) Mick Anglo   50p–£1.00

MERRY PLAY
1949 (1)
PM (Marx)
1 (nn) (tabloid) (gravure) Walter Bell   75p–£1.25

MERRY PLAY COMIC
Sep 1947 (1)
Philmar (Marx)
1 (nn) (8p) Walter Bell   50p–£1.00

MERRY TALES
1970 (4)
Top Sellers
to: *Pellephant*
1–4 (36p) (4C) foreign reprint   15p–25p

MERRY-THOUGHT
Henderson
registration copies for title copyright only:
5 Feb 1910–30 Apr 1910 (13)   £2.50–£5.00
1 Oct 1910–31 Dec 1910 (14)   £2.50–£5.00

MERRY-THOUGHT AND SCRAPS
7 May 1910–24 Sep 1910 (21)
Henderson
1 (16p) (magazine) (4C)   £3.00–£5.00
2–21   £2.00–£2.50

MERRYMAKER
1947 (1)
National Sport
1 (nn) (12p)   50p–£1.00

METEOR
1948 (1)
Childrens Press
1 (nn) (20p) Sam Fair   £1.00–£2.00

METEOR
1948 (6)
Paget
1–5 (8p) Harry Banger   50p–£1.00
1 (8p) (larger) S. K. Perkins   50p–£1.00

MICK MARTIN
1949 (1)
Martin & Reid (Gower)
1 (8p) (tabloid) Mick Anglo   75p–£1.25

MICKEY AND DONALD
6 Sep 1975–18 Oct 1975 (7)
IPC (Disney)
to: *Mickey Mouse*
1–7   10p–15p

MICKEY MAGAZINE
6 Dec 1980–28 Mar 1981 (17)
IPC (Disney)
& *Walt Disney's Puzzle Time*: Jan 1981
1 (264) (32p) US reprints   20p–30p
265–280   10p–20p

MICKEY MOUSE
25 Oct 1975–29 Nov 1980 (263)
IPC (Disney)
& *Donald Duck*: 31 Jan 1976
& *Wonderful World of Disney*: 21 Feb 1976
& *Disneyland*: 20 Nov 1976
& *Disney Time*: 25 Jun 1977
to: *Mickey Magazine*
1 (24p) (4C) Basil Reynolds   25p–35p
2–263 Colin Wyatt   15p–20p

MICKEY MOUSE HOLIDAY SPECIAL
1936–1939 (4)
Willbank/Odhams (Disney)
1 (64p) (gravure) Basil Reynolds   £5.00–£15.00
2–4 (4: *Xmas Special*)   £5.00–£10.00

MICKEY MOUSE SPECIALS
May 1976–Jun 1980 (10)
IPC (Disney)
1: *Fun Time Extra 1976* (40p)   30p–50p
2: *Holiday Special 1976*   25p–45p
3: *Fun Time Extra 1977*   25p–45p
4: *Holiday Special 1977*   25p–45p
5: *Fun Time Extra 1978*   25p–45p
6: *Holiday Special 1978*   25p–45p
7: *Fun Time Extra 1979*   20p–40p
8: *Summer Special 1979*   20p–40p
9: *Fun Time Holiday Special 1980*   20p–40p
10: *Summer Special 1980*   20p–40p

MICKEY MOUSE WEEKLY
8 Feb 1936–28 Dec 1957 (920)
Willbank/Odhams (Disney)
aka: *Mickey Mouse*: 13 Sep 1941
     Mickey Mouse Weekly: 4 Mar 1950
     Mickey's Weekly: 1 Oct 1955
to: *Zip; Walt Disney's Mickey Mouse*
1 (12p) (tab) (gravure) Wilfred
     Haughton   £10.00–£20.00
1936–1939 Basil Reynolds   £2.50–£7.50
13 Jan 1940: size reduced   £2.50–£3.50
25 May 1940: 8p issues   £2.00–£3.00
5 Jul 1941: size reduced   £2.00–£3.00
13 Sep 1941: fortnightly   £2.00–£2.50
11 Apr 1942: size reduced   £2.00–£2.50
25 Dec 1948: enlarged   £1.00–£1.50
3 Sep 1949: 12p issues   £1.00–£1.50
4 Mar 1950: weekly   £1.00–£1.50
21 Oct 1950: enlarged   £1.00–£1.50
1951–1957   50p–75p

MICKEY'S WEEKLY
see: *Mickey Mouse Weekly*

MIDGET
5 Jun–5 Sep 1931 (13)
Provincial
to: *Merry Midget*
1 (a) 8p issue   £3.00–£5.00
  (b) 12p issue   £4.00–£6.00
2–13   £2.00–£2.50

MIDGET COMIC
23 Aug–12 Sep 1930 (4)
Thomson (*Wizard* giveaway)
1–4 (32p) (small) Alan Morley   £2.00–£3.50

MIDGET COMIC
21 Aug 1937 (1)
Thomson (*Red Letter* giveaway)
1 (nn) (36p) Allan Morley   £2.50–£3.00

MIDGET COMIC
1946 (1)
Locker
1 (nn) (folder) R. Beaumont   50p–£1.00

MIDGET COMICS
1944 (1)
PM (Marx)
1 (nn) (8p) (small) G. Protheroe   50p–£1.00

MIGHTY ATOM
1948 (1)
Denlee
1 (nn) (16p) (large) P. Mendoza   75p–£1.50

MIGHTY COMIC
1945 (1)
Marx
1 (nn) (16p) Glyn Protheroe   50p–£1.00

MIGHTY COMIC ANNUAL
1952 (1)
Swan
rebound remainders in new cover (Williams)
1 (nn) *Topical Funnies* 36
        Western War Comic 1
        Comicolour 7
        Scramble 53
        New Funnies 42
        Thrill Comics 35
        Kiddyfun 3, 6, 7
        Boys Fun (coverless)   £2.00–£3.50

MIGHTY MIDGET
18 Sep 1976–25 Sep 1976 (2)
Polystyle (supplement: *Mighty TV Comic*)
1: *Doctor Who Comic* (16p) reprint   50p–£1.00
2: *Star Trek* (16p) reprint   35p–75p

MIGHTY MIDGET COMIC
5 Jul–26 Jul 1958 (4)
AP (*Knockout* giveaway)
1–4 Hugh McNeill   50p–75p

MIGHTY MOTH SPECIAL
Nov 1980–May 1981 (2)
Polystyle
1: *Winter Special* (48p) Dick Millington
   reprints   35p–50p
2: *Summer Special*   20p–35p

MIGHTY TV COMIC
see: *T.V. Comic*

MIGHTY THOR
20 Apr 1983–
Marvel
& *Original X-Men*: 31 Aug 1983
1: (4C) US reprints   15p–25p
2–   10p–20p

MIGHTY WORLD OF MARVEL
7 Oct 1972–17 Jan 1979 (329)
Marvel
& *Avengers*: 21 Jul 1976
& *Planet of the Apes*: 2 Mar 1977
& *Fury*: 7 Sep 1977
& *Fantastic Four*: 15 Jun 1978
to: *Marvel Comic*
1 (40p) (US reprints)   50p–£1.00
2–329   25p–35p

MIGHTY WORLD OF MARVEL (MONTHLY)
Jun 1983–Oct 1984 (17)
Marvel
& *Daredevils*: Dec 1983
to: *Savage Sword of Conan*
1 (52p) (4C) US reprints   50p–65p
2–17   25p–50p

MIGHTY WORLD OF MARVEL SUMMER
SPECIAL

Jun 1983
Marvel
1 (48p) US reprints   40p–60p

MIKE
Nov 1984–
Trustee Savings Bank/BMC
1 (24p) (4C) promo   15p–25p
2–   10p–15p

MIKE BARNETT MAN AGAINST CRIME
1952 (5)
Miller (Fawcett)
1 (50) (28p) US reprint   50p–£1.00
51–54   50p–75p

MIKE DONOVAN DETECTIVE COMIC
1951 (1)
Arnold
1 (50) (36p)   50p–£1.00

MIKE SHAYNE PRIVATE EYE
1962 (1)
Top Sellers (Dell)
1 (68p) US reprint   35p–75p

MINIATURE COMIC
Aug 1944 (2)
PM (Marx)
1–2 (nn) (small)   50p–£1.00

MINI-COMIC SERIES
20 Feb–6 Mar 1965 (3)
City (*Huckleberry Hound* giveaway)
1: *Huckleberry Hound*   25p–50p
2: *Yogi Bear*   25p–50p
3: *Flintstones*   25p–50p

MINI MONSTER COMIC BOOK
12 Oct–2 Nov 1974 (4)
IPC (*Whoopee* giveaway)
1 (32p in 4 parts) Reg Parlett   25p–50p

MIRABELLE
10 Sep 1956–22 Oct 1977 (1099)
Pearson/IPC
aka: *New Mirabelle* 19 Feb 1977
& *New Glamour*: 7 Oct 1958
& *Marty*: 2 Feb 1963
& *Valentine*: 16 Nov 1974
to: *Pink*
1 (32p)   £1.00–£1.75
2–1099   25p–75p

MIRABELLE POP FILM AND TV STAR
LIBRARY
3 Sep 1959–
Pearson
1 (68p)   75p–£1.00
2–   50p–75p

MIRABELLE SUMMER SPECIAL
1977 (1)
IPC
1 (56p)   25p–50p

MIRACLE MAN
1965 (13)
Top Sellers
1– (68p) foreign reprint   35p–75p

MIRACULOUS CIRCUMSTANCES
1981
Luddite Enterprises
1 (16p) (adult)   25p–50p

MIRROR MAN COMIC
1950 (1)
Peters (United Features)
1 (21) (20p) US reprint   50p–£1.00

MIRTH COMIC
1948 (1)
Philmar (Marx)
1 (nn) (8p) Tony Speer   50p–£1.00

MISHA
Jul 1983–
Soviet Union
1 (32p) (4C) Russian reprints   25p–50p
2–   20p–40p

MISTY
4 Feb 1978–12 Jan 1980 (102)
IPC
to: *Tammy*
1 (32p)   15p–25p
2–102   10p–15p

MISTY SPECIALS
Apr 1978–Apr 1980 (3)
IPC
1 (64p) *Summer Special*   25p–40p
2–3 *Holiday Special*   15p–25p

MOBY DICK
1951 (2)
Streamline
1 (nn) (28p) US reprint   50p–75p
2 (nn) (68p)   35p–75p

MODERN COMICS
Oct 1949 (1)
Modern Fiction
1 (8p) Bob Monkhouse   75p–£1.25

MODESTY BLAISE
Apr 1978–
Star Books (*Evening Standard* reprints)
1: *Black Pearl*   70p–£1.00
2–   50p–70p

MONEY FUN
1981–1982 (2)
National Savings/Creative Comics (giveaway)
1 (8p) (4C) Jim Baikie   25p–50p
2 Basil Reynolds   15p–25p

MONEYBOX
1945? (2)
National Savings (giveaway)
1 (221) (4p) (4C)   75p–£1.50
2 (257) (4p) (4C)   50p–£1.25

MONSTER CLUB
1980 (1)
Chips/Pioneer Press (giveaway)
1 (nn) (32p) film promo; John Bolton   50p–£2.00

MONSTER COMIC
9 Mar 1898–14 Jun 1898 (14)
Shurey
1 (16p)   £5.00–£10.00
2–14   £2.00–£2.50

MONSTER COMIC
23 Sep 1922–25 Jan 1930 (383)
United/Federated/Fleetway/AP
1 (8p) (tabloid) Reg Carter   £5.50–£7.50
1922–1927 Walter Bell   £1.75–£2.50
21 Jan 1928: first AP   £1.50–£2.00
1928–1930 Harry Banger   £1.25–£1.75

MONSTER COMIC
Jun–Nov 1939 (2)
Pearson
1 (nn) (32p)   £3.50–£5.00
2 (nn) (Xmas) Hugh McNeill   £3.50–£5.00

MONSTER COMIC
1945 (1)

Marx
1 (nn) (16p) Glyn Protheroe   50p–£1.00

MONSTER FUN COMIC
14 Jun 1975–30 Oct 1976 (72)
IPC
to:*Buster*
1 (32p) Leo Baxendale   25p–35p
2–72 Robert Nixon   10p–20p

MONSTER FUN COMIC SUMMER SPECIAL
1976 (1)
IPC
1 (64p) Robert Nixon   25p–35p
see: *Buster & Monster Fun Specials*

MONSTER MONTHLY
Apr 1982–Dec 1982 (9)
Marvel
1 (56p) US reprints   25p–50p
2–9   20p–40p

MONTE HALE WESTERN
Sep 1950–1959 (69)
Miller (Fawcett)
1 (nn) (16p) (gravure) US reprint   75p–£1.50
50 (Jun 1951)–118   50p–£1.00

MONTHLY PLAYBOX
Nov 1904–Apr 1905 (6)
AP (supplement: *World and his Wife*)
to: *Playbox*
1 (4C) (first Tiger Tim)   £5.00–£10.00
2–6   £3.50–£5.00

MOON COMICS
1948 (1)
Halle
1 (nn) (8p) *Comic Capers* reprint   50p–£1.00

MOON COMIX
1977 (2)
Birmingham Arts Lab
1 (32p) Hunt Emerson (adult)   50p–75p
2 (40p) David Noon   50p–75p

MORECAMBE AND WISE COMIC BOOK
1977 (1)
Corgi/Carousel
1 (100p) Terry Wakefield (small)   50p–£1.00

MOSES DESERT COMMANDER
1979 (1)
Lion/Fleurus
1 (nn) (52p) (4C) French reprint   50p–95p

MOTION PICTURE COMICS
Mar 1951–1952 (10)
Miller (Fawcett)
1: *Code of the Silver Sage*   £1.00–£2.00
2–10 US reprints   £1.00–£1.75

MOVIE CLASSICS
1955–1960 (88)
World (Dell)
1 (36p) (4C) *Sir Walter Raleigh*   50p–£1.00
2–88 US reprints   35p–75p

MR BENN SUMMER SPECIAL
May 1981 (1)
Polystyle
1 (nn) (48p) reprints (TV series)   35p–50p

MR CRABTREE GOES FISHING
1951 (1)
Mirror Books (*Daily Mirror* reprints)
1 (96p) (oblong)   50p–75p

MR CRABTREE'S FISHING WITH THE
EXPERTS
May 1978 (1)
Mirror Books (*Daily Mirror* reprints)
1 (nn) (160p) Bernard Venables (oblong)   50p–75p

MR DIGWELL'S EVERYDAY GARDEN BOOK
Mar 1980 (1)
Mirror (*Daily Mirror* reprints)
1 (nn) Books Bernard Venables (oblong)   50p–95p

MR DIGWELL'S GARDENING BOOK
1969–1975 (2)
Mirror/Hamlyn (*Daily Mirror* reprint)
1 (1969) Bernard Venables (oblong)   35p–50p
2 (1975)   25p–35p

MR DISTRICT ATTORNEY
1953 (23)
Strato/Thorpe & Porter (DC)
1 (68p) US reprint   50p–£1.00
2–23   35p–75p

MR MEN
1978 (2)
Mirror Books (*Daily Mirror* reprints)
1 (84p) (oblong) Roger Hargreaves   25p–50p
2   20p–45p

MR MEN SPECIALS
1975–1980 (2)
IPC
1: *Playhour Mr Men Special* (48p)   25p–35p
2: *Mr Men Holiday Special* (40p)   25p–30p

MR PERRY WINK'S SUBMARINE
ADVENTURES
1860 (1)
Kershaw
1 (12p) (oblong) T. Onwhyn   £5.00–£10.00

MRS WEBER'S DIARY
1982 (1)
Fontana (Cape)
1 (nn) (68p) (oblong)   £1.50–£2.50
Posy Simmonds *Guardian* strip reprints

MUFFIN AND HIS FRIENDS
1953 (1)
Brockhampton
1 (68p) (oblong)   50p–£1.00

THE MUMMY
1963 (1)
Top Sellers (Dell)
1 (nn) (68p) US reprint   50p–£1.00

MUNCHER
1978–1981 (3)
Trent Press/Wimpy (giveaway)
1 (8p) (4C) hamburger promo   25p–50p
2 (nn) (1979) 3 (nn) (1981)   20p–25p

MURDER BAG
11 Apr–21 Sep 1959 (3)
Pearson (*T.V. Picture Stories*)
1 (TVP 7) *Prison Break Murders*   25p–£1.00
2 (TVP 14) *Death of Big Foot*   25p–75p
3 (TVP 21) *Too Tidy Murder*   25p–75p

MUSTANG GREY AND THE TEXAS RANGERS
see: *Western Picture Library*

MY FAVOURITE
28 Jan 1928–13 Oct 1934 (351)
AP
to: *Sparkler*
1 (12p) (tabloid) G. Wakefield   £5.00–£10.00
2–351   £1.50–£2.00

MY FUNNYBONE
4 Sep 1911–22 Apr 1913 (86)
Belvedere/Milford
1 (8p) (tabloid) George Davey   £5.00–£10.00
2–32   £1.50–£2.00
33–86 (Milford; reprints)   £1.25–£1.50

MY GUY
4 Mar 1978–
IPC
& *Heartbeat*: 17 Apr 1982
& *Oh Boy*: 19 Jan 1985
1 (40p) (photos)   10p–25p
2–   5p–10p

MY GUY HOLIDAY SPECIAL
Apr 1979–
IPC
1 (56p) (photos)   20p–40p
2–

MY GUY MONTHLY
Aug 1984–
IPC
1 (5) (68p) (reprints)   10p–15p
6–   10p–15p

MY GUY SUMMER SPECIAL
Jun 1979–
IPC
1 (56p) (photos)   20p–40p
2–   15p–20p

MY HORSE
May 1973–1974
Top Sellers
1– (36p) (4C)   20p–35p

MY OWN ROMANCE
195– (13)
Miller (Atlas)
1 (28p) US reprint   25p–50p
2–13   15p–25p

MY SECRET CONFESSIONS
1955 (1)
Class (Sterling)
1 (68p) US reprint   35p–50p

MYRA
1982–
Myra Magazines
1– (20p) Myra Hancock   25p–50p

MYSTERIES OF SCOTLAND YARD
1955 (1)
Cartoon Art (Magazine Enterprises)
1 (28p) US reprint   75p–£1.00

MYSTERIES OF UNEXPLORED WORLDS
1956
Miller (Charlton)
1– (68p) US reprint   £1.00–£1.25

MYSTERY COMIC
30 Sep 1978 (1)
IPC
supplement to *Cheeky*
1 (nn)   5p–10p

MYSTERY COMICS
1940–1941 (5)
Boardman (Quality)
1 (7) (36p) (4C) US reprint   £2.00–£3.50
8–11 (20p)   £1.50–£2.00

MYSTERY IN SPACE
1952–1954 (9)
Miller (DC)
1 (28p) US reprint   £1.00–£1.50
2–9   75p–£1.00

MYSTERY IN SPACE
1954–1955 (13)
Strato (DC)
1 (68p) US reprint   £1.00–£1.50
2–13   75p–£1.00

MYSTIC
1961–1966 (66)
Miller (Atlas/EC)
1 (68p) US reprint   £1.50–£2.00
2–66   50p–£1.00

NAPALM KISS
Oct 1977 (1)
Birmingham Arts Lab
1 (32p) (adult) M. Mathews   50p–75p

NASTY TALES
Apr 1971–1972 (7)
Bloom/Meep Comix
1 Chris Welch (adult)   75p–£2.00
2–7 Edward Barker   75p–£1.00

NATURE BOY
1957 (2)
Miller (Charlton)
1–2 (28p) US reprint   50p–75p

NAVY PATROL
1955 (1)
Streamline/United Anglo-American (Key)
1 (68p) US reprint   50p–75p

NAVY TASK FORCE
1955 (1)
Streamline/United Anglo-American (Stanmor)
1 (28p) US reprint   50p–75p

NEAR MYTHS
Sep 1978–Dec 1978 (3)
Galaxy Media
1 (44p) (adult) Bryan Talbot   50p–£1.00
2–3 (52p) Graham Manley   50p–75p

NEW ADVENTURES OF BARBARELLA
1981 (4)
Virgin
1–4 (24p) French reprints   £1.00–£2.00

NEW ADVENTURES OF CHARLIE CHAN
Jun 1958–16 May 1959 (6)
Pearson (*T.V. Picture Stories*)
1 *Three Men on a Raft*   50p–£1.00
2 *Dateline Execution*   25p–75p
3 *Death of Don*   25p–75p
4 *The Sweater*   25p–75p
5 (TVP 3) *No Future for Fred*   25p–75p
6 (TVP 12) *Noble Art of Murder*   25p–75p

NEW ADVENTURES OF DON JUAN
1948 (1)
Pett
1 (20p) (Errol Flynn film) Norman Pett   £2.00–£5.00

NEW COMICS
1942 (2)
Marx
1 (nn) (blue) (tabloid) Frank Jupo   £2.00–£3.50
2 (nn) (blue/green)   £2.00–£3.00

NEW DIANA
see: *Diana*

NEW FUNNIES
Feb 1940–Jan 1951 (49)
Swan
1 (64p) William Ward   £2.50–£5.00
2–4 (64p) Harry Banger   £2.00–£3.50
5–14 (36p) John McCail   £1.75–£2.50
15 (28p) D. L. West   £1.50–£2.00

16–25 (20p) G. Protheroe   £1.25–£1.50
26–28 (16p) John Turner   £1.00–£1.25
29 (16p) format change   £1.00–£1.25
30–38 (16p) William McCail   £1.00–£1.25
39–42 (20p) Murdock Stimpson   £1.00–£1.25
Specials:
Spring/Autumn/Winter 1941 (52p)   £2.00–£3.00
Winter 1942 (44p)   £2.00–£3.00
Spring/Special 1943 (36p)   £2.00–£2.50
Winter 1944   £2.00–£2.50
see: *Bumper New Funnies*

NEW GLAMOUR
16 Oct 1956–30 Sep 1958 (102)
Pearson
aka: *Glamour*
to: *Mirabelle*
1 (32p) (women's comic)   75p–£1.50
2–102   25p–50p

NEW HOTSPUR
24 Oct 1959–9 Feb 1963 (173)
Thomson
to: *Hotspur*
1 (28p) Dudley Watkins   50p–£1.00
2–173   25p–35p

NEW JOKER
4 Nov 1897–13 Jan 1898 (11)
Greyfriars
to: *Jokes*
1 (24p) (magazine)   £5.00–£7.50
2–11   £1.50–£2.00

NEW JUNGLE COMICS
1950 (1)
Cartoon Art
1 (nn) (36p) Dennis Reader   £1.50–£2.50

NEW LADY PENELOPE
see: *Lady Penelope*

NEW PRINCESS AND GIRL
see: *Princess*

NEW ROBIN AND STORYTIME
see: *Robin*

NEW SHOOT
see: *Shoot*

NEW WORLDS COMIC
1947 (1)
Cardal
1 (8p) Crewe Davies   75p–£1.25

NEWSPAPER COMIC PRESENTS SCOOPS
10 Sep 1982–7 Dec 1982 (13)
25 Jan 1983–19 Apr 1983 (13)
Newsdesk Promotions
Portsmouth News supplement (1–26)
Basildon Evening Echo supplement (1–13)
East Hampshire Post (1–13)
1 (4p) (tabloid) Ron Smith   10p–20p
2–26 Sandy Calder   5p–10p

NICHOLAS THOMAS STRIP BOOKS
1953 (1)
Sampson Low Marston
1: *Nicholas & Timothy's Adventure*   50p–75p

NIGHTMARE
197–
Top Sellers
1 (36p) US reprints   20p–50p
2–   15p–25p

NIGHTMARE SUSPENSE PICTURE LIBRARY
1966–1967 (14)
MV Features

1 (68p) *March of Boneless One*	35p–75p	
2–14	25p–50p	

NIMBLE NORMAN
1948 (2)

1 (nn) (toll bridge cover) (4C)	50p–£1.00
2 (nn) (cup-tie cover)	50p–£1.00

NIPPER
Jun 1944 (1)
White

1 (nn) (small) (20p) Brian White	75p–£1.25

NIPPER ANNUAL
1934–1941 (8)
Daily Mail

1 (undated) (132p) Brian White reprints	£3.00–£5.00
2–3 (16p in 2C)	£2.50–£4.00
4–6 (16p in 4C)	£2.50–£4.00
7–8 (small; wartime)	£2.50–£3.50

NIPPER CARTOONS: 100 OF THE BEST
Oct 1946 (1)
White

1 (nn) (36p) Brian White reprints	£1.00–£1.50

NIPPER OMNIBUS OF COMIC STRIPS
1948 (1)
White

1 (nn) (100p) Brian White reprints	£1.50–£2.50

NODDY AND HIS FRIENDS
9 Mar 1974–30 Apr 1975 (49)
Hudvale
to: *Noddy Time*

1 (16p) Enid Blyton	35p–50p
2–49	20p–25p

NODDY AND HIS FRIENDS SUMMER SPECIAL
Jun 1974 (1)
Hudvale

1 (48p) Enid Blyton	35p–50p

NODDY AND HIS FRIENDS CHRISTMAS
SPECIAL
Dec 1974 (1)
Hudvale

1 (48p) Enid Blyton	35p–50p

NODDY STRIP BOOKS
1952–1953 (9)
Sampson Low Marston (Enid Blyton)

1: *Noddy's Car Gets a Squeak* (oblong)	£1.00–£2.00
2: *Noddy's Penny Wheel Car*	50p–£1.50
3: *Noddy & the Witch's Wand*	50p–£1.50
4: *Noddy & the Cuckoo's Nest*	50p–£1.50
5: *Noddy Gets Captured*	50p–£1.50
6: *Noddy Is Very Silly*	50p–£1.50
7: *Noddy the Cry Baby*	50p–£1.50
8: *Noddy Goes Dancing*	50p–£1.50
9: *Noddy & the Snow House*	50p–£1.50

NODDY TIME
10 May 1975–
Woman's Way

1 (16p) Enid Blyton	35p–50p
2–	25p–30p

NODDY TIME SPECIALS
May–Nov 1975 (2)

1: *Summer Special 1975* Enid Blyton	25p–50p
2: *Christmas Special 1975*	25p–35p

NORTHERN LOOKING GLASS
18 Aug 1925–3 Aug 1926 (12)
John Watson
(change of title from *Glasgow Looking Glass*)

1 (6) (4p) (tabloid)	£5.00–£10.00
7–17	£5.00–£10.00

NB: facsimile (reduced) editions

1906 (D. Brycc)	£1.00–£2.00

NOSEY PARKER'S HOLIDAY COMIC
2 Jul 1938 (1)
Thomson
supplement to *Rover* (story-paper)

1 (nn) (16p) (small) Allan Morley	£1.50–£2.50

NOSEY PARKER'S MIDGET COMIC
21 Dec 1935 (1)
Thomson (*Rover* giveaway)

1 (nn) (32p) (small) Allan Morley	£2.50–£3.50

NOW I KNOW
see: *Walt Disney's Now I Know*

NUGGETS
26 Nov 1892–28 Jan 1905 (636)
Henderson
& *Garland*: 5 Aug 1900
to: *New Series*

1 (30) (16p) Julius Stafford Baker	£5.00–£7.50
31–636	£1.75–£2.25

NUGGETS NEW SERIES
4 Feb 1905–22 Jul 1905 (25)
Henderson
to: *New Series*

1 (24p)	£5.00–£7.50
2–25	£1.50–£2.00

NUGGETS NEW SERIES
29 Jul 1905–10 Mar 1906 (34)
Henderson
to: *Lot-O'-Fun*

1 (16p)	£5.00–£7.50
2–34	£1.75–£2.25

NUMBER TEN (NO.10)
1973 (1)
Beaverbrook (*Sunday Express* reprints)

1 (nn) (76p) Peter Maddocks	50p–75p

NURSE LINDA LARK
1965 (1)
Top Sellers (Dell)

1 (68p) US reprint	20p–30p

NURSERYLAND SERIES
1945? (4)
Cooke

1 (oblong) *Simple Simon*	50p–75p
2 *Simple Simon in Nurseryland*	50p–75p
3 *London Bridge is Broken Down*	50p–75p
4 *Tom Tom the Pipers Son*	50p–75p

NUTTY
23 Feb 1980–
Thomson

1 (24p)	15p–25p
2–	10p–15p

NUTTY BOYS
Jan 1981–
Madness Comix

1 (24p) (pop group fan club comic)	50p–£1.00
2–	25p–50p

NYOKA THE JUNGLE GIRL
1950–1959 (69)
Miller (Fawcett)

1 (nn) (16p) (gravure) US reprints	£1.00–£1.75
50–117	75p–£1.25

O.S.S.
Jun 1958–Nov 1959 (9)
Pearson (*T.V. Picture Stories*)

1: *Operation Flintaxe*	25p–£1.00
2: *Operation Fracture*	25p–75p
3: *Operation Payday*	25p–75p
4: *Operation Tulip*	25p–75p
5: *Operation Sweet Talk*	25p–75p
6: (TVP 5) *Operation Big House*	25p–75p

7: (TVP 18) *Operation Orange Blossom*   25p–75p
8: (TVP 26) *Operation Dagger*   25p–75p
9: (TVP 29) *Operation Lovebirds*   25p–75p

OFFICE HOURS
1931 (1)
Lane (*Daily Express* strips)
1 (nn) (68p) Batchelor reprints   £2.50–£4.00

OGOTH AND UGLY BOOT
Dec 1973 (1)
H. Bunch/Cozmic Comix
1 (36p) Chris Welch (adult)   25p–75p

OH BOY
23 Oct 1976–12 Jan 1985 (428)
IPC
& *Mates*: 5 Sep 1981
& *Photo Love*: 5 Feb 1982
to: *My Guy*
1 (40p)   10p–20p
2–428   5p–10p

OH BOY AND WONDERMAN
1951 (1)
Paget
1 (22) (28p) Stanley White   75p–£1.50

OH BOY COMICS
1948–1951 (24)
Paget
1 (8p) Bob Monkhouse   £1.50–£3.00
2–4   £1.00–£2.00
5–7 Mick Anglo   50p–£1.00
8–15 (12p issues)   50p–£1.00
16–20 (16p issues)   50p–£1.00
21, 23, 24 (12p)   35p–75p
22: see *Oh Boy and Wonderman*

OH BOY HOLIDAY/SUMMER SPECIAL
May 1977–1983 (7)
IPC
1 (56p)   20p–30p
2–   10p–15p

OH BOY MONTHLY
Nov 1984–
IPC
1 (68p) reprints   10p–15p
2–   10p–15p

OH WICKED WANDA
Jul 1976 (1)
Penthouse
1 (nn) (4C) Ron Embleton reprints   £1.50–£2.50

OKAY COMIC
Jan 1947–Apr 1949 (4)
International (1) Burnside (2–4)
1 (nn) (20p) J. R. Turner   75p–£1.50
2 (nn) (16p) J. R. Turner   75p–£1.00
3 (nn) (8p) Bob Monkhouse   75p–£1.00
4 (nn) (tabloid) P. Brennan   £1.00–£1.50

OKAY COMICS WEEKLY
16 Oct 1937–26 Feb 1938 (20)
Boardman (US Sunday comics reprint)
1 (16p) Eisner cover   £5.00–£10.00
2 Eisner cover   £2.00–£7.50
3–12 (Vol 1)   £2.00–£3.00
Vol 2; 1–7   £2.00–£2.50

OKLAHOMA KID
1957 (1)
Miller (Ajax)
1 (28p) US reprint   50p–75p

OLD MURPHY'S COMIC KALENDAR
Dec 1880–
Diprose & Bateman

1 (32p) H. Heath   £5.00–£7.50
2–   £3.50–£5.00

OMPA-PA
1977 (2)
Egmont/Methuen (Lombard)
1: *O & Brother Two Scalp* (36p) (4C)   50p–75p
2: *O Saves the Day* foreign reprint   25p–50p

ON THE LINE
1969 (1)
Kaye & Ward (*Evening News* reprints)
1 (116p) (oblong) George Stokes   35p–50p

ONLY MY FUN
22 Oct 1908 (1)
AP (free in *Wonder Box* 4)
1 (nn) (16p) (3C) J. S. Baker   £2.00–£5.00

OOJAH SKETCH
8 Oct 1921–23 Nov 1929 (422)
London Publishing Co
supplement to *Daily Sketch* newspaper
first issue only: *The Oojah's Paper*
1 (4p) (tabloid) Thomas Maybank   £2.00–£5.00
2–22 Apr 1922 (4p) Will Owen   £1.50–£2.00
29 Apr 1922–15 Jul 1922 (3p)   £1.25–£1.50
22 Jul 1922–23 Nov 1929 (2p)   50p–£1.00

OOJAH'S PAPER
6 Oct 1921
first issue of *Oojah Sketch*; see under this title

OOR WULLIE SUMMER FUN SPECIAL
Jun 1980–
Thomson
1 (36p)   25p–35p
2–   15p–20p

OPTIMIST
1976 (1)
Comic Collective
1 (16p) (tabloid) (2C) adult comic   25p–50p

ORANGE HAND
1974 (1)
Orange Hand (giveaway)
1 (nn) (6p) Batman (promo)   50p–£1.00

ORIGINAL X-MEN
27 Apr 1983–23 Aug 1983 (17)
Marvel
to: *Mighty Thor*
1 (4C) US reprints   15p–25p
2–17   10p–20p

OUR WONDERFUL EMPIRE
1938 (1)
Sunday Pictorial
1 (56p) (oblong) Hellier reprints   £1.00–£2.50

OUT-AND-OUT SMASHER COMIC
1947 (1)
PJ
1 (nn) (8p) R. Plummer   50p–£1.25

OUT OF THIS WORLD
Oct 1951–1953 (22)
Strato/Thorpe & Porter (Avon)
1 (68p) US reprint   50p–£1.50
2–22   50p–£1.00

OUT OF THIS WORLD
196–
Class (Charlton)
1 (nn) (68p) US reprint   50p–£1.00
2 (1)   50p–£1.00
3– (2–)   35p–50p
2nd series (Class Series)
1 (52p)   20p–35p
2–   15p–25p

OUTER SPACE
1958
Miller (Charlton)
1– (68p) US reprint   50p–£1.00

OUTER SPACE
1961 (9)
Class (Charlton)
1 (68p) US reprint   50p–£1.00
2–9   50p–75p

OUTLAWS
1955 (1)
Streamline/United Anglo-American
1 (68p) US reprint   50p–75p
see: *Blue Bolt Series*

OUTLAWS OF THE WEST
1958
Miller (Charlton)
1– (28p) US reprint   35p–50p

OUTLAWS WESTERN STORIES
1954 (2)
Streamline/United Anglo-American
1–2 (28p) US reprint   50p–75p

OUTPOST ADVENTURE COMIC
1950 (1)
Martin & Reid (Gower)
1 (16p) Mick Anglo   50p–£1.00

OVALTINEY'S OWN COMIC
16 Oct 1935–2 Apr 1938 (128)
Target (supplement)
1 (4p) S. K. Perkins (promo)   £3.00–£5.00
2–128 Louis Diamond   £1.50–£2.00

PADDINGTON'S CARTOONS
1979 (1)
Collins/Fontana Picture Lions
1 (nn) (36p) (4C) Ivor Wood   50p–75p

PAGET ACE COMIC
1949 (1)
1 (nn) (12p) Harry Banger   50p–£1.00

PAGET ACME COMIC
1949 (1)
1 (nn) (12p) Wally Robertson   50p–£1.00

PAGET ACTION COMIC
1949 (1)
1 (nn) (12p) S. K. Perkins   50p–£1.00

PAGET BAGS O' FUN COMIC
1949 (1)
1 (nn) (12p) Harry Banger   50p–£1.00

PAGET BUDGET O' FUN COMIC
1949 (1)
1 (nn) (12p) Harry Banger   £1.00–£2.00

PAGET BUMPER TOTS COMIC
1950 (1)
1 (nn) (8p) (tabloid) Mick Anglo   50p–£1.00

PAGET DADDLE TUPNEY
1949 (1)
1 (nn) (12p) Dick Brook   50p–£1.00

PAGET DALLY COMIC
1949 (1)
1 (nn) (12p) S. K. Perkins   50p–£1.00

PAGET DANDY TUPNEY
1949 (1)
1 (nn) (12p) Harry Banger   50p–£1.00

PAGET DAPPER COMIC
1949 (1)
1 (nn) (12p) S. K. Perkins   50p–£1.00

PAGET DASHING TUPNEY
1949 (1)
1 (nn) (12p) Harry Banger   50p–£1.00

PAGET DAZZLE TUPNEY
1949 (1)
1 (nn) (12p) Harry Banger   50p–£1.00

PAGET DEBONAIR TUPNEY
1949 (1)
1 (nn) (12p) Dick Brook   50p–£1.00

PAGET DEMON TUPNEY
1949 (1)
1 (nn) (12p) Jack Bridges   50p–£1.00

PAGET DEPENDABLE TUPNEY
1949 (1)
1 (nn) (12p) Harry Banger   50p–£1.00

PAGET DIAMOND TUPNEY
1949 (1)
1 (nn) (12p) Harry Banger   50p–£1.00

PAGET FUN COMIC
1949 (1)
1 (nn) (12p) Harry Banger   50p–£1.00

PAGET FUNNY CUTS COMIC
1949 (4)
1–4 (12p) Wally Robertson   50p–£1.00

PAGET GUSTO
1948 (1)
1 (nn) (8p) Mick Anglo   50p–£1.00

PAGET HAPPY FUNNY CUTS COMIC
1949 (1)
1 (nn) (12p) Wally Robertson   50p–£1.00

PAGET HAPPY LAUGHS
1949 (1)
1 (nn) (12p) Harry Banger   50p–£1.00

PAGET HEADY FUNNY CUTS COMIC
1949 (1)
1 (nn) (12p) Wally Robertson   50p–£1.00

PAGET HEARTY FUNNY CUTS COMIC
1949 (1)
1 (nn) (12p) Wally Robertson   50p–£1.00

PAGET HELLO FUNNY CUTS COMIC
1949 (1)
1 (nn) (12p) Wally Robertson   50p–£1.00

PAGET JOLLY LAUGHS
1949 (1)
1 (nn) (12p) Harry Banger   50p–£1.00

PAGET MERRY LAUGHS
1949 (1)
1 (nn) (12p) Harry Banger   50p–£1.00

PAGET PAGEANT COMIC
1948 (1)
1 (nn) (8p) Harry Banger   50p–£1.00

PAGET PARADE COMIC
1949 (1)
1 (nn) (12p) Harry Banger   50p–£1.00

PAGET PEP COMIC
1948 (1)
1 (nn) (8p) Harry Banger   50p–£1.00

PAGET PICNIC COMIC
1949 (1)
1 (nn) (12p) Harry Banger   50p–£1.00

PAGET PINNACLE COMIC
1949 (1)
1 (nn) (12p) Harry Banger   50p–£1.00

PAGET PLAY COMIC
1948 (1)
1 (nn) (8p) Harry Banger   50p–£1.00

PAGET PLEASURE COMIC
1948 (1)
1 (nn) (8p) Harry Banger   50p–£1.00

PAGET PLUS COMIC
1948 (1)
1 (nn) (8p) Harry Banger   50p–£1.00

PAGET POPULAR COMIC
1948 (1)
1 (nn) (8p) Harry Banger   50p–£1.00

PAGET PRINCE OF COMICS
1949 (1)
1 (nn) (12p) S. K. Perkins   50p–£1.00

PAGET PRIZE COMIC
Mar 1949 (1)
1 (nn) (8p) Harry Banger   50p–£1.00

PAGET PUKKA COMIC
1948 (1)
1 (nn) (8p) Harry Banger   50p–£1.00

PAGET SLAM COMIC
1948 (1)
1 (nn) (8p) Harry Banger   50p–£1.00

PAGET SLICK COMIC
Mar 1949 (1)
1 (nn) (8p) HarryBanger   50p–£1.00

PAGET SNAPPY COMIC
Mar 1949 (1)
1 (nn) (8p) Harry Banger   50p–£1.00

PAGET SNIPS
1948 (1)
1 (nn) (8p) Harry Banger   50p–£1.00

PAGET SPARKLE COMIC
1948 (1)
1 (nn) (8p) Harry Banger   50p–£1.00

PAGET SPREE COMIC
1948 (1)
1 (nn) (8p) Harry Banger   50p–£1.00

PAGET SUPER
Mar 1949 (1)
1 (nn) (8p) Harry Banger   50p–£1.00

PAGET SUPER DUPER COMIC
1950 (1)
1 (nn) (16p) Harry Banger   50p–£1.25

PAGET SURE-FIRE COMIC
1948 (1)
1 (nn) (8p) Harry Banger   50p–£1.00

PAGET TUPNEY
1949 (2)
1–2 (12p) Harry Banger   50p–£1.00

PAGET ZEST
1948 (1)
1 (nn) (8p) Harry Banger   50p–£1.00

PANCHO VILLA WESTERN COMIC
1954–1959 (63)
Miller (King-Ganteaume)
1 (28p) Colin Andrew   50p–£1.00
2–63 George Bunting   25p–50p

PANDA COMICS
1949 (1)
BB (Birn)
1 (nn) (16p) (gravure) Marten Toonder   £1.50–£3.50

PANGO
1953–1954
Mundial (Miller)
1 (no unknown) (28p) foreign reprint   50p–75p
–80   35p–50p

PANTO PLAYTIME
1948 (1)
Hotspur
1 (nn) (8p) Alan Fraser   50p–£1.00

PANTO PRANKS
1949 (1)
1 (nn) (8p) (gravure) D. Gifford   50p–£1.00

PARAMOUNT COMIC
Feb 1945 (1)
Locker
1 (nn) (8p) C. Compton   50p–£1.00

PATCHES
10 Mar 1979–
Thomson
1 (32p) (gravure) (photos)   10p–20p
2–242   5p–15p
243– (larger format)   5p–10p

PATCHES SUMMER SPECIAL
Jul 1980–
Thomson
1 (48p) (gravure) (photos)   25p–30p
2–   10p–20p

PATCHES POP SPECIAL
Sep 1982–Sep 1983 (2)
Thomson
1 (48p) (gravure) (photos)   20p–30p
2   15p–25p

PATSY'S CHRISTMAS REFLECTIONS
Oct 1948 (1)
Daily Mirror strips
1 (nn) (oblong) Jack Dunkley   50p–£1.00

PAUL MAN OF ACTION
1979 (1)
Lion/Fleurus
1 (nn) (52p) (4C) French reprint   50p–95p

PAUL TEMPLE LIBRARY
Mar 1964–(10)
Micron/Smith (*Evening News* strips)
1 (68p) *Magpie Mystery*   50p–£1.50
2–10   50p–75p

PEANUTS COLOUR KNIGHTS
1975 (6)
Knight/Brockhampton (United Features)
1: *Snoopy On Stage* (US reprint) (4C)   25p–45p
2: *Peanuts Season*   25p–45p
3: *Snoopy in Springtime*   25p–45p
4: *Colourful Charlie Brown*   25p–45p

5: *The Magic Lollipop* 25p–45p
6: *The Halloween Pumpkin* 25p–45p

PECOS BILL
Sep 1951–1959 (91)
Westworld (Mondiales)
1 (36p) foreign reprint 50p–£1.00
2– Vol 8 No 7 35p–50p

PECOS BILL
1971–1973
Top Sellers
1– (36p) (4C) foreign reprint 25p–30p

PECOS BILL PICTURE LIBRARY
1962–1964 (28)
Famepress
1–28 (68p) foreign reprint 25p–30p

PEEP SHOW
1 Jul 1901–17 Sep 1901 (12)
Strong
to: *Boys Peep Show*
1 £5.00–£7.50
2–12 £2.00–£3.00

PELICAN FUNNIES
1947 (1)
National Sport
1 (nn) (12p) 50p–£1.00

PELLEPHANT AND CO BUMPER ISSUE
1972 (1)
Top Sellers
1 (nn) (52p) (4C) foreign reprint 25p–50p

PELLEPHANT AND HIS FRIENDS
1973 (1)
Top Sellers
1 (130p) (4C) (small) foreign reprint 35p–50p

PELLEPHANT AND HIS FRIENDS
1972–1974
Top Sellers/Williams
1– (36p) (4C) foreign reprint 10p–25p

PENELOPE
25 May 1968–6 Dec 1969 (81)
City
to: *Princess Tina*
1 (123) (gravure) 50p–75p
124–203 25p–50p

PENGUIN BRISTOW
see: *Bristow*

PENGUIN COLONEL PEWTER
see: *Colonel Pewter*

PENNY
24 Apr 1979–5 Apr 1980 (49)
IPC
to: *Jinty*
1 (32p) J. Edward Oliver 15p–25p
2–49 10p–15p

PENNY COMIC
1944 (1)
PM (Marx)
1 (nn) (8p) (folded strip) 50p–£1.00

PENNY COMICS OF THE THIRTIES
1975
'Collectors Comics' No 1
New English Library
4 facsimiles in 4C cover: £1.00–£2.00
Merry Midget 1: 12 Sep 1931 25p–50p
Sparkler 20: 23 Jan 1932 25p–50p

Rattler 105: 24 Aug 1935 25p–50p
Target 53: 30 Jun 1936 25p–50p

PENNY SPECIALS
Jun 1979–1980 (2)
IPC
1: *Summer Special 1979* (64p) 20p–40p
2: *Holiday Special 1980* 15p–25p

PENNY WONDER
10 Feb 1912–28 Dec 1912 (47)
AP
to: *Wonder*
1 (16p) (tabloid) G. M. Payne £5.00–£10.00
2–47 Bertie Brown £1.50–£2.00

PERCY VERSES
1950? (1)
ROSPA
1 (nn) (32p) (4C) (small) Mendoza £1.00–£2.00

PERFECT CRIME
1951 (2)
Pemberton/World (Cross)
1–2 (36p) US reprint 50p–£1.00

PERISHERS
1963–
Mirror (*Daily Mirror* reprints)
1963: *Meet the Perishers* (oblong) £2.00–£3.00
1965: *Perishers Strike Again* £1.00–£2.00
1968: *Perishers Back Britain* £1.00–£2.00
1968: *Playtime With Perishers* 75p–£1.50
1969: *Flat Out With Perishers* 75p–£1.50
1969: *Perishers Pop Up Again* 75p–£1.50
1970: *Perishers Do Their Thing* 75p–£1.50
1970: *Perishers No 8* 75p–£1.50
1971– (numbered) 75p–£1.50

PERISHERS BOOK OF FUN AND GAMES
Jun 1979 (1)
Mirror
1 (nn) Dennis Collins 25p–50p

PERISHERS OMNIBUS
1964–
Mirror (*Daily Mirror* reprints)
1 (244p) (oblong) D. Collins £1.50–£2.50
2– 75p–£1.50

PERISHERS SPECTACOLOUR
Nov 1979 (1)
Mirror Books (*Daily Mirror* reprints)
1 (nn) (52p) (4C) Dennis Collins 50p–£1.50

PERSUADERS HOLIDAY SPECIAL
May 1972 (1)
Polystyle
1 (nn) (48p) 50p–£1.00

PETE MANGAN OF THE SPACE PATROL
Jul 1953–Dec 1953 (6)
Miller
1 (50) (28p) 50p–£1.00
51–55 35p–75p

PETE REVELL–VENTURER
1972 (2)
Revell (promotional)
1 (8p) (large) (4C) 50p–£1.00
2 35p–75p

PETER PAUL AND PERCY SERIES
1941–1944 (2)
Faber
1–2 (oblong) C. H. Chapman £1.00–£2.00

PETS PLAYTIME COMIC
1949 (1)
Philmar (Marx)
1 (nn) (8p) Walter Bell 50p–£1.00

PETT'S ANNUAL
see: *Jane*

PHANTOM
1961–1962 (18)
Miller (King Features)
1 (68p) US reprint   50p–£1.00
2–18   35p–75p

PHANTOM RANGER COMIC
1955 (18)
World (Frew)
1 (28p) Australian reprint   50p–75p
2–18   35p–50p

PHANTOM WORLD ADVENTURE LIBRARY
Jan–Aug 1967 (8)
World (King Features)
1 (68p) *Deadly Catch*   35p–50p
2–8   15p–25p

PHILBERT DESANEX 100,000TH DREAM
1979 (1)
Hassle Free Press
1 (nn) (52p) (small) US reprint   35p–50p

PHOTO LOVE
31 Mar 1979–29 Jan 1983 (197)
IPC
& *Photo Secret Love*: 6 Feb 1981
to: *Oh Boy*
1 (32p) photos   10p–20p
2–197   5p–10p

PHOTO LOVE SUMMER SPECIAL
Jun 1979 (1)
IPC
1 (nn) (64p) photos   20p–40p

PHOTO LOVE SUMMER SPECTACULAR
Aug 1980 (1)
IPC
1 (nn) (56p) photos   25p–50p

PHOTO ROMANCE
Nov 1956–
Rolls House
1: *Merchant of Love* (68p)   20p–35p
2–   15p–25p

PHOTO ROMANCE
20 Mar 1973–22 May 1973 (10)
Simavi
1 (24p) (tabloid) photos   25p–50p
2–10   20p–50p

PHOTO ROMANCES
Jan 1960–
Pearson
1: *Dream Lover* (36p) photos   25p–50p
2–   20p–25p

PHOTO SECRET LOVE
15 Mar 1980–30 Jan 1981 (99)
IPC
to: *Photo Love*
1 (32p) photos   10p–25p
2–99   5p–10p

PHOTO SECRET LOVE HOLIDAY SPECIAL
Apr 1983–Apr 1984 (2)
IPC
1–2 photos   15p–30p

PIC POINTS
1981 (1)
Redemptorist
1 (nn) (36p) (advice for teens)   50p–90p

PICCOLO FISHING BOOK
1981 (1)
Pan/Piccolo
1 (nn) (132p) (small) Bernard Venables   50p–95p

PICTORIAL COMEDY
Apr 1899–Jun 1908 (111)
Henderson
to: *Life's Pictorial Comedy*
1 (40p) (magazine) US reprints (adult)   £2.00–£3.00
2–111   £1.00–£2.00

PICTORIAL COMIC LIFE
2 Jul 1898–23 Dec 1899 (78)
Henderson
to: *Comic Life*
1 (8p) (outsize)   £5.00–£10.00
2–78   £1.50–£2.00

PICTORIAL NUGGETS
26 Sep 1903–9 Jul 1904 (41)
Henderson
1 (16p supplement to *Nuggets*)   £1.50–£2.00
2–41   £1.00–£1.50

PICTORIAL PAGES
Aug 1853–1855
Houlston & Stoneman
1 (religious)   £1.50–£2.50
2–   £1.50–£2.00

PICTORIAL VARIETIES
7 Aug 1893–
Henderson
1 (25) (16p supplement to *Varieties*)   £1.00–£1.50
26–   £1.00–£1.25

PICTURE CLASSICS
1980
Watts (Syndication International)
reprints from *Look & Learn*
1 (36p) *King Solomon's Mines*   50p–£1.00

PICTURE EPICS
Oct 1952–Nov 1952 (4)
Swan (reprints)
1: *Back From the Dead*   £1.00–£2.00
2: *Old Hooky Buccaneer*   £1.00–£2.00
3: *Space Conquerors*   £1.50–£2.50
4: *Ah Wong v The Cobra*   £1.50–£2.50

PICTURE FUN
16 Feb 1909–24 Jul 1920 (595)
Trapps Holmes
to: *Film Fun*
1 (8p) (tabloid) Charles Genge   £5.00–£10.00
2–595 Frank Holland   £1.25–£1.75

PICTURE MAGAZINE
Jan 1893–Jun 1896 (42)
Newnes
1 (64p) (magazine) (adult)   £2.50–£5.00
2–42   £1.50–£2.00

PICTURE POLITICS
Nov 1893–Feb 1914 (244)
Westminster Gazette
1 (16p) F. Carruthers Gould (adult)   £2.50–£3.50
2–244   £1.00–£1.50

PICTURE PRANKS COMIC
1944 (1)
Martin & Reid
1 (nn) (8p)   50p–£1.00

PICTURE ROMANCE
1970–
World (*Illustrated World Library*)
1 (68p) (small) reprints   10p–20p
2–   10p–15p

PICTURE ROMANCE LIBRARY
Oct 1956–
Pearson
1: *Her Forgotten Past* (68p)   25p–45p
2–   10p–20p

PICTURE-SHOW OF ROBIN HOOD
194– (1)
Juvenile Productions
1 (6701) (16p) (4C)   £1.00–£2.00

PICTURE-SHOW OF ROBINSON CRUSOE
194– (1)
Juvenile Productions
1 (6700) (16p) (4C)   £1.00–£2.00

PICTURE STORIES
1976 (1)
Puffin/Penguin
1 (nn) (28p) (4C) Rodney Peppe   25p–50p

PICTURE STORIES OF WORLD WAR TWO
Aug 1960– (56)
Pearson
1: (68p) (small)   25p–50p
2–56   20p–30p

PICTURE STORY (CAN HEIRONYMUS MERKIN)
1969 (1)
City (Parade Special)
1 (60p) photos (film)   75p–£1.00

PICTURE STORY POCKET WESTERN
1958–
World
1– (68p) (small) US reprint   20p–25p

PICTURE STORY READERS
1956 (8)
Murray (*Childrens Newspaper* reprints)
1: *Coral Island*   50p–75p
2: *Lorna Doone*   25p–50p
3: *Treasure Island*   25p–50p
4: *Kidnapped*   25p–50p
5: *Lost World*   35p–75p
6: *Vice Versa*   25p–50p
7: *Marco Polo's Amazing Adventure*   25p–50p
8: *Invisible Man*   35p–75p

PICTURE STRIP BOOKS
195? (3)
Collins
1: *Oliver Twist* (16p) (4C)   50p–£1.00
2: *Prince the Pony*   50p–75p
3: *Jungle Giants*   50p–75p

PIGMY COMIC
1944 (1)
PM (Marx)
1 (nn) (8p) (small) Reg Carter   50p–£1.00

PILLAR BOX COMIC
1947 (1)
Reynard
1 (nn) (8p) Tom Cottrell   50p–£1.00

PINK
24 Mar 1973–14 Jun 1980 (377)
IPC
& *Princess Tina*: 1973
& *New Mirabelle*: 29 Oct 1977
to: *Mates*
1   35p–75p
2–377   20p–30p

PINK DRESS COMICS
1983 (1)
Community Arts Workshop
1 (32p) (small) comic of stage show   50p–75p

PINK PANTHER SPECIALS
1973–
World/Polystyle
1: *Summer Special 1973* (32p)   25p–50p
2: *Summer Special 1974*   20p–45p
3: *Holiday Special 1975* (48p)   30p–35p
4: *Holiday Special 1976*   30p–35p
5: *Holiday Special 1977*   25p–30p
6: *Holiday Special 1978*   25p–30p
7: *Holiday Special 1979*   25p–30p
8: *Holiday Special 1980*   25p–30p
9: *Summer Special 1981*   25p–30p
10: *Holiday Special 1982*   25p–30p
11: *Holiday Special 1983*   25p–30p
12: *Holiday Special 1984*   25p–30p

PINK SPECIALS
1976–1980 (6)
IPC
1: *Pink Pop Special 1976* (64p)   25p–50p
2: *Pink Summer Special 1977*   20p–40p
3: *Pink Summer Special 1978*   20p–40p
4: *Pink Summer Special 1979*   20p–30p
5: *Pink Holiday Special 1980*   20p–30p
6: *Pink Summer Special 1980*   20p–30p

PINTA POW
1979 (1)
Scottish Dairy Council (giveaway)
1 (nn) (8p) (4C) milk promo   25p–50p

PINWHEEL
1948 (1)
McKenzie Vincent
1 (nn) (8p)   50p–£1.00

PIONEER WESTERN COMIC
1950 (2)
Wyndham/Timpo Toys
1–2 (16p) Mick Anglo   75p–£1.25

PIP AND SQUEAK
15 Oct 1921–23 May 1925 (189)
Daily Mirror
supplement to *Daily Mirror* newspaper
1 (4p) (tabloid) A. B. Payne   £2.50–£5.00
2–18 Mar 1922 (4p) Arthur Mansbridge   £1.00–£1.75
25 Mar 1922–1 Jul 1922 (3p) P. Simmonds   75p–£1.00
8 Jul 1922–23 May 1925 (2p) H. Batho   50p–75p

PIP POP COMIC
Philmar (Marx)
1949 (1)
1 (nn) (8p) (tabloid) (gravure) F. Minnitt   50p–£1.50

PIPPIN
24 Sep 1966–5 Jul 1975 (459)
Polystyle
to: *Pippin in Playland*
1 (16p) (gravure) Fred Robinson   50p–75p
2–459 (*Rupert* by Bestall reprints from 1974)   10p–25p

PIPPIN HOLIDAY SPECIAL
1969–
Polystyle
1 (nn) (48p) reprints   40p–50p
2–   25p–30p

PIPPIN IN PLAYLAND
12 Jul 1975–
Polystyle
& *Read to Me*: 13 Aug 1977
1 (460) (16p)   10p–15p
461–   10p–15p

PIPPIN WINTER SPECIAL
1974 (1)
Polystyle
1 (nn) (48p) reprints   35p–40p

PIRATES ADVENTURE COMIC
see: *Pirates Comics*

PIRATES COMICS
1951–1952 (7)
Streamline/United Anglo-American (Hillman)
aka: *Pirates Adventure Comic*
1 (nn) (4C) US reprint   75p–£1.00
2–7 (nn) (68p)   35p–75p

PIXI TALES
195– (66)
Strato/Thorpe & Porter
1: *Queen Bee* (36p) (4C) foreign reprints   25p–50p
2–66   25p–35p

PIXIE
24 Jun 1972–13 Jan 1973 (30)
AP
to: *June*
1 (24p) Hugh McNeill   25p–35p
2–30 Michael Hubbard   15p–20p

PLANET
1949 (2)
Allen
to: *Children's Rocket Book*
1 (32p) (small) Bill Holroyd   50p–£1.00
2 (nn) (12p) Jack Pamby   50p–75p

PLANET COMICS
1950 (1)
Cartoon Art (Fiction House)
1 (nn) (28p) US reprint   50p–£1.00

PLANET COMICS
1951 (5)
Locker (Fiction House)
1 (68p) US reprint   75–£1.75
2–5   50p–£1.50

PLANET OF THE APES
26 Oct 1974–23 Feb 1977 (123)
Marvel
& *Dracula Lives*: 23 Jun 1976
to: *Mighty World of Marvel*
1 (36p) US reprint   50p–75p
2–123   20p–35p

PLANET STORIES
Jun 1961–
Atlas (Fiction House)
1 (28p) US reprint   50p–£1.00
2–   50p–75p

PLASTIC MAN
Mar 1951–
Popular (Boardman) (Quality)
1 (2) (36p) (4C) US reprint   £1.00–£1.75
5; 60; etc   75p–£1.00

PLAY SCHOOL HOLIDAY SPECIAL
Jun 1982–Jul 1984 (3)
Polystyle
1 (nn) (48p) TV characters   20p–35p
2–3   20p–30p

PLAYBOX
29 Oct 1898–
Harmsworth/AP
1 (4p) supplement: *Home Chat*   £1.00–£3.00
2– Mabel Taylor   £1.00–£1.25
Double numbers (Xmas/Spring) 8p   £1.00–£1.50

PLAYBOX
May 1905–May 1910 (61)
AP
supplement: *World & his Wife*
1 (nn) (16p) J. S. Baker   £3.50–£5.00
2–61 (nn) Louis Wain   £2.50–£3.00

PLAYBOX
May 1910–Dec 1913 (44)
AP

supplement: *New Children's Encyclopedia*
1 (4) (8p) J. S. Baker   £1.50–£2.00
5–47 S. J. Cash   £1.00–£1.25

PLAYBOX
14 Feb 1925–11 Jun 1955 (1279)
AP
to: *Jack & Jill*
1 (12p) (tabloid) H. Foxwell   £5.00–£10.00
1925–1939 Walter Bell   £1.50–£2.00
4 Nov 1939: first small (24p)   £1.50–£2.00
8 Jun 1941: (16p) Bert Wymer   £1.50–£2.00
1941–1947 Fred Crompton   £1.00–£1.50
1947: (8p) (tabloid) Anton Lock   50p–£1.00
1947–1955 P. J. Hayward   50p–75p

PLAYBOX
3 Apr 1982–9 Oct 1982 (28)
IPC
to: *Jack & Jill*
1 (16p)   10p–20p
2–28   5p–10p

PLAYGROUP
24 Mar 1984–
IPC
1   15p–25p
2–   10p–15p

PLAYHOUR
15 Feb 1910–15 Apr 1910 (3)
AP
supplement: *New Children's Encyclopedia*
to: *Playbox*
1 (8p) (4C) J. S. Baker   £1.50–£2.00
2–3   £1.00–£1.25

PLAYHOUR
21 May 1955–
AP/Fleetway/IPC
& *Chicks Own*: 15 Mar 1957
& *Tiny Tots*: 31 Jan 1959
& *Harold Hare*: 11 Apr 1964
& *TV Toyland*: 2 Mar 1968
& *Robin*: 1 Feb 1969
& *Hey Diddle Diddle*: 22 Sep 1973
& *Bonnie*: 17 May 1975
& *Fun To Do*: 13 Mar 1982
& *Chips Comic*: 6 Aug 1983
1 (32) (16p) Basil Reynolds   35p–50p
33– Hugh McNeill   20p–25p

PLAYHOUR HOLIDAY SPECIAL
1969
IPC
1 (48p)   35p–50p
2–   20p–35p

PLAYHOUR PICTURES
16 Oct 1954–14 May 1955 (31)
AP
to: *Playhour*
1 (16p) Sep E. Scott   35p–50p
2–31 Hugh McNeill   20p–25p

PLAYLAND
13 Jan 1968–5 Jul 1975 (391)
TV/Polystyle
& *Toytown*: 24 Mar 1973
to: *Pippin in Playland*
1 (16p) Fred Robinson   35p–50p
2–391 John Ryan   10p–25p

PLAYLAND FUN SPECIAL
Oct 1979–Oct 1980 (2)
Polystyle
1 (48p) Fred Robinson   25p–40p
2 John Ryan   20p–30p

PLAYLAND HOLIDAY/SUMMER SPECIAL
May 1969–
Polystyle

1 (48p) TV characters: reprints   35p–50p
2–   25p–35p

PLAYTIME
Jul 1949–
Kilburn
1 (16p) Catholic comic   £1.00–£2.00
2–   50p–£1.50

PLAYTIME
29 Mar 1919–17 Nov 1923 (243)
AP
& *Young Folks Tales:* 18 Mar 1922
to: *New Series*
1 (24p) Harry Rountree   £5.00–£10.00
2–243 Phil Swinnerton   £2.00–£2.50

PLAYTIME NEW SERIES
24 Nov 1923–12 Oct 1929 (307)
AP
to: *Bo-Peep*
1 (12p) (tabloid) Walter Holt   £5.00–£10.00
2–307 Harry Banger   £1.50–£2.00

PLUG
24 Sep 1977–24 Feb 1979 (75)
Thomson
to: *Beezer*
1 (20p) (gravure) Bob Dewar   25p–35p
2–75 Graham Allen   15p–20p

PLUS
Dec 196–
Christian Publicity
1 (8p) Harold Johns   50p–£1.00
2–   25p–50p

POCKET CHILLER LIBRARY
1971
Top Sellers
aka: *Pocket Horror Library*
1: *The Body* (68p) reprints   25p–50p
2–   10p–25p

POCKET COMIC
1944 (1)
PM (Marx)
1 (nn) (small) (8p) Reg Carter   50p–£1.00

POCKET COR-MIC
Oct 13–Nov 4 1973 (4)
IPC
1–4 (supplement to *Cor*)   15p–25p

POCKET DETECTIVE LIBRARY
1971
Top Sellers
1: *The Big Snatch* (68p) reprints   15p–35p
2–   15p–20p

POCKET ROMANCE LIBRARY
1971
Top Sellers
1– (68p) US reprints   10p–15p

POCKET WAR LIBRARY
1971
Top Sellers
1: *A Man's Honour* (68p) reprints   15p–20p
2–   10p–15p

POCKET WESTERN LIBRARY
1971
Top Sellers
1: *The Lost Expedition* (68p) reprints   15p–25p
2–   10p–15p

POLE POSITION
Nov 1983 (1)
Atari
1 (nn) (poster) (4C) game promo   5p–10p

POLICE COMIC
1953 (6)
Archer (Quality)
1 (68p) US reprints   50p–£1.00
2–6   50p–75p

POLICE FILES
1951 (1)
Streamline/United Anglo-American (Fox)
1 (nn) (28p) US reprint   50p–£1.00

POLLY PIGTAILS
1948 (2?)
Cartoon Art (Parents Magazine)
1 (20p) (4C) US reprints   75p–£1.25
2–   50p–£1.00

PONTY AND POP
Dec 1974 (1)
South Wales Echo
1 (nn) (72p) (oblong) Gren Jones reprint   £1.00–£2.00

POOR KID
Jun 1974–
Wild Wind/Children of God
1 (20p) (small)   10p–25p
2– (religious sect promo)   5p–10p

POP ANNUAL
18 Jul 1925–195– (24)
Daily Sketch strip reprints
1 (1925) (hardback) Millar Watt   £5.00–£7.50
2 (1926) (hardback)   £5.00–£6.50
1927–1939   £3.50–£5.00
1942–1944 (oblong)   £3.50–£4.00
1945–1949 (last Millar Watt)   £2.00–£3.00
Pop At His Best (large oblong)   £1.00–£2.00

POP PIC LIBRARY
1965–
Micron
1– (68p)   20p–35p

POP SHOTS
1946 (1)
Fisher
1 (nn) (8p) W. Forshaw   50p–£1.00

POPEYE
(a) Pemberton/Thorpe & Porter (Dell)
     1952–1953 (19)
     1–19 (28p) US reprint   50p–£1.00
(b) World (Dell)
     1957 (7)
     1–7 (28p) US reprint   50p–75p
(c) Miller (King Features)
     1959–1963 (30)
     1–30 (28p) US reprint   50p–£1.00

POPEYE HOLIDAY SPECIAL
1965–1984 (20)
TV/Polystyle
aka: *TV Comic's Popeye Holiday Special*
1 (48p) (King Features) US reprint   50p–£1.00
2–20   50p–75p

POPEYE OFFICIAL FILM POSTER MAGAZINE
1980 (1)
Phoenix
1 (16p) (4C) (poster)   10p–30p

POPEYE THE SAILOR
1977 (4)
Egmont/Methuen (King Features)
1: *P to the Rescue* (52p) (4C) US reprints   50p–85p
2: *P in Space*   25p–50p
3: *P Rules OK*   25p–50p
4: *The Thing Next Door*   25p–50p

POPEYE WINTER SPECIAL
1974–1980 (7)

Polystyle
aka: *TV Comic's Popeye Winter Special*
1– (48p) (King Features) US reprints   35p–75p
2–7   35p–50p

POPPET
5 Oct 1963–11 Jul 1964 (41)
Fleetway
to: *June*
1 (28p) Michael Hubbard   25p–45p
2–41   10p–25p

POPS PUPPET COMICS
Dec 1949–Jan 1950 (2)
Apollo
1–2 (8p) 'Eulalie'   50p–£1.00

POSTMAN PAT SUMMER SPECIAL
Jun 1983–May 1984 (2)
Polystyle
1 (48p) (TV series) reprints   15p–30p
2   10p–15p

POW
21 Jan 1967–7 Sep 1968 (86)
Odhams
& *Wham:* 20 Jan 1968
to: *Smash*
1 (28p) Leo Baxendale   50p–£1.00
2–86 Ken Reid   25p–50p

POWER COMIC
1950 (1)
Martin & Reid (Gower)
1 (nn) (8p) Mick Anglo   50p–£1.00

PRAIRIE GUNS
see: *Action Series*

PRAIRIE WESTERN
1952 (3)
Scion
1 (24p) Ron Embleton   50p–£1.00
2–3 (20p) Norman Light   35p–£1.00

PRANG COMIC
1948 (1)
Hotspur
1 (nn) (8p)   50p–£1.00

PREMIER
1948 (7)
Paget
1–7 (8p) Mick Anglo   50p–£1.00

PRIMO
1965–1966 (13)
Lyons/Circle Service (giveaway)
1 (12p) (4C) Premium Tea promo   50p–£1.00
2–13   25p–50p

PRINCE COMIC
1947 (2)
Ensign
1 (nn) (8p) (gravure) W. Forshaw   50p–£1.00
2   50p–£1.00

PRINCESS
30 Jan 1960–16 Sep 1967 (346)
AP/Fleetway
& *Girl:* 10 Oct 1964
aka: *New Princess & Girl* (1964)
to: *Princess Tina*
1 (20p) (gravure) H.M. Brock   50p–75p
2–346 Eric Parker   25p–50p

PRINCESS
24 Sep 1983–31 Mar 1984 (28)
IPC
to: *Tammy*

1 (24p) (4C)   10p–20p
2–28   10p–15p

PRINCESS HOLIDAY SPECIAL
1964 (1)
Fleetway
1 (nn) (48p)   35p–50p

PRINCESS OF ASGAARD
1971 (1)
Danish Bacon (giveaway)
1 (nn) (8p) (4C) promo   50p–75p

PRINCESS PICTURE LIBRARY
Jul 1961–1966
Fleetway
to: *June & School Friend Picture Library*
1: *Sue Day Detective* (68p)   25p–50p
2–   20p–25p

PRINCESS TINA
23 Sep 1967–1973
IPC
& *Penelope:* 13 Dec 1969
to: *Pink*
1 Michael Hubbard   35p–50p
2– Hugh McNeill   20p–30p

PRINCESS TINA SUMMER SPECIAL
1969–1972 (4)
IPC
to: *Tina Summer Special*
1–4 (96p)   35p–45p

PRIVATE EYE PICTURE STORIES
1963–
Pearson
1: *Rats of Paris* (68p) (small)   35p–50p
2–   20p–35p

PRIVATE LIVES ROMANCES
1959 (7)
Miller (Standard)
1–7 (68p) US reprint   25p–35p

PRIZE COMICS WESTERN
1950 (2)
Streamline/United Anglo-American (Prize)
1 (nn) (28p) (4C) US reprint   50p–£1.00
2 (nn) (36p)   50p–75p

PRO JUNIOR
undated: no imprint
1 (nn) (20p) US/UG reprint   25p–50p

PSSST
Jan 1982–Oct 1982 (10)
Never/Artpool
1 (52p) (adult)   50p–£1.00
2–10 Bryan Talbot   50p–75p

PSYCHO
197–
Top Sellers
1 (36p) US reprints   20p–50p
2–   15p–25p

PUB DOG BOOK
Jun 1984 (1)
Daily Express
1 (nn) Graham Allen strips reprint   35p–75p

PUBLIC ENEMIES
1949 (8)
Locker (DS)
1 (58p) US reprint   50p–£1.00
2–8   50p–75p

PUCK
30 Jul 1904–11 May 1940 (1867)
AP
to: *Sunbeam*

1 (12p) (tabloid) J. B. Yeats	£5.00–£10.00
1904–1929 Walter Booth	£2.00–£2.50
1930–1940 Roy Wilson	£1.50–£2.50

PUPPETOONS
1951 (2)
Miller (Fawcett)
aka: *George Pal's Puppetoons*

1–2 (28p) US reprint	50p–£1.00

PUNCH AND JUDY COMIC
1949 (1)
Martin & Reid (Gower)

1 (nn) (gravure) Frank Minnitt	50p–£1.00

PUNCH AND JUDY COMIC (Uncle Tony's)
1979 (1)
Drewitt

1 (8p) (2C) entertainer's promo	25p–50p

PURPLE HOOD
196– (2)
Spencer

1–2 (52p) Michael Jay	35p–50p

PUSS IN BOOTS
1969–1970 (2)
IPC

1 (24p) (4C) 1969 pilot issue	£1.00–£2.00
2 (24p) (4C) 1970 pilot issue	£1.00–£2.00

(different editions of unpublished comic)

QUEST FOR THE GLOOP
1982 (1)
Puffin/Penguin

1 (nn) (36p) (4C) Jan Pienkowski	50p–£1.50

QUICK TRIGGER WESTERN
1956 (4)
Miller (Atlas)

1 (28p) US reprint	50p–75p
2–4	35p–50p

QUIZZER
1974 (1)
Williams
to: *Junior Quizzer*

1 (nn) (52p) R. Turner	20p–30p

QUIZZER MONTHLY
Jul 1979–Jul 1980 (13)
Byblos

1 (36p) R. Turner (reprints)	10p–20p
2–13	10p–15p

QUIZZER SPECIALS
May 1978–Nov 1981 (5)
Byblos

1: *Summer Special 1978* (68p)	10p–25p
2: *Winter Special 1979* (52p)	10p–20p
3: *Winter Special 1980*	10p–20p
4: *Summer Special 1981*	10p–20p
5: *Winter Special 1981*	10p–20p

RACE FOR THE MOON
1959–1960 (24)

(a) Class (Harvey)	
1 (nn) (68p) US reprint	50p–£1.00
(b) Strato (Harvey)	
1– (68p) US reprint	50p–£1.00
(c) Top Sellers (Harvey)	
–23 (68p) US reprint	50p–£1.00

RACE INTO SPACE
1961 (1)
Class

1 (68p) US reprint	35p–75p

RADAR THE MAN FROM THE UNKNOWN
1962 (16)

Famepress

1 (68p) (small) Italian reprint	25p–50p
2–16	20p–25p

RADIANT COMICS
Dec 1943 (1)
PM (Marx)

1 (nn) (16p) Frank Jupo	50p–£1.00

RADIO FUN
15 Oct 1938–18 Feb 1961 (1167)
AP
& *Wonder*: 19 Sep 1953
to: *Buster*

1 (28p) Roy Wilson	£5.00–£15.00
2–53 Reg Parlett	£3.50–£5.00
54–63 (24p) George Parlett	£3.00–£4.50
64 (first 2C) John Jukes	£3.00–£4.00
1941–1945 (16p) George Heath	£2.50–£3.00
1946–1950 Bertie Brown	£1.00–£1.50
1951–1961 Albert Pease	50p–£1.00

RAINBOW
14 Feb 1914–28 Apr 1956 (1898)
AP
& *Tiger Tims Weekly*: 25 May 1940
to: *Tiny Tots*

1 (12p) (tabloid) J. S. Baker	£5.00–£10.00
2– H. S. Foxwell	£2.50–£5.00
1920–1929 Vincent Daniel	£1.50–£2.00
1930–1939 T. Gilson	£1.00–£1.75
1940–1956 Albert Lock	£1.00–£1.50

RAMAR OF THE JUNGLE
1956 (4)
Miller (Charlton)

1 (28p) US reprint	50p–£1.00
2–4	35p–75p

RAMPAGE (WEEKLY)
19 Oct 1977–31 May 1978 (35)
Marvel
to: *Rampage* (monthly)

1 (36p) US reprints	10p–25p
2–35	10p–20p

RAMPAGE (MONTHLY)
Jul 1978–Dec 1982 (54)
Marvel
& *Blockbuster*: Mar 1982
to: *Marvel Superheroes*

1 (68p) US reprints	25p–45p
2–54 (52p)	20p–35p

RANCHER
Jul 1950 (1)
Martin & Reid (Gower)

1 (16p) Paddy Brennan	50p–£1.00

RANGE BUSTERS
1951 (1)
Streamline/United Anglo-American (Fox)

1 (nn) (28p) (gravure) US reprints	50p–£1.00

RANGELAND WESTERN
1949 (1)
Martin & Reid (Gower)

1 (8p) (gravure) John McCail	50p–£1.25

RANGER
18 Sep 1965–18 Jun 1966 (40)
Fleetway
to: *Look & Learn*

1 (40p) Don Lawrence (Trigan)	£1.00–£1.50
2–40	50p–£1.00

RANGER WESTERN COMIC
1955–1956 (17)
Peters

1 (V2N1) (28p) Douglas Reay	50p–£1.00
2–V3N5 John Wheeler	50p–£1.00

RANGERS COMICS
1952
Thorpe & Porter (Fiction House)
1– (28p) US reprint   50p–75p

RANGERS COMICS
1950
Cartoon Art (Fiction House)
1 (nn) (20p) (4C) US reprint   75p–£1.00

RATTLER
19 Aug 1933–15 Oct 1938 (269)
Target
to: *Rattler & Chuckler*
1 (12p) (tabloid) Harry Banger   £5.00–£7.50
2–60 (12p) Bert Hill   £2.00–£3.00
61–269 (8p) Louis Diamond   £2.00–£2.50

RATTLER AND CHUCKLER
22 Oct 1938–8 Apr 1939 (25)
Target
to: *Tip-Top*
1 (12p) (tabloid) Harry Banger   £2.50–£5.00
2–22 (12p) Bert Hill   £2.00–£2.50
23–25 (8p) Louis Diamond   £1.75–£2.00

RAW PURPLE
1977 (1)
Beyond the Edge
1 (nn) (52p) (adult) A. Ghura   £1.00–£1.25

RAY REAGAN
Apr 1949 (1)
Modern Fiction
1 (16p) (gravure) Ron Embleton   £1.00–£2.00

RAZZLE DAZZLE
1946–1947 (2)
Cartoon Art
1 (8p) G. F. Christie   50p–£1.00
2 Dennis Reader   50p–£1.00

READ TO ME
27 Jan 1977–4 Aug 1977 (28)
Polystyle
to: *Pippin*
1 (16p) Fred Robinson   10p–20p
2–28   10p–15p

READ TO ME HOLIDAY SPECIAL
May 1977 (1)
Polystyle
1 (48p) Fred Robinson   20p–25p

REAL CLUE CRIME STORIES
1951 (2)
Streamline/United Anglo-American (Hillman)
1–2 (36p) US reprint   50p–£1.00

REAL LIFE STORIES
1962 (1)
Cartoon Art
1 US reprint   50p–75p

REAL WESTERN HERO
1949 (1)
Arnold (Fawcett)
1 (70) (32p) US reprint   50p–75p

RED ARROW COMICS
1948 (1)
Cartoon Art
1 (nn)   50p–£1.50

RED COMET INTERPLANETARY
ADVENTURES
1961–1962
Atlas (Fiction House)
1 (28p) US reprint   75p–£1.00
2–   50p–75p

RED DAGGER
Oct 1979–Jun 1984 (30)
Thomson
1 (68p) *Twisty* (reprints)   25p–35p
2–30   15p–25p

RED FLASH COMIC
1948–1949 (2)
Philmar/PM
1 (16p) Wally Robertson   50p–£1.25
2 (16p) Frank Minnitt   50p–£1.00

RED HAWK
1953 (1)
Cartoon Art (Magazine Enterprises)
1 (28p) US reprint   50p–£1.00

RED MASK
see: *Action Series*

RED RANGER
Apr 1949 (1)
Modern Press
1 (8p) R. Beaumont   50p–£1.00

RED RYDER COMICS
1954–1959 (60)
World (Dell)
1 (36p) US reprint   50p–£1.00
2–56 (28p)   50p–75p
57–60 (68p)   50p–75p

RED SPOT COMIC
1944 (1)
Martin & Reid
1 (nn) (8p) Bob Wilkin   50p–£1.00

RED STAR COMIC
1948 (1)
Halle (*All Star* reprint)
1 (nn) (8p) Nat Brand   50p–75p

REDSKIN
195– (2)
Streamline/United Anglo-American (Youthful)
1–2 (28p) US reprint   50p–75p

REEL COMICS
Oct 1944 (1)
Locker
1 (nn) (16p)   50p–£1.00

REFLECTIONS FOR CHILDREN
1947 (1)
Daily Mirror
1 (nn) (52p) A. B. Payne   £1.00–£3.50

REGAL COMIC
195–
Miller (Fawcett)
1– (28p) (*Bill Boyd* etc) US reprint   50p–75p

RESISTANCE COMIX
1981–
Resistance Comix
1– (8p) (Belfast UG)   15p–25p

REVEILLE EXTRA
30 Apr 1976–14 Jul 1976 (12)
Reveille Newspapers
supplement to *Reveille*
1 (4p) Terry Wakefield   10p–25p
2–12 Geoff Jones   10p–15p

REWARD
195–
Arnold
1– US reprint   50p–£1.00

REX ALLEN
Apr 1953–1954 (16)
World (Dell)
1 (28p) US reprint   75p–£1.00
2–16   50p–75p

RIDER
1957 (2)
Miller (Ajax)
1–2 (28p) US reprint   50p–75p

RIN TIN TIN
1955–1956 (13)
World (Dell)
1 (28p) US reprint   50p–£1.00
2–13   50p–75p

RIN TIN TIN
1972–1974
Top Sellers
1– (36p) (4C) US reprint   25p–30p

RINGO KID WESTERN
1955–1956 (17)
Miller (Atlas)
1 (28p) US reprint   50p–£1.00
2–17   50p–75p

RINGOS GIGGLE AND THINK BOOK
1980? (1)
Golden Wonder Crisps
1 (nn) (16p) (4C) promo   50p–£1.00

RIP CARSON
1950 (1)
Cartoon Art (Fiction House)
1 (16p) (4C) US reprint   50p–£1.00

RIP CARSON COMICS
1951 (1)
Streamline (Fiction House)
1 (28p) US reprint   50p–75p

RIP KIRBY SERIES
1948–1956 (5)
Associated Newspapers (King Features)
1: *Menace of the Mangler* (16p) US reprint £1.00–£3.00
2: *Poison and Paradise* (52p)   £1.00–£3.00
3: *Moray's Last Gamble* (52p)   £1.00–£2.50
4: *Man Who Stole a Million* (44p) £1.00–£2.50
5: *Beaumont Case* (84p)   £1.00–£2.50

RIPPING COMIC
1948 (2)
JT Comics
1 (nn) (8p) John Turner   50p–£1.00
2 (2C) Bob Monkhouse   50p–£1.00

ROARING WESTERN
1952 (1)
Streamline
1 (28p) US reprint   50p–75p

ROBIN
Feb 1952–1953
SNPI/Miller
to: *Pango*
1 (50) (24p) foreign reprint 50p–75p
51–   25p–50p

ROBIN
28 Mar 1953–25 Jan 1969 (836)
Hulton/Longacre/IPC
& *Story Time*: 13 May 1967
to: *Playhour*
1 (12p) (gravure) Mike Noble £1.00–£1.50
2–836 Bob Wilkin   20p–25p

ROBIN HOOD
1955 (4)
World

1 (28p) US reprint   50p–75p
2–4   25p–50p

ROBIN HOOD
1957–1959 (34)
Miller
aka: *Robin Hood Tales*
1 (28p) Colin Andrew   50p–£1.00
2–34 (some issues US reprints) 35p–75p

ROBIN HOOD AND HIS MERRY MEN
1956 (2)
Streamline/United Anglo-American (Charlton)
1 (nn) (28p) US reprint   50p–75p
2 (nn) (68p)   50p–75p

ROBOT REBELLION
1951 (1)
Streamline
1 (28p) US reprint   £1.00–£1.50

ROCK'N'ROLL MADNESS FUNNIES
Jun 1973–Mar 1974 (2)
H. Bunch/Cosmic Comics
1 (36p) (adult) Dave Gibbons 50p–£1.00
2 Edward Barker   35p–75p

ROCKET
26 Oct 1935–22 Oct 1938 (157)
Target
to: *Target & Rocket*
1 (8p) Harry Banger   £5.00–£7.50
2–93 (8p) Bert Hill   £2.00–£3.00
94–109 (12p) Louis Diamond   £2.00–£3.00
110–157 (8p) G. Larkman   £2.00–£2.50

ROCKET
21 Apr 1956–24 Nov 1956 (32)
News of the World
to: *Express Weekly*
1 (16p) (gravure) Ley Kenyon £2.00–£4.00
2–32 Cyril Price   £1.00–£2.00

ROCKET
see: *Children's Rocket Book*

ROCKET COMIC
1948 (1)
Hotspur
1 (8p)   50p–£1.00

ROCKET COMIC
1948–1949 (2)
PM (Marx)
1 (16p) Frank Minnitt   50p–£1.00
2 (gravure) Wally Robertson 50p–£1.00

ROCKETSHIP X
1951 (1)
Streamline/United Anglo-American (Fox)
1 (nn) (28p) US reprint   £1.00–£1.50

ROCKY LANE WESTERN
Jun 1950–1959 (90)
Miller (Fawcett)
1 (nn) (12p) (gravure) US reprint 50p–£1.00
50–139 (28p)   50p–75p

ROCKY MOUNTAIN KING WESTERN COMIC
1955–1959 (65)
Miller
1 (28p) Tom Barling   50p–75p
2–65 Terry Patrick   35p–50p

ROD CAMERON WESTERN
1950–1960
Miller (Fawcett)
1 (1950 (gravure) (32p)   75p–£1.25
8 (gravure) (large) US reprint 75p–£1.00
50–64 (1951) (24p)   50p–75p
1– (1960) (68p)   35p–50p

ROM SUMMER SPECIAL
May 1982 (1)
Marvel
1 US reprints   40p–50p

ROMANCE IN PICTURES/ROMANCE PICTURE LIBRARY
195 –1963
Brown Watson (Selecciones Ilustradas)
1 (68p) Spanish reprint   20p–40p
2–   10p–15p

ROMANCE STRIP STORIES
1959
Miller
1– (68p) US reprint   20p–25p

ROMANTIC ADVENTURE LIBRARY
1962–
Micron
1: *Goddess in Love* (68p)   15p–20p
2–   10p–15p

ROMANTIC CONFESSIONS PICTURE LIBRARY
1961–
Fleetway
1 (45) (68p)   20p–25p
46–   15p–20p

ROMANTIC SECRETS
1950 (24)
Miller (Fawcett)
1 (68p) US reprint   20p–25p
2–24   15p–20p

ROMANTIC STORY
1955 (12)
Miller (Fawcett)
1 (50) (28p) US reprint   20p–25p
51–61   15p–20p

ROMEO
31 Aug 1957–14 Sep 1974 (887)
Thomson
& Cherie: 26 Oct 1963
to: *Diana*
1 (28p)   50p–60p
2–887   20p–25p

ROMEO BROWN/GARTH
1958 (1)
Mirror (strip reprints)
1 (nn) (132p) James Holdaway £1.50–£2.50

ROMEO TUBBS
1951 (1)
Streamline/United Anglo-American (Fox)
1 (nn) (28p) US reprint   35p–75p

ROOKIE COP
1956
Miller (Charlton)
1– (28p) US reprint   35p–75p

ROSE OF BAGDAD
1952 (1)
Gaywood
1 (nn) (36p) (Italian cartoon film) 50p–£1.50

ROSPA ROCKET
1951 (1)
Rospa
1 (8p) Bob Wilkin (promo)   50p–£1.00

ROUND THE NURSERY FIRE
20 Nov 1915–18 Dec 1915 (5)
AP
supplement to *Family Journal*
1: 'Blue Book' (16p) H. Foxwell £1.50–£3.00
2: 'Pink Book'   £1.00–£2.00
3: 'Green Book'   £1.00–£2.00

4: 'Mauve Book'   £1.00–£2.00
5: 'White Book'   £1.00–£2.00

ROUNDUP BUDGET OF FUN AND ADVENTURE
1948 (1)
Childrens Press (Mallard)
1 (nn) (20p) Sam Fair   50p–£1.25

ROVER MIDGET COMIC
11 Feb 1933 (1)
Thomson (*Rover* giveaway)
1 (nn) (32p) (small) D. Watkins £2.50–£3.50

ROVER SUMMER FUN BOOK
6 June 1936 (1)
Thomson
supplement to *Rover* (story-paper)
1 (nn) (8p) Dudley Watkins £1.00–£2.50

ROXY
15 Mar 1958–14 Sep 1963 (235)
AP
to: *Valentine*
1 (28p)   50p–75p
2–235   25p–50p

ROY CARSON
1948–1951 (8)
Boardman
to: *Roy Carson Comic*
1 (nn) (12p) (gravure) D. McLoughlin £1.00–£2.50
nos: (2) (3) (4) 13; 23; 34; 36 £1.00–£2.00

ROY CARSON COMIC
1953 (2)
Popular (Boardman)
1 (46) 2 (54) (28p) D. McLoughlin £1.00–£2.00

1954 (1)
Moring (Boardman reprints)
1 (nn) (68p) D. McLoughlin £1.00–£1.50

ROY OF THE ROVERS
25 Sep 1976–
IPC
1 (32p)   10p–25p
2–   10p–15p

ROY OF THE ROVERS HOLIDAY SPECIAL
May 1977–
IPC
1 (64p)   25p–40p
2–   20p–40p

ROY ROGERS AND TRIGGER
see: *Roy Rogers Comics*

ROY ROGERS COMICS
Apr 1951–1959 (100)
Pemberton/World (Dell)
aka: *Roy Rogers and Trigger* (57–84)
1 (36p) US reprint   50p–£1.50
2–15   50p–75p
16–18 (2C)   50p–75p
19– (4C)   75p–£1.00
95–100 (68p)   50p–75p

ROY ROGERS' TRIGGER
1952–1953 (14)
Pemberton/World (Dell)
1 (28p) US reprint   50p–£1.00
2–14   50p–75p

RUDIMENTS OF WISDOM
1974 (1)
Hutchinson (*Observer* strip reprints)
1 (52p) (oblong) Tim Hunkin 50p–75p

RUMBELOWS CHRISTMAS COMIC
1981 (1)

Rumbelows (giveaway)
1 (nn) (4p) (4C) promo   5p–10p

RUMPEL-STILTS-KIN
1944? (1)
Guardian Press
1 (nn) (20p) Fred Robinson   £1.00–£2.00

RUPERT
197–
Has
1 (16p) (4C) (poster)   30p–50p
2–   20p–30p

RUPERT ADVENTURE BOOK
1973 (2)
Daily Express (reprints)
1 (32p) (4C) *R in Mysteryland*   50p–75p
2 *R at Rocky Bay*   35p–50p

RUPERT ADVENTURE SERIES
Sep 1948–Jun 1963 (50)
Daily Express (reprints)
1: *Rupert & Snuffy*   £1.50–£3.00
2–50   £1.00–£1.50

RUPERT GIANT FOLDOUT WALL POSTER
1978 (1)
Jeenaroy
1 (folder) (4C)   30p–50p

RUPERT HOLIDAY SPECIAL
May 1979–May 1981 (3)
Polystyle (*Daily Express* reprints)
1 (nn) (48p) Alfred Bestall   25p–50p
2–3   20p–40p

RUPERT IN STORYLAND
see: *Storyland*

RUPERT SUMMER SPECIAL
May 1983
Marvel (*Daily Express* reprints)
1 (nn) (52p)   20p–35p

RUPERT T.V. PLAYBOOKS
1975 (4)
Stanfield
1: *Rupert Goes to the Moon* (16p)   20p–50p
2: *R and the Blue Mist*   15p–35p
3: *R and the Postman*   15p–35p
4: *R and the Magician's Hat*   15p–35p

RUPERT T.V. STORYBOOKS
1978 (6)
Stanfield
1 (28p) (4C) (small) Mick Wells   25p–30p
2–6   20p–25p

RUPERT WEEKLY
20 Oct 1982–15 Sep 1984 (100)
Marvel
& *Worzel Gummidge*: 28 Sep 1983
to: *Storyland*
1 (20p) *Daily Express* reprints   10p–20p
2–100   10p–15p

RUPERT'S FAMOUS YELLOW LIBRARY
1949 (2)
Sampson Low Marston (*Daily Express*)
1: *R & His Friend Margo* (20p)   £7.00–£8.00
2: *R the Knight & the Lady*   £5.00–£6.00
(Mary Tourtel; comic format)

RUTHERCOTE BUMPER BOOK OF FAMOUS COMICS
1968 (1)
Clyde Paper Co (giveaway)
1 (nn) (8p) (4C) printing promo: comic covers 25p–50p

S.A.T.A.N. PICTURE LIBRARY
Jan 1966–
Famepress
1– (68p) *Cold the Kiss of Fear* foreign reprint   20p–25p
2–   10p–20p

SABRE ROMANTIC STORIES IN PICTURES
1971–
Sabre
1– (68p) foreign reprint   15p–20p
2–   10p–15p

SABRE THRILLER PICTURE LIBRARY
1971–
Sabre
1– (68p) *Night of the Vulture* foreign reprint   15p–25p
2–   10p–15p

SABRE WAR PICTURE LIBRARY
1971–
Sabre
1: (68p) *Operation Breakthrough* foreign
reprint   15p–25p
2–   10p–15p

SABRE WESTERN PICTURE LIBRARY
1971–
Sabre
1: (68p) *Time to Fight* foreign reprint   15p–25p
2–   10p–15p

SABU
1951 (4)
Streamline/United Anglo-American (Fox)
1 (28p) US reprint   50p–£1.00
2–4   50p–75p

SAD SACK
1973–
Top Sellers (Harvey)
1– (36p) (4C) US reprint   25p–35p
2–   15p–20p

SAFETY FUN
1946? (1)
Cambridge Accident Prevention (giveaway)
1 (8p) Ronald Searle   £1.00–£2.50

SAFETY LIGHT
1939? (1)
ROSPA
1 (nn) (8p) (2C) road safety   £1.50–£3.00

SAINT
1966 (5)
Top Sellers
1 (68p) US reprint   75p–£1.00
2–5   50p–75p

SAINT DETECTIVE CASES
Oct 1951–
Thorpe & Porter (Avon)
1– (68p) US reprint   75p–£1.00

SALLY
14 Jun 1969–27 Mar 1971 (94)
IPC
to: *Tammy*
1 (36p) Ernest Ratcliff   35p–50p
2–94 Arthur Martin   20p–25p

SALLY SUMMER SPECIAL
1970 (1)
IPC
1 (nn) (96p)   35p–50p

SAM HILL PRIVATE EYE COMICS
1952 (5)
Thorpe & Porter (Closeup)
1 (68p) US reprints   75p–£1.00
2–5   50p–75p

SAMSON
1955 (3)
Miller (Ajax)

1 (28p) US reprint	75p–£1.00
2–3	50p–75p

SAMSON AND DELILAH
1950 (1)
Streamline/United Anglo-American (Fox)

1 (nn) (28p) US reprint	75p–£1.00

SANDIE
12 Feb 1972–20 Oct 1973 (89)
IPC
to: *Tammy*

1 (40p)	25p–35p
2–89	15p–20p

SATURDAY COMIC
31 Mar 1984–
Exeter Express & Echo (supplement)

1 (4p) US reprints	10p–15p
2–	5p–10p

SAVAGE ACTION
Nov 1979–Jan 1982 (15)
Marvel
to: *Marvel Super Heroes*

1 (52p) US reprints	30p–45p
2–15	25p–40p

SAVAGE SWORD OF CONAN
8 Mar 1975–5 Jul 1975 (18)
Marvel

1 (36p) US reprints	25p–50p
2–18	20p–35p

SAVAGE SWORD OF CONAN (MONTHLY)
Nov 1977–
Marvel
& Mighty World of Marvel: Nov 1984

1 (52p) US reprints	25p–50p
2–	

SBONCYN
May 1980–
Cyhoeddiadau Mei

1 (16p) Welsh language	25p–50p
2–	15p–20p

SCHOOL FRIEND
20 May 1950–23 Jan 1965 (766)
AP
& Girls Crystal: 25 May 1963
to: *June*

1 (20p) Evelyn Flinders	75p–£1.00
2–766 Basil Reynolds	25p–35p

SCHOOL FRIEND PICTURE LIBRARY
Feb 1962–Sep 1965
AP
to: *June & School Friend Pic. Lib.*

1: *Tracy's Fabulous Fur* (68p)	25p–50p
2–	15p–25p

SCHOOL FUN
15 Oct 1983–26 May 1984 (33)
IPC
to: *Buster*

1 (32p) Frank McDiarmid	5p–10p
2–33 Trevor Metcalfe	5p–10p

SCHOOL FUN HOLIDAY SPECIAL
May 1984 (1)
IPC

1 (64p)	20p–35p

SCHOOLGIRL
1951 (1)
Swan

1 (36p) John McCail	50p–£1.00

SCHOOLGIRLS PICTURE LIBRARY
Jul 1957–Sep 1965 (327)
AP
to: *June & School Friend Picture Lib.*

1: *Leader of Secret Avengers* (68p)	25p–35p
2–	15p–25p

SCOOBY-DOO AND HIS TV FRIENDS
24 Feb 1982–2 Jun 1983 (68)
Marvel/Hanna-Barbera

1 (32p) US reprints	15p–25p
2–68	10p–20p

SCOOBY DOO SPECIAL
May 1982–May 1984 (4)
Marvel (Hanna-Barbera)

1 *Summer 1982* (48p) US reprints	25p–50p
2 *Winter 1982*	20p–45p
3 *Summer 1983*	20p–45p
4 *Summer 1984*	20p–40p

SCOOBY DOO'S FUNTASTIC WORLD
HOLIDAY SPECIAL
Oct 1979–May 1980 (2)
Polystyle/Hanna-Barbera

1 (48p) US reprints	25p–40p
2	25p–35p

SCOOP
21 Jan 1978–3 Oct 1981 (194)
Thomson
to: *Victor*

1 (32p) (gravure)	15p–35p
2–194	10p–15p

SCOOP WESTERN
1950 (1)
Martin & Reid (Gower)

1 (16p) John McCail	50p–£1.00

SCOOPS
see: *Newspaper Comic*

SCOOPS COMIC
1948 (1)
Hotspur

1 (nn) (8p)	50p–£1.00

SCORCHER
10 Jan 1970–26 Jun 1971 (125)
IPC
to: *Scorcher & Score*

1 (32p) Ken Reid	25p–35p
2–125	20p–25p

SCORCHER AND SCORE
3 Jul 1971–5 Oct 1974 (171)
IPC
to: *Tiger*

1 (32p) Ken Reid	25p–35p
2–171	20p–25p

SCORCHER SPECIALS
May 1971–May 1980 (6)
IPC

1: *Holiday Special 1971* (96p)	30p–50p
2: *Holiday Special 1972*	25p–45p
3: *Holiday Special 1973*	25p–45p
4: *Holiday Special 1974* (80p)	25p–45p
5: *Summer Special 1979* (64p) reprints	20p–35p
6: *Holiday Special 1980*	20p–35p

SCORCHY
1972 (1)
Gold Star

1 (68p) US reprint (adult)	75p–£1.00

SCORE 'N' ROAR
19 Sep 1970–26 Jun 1971 (41)
IPC

to: *Scorcher & Score*
1 (32p)   25p–35p
2–41   15p–20p

SCOTLAND YARD
Nov 1965–
Famepress
1: *Innocent Crook* (68p)   20p–35p
2– (small) foreign reprints   15p–20p

SCOTTISH DAILY EXPRESS CHILDREN'S OWN
8 Apr 1933–27 Oct 1934 (82)
London Express Newspapers
supplement to *Scottish Daily Express*
1 (nn) (8p) (2C) (tabloid) George Parlett   £2.50–£5.00
2–82 Basil Reynolds   £1.00–£2.00
(*NB*: numbered same as newspaper)
see: *Daily Express Children's Own*

SCOTTY COMIC
1963 (2)
3M Scotch Tape (giveaway)
1 (nn) (8p) (4C) (small) Tomahawk   50p–£1.00
2 (nn) (8p) (4C) (small) Sticky Business 50p–£1.00

SCRAPS
29 Aug 1883–30 Apr 1910 (1394)
Henderson
to: *Merry-Thought & Scraps*
1 (8p) (tabloid)   £5.00–£10.00
2–   £1.50–£2.00
Xmas Triple Numbers   £2.00–£3.00
1900–1910   £1.00–£2.00

SCREAM
24 Mar 1984–30 Jun 1984 (30)
IPC
to: *Eagle*
1–30 (32p)   10p–25p

SEA DEVIL
1952 (1)
Scion
1 (20p) Terry Patrick   50p–£1.00

SEA HERO
1951 (1)
Scion
1 (nn) (24p) King-Ganteaume   50p–£1.00

SEASIDE COMIC
1930–1939 (10)
Pearson
1 (27 Jun 1930) Walter Bell   £2.50–£5.00
2 (20 Jun 1931) Walter Bell   £2.00–£3.50
3 (18 Jun 1932) Walter Bell   £2.00–£3.50
4 (17 Jun 1933) A. W. Browne   £2.00–£3.00
5 (14 Jun 1934) A. W. Browne   £2.00–£3.00
6 (14 Jun 1935) R. Plummer   £2.00–£3.50
7 (28 May 1936) Walter Bell   £2.00–£3.50
8 (4 Jun 1937) Ray Bailey   £2.00–£3.50
9 (3 Jun 1938) Norman Ward   £2.00–£3.50
10 (2 Jun 1939) R. Plummer   £2.00–£3.50

SECRET AGENT PICTURE LIBRARY
1961
Pearson
1 (68p) (small)   50p–75p
2–   35p–50p

SECRET AGENT PICTURE LIBRARY HOLIDAY
SPECIAL
1969–
Fleetway
1 (224p) reprints   50p–75p
2– (192p)   25p–50p

SECRET AGENT SERIES
Jan 1967–Jan 1968 (26)
Fleetway
1: *Meet Johnny Nero* (68p) (small)   35p–50p
2–26   25p–35p

SECRET AGENT X9
see: *Action Series*

SECRET HEARTS
1955 (8)
Trent (DC)
1–8 (68p) (US reprints)   25p–35p

SECRET LOVE
Jul 1983–
Micron (Eurediff)
1 (36p) photos: foreign reprint   15p–30p
2–   15p–20p

SECRET MISSIONS
1951 (1)
Streamline (Fox)
1 (nn) (28p) US reprint   50p–£1.00

SECRET SERVICE
1951 (1)
Streamline
1 (nn) (28p) US reprint   50p–£1.00

SECRET SERVICE PICTURE LIBRARY
Jun 1965–
MV Features
1: *The Defector* (68p)   25p–35p
2–   15p–25p

SECRET SERVICE SERIES
1948–1949 (6)
see: *Jet Plane Raiders*; *Wreckers*; *Crime Syndicate*;
Forgers; *Smugglers Creek*; *Atomic Spyring*

SECRETS OF LOVE
1954
Swan (Star)
1 US reprint   50p–75p
2–   35p–50p

SECRETS OF THE UNKNOWN
Oct 1962–
Class (Atlas)
1 (68p) US reprint   50p–£1.00
2–   20p–50p

SEE-SAW
9 Oct 1976–16 Jul 1977 (41)
IPC
to: *Toby*
1 (16p) TV characters   10p–15p
2–41   5p–10p

SENORITA RIO
1950 (1)
Cartoon Art (Fiction House)
1 (16p) US reprint   50p–£1.00

SERENADE
22 Sep 1962–9 Feb 1963 (25)
Fleetway
to: *Valentine*
1 (32p)   35p–50p
2–25   20p–25p

SERGEANT O'BRIEN
Feb 1952–1954 (42)
SNPI/Miller
1 (50) (24p) foreign reprint   35p–75p
51–91   25p–50p

SERGEANT PAT OF RADIO PATROL
Aug 1948 (1)
Modern Fiction (King Features)
1 (nn) (16p) (gravure) US reprint   50p–£1.00

SERGEANT PRESTON OF THE YUKON
1953–1954 (16)
World (Dell)

1 (28p) US reprint   35p–75p
2–16   35p–50p

SERIOUS COMICS
1975 (1)
H. Bunch/Cosmic Comics
1 (36p) (adult) William Rankin   35p–75p

SERVICE
May 1952–1953 (7)
Shell Mex-BP
6–12 (giveaway) (gravure)   50p–£1.00

SEVEN
20 Feb 1971–5 Jun 1971 (16)
Gresham
to: *Esmeralda*
1 (24p) (gravure)   35p–50p
2–16   25p–30p

SEXY TALES
1974 (3)
Top Sellers
1–3 (132p) foreign reprint   25p–35p

SHARI LEWIS' LAMBCHOP WEEKLY
Nov 1972–1974
Shelbourne
1 (16p)   20p–25p
2–   10p–15p

SHELL
Feb 1951–Jan 1952 (5)
Shell Mex-BP (giveaway)
to: *Service*
1 (gravure)   £1.00–£2.00
2–5   50p–£1.00

SHERIFF
1948–1949 (4)
Screen Stories
to: *Sheriff & Elmo's Own*
1 (8p) Denis Gifford   50p–£1.50
2–4   50p–£1.00

SHERIFF AND ELMO'S OWN
15 Jul 1949–1950 (5)
Screen Stories
1 (tabloid) (8p) Mick Anglo   50p–£1.00
2–5   50p–£1.00

SHERIFF OF COCHISE
June 1959–Sep 1959 (3)
Pearson (*T.V. Picture Stories*)
1 (TVP 18) *Kingdom* (68p)   50p–£1.00
2 (TVP 20) *Safe Men*   25p–50p
3 (TVP 22) *Hold-up*   25p–50p

SHERIFF OF TOMBSTONE
1959 (6)
Miller (Charlton)
1 (50) (28p) US reprint   50p–75p
51–55   35p–50p

SHIVER AND SHAKE
10 Mar 1973–5 Oct 1974 (83)
IPC
to: *Whoopee*
1 (36p) Robert Nixon   25p–50p
2–83 Brian Walker   15p–20p

SHIVER AND SHAKE CHRISTMAS HOLIDAY SPECIAL
1973 (1)
IPC
1 (nn) (96p)   25p–50p

SHIVER AND SHAKE HOLIDAY SPECIAL
Jul 1974–Jui 1980 (7)
IPC

SHOCK
Oct 1979–1980 (4)
Portman
1 (52p) US reprints   15p–35p
2–4   10p–15p

SHOOT
16 Aug 1969–
IPC
aka: *New Shoot* 1984
& *Goal:* 15 Jun 1974
1 (magazine)   20p–25p
2–   10p–15p

SHOOTING STAR COMIC
1948 (1)
Scion
1 (nn) (8p) Bob Wilkin   50p–£1.00

SHOTS FROM THE FILMS
1948 (1)
McKenzie
1 (nn) (8p) (photos)   50p–£1.00

SHOWBOAT COMIC
Sep 1948 (1)
Pictorial Art
1 (nn) (8p) Bob Wilkin   50p–£1.00

SIDE SPLITTERS
6 Aug 1894–1 Oct 1894 (9)
Trapps Holmes
to: *Worlds Comic*
1 (16p)   £5.00–£10.00
2–9   £1.50–£2.00

SILVER KID WESTERN
1955 (2)
Streamline/United Anglo-American (Stanmor)
1 (nn) (28p) US reprint   50p–75p
2 (nn) (68p)   35p–75p

SILVER KING
1946 (1)
PM (Marx)
1 (nn) (8p) (silver paper) Denis Gifford   50p–£1.50

SILVER SPARKS COMIC
1946 (1)
Marx
1 (nn) (8p) (silver paper)   50p–£1.00

SILVER STAR LIBRARY
Apr 1952–
Newnes Pearson
1: *Romantic Secrets* (32p) (4C) US reprint   50p–75p
2–   35p–50p

SILVER STAR FUN COMIC
1946 (1)
PM (Marx)
1 (nn) (8p) (silver paper) Denis Gifford   50p–£1.50

SILVER SURFER WINTER SPECIAL
Nov 1982 (1)
Marvel
1 (52p) US reprints   30p–60p

SINBAD AND THE EYE OF THE TIGER
1977 (1)
General Books
1 (nn) (32p) (film) Ian Gibson   35p–75p

SINGBAD THE SAILOR
1948 (1)
Childrens Press (Mallard)
1 (nn) (20p) Sam Fair   50p–£1.25

SINISTER TALES
Jan 1964–
Class (Atlas)
1 (68p) US reprint   50p–£1.00
2–   25p–35p

SIX COMICS OF WORLD WAR ONE
1972 (1)
Way (facsimiles)
set: *Lot-O-Fun* 4 Nov 1914
    Picture Fun 26 Dec 1914
    Comic Life 31 Jul 1915
    Funny Wonder 7 Aug 1915
    Rainbow 28 Apr 1917
    Illustrated Chips 21 Dec 1918
as single copies: 25p–£1.00
as set: £1.00–£2.50

SIX-GUN HEROES
Sep 1950–1959
Miller (Fawcett)
1– (Sep 1950) (28p) US reprint   75p–£1.00
50 (Jul 1951)   75p–£1.00
51–114   50p–75p

SIXGUN WESTERN
1957 (7)
Miller (Atlas)
1 (28p) US reprint   50p–£1.00
2–7   35p–75p

SKIPPER MIDGET COMIC
10 Nov 1934 (1)
Thomson (Skipper giveaway)
1 (nn) (32p) Dudley Watkins   £1.00–£2.00

SKITS
27 Jun 1891–28 Nov 1891 (23)
British Pub.
1 (8p) (tabloid)   £5.00–£10.00
2–23   £1.50–£2.00

SKY HERO COMIC
1952 (1)
Scion
1 (nn) (28p) King-Ganteaume   75p–£1.00

SKY HIGH COMIC
1949 (1)
PM (Marx)
1 (nn) (16p) Colin Merritt   50p–£1.00

SKY POLICE COMICS
1949 (1)
Cartoon Art (Fiction House)
1 (nn) (20p) (4C) US reprint   75p–£1.50

SKY SHERIFF
1951
Pemberton/World (DS)
aka: *Breeze Lawson*
1 (36p) US reprint   50p–75p

SKYLINE COMIC
1952 (1)
Scion
1 (20p) King-Ganteaume   50p–£1.00

SLAM BANG COMICS
1954 (8)
Miller (Fawcett)
1 (28p) US reprints   50p–£1.00
2–8   50p–75p

SLEEP CLINIC
1979 (1)
Express Books (*Daily Express* reprints)
1 (nn) (100p) (oblong) Neville Colvin 50p–75p

SLEEPYTIME STORIES
1972

Shelbourne
to: *Golden Hours*
1–   10p–20p

SLICK FUN
Jun 1940–1945 (21)
Swan
to: *Coloured Slick Fun*
1 (36p) William Ward   £2.50–£5.00
2–10 (36p) Harry Banger   £1.50–£2.00
11–12 (28p) John McCail   £1.00–£1.50
13–19 (20p) Glyn Protheroe   £1.00–£1.25
Spring 1942 (double) M. Stimpson £1.50–£2.50
Winter 1942 (double) Lovern West £1.50–£2.50

SLY SINISTER SCURVY ADVENTURES OF
CAPTAIN REILLY-FFOULL
194– (1)
Daily Mirror
1 (nn) (36p) *Just Jake* strips reprint £2.00–£3.50

SMASH
5 Feb 1966–3 Apr 1971 (265)
Odhams/IPC
& *Pow*: 14 Sep 1968
& *Fantastic*: 2 Nov 1968
to: *Valiant*
1 (24p) Leo Baxendale   £1.00–£2.00
2– Brian Lewis   25p–50p
15 Mar 1969: IPC issues   15p–20p

SMASH COMICS
1940–1941 (5)
Boardman (Quality)
1 (7) (36p) (4C) US reprints   £2.00–£3.50
8–11 (20p)   £1.50–£2.00

SMASH HOLIDAY SPECIAL
1969–1970 (2)
IPC
1–2 (96p) Leo Baxendale   25p–50p

SMASHER COMIC
1947 (1)
CAS
1 (nn) (8p) Bob Wilkin   50p–£1.00

SMASHER COMIC
see: *Out-and-Out Smasher Comic*

SMASHER COMICS
1947 (1)
Tongard
1 (8p) Bob Monkhouse   50p–£1.00

SMILER (adventures of)
1982 (1)
Boots (giveaway)
1 (nn) (12p) (3C) dental hygiene promo 5p–10p

SMILES
5 May 1906–10 Nov 1908 (133)
Trapps Holmes
to: *Funny Cuts*
1 (16p) (tabloid) Oliver Veal   £5.00–£10.00
2–133 Chas Genge   £1.50–£2.00

SMILEY BURNETTE WESTERN
1950 (4)
Miller (Fawcett)
1 (28p) US reprint   75p–£1.00
2–4   50p–75p

SMOKING GUNS WESTERN
1951 (1)
Scion
1 (24p) Ron Embleton   50p–£1.00

SMUGGLERS CREEK
1949 (1)
Hotspur (*Secret Service Series* 5)

1 (8p) (gravure) Bob Wilkin   50p–£1.00

SMURFS
see: *It's the Smurfs*
    King Smurf

SNACKS
15 Jun 1889–21 Jun 1890 (51)
Snacks
1 (8p) (tabloid)   £5.00–£10.00
2–51   £1.50–£2.00

SNAP-SHOTS
28 Jul 1890–30 Apr 1910 (1394)
Henderson
& Comic Pictorial Sheet: 5 Oct 1904
& Pictorial Comedy: 20 Oct 1904
1 (16p)   £5.00–£10.00
2–   £1.50–£2.00
Club Edition (1899–) (24p)   £1.25–£1.75

SNATCH COMICS
undated/no imprint
1 (36p) (small) US/UG reprint   25p–50p

SNOOZY SERIES
1959–1960 (2)
Brockhampton
1: *Snoozy the Sea Lion* (36p)   50p–£1.00
2: (oblong)   35p–50p

SNOW WHITE
1974 (1)
Top Sellers
1 (nn) (132p) (adult) foreign reprint   25p–35p

SOCCER
Dec 1973–1974
Top Sellers
1– (36p) (4C) foreign reprint   20p–25p

SOLDIER COMICS
1952 (6)
Miller (Fawcett)
1 (28p) US reprint   35p–75p
2–6   25p–50p

SOLO
18 Feb 1967–16 Sep 1967 (31)
City
to: *TV Tornado*
1 (24p) (Disney reprints)   50p–75p
2–31 Reg Parlett   35p–50p

SOMETIME STORIES
May 1977 (1)
Hourglass Comics
1 (32p) (adult) McCarthy & Ewins   50p–75p

SON OF TARZAN SPECIAL
Oct 1980–Aug 1981 (4)
Byblos
1: *Autumn Special* (52p) reprints   25p–40p
2: *Winter Special*   25p–35p
3: *Summer Special*   25p–35p
4: *Autumn Special*   25p–35p

SOOTY SPECIALS
May 1976–May 1982 (10)
Polystyle
1: *Holiday Special 1976* (48p) reprints   35p–50p
2: *Holiday Special 1977*   25p–30p
3: *Winter Special 1977*   25p–30p
4: *Holiday Special 1978*   25p–30p
5: *Winter Special 1978*   25p–30p
6: *Holiday Special 1979*   25p–30p
7: *Sooty's Special 1979*   25p–30p
8: *Holiday Special 1980*   25p–30p
9: *Summer Special 1981*   25p–30p
10: *Holiday Special 1982*   25p–30p

SOUR CREAM
May 1980–June 1982 (3)
Sourcream/Sisterwrite
1 (8p) (folder) (2C) women's lib   50p–£1.00
2–3   25p–50p

SOUTH WALES ECHO & EXPRESS CHILDREN'S
SUPPLEMENT
27 May 1933–8 Jun 1935 (107)
South Wales Echo & Express
supplement to newspaper
aka: *Children's South Wales Echo & Express; Boys and
Girls Own South Wales Echo*
1 (nn) (4p) (tabloid) Reg Perrott   £2.00–£3.00
2–107 Stanley White   £1.00–£1.50

SPACE ACE
Aug 1960–Mar 1963 (32)
Atlas
1 (28p) R. Turner   50p–£1.00
2–32 Colin Andrew   35p–75p

SPACE ADVENTURES
195–
Miller (Charlton)
1– (68p) (small) US reprint   35p–50p

SPACE ADVENTURES
1953–
Miller (Charlton)
1 (50) (28p) US reprint   50p–75p
51–   50p–65p

SPACE ADVENTURES PRESENTS SPACE TRIP
TO THE MOON
1961 (1)
Class (Charlton)
1 (68p) US reprint   50–75p

SPACE AND ADVENTURE COMICS
1961 (2)
Miller
1 (reprints) (68p)   £1.00–£2.00
2   £1.00–£1.50

SPACE COMICS
May 1953–1954 (32)
Arnold (Gower)
aka: *Captain Valiant*
1 (50) (32p) Mick Anglo   50p–£1.00
51–54 Denis Gifford   35p–75p
55–81 (weekly: 28 Nov 1953)   35p–75p

SPACE COMICS OMNIBUS
1954 (1)
Arnold
Space Comics 55–60 rebound   £2.00–£3.00

SPACE COMMANDER KERRY
Aug 1953–1954 (6)
Miller (Gower)
1 (50) (28p) Mick Anglo   50p–£1.00
51–55 Denis Gifford   35p–75p

SPACE COMMANDO COMICS
Sep 1953–1954 (10)
Miller (Gower)
1 (50) (28p) Mick Anglo   50p–£1.00
51–59 Denis Gifford   35p–75p

SPACE HERO COMIC
1951 (2)
Scion
1 (24p) Norman Light   50p–£1.00
2   35p–75p

SPACE PATROL
Jun 1964–Dec 1964 (2)
Young World
1 (*Super Mag* 12) Paul Hoye   50p–75p
2 (*Super Mag* 24)   50p–75p

SPACE PICTURE LIBRARY HOLIDAY SPECIAL
May 1977–May 1981 (5)
IPC
1 (nn) (196p) reprints   30p–50p
2–5   20p–30p

SPACE SQUADRON
1951 (2)
Streamline/United Anglo-American (Atlas)
1–2 (28p) US reprint   50p–£1.00

SPACE TRAVELLERS
195– (10)
Peters (United Features)
1 (28p) *Twin Earths* reprint   50p–£1.00
2–10   50p–75p

SPACE WORLDS
1954 (1)
Streamline/United Anglo-American (Atlas)
1 (28p) US reprint   50p–£1.00

SPACEHAWKS
see: *Blue Bolt Series*

SPACEMAN
1953–1954 (15)
Gould-Light
1 (28p) Ron Embleton   £1.00–£1.25
2–15 Norman Light   75p–£1.00

SPACEMAN COMICS
1950 (1)
Cartoon Art (Fiction House)
1 (28p) US reprint   75p–£1.25

SPACEWAYS COMIC
Nov 1953 (1)
Popular (Boardman)
1 (52) (28p) Denis McLoughlin   £1.00–£2.00

SPARK MAN
1950 (1)
Peters (United Features)
1 (19) (20p) (gravure) US reprint   50p–£1.00

SPARKLE
4 Nov 1953–3 Feb 1954 (14)
Pearson
1 (4p) supplement: *Silver Star*   50p–£1.00
2–14   25p–50p

SPARKLER
12 Sep 1931–23 Jun 1932 (20)
Provincial
1 (8p) (tabloid) Bert Hill   £5.00–£7.50
2–20 Louis Diamond   £2.00–£2.50

SPARKLER
20 Oct 1934–5 Aug 1939 (251)
AP
to: *Crackers*
1 (12p) (tabloid) Bertie Brown   £5.00–£10.00
2–251 George Wakefield   £2.00–£2.50

SPARKLER AND MERRY MIDGET
12 Sep 1931–23 Jun 1982 (20)
overseas edition: two comics   £2.50–£3.00

SPARKLER COMIC BOOK SERIES
1948–1949 (16)
Peters (United Features)
to: *Comics on Parade*
1 (16p) (gravure) US reprint   75p–£1.25
2–16   50p–£1.00

SPARKLER COMICS
Feb 1948 (1)
Miller (United Features)
1 (16p) (gravure) US reprints   50p–£1.00

SPARKLET COMIC
1948 (2)
Philmar/PM (Marx)
1–2 (8p) Arthur Martin   50p–£1.00

SPARKLING COMIC
1945 (3)
International
(a) (12p) inc: *Super Science Thrills*   50p–£1.00
(b) (8p) John Turner   50p–£1.00
(c) (8p) b/w edition   50p–£1.00

SPARKLING COMIC
1945 (1)
Marx
1 (nn) (16p) Reg Carter   50p–£1.00

SPARKS
2 May 1896–
Bradley
1 (16p) (tabloid)   £5.00–£10.00
2–   £2.00–£3.50

SPARKS
21 Mar 1914–29 Dec 1917 (198)
Henderson
to: *Big Comic & Sparks*
1 (12p) Walter Booth   £5.00–£10.00
2– Louis Briault   £1.50–£2.00
1915: red/black issues   £2.00–£2.25
1916: small issues   £1.50–£2.00
1917: b/w issues   £1.50–£1.75

SPARKS AND THE BIG COMIC
5 Oct 1918–26 Apr 1919 (30)
Henderson
to: *Sparks*
247–276 (8p) (tabloid) Walter Booth   £1.50–£1.75

SPARKS (NEW SERIES)
3 May 1919–17 Apr 1920 (51)
Henderson/AP
to: *Little Sparks*
1 (277) (8p) (tabloid) Walter Booth   £2.00–£2.50
278–322   £1.50–£2.00
323–327: AP issues Don Newhouse   £1.50–£2.00

SPARKY
23 Jan 1965–16 Jul 1977 (652)
Thomson
to: *Topper*
1 (24p) Jack Monk   50p–75p
2–652 Bob Nixon   15p–35p

SPARKY WATTS
1950–1951 (2)
Streamline/United Anglo-American (Columbia)
1–2 (nn) (4C) (36p) US reprint   75p–£1.25

SPECTACULAR COLOUR COMIC
1951 (2)
Scion
1–2 (24p) King-Ganteaume   50p–£1.00

SPECTACULAR CRIMES
1951 (2)
Streamline/United Anglo-American (Fox)
1–2 (28p) US reprint   75p–£1.00

SPECTACULAR FEATURES
1951 (1)
Streamline/United Anglo-American (Fox)
1 (28p) US reprint   75p–£1.00

SPECTRE STORIES
196 (6)
Spencer
1–6 (52p) Ron Embleton   35p–75p

SPEED
23 Feb 1980–25 Oct 1980 (36)

IPC
to: *Tiger*
1 (32p) R. Turner   20p–30p
2–36   10p–15p

SPEED AND POWER
22 Mar 1974–22 Nov 1975 (87)
IPC
to: *Look & Learn*
1 (magazine)   15p–20p
2–87   10p–15p

SPEED AND POWER CHRISTMAS SPECIAL
1974 (1)
IPC
1 (nn) (48p)   20p–30p

SPEED GALE COMICS
1947 (1)
Cartoon Art
1 (nn) (16p) (reprints)   50p–£1.00

SPEED KINGS COMIC
Nov 1953–Apr 1954 (6)
Mans World (Atlas)
1 (12) (28p)   50p–75p
13–17   50p–75p

SPEED SUMMER SPECIAL
Aug 1980 (1)
IPC
1 (nn) (64p) Geoff Campion   25p–45p

SPELLBOUND
1961–1966 (66)
Miller (Atlas)
1 (68p) US reprint   50p–£1.00
2–66   35p–50p
see: *Comics to Hold You Spellbound*

SPELLBOUND
25 Sep 1976–14 Jan 1978 (69)
Thomson
to: *Debbie*
1 (32p)   15p–25p
2–69   10p–15p

SPELLBOUND MAGAZINE
1952 (1).
Cartoon Art
1 (nn) (68p) US reprints   £1.00–£2.50

SPIDERMAN COMICS WEEKLY
17 Feb 1973–
Marvel
aka: *Super Spiderman* 158–
      Spiderman Comic 311–
      Super Spiderman TV Comic 450–
      Spiderman & his Amazing Friends 553–
& *The Super Heroes:* 21 Feb 1976
& *The Titans:* 1 Dec 1976
& *Captain Britain:* 13 Jul 1977
& *Marvel Comic:* 1 Aug 1979
& *Hulk:* 22 May 1980
& *Team-Up:* 11 Mar 1981
& *Incredible Hunk:* 6 Oct 1982
& *Fantastic Four:* 21 Apr 1983
& *Big Ben:* 26 Jul 1984
1 (40p) US reprints   50p–£1.00
2–   25p–35p

SPIDERMAN POCKET BOOK
Mar 1980–Jul 1982 (28)
Marvel
1 (52p) (small) US reprints   15p–25p
2–28   10p–15p
9, 20 Xmas double numbers (100p)   20p–30p

SPIDERMAN SPECIALS
May 1979–
Marvel
1: *Summer Special 1979* (52p)   25p–50p
2: *Winter Special 1979*   25p–50p

3: *Summer Special 1980*   25p–40p
4: *Winter Special 1980*   25p–40p
5: *Summer Special 1981*   25p–45p
6: *Winter Special 1981*   25p–45p
7: *Summer Special 1982*   30p–50p
8: *Winter Special 1982*   30p–50p
9: *Summer Special 1983*   30p–50p
10: *Winter Special 1983*   25p–50p
11: *Summer Special 1984*   25p–50p
12: *Winter Special 1984*   25p–50p

SPIDERMAN'S JUNIOR PUZZLE FUN
Oct 1981 (1)
Marvel
1 (52p) US reprints   25p–45p

SPIDERMAN'S PLAYTIME FUN-BOOK
Nov 1981 (1)
Marvel
1 (52p) US reprints   25p–45p

SPIKE
22 Jan 1983–28 Apr 1984 (67)
Thomson
to: *Champ*
1 (36p)   15p–20p
2–67 (32p)   10p–15p

SPIRIT
1949 (2)
Boardman (Quality)
1 (12) (12p) (gravure) US reprint   £1.50–£2.50
17   £1.00–£2.00

SPORT KOMIC
1948 (1)
Merseyside Sporting News
1 (nn) (8p) Charles Ross   50p–£1.00

SPORTING SAM
1979 (1)
Express Books (*Sunday Express* reprints)
1 (nn) (132p) (oblong) Reg Wootton   50p–£1.00

SPORTS FUN
11 Feb 1922–6 May 1922 (13)
AP
to: *New Series* (story-paper)
1 (20p) Tom Webster   £4.00–£6.00
2–13 George Wakefield   £1.75–£2.00

SPORTS PARADE
1947 (1)
Mirror (*Sunday Pictorial* strips)
1 (nn) (28p) 'Jon' reprints   £1.50–£2.00

SPRING COMIC
1932–1934 (3)
Pearson
1: 21 Mar 1932 (12p) (tabloid)   £2.50–£5.00
2: 21 Mar 1933 Walter Bell   £2.00–£3.50
3: 26 Mar 1934 A. W. Browne   £2.00–£2.50

SPY SMASHER
Jul 1953– (4)
Miller (Fawcett)
1 (50) (28p) US reprint   75p–£1.00
51–54   50p–75p

SPY 13 SUMMER SPECIAL
Jun 1966 (1)
Fleetway
1 (224p) reprints (small)   50p–75p

SPYMASTER COMICS
1951–1952 (3)
Scion
1–3 (24p) King-Ganteaume   50p–£1.00

SQUIBS FUN COMIC
1949 (1)

Martin & Reid (Gower)
1 (nn) (8p) (tabloid) Frank Minnitt   50p–£1.25

SRADAG
1960
Comunn Gaidhealach
1 (4p) (4C) (large) Gaelic comic   £1.00–£2.00

STANLEY BAGSHAW
1982–1983 (2)
Picture Puffins (Hamish Hamilton)
1: *SB & the 14 Foot Wheel* (36p) (4C)   50p–£1.10
2: *SB & the 22 Ton Whale*   60p–£1.25

STAR COMIC
1954 (2)
Peters
1 (20p) Bert Hill   50p–£1.00
2 James Bleach   50p–£1.00

STAR COMICS
Dec 1943 (1)
PM (Marx)
1 (nn) (16p) Frank Jupo   50p–£1.00

STAR FLASH COMIC
1948 (2)
PM (Marx)
1 (8p) Colin Merritt   50p–£1.00
2 Wally Robertson   50p–£1.00

STAR HEROES
Oct 1979 (1)
Marvel
1 (52p) US reprints   25p–40p

STAR HEROES POCKET BOOK
Mar 1980–May 1981 (13)
Marvel
to: *X-Men Pocket Book*
1 (52p) (small) US reprints   15p–25p
2–8   10p–15p
9 (100p)   20p–30p
10–13   10p–20p

STAR LORD
13 May 1978–7 Oct 1978 (22)
IPC
to: *2000 AD*
1 (32p) Ian Kennedy   50p–75p
2–22 Carlos Esquerra   25p–50p

STAR LORD SUMMER SPECIAL
22 Jul 1978 (1)
IPC
1 (48p) John Cooper   35p–50p

STAR LOVE STORIES
196 –197–
Thomson
1– (small) (68p)   15p–20p

STAR PIRATE COMICS
1950 (1)
Cartoon Art (Fiction House)
1 (nn) (20p) US reprint   50p–£1.00

STAR ROCKET
1953–(5)
Comyns (4); Moring (5)
1–4 (28p) Ron Embleton   50p–£1.00
5 (nn) (68p) (Moring reprint)   50p–£1.00

STAR STREAMLINE COMICS
195–(1)
Streamline/United Anglo-American
1 (nn) (132p) US reprints   £1.50–£2.50

STAR TREK
see: *Mighty Midget*

STAR TREK SPECIALS
Nov 1975–Nov 1982 (4)
Polystyle (1) IPC (2) Marvel (3–4)
1: *Winter Special 1975* (48p)   35p–50p
2: *Special 1978* (48p)   35p–50p
3: *Summer Special 1981* (52p)   30p–45p
4: *Winter Special 1982*   40p–60p

STAR WARS
Apr 1978 (1)
Sphere (Marvel)
1 (nn) (128p) US reprint   75p–£1.00

STAR WARS WEEKLY
8 Feb 1978–22 May 1980 (117)
Marvel
to: *Star Wars: Empire Strikes Back*
1 (28p) US reprints   25p–50p
2–117   25p–35p

STAR WARS: THE EMPIRE STRIKES BACK
WEEKLY
29 May 1980–23 Oct 1980 (22)
Marvel
to: *Star Wars: Empire Strikes Back Monthly*
1 (118) (28p) US reprints   15p–25p
119–139   15p–20p

STAR WARS: THE EMPIRE STRIKES BACK
MONTHLY
Nov 1980–Jul 1983 (32)
Marvel
to: *Star Wars: Return of the Jedi*
1 (140) (44p) US reprints   25p–40p
141–171   20p–40p

STAR WARS: RETURN OF THE JEDI
22 Jun 1983–
Marvel
1 (28p) (4C) US reprints   15p–25p
2–   15p–20p

STAR WARS SPECIALS
May 1983–Nov 1984
Marvel
1: *Summer Special 1983* (48p) US reprint   35p–60p
2: *Winter Special 1983*   30p–50p
3: *Summer Special 1984*   30p–50p
4: *Winter Special 1984*   30p–50p

STARBLAZER
Apr 1979–
Thomson
1 (68p) (small) *Omega Experiment*   15p–25p
2–   10p–15p

STARK TERROR
Oct 1979–1980 (4)
Portman (Stanley)
1 (52p) US reprints   15p–35p
2–4   10p–15p

STARLIGHT COMICS
1947 (1)
Bear Hudson
1 (nn) (12p)   50p–£1.00

STARRY SPANGLES COMIC
1948 (1)
Philmar (Marx)
2 (nn) (8p) Walter Bell   50p–£1.00

STARTLING DETECTIVE
1951 (1)
Streamline (Fox)
1 (28p) US reprint   75p–£1.00

STARTLING TERROR TALES
1952 (1)
Arnold (Star)
1 (68p) US reprint   £1.50–£2.50

STEVE SAMSON
Jan 1953–1955 (40)
Sports Cartoons (Miller)
& Capt. Vigour, Dick Hercules, Supersonic: 18
1 (28p) Nat Brand   50p–£1.00
2–40 (weekly from 18)   35p–50p

STEWPOT'S FUN BOOK
1977 (1)
ITV/Arrow
1 (100p) Trevor Metcalfe (small)   50p–75p

STICK-IT COMICS
Feb 1951 (1)
News of the World
1 (nn) (16p) Cyril Price   50p–£1.00

STINGRAY SUMMER SPECIAL
Jun 1983 (1)
Polystyle
1 (48p) (TV series) reprints   40p–60p

STORIES OF BILLY THE BEE
196– (1)
Beaverbrook (*Evening Standard* strips)
1 (nn) (68p) Harry Smith   £1.00–£2.00

STORIES TO HOLD YOU SPELLBOUND
see: *Comics To Hold You Spellbound; Spellbound*

STORM
Aug 1982 (1)
BEAP/Oberon
1 (nn) (52p) (4C) Don Lawrence   50p–80p

STORMBRINGER
1980? (1)
Savoy Books
1 (nn) (32p) (tabloid) James Cawthorn   £1.50p–£3.00

STORMER
23 Mar 1981 (1)
NSIWP/NSPUK
1 (4p) (tabloid) National Front propaganda 50p–£5.00

STORY LAND
28 Mar 1984–
Marvel
& Rupert: 22 Sep 84
1   15p–20p
2–   10p–15p

STORY TELLER
5 Jan 1983–17 Dec 1983 (26)
Marshall Cavendish
to: *Story Teller 2*
1 (with sound cassette) (32p) (4C)   £1.00–£2.00
2–26 (with sound cassettes)   75p–£1.00
without sound cassettes   10p–25p
see: *Christmas Story Teller*

STORY TELLER 2
17 Dec 1983–19 Jan 1984 (26)
Marshall Cavendish
1 (nn) (free preview issue) (32p) (4C)   50p–£1.00
1– (with sound cassette)   £1.00–£1.50
2–26   75p–£1.00
without sound cassettes   10p–25p

STORY TIME
aka: *Woman's Realm Story Time*
11 Sep 1965–6 May 1967 (87)
Odhams
to: *Robin*
1 (16p)   25p–25p
2–87   15p–20p

STORYTIME FAVOURITES
1973

Top Sellers (Gilberton)
1– (36p) (4 col) US reprint   25p–50p

STRAIGHT ARROW
1951 (1)
Streamline/United Anglo-American (ME)
1 (28p) US reprint   50p–75p

STRAIGHT ARROW
1952– (20)
Compix/Cartoon Art (Magazine Ent.)
1 (24p) US reprint   75p–£1.00
2–20   50p–75p

STRANGE STORIES
196 (6)
Spencer
1–6 (52p) Ron Embleton   25p–75p

STRANGE WORLDS
Oct 1951–
Thorpe & Porter (Avon)
1 (68p) US reprint   50p–75p

STRANGE WORLDS
Nov 1953–1954 (6)
Mans World/Atlas
1 (12) (28p) Sydney Jordan   50p–£1.00
13–17   50p–75p

STREAMLINE COMICS
1947 (4)
Cardal
1 (20p) Denis Gifford   50p–£1.00
2–4 Bryan Berry   50p–£1.00

STREAMLINE COMICS
see: *Action Streamline Comics*
     Adventure Streamline Comics
     Flash Streamline Comics
     Star Streamline Comics
     Super Streamline Comics

STREAMLINE PICTORIAL ROMANCE
195? (7?)
Streamline
1: *He Dared Her* (28p) US reprints   25p–50p
2: *He Scorned Her*   25p–50p
3: *Honeymoon Without Love*   25p–50p
4: *I Wanted Both Men*   25p–50p
5: *Man Downstairs*   25p–50p
6: *My Father's Past*   25p–50p
7: *They Called Me a Flirt*   25p–50p

STREET COMIX
1976–1978 (5)
Birmingham Arts Lab
1 (12p) (adult) (giveaway)   25p–50p
2–5 (40p) Hunt Emerson   50p–75p

STRIKER
10 Jan 1970–
City
1   25p–50p
2–   15p–20p

STRIP CARTOON SECTION
17 Apr 1938–11 Dec 1938 (35)
Sunday Pictorial
supplement to *Sunday Pictorial* newspaper
1 (nn) (4p) (tabloid) Arthur Ferrier   £1.00–£2.00
2–35 Harry Dodd   50p–£1.00
(absorbed into newspaper, no longer a section)

STRIP COMICS
1944 (1)
Fairylite
1 (nn) (16p) (4C) Bob Wilkin   50p–£1.00

STUPENDOUS SERIES
Feb 1967–Jan 1968 (24)

Fleetway
1 (3) (132p) (small)   25p–50p
4–24   15p–25p

SUCCESSORS
Dec 1979 (1)
Kelly
1 (24p) Keith Luck   15p–30p

SUMMER COMIC
1932–1938 (4)
Pearson
1 (25 Jun 1932) A. W. Browne   £2.50–£5.00
2 (28 May 1936) R. Plummer   £2.00–£3.00
3 (4 Jun 1937) F. Minnitt   £2.00–£3.00
4 (3 Jun 1938) Norman Ward   £2.00–£3.00

SUMMER HOLIDAY COMIC
14 Jun 1935 (1)
Pearson
1 (nn) (12p) (tabloid) R. Plummer   £2.50–£3.50

SUN
11 Nov 1947–17 Oct 1959 (558)
Allen (1–41); AP
aka: *Fitness & Sun* (4); *Sun Comic*; *Sun Adventure
Weekly*; *Cowboy Sun*; *Sun Weekly*
to: *Lion*
1 (8p) (tabloid) Harry Banger   £1.50–£2.00
41 (first AP issue) Fred Robinson   75p–£1.25
164 (comicbook format) Hugh McNeill   75p–£1.00
490 (20p) (letterpress) Geoff Campion   25p–50p

SUN FUN CARTOON SPECIAL
28 Aug 1978 (1)
Sun
supplement to *Sun* newspaper
1 (4p) (tabloid) US reprints   10p–25p

SUNBEAM
7 Oct 1922–23 Jan 1926 (173)
AP
to: *New Series*
1 (12p) (tabloid) Walter Booth   £5.00–£10.00
2–173 Walter Bell   £1.50–£2.00

SUNBEAM NEW SERIES
30 Jan 1926–25 May 1940 (747)
AP
& *Puck*: 18 May 1940
to: *Tiny Tots*
1 (12p) (tabloid) Fred Crompton   £5.00–£10.00
2–731 Don Newhouse   £1.50–£2.00
732–747 (small format)   £2.00–£3.00

SUNDANCE WESTERN
1970
World
1– (68p) (small) US reprint   20p–25p

SUNDAY EXTRA
6 June 1965–10 Jul 1967 (110)
Sunday Citizen
supplement to *Sunday Citizen* newspaper
1 (4p) (tabloid) (green paper) F. Langford   25p–50p
2–14 Nov 1965 Sally Artz   15p–20p
21 Nov 1965–10 July 1967 (white paper)   15p–20p

SUNDAY FAIRY
10 May 1919–4 Oct 1919 (22)
AP
to: *Childrens Sunday Fairy*
1 (12p) Helen Jacobs   £5.00–£7.50
2–22 Julius Baker   £1.50–£2.00

SUNDAY GANG SPECIAL
Oct 1978 (1)
Lion/BBC
1 (nn) (36p) Bob Bond (religious)   25p–50p

SUNDAY POST FUN SECTION
8 Mar 1936–
Thomson
supplement to *Sunday Post* newspaper
1 (nn) (8p) Dudley Watkins   £2.50–£5.00
2–2 Jun 1940 Allan Morley   £1.00–£1.50
9 Jun 1940–6 Apr 1941 (6p)   £1.00–£1.25
13 April 1941–22 Mar 1942 (4p)   50p–75p
29 Mar 1942– (2p)   25p–50p
(4p)   10p–15p

SUNDAY TRIBUNE COMIC
13 Dec 1981–
Dublin Sunday Tribune
supplement to *Sunday Tribune*
1 (8p) (4C) (tabloid) US reprints   25p–50p
2–   10p–15p

SUNNY COMIC
17 Sep 1928–20 Apr 1929 (28)
Ransom (*Monster Comic* reprints)
1 (8p) (tabloid) Reg Carter   £3.00–£5.00
2–28 Louis Diamond   £1.50–£2.00

SUNNY COMIC
1945 (1)
International
1 (nn) (8p) J. R. Turner   50p–£1.00

SUNNY COMIC
1945 (1)
PM (Marx)
1 (nn) (16p) Reg Carter   50p–£1.00

SUNNY FUN COMIC
1948 (1)
Philmar (Marx)
1 (8p) Wally Robertson   50p–£1.00

SUNNY SANDS
2 Jun 1939 (1)
Pearson
1 (12p) (tabloid) Norman Ward   £3.50–£5.00

SUNNY STORIES NEW SERIES
12 Jul 1958–19 Jun 1971
Newnes/IPC
to: *Disneyland*
1 (previously story-paper)   25p–35p
2–   20p–25p

SUNNYTIMES COMIC
1948 (1)
Rayburn (Martin & Reid)
1 (8p) Bob Wilkin   50p–£1.00

SUNSHINE
16 Jul 1938–8 Apr 1939 (39)
Target
to: *Jingles*
1 (8p) (tabloid) Harry Banger   £5.00–£7.50
2–15 (8p) Bert Hill   £2.00–£3.00
16–29 (12p) Louis Diamond   £1.50–£2.00

SUNSHINE PICTURE STORY BOOK
1944 (1)
no imprint
1 (nn) (14p) (oblong) Fred Robinson   50p–£1.00

SUPER ADVENTURE
Jan 1968–1969 (36)
White
1: *Bitter Bargain* (68p) (small)   20p–25p
2–36 foreign reprints   15p–20p

SUPER ADVENTURES
1946 (1)
John Matthew (Martin & Reid)
1 (8p) (2C)   50p–£1.00

202

SUPER-BUMPER COMIC
1948 (1)
Valentine (Mallard)
1 (nn) (16p) Nat Brand ... 50p–£1.25

SUPER CLASSICS ILLUSTRATED
May 1952–
Thorpe & Porter (Gilberton)
1: *Westward Ho* (48p) US reprint ... 50p–£1.00
2– ... 50p–75p

SUPER COMIC STRIPS
1949 (1)
Martin & Reid (Gower)
1 (8p) (tabloid) Harry Banger ... 50p–£1.25

SUPER COMICS
Dec 1943 (1)
PM (Marx)
1 (16p) Frank Jupo ... 50p–£1.00
1946 reprint (larger) ... 50p–£1.00

SUPER D.C.
June 1969–Jul 1970 (14)
Top Sellers (DC)
1 (40p) US reprints ... 35p–75p
2–14 ... 25p–50p

SUPER DETECTIVE LIBRARY
Mar 1953–Dec 1960 (188)
AP
aka: *Super Detective Picture Library*
1: *Meet the Saint* (68p) ... £1.50–£2.50
2–188 ... 75p–£1.00
NB: Sherlock Holmes/Edgar Wallace/Buck Ryan
issues may cost more

SUPER DUPER COMICS
1946–1960 (21)
Cartoon Art
aka: *Super Duper Boys Magazine/It's Super-Duper*
1 (8p) ... 50p–£1.00
2–3 (8p) (tabloid) ... 50p–£1.50
   (3 varies: some Powerman)
4 (16p) Dennis Reader ... 50p–£1.00
Special (nn) (16p) Dennis Reader ... 50p–£1.00
5–14 (36p) Dennis Reader ... 50p–£1.50
15–18 (20p) Dennis Reader ... 50p–£1.00
19 (68p) (inc US reprints) ... 50p–£1.00
20 (36p) ... 50p–£1.00

SUPER FUNNIES
1940–1941 (5)
Boardman (Quality)
1 (29) (36p) US reprints (4C) ... £2.00–£3.50
30–33 (20p) ... £1.50–£2.00

SUPER HERO FUN AND GAMES
Oct 1979 (1)
Marvel
1 (nn) (36p) US reprints ... 20p–25p

SUPER HERO FUN AND GAMES
Mar 1980–Nov 1981 (21)
Marvel
1 (36p) US reprints ... 20p–25p
2–21 ... 15p–20p

SUPER-HEROES
8 Mar 1975–14 Feb 1976 (50)
Marvel
to: *Spiderman*
1 (36p) US reprints ... 25p–50p
2–50 ... 15p–20p

SUPER HEROES MONTHLY
1980–Jun 1982 ( )
Egmont/London Editions (DC)
1 (52p) US reprints ... 40p–50p
2– ... 25p–45p

SUPER JOLLY ROGER
1949 (1)
Martin & Reid (Gower)
1 (8p) (tabloid) Bob Monkhouse ... 50p–£1.25

SUPER MAG
Jan 1964–
Young World (Gold Key)
1 (36p) *Flight of White Stallion* US reprint ... 35p–50p
2– ... 25p–35p
see: *Space Patrol*; *Terrible Ten*

SUPER MOUSE
195– (1)
Class (Charlton)
1 (68p) US reprints ... 25p–45p

SUPER PICTURE SPECIAL
1969 (1)
IPC
1 (448p) (reprints) (small) ... 35p–50p

SUPER SCIENCE THRILLS
1945 (1)
International
1 (nn) (8p) ... 50p–£1.00

SUPER SMASHER COMIC
1947 (1)
Coordination
1 (nn) (8p) Peit Van Elk ... 50p–75p

SUPER-SONIC THE SUPER COMIC
Dec 1953–May 1954 (6)
Mans World (Miller)
to: *Steve Samson*
1 (12) (28p) ... 50p–£1.00
13–17 ... 50p–75p

SUPER SPORTS
May 1979–Aug 1980 (6)
Byblos
1: *Summer Special* (52p) Spanish reprint ... 20p–40p
2: *Autumn Special* ... 20p–35p
3: *Winter Special* ... 20p–35p
4: *Spring Special* ... 20p–35p
5: *Summer Special* ... 20p–35p
6: *Autumn Special* ... 20p–35p

SUPER STAR
Oct 1948–Oct 1949 (4)
Berkeley Thompson (Martin & Reid)
1 (8p) (tabloid) Bob Monkhouse ... 50p–£1.50
2–4 John McCail ... 50p–£1.00

SUPER STREAMLINE COMICS
195– (1)
Streamline/United Anglo-American
1 (nn) (132p) US reprints; *Masterman* ... £1.50–£2.50

SUPER SUNDAY
15 Sep 1974–19 Jan 1975 (27)
Simavi
1 (8p) (outsize) (4C) ... 25p–50p
2–27 ... 20p–25p

SUPER WESTERN COMICS
1951 (2)
Streamline/United Anglo-American (Youthful)
1 (28p) US reprint ... 35p–50p
2 (68p) ... 35p–50p

SUPERMAN
Feb 1981–Oct 1982 (2)
Health Education Council
1 (AS26) (8p) (4C) anti-smoking promo ... 10p–20p
2 (AS30) ... 5p–10p

SUPERMAN AND SPIDERMAN
1982 (1)

Marvel
1 (68p) (4C) US reprint — 50p–£1.00

SUPERMAN POCKETBOOK
Apr 1978–
Egmont/Methuen (DC)
1 (100p) (4C) (small) US reprints — 20p–35p
2– — 15p–25p

SUPERMAN SPECTACULAR
20 Mar 1982 (1)
London Editions (DC)
1 (52p) (4C) US reprint — 50p–75p

SUPERTED HOLIDAY SPECIAL
May 1984 (1)
Polystyle
1 (48p) T.V. character — 25p–45p

SUPERTHRILLER
1947–195– (29)
Foldes/World
aka: *Super Thriller Comic*
to: *Western Super Thriller Comics*
1 (5) (12p) Rex Hart — 50p–£1.00
6 (nn) (20p) — 50p–£1.00
7–33 Terry Patrick — 35p–75p

SUREFIRE COMIC
1949 (2)
Philmar (Marx)
1–2 (16p) (gravure) Arthur Martin — 50p–£1.00

SURPRISE COMIC
1948 (5)
Paget
1 (nn) (8p) Harry Banger — 50p–£1.00
2–5 — 50p–£1.00

SUSIE OF THE SUNDAY DISPATCH
1956 (1)
Sunday Dispatch strips reprint
1 (nn) (84p) Norman Pett — £2.00–£5.00

SUSPENSE MAGAZINE
1952 (1)
Cartoon Art (Magazine Enterprises)
1 (28p) US reprint — 75p–£1.25

SUSPENSE PICTURE LIBRARY HOLIDAY
SPECIAL
May 1977–May 1981 (5)
IPC
1 (196p) reprints — 30p–50p
2–5 — 20p–30p

SUSPENSE STORIES
May 1963–
Class (Atlas)
1 (68p) US reprint — 50p–£1.00
2– — 25p–35p

SUZIE AND JONNIE (Laid Back Adventures of)
1981 (1)
Ghura
1 (nn) (52p) Antonio Ghura (adult) — 75p–£1.00

SUZY
11 Sep 1982–
Thomson
& *Tops*: 4 Feb 1984
1 (32p) gravure — 15p–25p
2– — 10p–15p

SWEETHEARTS LIBRARY
196–
World (ACG)
1– (68p) US reprint — 10p–25p

SWELL COMIC
1948–1949 (2)

PM (Marx)
1 (8p) George Parlett — 50p–£1.00
2 (8p) (tabloid) Reg Parlett — 50p–£1.20

SWIFT
20 Mar 1954–2 Mar 1963 (477)
Hulton/Longacre
& *Zip*: 10 Oct 1959
to: *Eagle*
1 (16p) (gravure) Harry Bishop — 50p–£1.00
2–477 Don Lawrence — 25p–50p

SWIFT ARROW
1957
Miller (Ajax)
1– (28p) US reprint — 50p–75p

SWIFT MORGAN
1948–1951 (7)
Boardman
1 (nn) (12p) *in Lost World* — £1.00–£2.50
2 (nn) & *Ancient Romans* — £1.00–£2.00
3 (nn) & *Ancient Egyptians* — £1.00–£2.00
4 (9) & *Feathered Serpent* — £1.00–£2.00
5 (16) & *Atlantis* — £1.00–£2.00
6 (30) & *Flying Saucers* — £1.00–£2.00
7 (38) & *Greek Wars* — £1.00–£2.00

SWIFT MORGAN SPACE COMIC
Mar 1953 (1)
Popular
to: *Spaceways Comic*
1 (50) (28p) D. McLoughlin — £1.00–£2.00

SWORD OF FREEDOM
Feb 1959–20 Jun 1959 (4)
Pearson (*T.V. Picture Stories*)
1 (68p) *Vendetta* (small) — 25p–£1.00
2 (TVP 4) *Adriana* — 25p–75p
3 (TVP 9) *Violetta* — 25p–75p
4 (TVP 17) *Assassin* — 25p–75p

SWORDS OF HEAVEN, FLOWERS OF HELL
1979 (1)
Star (Heavy Metal)
1 (nn) (72p) (4C) US reprint — £1.50–£2.95

T-MAN
1953 (6)
Archer (Quality)
1 (68p) US reprint — 50p–£1.00
2–6 — 50p–75p

T.V. ACTION
1 Apr 1972–15 Sep 1973 (72)
Polystyle
aka: *New T.V. Action* 21 Jan 1973–
to: *T.V. Comic*
1 (59) (24p) John Burns — 50p–£1.00
60–130 Brian Lewis — 35p–50p

T.V. ACTION AND COUNTDOWN HOLIDAY
SPECIAL
1972 (1)
Polystyle
1 (nn) (48p) — 50p–£1.00

T.V. ACTION HOLIDAY SPECIAL
Mar 1973 (1)
Polystyle
1 (nn) (48p) Martin Asbury — 50p–£1.00

T.V. CENTURY 21
23 Jan 1965–30 Dec 1967 (154)
City
to: *T.V. 21*
1 (20p) Ron Embleton — £2.00–£7.50
2–154 R. Turner — £1.00–£2.00

T.V. CENTURY 21 INTERNATIONAL EXTRA
1965 (1)

City
1 (nn) (48p) R. Turner £5.00–£10.00

T.V. CENTURY 21 STINGRAY SPECIAL
1965 (1)
City
1 (nn) (48p) R. Turner £5.00–£10.00

T.V. CENTURY 21 SUMMER EXTRA
1965 (1)
City
1 (nn) (48p) Frank Hampson £5.00–£10.00

T.V. COMEDY SCENE
1976 (1)
ITV
1 (nn) (52p) (4C) Harry North 50p–£1.00

T.V. COMIC
9 Nov 1951–29 Jun 1984 (1697)
NoW/Beaverbrook/TV/Polystyle
& *T.V. Express*: 13 Jan 1962
& *T.V. Land*: 20 Jan 1962
& *T.V. Action*: 22 Sep 1973
& *Tom & Jerry Weekly*: 10 Aug 1974
& *Target*: 19 Aug 1978
aka: *Mighty T.V. Comic*
1 (8p) (gravure) Marten Toonder £1.00–£2.00
2–3 (8p) Cyril Price £1.00–£1.25
4– (12p) Lunt Roberts 75p–£1.00
6 Feb 1953 (16p) Roland Davies 25p–50p
1961: 'Supercar' 50p–75p
1962: 'Fireball XL5' 50p–75p
1965: 'Dr Who' 50p–75p
1970–1984 20p–25p

T.V. COMIC HOLIDAY SPECIAL
Jun 1963–Apr 1984 (26)
T.V./Polystyle
1 (48p) (gravure) reprints 50p–£1.00
2–26 35p–75p

T.V. COMIC SUMMER SPECIAL
1962 (1)
T.V.
to: *T.V. Comic Holiday Special*
1 (48p) reprints 75p–£1.25

T.V. EXPRESS
23 Apr 1960–6 Jan 1962 (108)
T.V.
to: *T.V. Comic*
1 (286) (16p) (gravure) Ron Embleton 50p–£1.00
287–375 John Burns 50p–75p

T.V. FAN
12 Sep 1959–30 Jan 1960 (21)
Fleetway
to: *Valentine*
1(313) (16p) Arthur Martin 50p–75p
314–333 25p–50p

T.V. FAVOURITES (A Pippin Special of)
Nov 1979–Nov 1980 (2)
Polystyle
1 (48p) reprints 25p–40p
2 20p–30p

T.V. FEATURES
Nov 1960–Jun 1961 (8)
Anglo
1 (28p) George Parlett (reprints) 50p–75p
2–8 Denis Gifford 50p–65p

T.V. FUN
19 Sep 1953–5 Sep 1959 (312)
AP
& *Jingles*: 29 May 1954
& *Tip Top*: 29 May 1954
to: *T.V. Fan*
1 (20p) Arthur Martin 75p–£1.00
2–312 Roy Wilson 35p–50p

T.V. HEROES
Jul 1958–Aug 1960 (26)
Miller
1 (32p) Colin Andrew (large) 50p–£1.00
2–7 Arthur Barker 35p–75p
8–26 Denis Gifford (standard) 35p–75p

T.V. LAND
1 Oct 1960–13 Jan 1962 (68)
T.V.
to: *T.V. Comic*
1 (16p) (gravure) Tony Hart 35p–50p
2–68 Fred Robinson 25p–30p

T.V. MINI-BOOK
1955 (12)
News of the World
1: *Seven Muffin Advs*, (32p) (oblong) (4C) 50p–£1.50
2–12 50p–£1.00

T.V. PHOTO STORIES
Jan–Mar 1960 (6)
Pearson
1; 5 *O.S.S.* (36p) 50p–75p
2; 6 *William Tell* 50p–75p
3 *Dial 999* 50p–75p
4 *Buccaneers* 50p–75p

T.V. PICTURE STORIES
see: *Adventures of Robin Hood*
Buccaneers
Dixon of Dock Green
Emergency Ward 10
Hawkeye & Last of Mohicans
Highway Patrol
Murder Bag
New Adventures of Charlie Chan
O.S.S.
Sheriff of Cochise
Sword of Freedom
William Tell

T.V. POSTER MAGAZINE
1975–1976 (4)
Imperial/NEL
1 (16p) (4C) *Sooty & Sweep* 15p–20p
2–4 10p–20p

T.V. TORNADO
14 Jan 1967–14 Sep 1968 (88)
City
& *Solo*: 23 Sep 1967
to: *T.V. 21*
1 (24p) Mick Anglo 50p–£1.00
2–88 Harry Bishop 35p–50p

T.V. TOYLAND
28 May 1966–23 Feb 1968 (92)
Fleetway
to: *Playhour*
1 (16p) Philip Mendoza 50p–75p
2–92 25p–30p

T.V.21
6 Jan 1968–20 Sep 1969 (90)
City
& *T.V. Tornado*: 21 Sep 1968
to: *T.V.21 & Joe 90*
1 (154) (20p) Mike Noble £1.00–£1.50
155–242 50p–£1.00

T.V.21 AND JOE 90
27 Sep 1969–25 Sep 1971 (105)
City/IPC
aka: *T.V. 21*
to: *Valiant*
1 (24p) Martin Asbury 75p–£1.00
2– Don Lawrence 35p–75p
3 Jul 1971: first IPC 25p–50p

T.V.21 SPRING EXTRA THUNDERBIRDS
Mar 1967 (1)

City
1 (nn) (48p)   £5.00–£10.00

TALES FROM THE CRYPT
1952 (2)
Arnold (EC)
1–2 (68p) US reprint   £1.00–£1.50

TALES FROM THE FRIDGE
Mar 1974 (1)
H. Bunch/Cozmic Comix (Kitchen Sink)
1 (nn) (36p) US reprint   25p–50p

TALES OF ACTION
196– (2)
Class
1–2 (68p) US reprint   35p–50p

TALES OF RHUBARB
Aug 1981 (1)
Abbott
1 (28p) Jon Abbott (adult)   50p–75p

TALES OF TERROR
Sep 1978–
Portman (Marvel)
1 (68p) US reprints   20p–50p
2–   15p–25p

TALES OF TERROR PICTURE LIBRARY
1966 (12)
Famepress
1– Terror of Living Pulp foreign reprint   20p–25p
2–12   15p–20p

TALES OF THE SUPERNATURAL
196– (1)
Class
1 (68p) US reprints   50p–£1.00

TALES OF THE UNDERWORLD
1960 (5)
Class (Charlton)
1–5 (68p) US reprint   50p–75p

TAMMY
6 Feb 1971–23 Jun 1984
IPC
& Sally: 3 Apr 1971
& Sandie: 27 Oct 1973
& June: 22 Jun 1974
& Misty: 15 Sep 1979
& Jinty: 28 Nov 1981
& Princess: 5 May 1984
to: Girl
1 (36p)   35p–50p
2–   10p–15p

TAMMY AND JUNE SUMMER SPECIAL
1975 (1)
IPC
1 (80p)   25p–35p

TAMMY AND SANDIE SUMMER SPECIAL
1974 (1)
IPC
1 (nn) (80p)   25p–35p

TAMMY HOLIDAY SPECIAL
1971–1984 (14)
IPC
1 (nn) (96p)   25p–35p
2–14   20p–25p

TARGET
15 Jun 1935–22 Oct 1938 (176)
Target
to: Target & Rocket
1 (8p) (tabloid) Louis Diamond   £5.00–£7.50
2–112 (8p) Harry Banger   £2.00–£3.00

113–130 (12p) Bert Hill   £2.00–£3.00
131–176 (8p) S. Perkins   £2.00–£2.50

TARGET
22 Apr 1972–
NEL
1 (32p) (magazine)   25p–50p
2–   15p–20p

TARGET
1969–1970
Methodist Youth (giveaway)
1 (4p) (4C) (small) religious promo   15p–25p
2–   10p–15p

TARGET
14 Apr 1978–12 Aug 1978 (18)
Polystyle
to: TV Comic
1 (20p) TV characters   15p–25p
2–18   10p–20p

TARGET
see: Blue Bolt Series

TARGET AND ROCKET
29 Oct 1938–8 Apr 1939 (24)
Target
to: Jolly Comic
1 (12p) Harry Banger   £5.00–£7.50
2–19 (12p) Bert Hill   £2.00–£3.00
20–24 (8p) Louis Diamond   £2.00–£2.50

TARGET COMICS
1952 (6)
Miller (Star)
1 (28p) US reprint   50p–£1.00
2–6   50p–75p

TARKAN
3 Mar 1973–20 Oct 1973 (34)
Simavi
1–34 (16p) (4C) foreign reprint   15p–25p

TARZAN ADVENTURES
8 Apr 1953–26 Dec 1959 (344)
Westworld (United Features)
1 (V3N1) (28p) US reprints   75p–£1.00
V3 2–52 George Bunting   50p–75p
V4 1–52 James Bleach   50p–75p
V5 1–52 J&M Thomas   50p–75p
V6 1–52 A. Graham   50p–75p
V7 1–52 James Cawthorn   50p–75p
V8 1–52 Drummond Riddell   50p–75p
V9 1–32 King-Ganteaume   50p–75p

TARZAN COMIC
1950–Oct 1951 (19)
Peters (United Features)
V1 1–4 (68p) (gravure)   £1.00–£2.00
V2 1–15 (36p) US reprints   50p–£1.00

TARZAN MONTHLY
(a) 1980
(b) 18 Feb 1981–25 Feb 1982 (13)
Byblos
1– (68p) US reprint   20p–30p
1–13 (52p) foreign reprint   20p–30p

TARZAN OF THE APES
1972 (1)
Top Sellers (Dell)
1 (260p) (small) US reprint   25p–35p

TARZAN OF THE APES
1970–1971
Top Sellers (Dell)
1– (36p) (4C) (monthly) US reprint   15p–25p

TARZAN OF THE APES
1971–1975 (100?)

Top Sellers (Dell)
1– (36p) (4C) (fortnightly) US reprint   10p–20p

TARZAN OF THE APES SPECIAL SUPER ADVENTURE
1972 (2)
Williams (Dell)
1–2 (52p) (4C) US reprints   25p–35p

TARZAN SPECIAL
May 1978–Nov 1981 (10)
Byblos
1: *Summer Special 1978* (68p) reprints   35p–50p
2: *Summer Special 1979* (52p)   25p–35p
3: *Autumn Special 1979*   25p–35p
4: *Winter Special 1979*   25p–35p
5: *Spring Special 1980*   25p–35p
6: *Summer Special 1980*   25p–35p
7: *Autumn Special 1980*   25p–35p
8: *Winter Special 1980*   25p–35p
9: *Summer Special 1981*   25p–35p
10: *Winter Special 1981*   25p–35p

TARZAN THE GRAND ADVENTURE COMIC
15 Sep 1951–3 Apr 1953 (59?)
Westworld
to: *Tarzan Adventures*
V1 1 (12p) (tabloid) (4-col)   £1.00–£2.00
V1 2–23? reprints   50p–£1.00
V2 1 (smaller) (1 Aug 1952)   50p–£1.00
V2 2–36   50p–75p

TARZAN WEEKLY
11 Jun 1977–
Byblos
1 (32p) US reprints   10p–25p
2–   10p–15p

TARZAN WORLD ADVENTURE LIBRARY
May–Aug 1967 (4)
World (Dell)
1–4 (68p) US reprints   10p–20p

TEDDY BEAR
21 Sep 1963–15 Sep 1973 (520)
Fleetway/IPC
to: *Jack & Jill*
1 (16p) (gravure)   25p–35p
2–520   15p–25p

TEDDY BEAR'S HOLIDAY SPECIAL
1965–1974 (10)
Fleetway/IPC
1–10 (nn) (48p) reprints   20p–30p

TEDDY BEAR'S PLAYTIME
20 Jun 1981–24 Oct 1981 (19)
IPC
to: *Jack & Jill*
1 (16p) reprints   15p–20p
2–19   5p–10p

TEDDY BEAR'S SUMMER SPECIAL
1979 (1)
IPC
1 (nn) (48p) reprints   20p–25p

TEDDY TAIL SERIES
1915–1926 (10)
Black (*Daily Mail* reprints)
1915: *Adventures of TT*   £3.50–£5.00
1915: *TT in Nursery Rhyme Land*   £2.50–£4.00
1916: *TT in Fairyland*   £2.50–£4.00
1917: *TT in Historyland*   £2.50–£4.00
1919: *TT's Fairy Tale*   £2.50–£4.00
1920: *TT at Seaside*   £2.50–£4.00
1921: *TT in Babyland*   £2.50–£4.00
1921: *TT's Alphabet*   £2.50–£4.00
1922: *TT in Toyland*   £2.50–£4.00
1926: *TT's Adventure ABSea*   £2.50–£4.00

TEDDY TAIL SERIES (2)
1950–1951 (6)
Daily Mail strip reprints
1: *TT & Magic Drink* (16p)   £1.00–£2.00
2: *TT & Pearl Thief*   75p–£1.50
3: *TT Goes West*   75p–£1.50
4: *Willow Pattern Story*   75p–£1.50
5: *TT & Cave Men* (24p)   75p–£1.50
6: *TT & Gnomes*   75p–£1.50

TEDDY'S ADVENTURES
1970 (4)
Clifford
1 (20p) (4C) (Dutch reprint)   25p–50p
2–4 George Lemann   25p–50p

TEEN
Apr 1953–
Thorpe & Porter
1– (28p) US reprints   25p–50p

TELEVISION FAVOURITES COMIC
Jan 1958–1959 (18)
World (Dell)
1 (28p) US reprints   50p–£1.00
2–17   35p–75p
18 (68p)   35p–75p

TELL ME WHY
31 Aug 1968–21 Nov 1970 (82)
Fleetway
to: *World of Wonder*
1 (24p) (4C) (magazine)   35p–75p
2–82   15p–25p

10–4 ACTION
Nov 1981–May 1982 (6)
CB News
1 (52p) (adult: CB radio)   25p–50p
2–6 Steve Chadburn   15p–25p

TENDER LOVE
Jul 1983–Aug 1984 (13)
Micron (Euredif)
1 (52p) (4C) photos; foreign reprint   30p–50p
2–13   15p–30p

TERRA NOVA
Jul 1983 (1)
Eco/Alec
1: (0) promo issue (32p) Martin Asbury   £1.00–50p

TERRIBLE TEN
Jun–Dec 1964 (2)
Young World
1 (*Super Mag* 11)   25p–50p
2 (*Super Mag* 23)   25p–50p

TERRIFIC
15 Apr 1967–3 Feb 1968 (43)
Odhams (Marvel)
to: *Fantastic*
1 (40p) US reprints   50p–£1.00
2–43   35p–50p

TEX AUSTIN
1959 (3)
Miller
1–3 (68p) (small) US reprint   25p–35p

TEX RITTER WESTERN
1951–1959 (49)
Miller (Fawcett)
1 (50) (36p) US reprint   50p–£1.00
51–99 (28p)   50p–75p

TEX WILLER
1971
Top Sellers
aka: *Western Classics*
1– (128p) (small) foreign reprint   10p–20p

207

TEXAN
1951 (8)
Pemberton/World (St John)
1–8 (32p) US reprint   50p–75p

TEXAS KID COMICS
1952 (2)
Thorpe & Porter (Atlas)
1–2 (68p) US reprint   50p–75p

TEXAS RANGERS IN ACTION
1959 (11)
Miller (Charlton)
1–11 (28p) US reprint   50p–75p

THAT'LL BE THE DAY
Jun 1975 (1)
IPC
1 (12p) (4C) (tabloid) (adult) Alf Saporito   25p–35p

THEO DRAKE DETECTIVE
1959
Miller
1– (Nero Wolfe) (68p) (small)   35p–50p

THING IS BIG BEN
see: Big Ben

THOSE GOOD OLD COMIC DAYS
Apr 1979 (1)
Birmingham Sunday Mercury Special
1 (nn) (20p) (4C) (tabloid)   20p–50p

THOUGHTS ARE THINGS
193? (1)
Greater World
1 (28p) (oblong) Justin Elliot   £3.00–£5.00

THREE CHEERS COMIC
1946 (1)
Lewis-King
1 (nn) (8p)   50p–£1.00

3-D DOLLY
1953 (1)
Streamline/United Anglo-American (Harvey)
1 (36p) (stereo/glasses) US reprint   £1.00–£2.00

THREE DIMENSION COMICS
1953 (2)
Monthly Magazines
1–2 (36p) (stereo/glasses) US reprint   £1.00–£2.00

THREE STAR ADVENTURES
1947 (2)
Turvey (1) BCM Demob (2)
1–2 (8p) Rex Hart   50p–£1.00

THREE WESTERNERS
1951 (4)
Cartoon Art
1 (20p) US reprints   75p–£1.00
2–4   50p–75p

THRILL COMICS
Apr 1940–1950 (38)
Swan
to: Girls Fun
1 (36p) William Ward   £2.50–£5.00
2–11 John McCail   £1.50–£2.00
12 (28p) Harry Banger   £1.00–£1.50
13–21 (20p) Glyn Protheroe   £1.00–£1.25
22–24 (16p) Dennis Reader   75p–£1.00
25–35 (16p) (format change)   50p–75p
specials:
Summer 1941 (52p) William McCail   £2.00–£3.00
Spring 1942 (36p) William Ward   £2.00–£2.50
Special 1943 (28p) John McCail   £1.50–£2.00

THRILLER
1946–1947 (4)
Foldes
to: Superthriller
1–4 (12p) Bob Wilkin   50p–£1.00

THRILLER
1970–
World
1– (68p) (small) reprint   20p–25p

THRILLER COMICS
Nov 1951–May 1963 (450)
AP
aka: Thriller Picture Library
1 (68p) Three Musketeers   £2.00–£4.00
2–60   £2.00–£3.00
61–200   £1.50–£2.00
201–450   50p–£1.00

THRILLER PICTURE LIBRARY
see: Thriller Comics

THRILLING HERO
Nov 1953–Feb 1954 (4)
Mans World/Atlas
1 (16) (28p) Nat Brand   75p–£1.00
17–19   50p–£1.00

THRILLS
1945 (1)
Pate
1 (nn) (8p) Frank Jupo   50p–£1.00

THRILLS AND FUN COMIC
1944 (1)
Martin & Reid
1 (nn) (8p)   50p–£1.00

THUNDA KING OF THE CONGO
see: Action Series

THUNDER
17 Oct 1970–13 Mar 1971 (22)
IPC
to: Lion
1 (36p) Denis McLoughlin   25p–35p
2–22 Leo Baxendale   20p–25p

THUNDER COMICS
1951 (1)
Streamline (Fiction House)
1 (28p) US reprint   50p–£1.00

THUNDERBIRDS
see: Gerry Anderson's Thunderbirds

THUNDERBIRDS EXTRA
1966 (1)
City
1 (48p) Ron Turner   £5.00–£10.00

THUNDERBIRDS SPECIAL
Jun 1982–Jun 1983 (2)
Polystyle
1 (48p) reprints   35p–50p
2   30p–45p

TIC TAC TOE COMICS
1951 (1)
Pemberton/World
1 (28p) US reprint   25p–50p

TIGER
11 Sep 1954–
AP/Fleetway/IPC
& Comet: 21 Oct 1959
& Champion: 26 Mar 1955
& Hurricane: 15 May 1965
& Jag: 5 Apr 1969
& Scorcher & Score: 12 Oct 1974

& *Speed*: 1 Nov 1980
1 (20p) Joe Colquhoun 50p–75p
2– 10p–35p

TIGER GIRL
1950 (1)
Cartoon Art (Fiction House)
1 (nn) (16p) US reprint .... 50p–£1.00

TIGER HOLIDAY SPECIAL
Jun 1971–
IPC
1–3 (96p) Geoff Campion 50p–75p
4–5 (80p) 35p–50p
6– (64p) 25p–30p

TIGER OLYMPIC SPECIAL
1976 (1)
IPC
1 (nn) (64p) (photos) .... 50p–£1.00

TIGER SPORTS LIBRARY
Jul 1961–
Fleetway
1: *Come On Carford* (68p) 25p–35p
2– 15p–20p

TIGER TIM'S TALES
1 Jun 1919–24 Jan 1920 (28)
AP
to: *Tiger Tim's Weekly*
1 (24p) (small) .... £3.00–£5.00
2–28 Herbert Foxwell .... £1.50–£2.00

TIGER TIM'S WEEKLY
31 Jan 1920–12 Nov 1921 (94)
AP
to: *New Series*
1 (12p) (small 2C) .... £5.00–£10.00
2–94 Herbert Foxwell .... £2.00–£2.75

TIGER TIM'S WEEKLY NEW SERIES
19 Nov 1921–18 May 1940 (965)
AP
to: *Rainbow*
1 (12p) (tabloid) H. Foxwell .... £7.50–£10.00
1921–1929 Albert Lock .... £2.00–£2.50
1930–1940 S. J. Cash .... £1.50–£2.00

TIM HOLT
1952 (2)
Cartoon Art (Magazine Enterprises)
1–2 (32p) US reprint .... 75p–£1.00

TIM HOLT
1953 (4)
Streamline (Magazine Enterprises)
1 (32p) (4C) US reprint .... 75p–£1.00
2–4 .... 50p–£1.00

TIM HOLT
1953–1954 (24)
World (Magazine Enterprises)
1 (28p) US reprint .... 50p–£1.00
2–24 .... 50p–75p

TIM TYLER
see: *Action Series*

TINA
25 Feb 1967–16 Sep 1967 (30)
Fleetway
to: *Princess Tina*
1 (32p) Michael Hubbard 25p–50p
2–30 Hugh McNeill 20p–25p

TINA SUMMER (HOLIDAY) SPECIAL
Jun 1973–Jun 1980 (8)
IPC
1–3 (80p) Jeff Jones 25p–35p
4–8 (64p) 20p–30p

TINY COMIC
1946 (1)
PM (Marx)
1 (nn) (folded strip) Reg Carter .... 50p–£1.00

TINY TOTS
22 Oct 1927–24 Jan 1959 (1334)
AP
& *Sunbeam*: 1 Jun 1940
& *Rainbow*: 5 May 1956
to: *Playhour*
1 (12p) (tabloid) Fred Crompton .... £7.50–£10.00
1927–1940 Terry Wakefield .... £1.50–£2.00
25 May 1940 (fortnightly) .... £1.00–£1.25
26 Oct 1951 (weekly) 50p–75p
5 May 1956 (all pictures) 35p–50p
27 Sep 1956 (gravure) 25p–35p

TIP TOP
21 Apr 1934–29 May 1954 (727)
AP
& *Butterfly*: 25 May 1940
to: *TV Fun*
1 (8p) (tabloid) Reg Parlett .... £5.00–£7.50
1934–1940 Roy Wilson .... £1.50–£2.00
6 Jan 1940: 4C issues. Bertie Brown ... £1.75–2.25
1 Jun 1940: fortnightly. Terry Wakefield £1.00–£1.25
25 Oct 1952: weekly. Albert Pease .... 50p–£1.00

TIP TOP COMIC
17 Sep 1928–20 Apr 1929 (28)
Ransom (reprints *Golden Penny*)
1 (8p) (tabloid) Reg Carter .... £3.00–£5.00
2–28 Louis Diamond .... £1.50–£2.00

TIP TOP COMICS
Dec 1940–Jan 1941 (2)
Miller (United Features)
to: *Comics On Parade*
1–2 (32p) (gravure) US reprint .... £2.00–£3.00

TIR NA NOG
Sep 1946–
Educational Co of Ireland
supplement to *Our Boys*
1 (4p) (2C) (Gaelic) 25p–50p
2– Alan Fraser 20p–25p
(8p) (4C) 10p–15p

TISWAS
30 Jan 1981–
Moore Harness
1 (36p) (puzzles) (TV series) 10p–25p
2– 10p–15p

TITANS
25 Oct 1975–24 Nov 1976 (58)
Marvel
to: *Super Spiderman*
1 (36p) (oblong) US reprints 20p–35p
2–58 .... 15p–25p

TITANS POCKET BOOK
25 Sep 1980–12 Nov 1981 (13)
Marvel
1 (52p) (small) US reprints 15p–25p
2 .... 10p–20p
3 (100p) 20p–30p
4–13 .... 15p–20p

TITBITS SCIENCE FICTION COMICS
1953 (6)
Pearson
1: *Terror of Titan* (68p) (small) .... £2.00–£2.50
2: *Planet X1* .... £1.50–£2.00
3: *Dome of Survival* .... £1.50–£2.00
4: *Diemos Deadline* .... £1.50–£2.00
5: *Captain Diamond* .... £1.50–£2.00
6: *Scourge of Carbon Belt* .... £1.50–£2.00

TITBITS WILD WEST COMICS
1953

Pearson
1: *Arizona Kid* (small) (68p)   50p–£1.00
2–   50p–75p

TOAST OF EUROPE
1982 (1)
Bluett
1 (nn) (82p) (small) Tom Mathews   £2.00–£3.75

TOBY
30 Jan 1976–30 Sep 1978 (88)
IPC
& See-Saw: 23 Jul 1977
to: *Jack & Jill*
1 (16p) John Donnelly   10p–20p
2–88 Doris White   5p–10p

TOBY SPECIALS
Jun 1976–Jun 1978 (3)
IPC
1: *Holiday Special 1976* (40p)   15p–25p
2: *Holiday Special 1977*   10p–20p
3: *Summer Special 1978*   10p–20p

TOBY TWIRL STRIP BOOKS
1953 (2)
Sampson Low Marston
1: *TT on Dapple Heath* (oblong)   75p–£1.00
2: *TT & the Talking Poodle*   50p–75p

TOM AND JERRY
1972 (3)
Nabisco (giveaway: *Shreddies*)
1–3 (nn) (16p) (oblong) promo   25p–35p

TOM AND JERRY BUMPER COMIC BOOK
1975 (1)
Polystyle
1 (68p) Bill Titcombe reprints   35p–50p

TOM AND JERRY COMICS
Jan 1953– (4)
Thorpe & Porter (Dell)
1–4 (28p) (gravure) US reprints   50p–75p

TOM AND JERRY SPECIALS
May 1973–Jul 1984 (16)
World/Polystyle
1: *Summer Special 1973* (32p) reprints   25p–45p
2: *Summer Special 1974*   20p–40p
3: *Holiday Special 1975* (48p)   25p–35p
4: *Holiday Special 1976*   25p–30p
5: *Winter Special 1976*   25p–30p
6: *Holiday Special 1977*   25p–30p
7: *Winter Special 1977*   25p–30p
8: *Holiday Special 1978*   25p–30p
9: *Winter Special 1978*   25p–30p
10: *Holiday Special 1979*   25p–30p
11: *Winter Special 1979*   25p–30p
12: *Holiday Special 1980*   25p–30p
13: *Holiday Special 1981*   25p–30p
14: *Holiday Special 1982*   250p–30p
15: *Holiday Special 1983*   25p–30p
16: *Holiday Special 1984*   20p–30p

TOM AND JERRY WEEKLY
13 Oct 1973–3 Aug 1974 (43)
Spotlight/World (Dell)
to: *T.V. Comic*
1 (24p) US reprints   25p–50p
2–43   15p–25p

TOM CORBETT SPACE CADET
Apr–Dec 1953 (9)
World (Dell)
1 (36p) US reprint   75p–£1.00
2–9   50p–75p

TOM MIX WESTERN COMIC
Aug 1950–1959 (88?)
Miller (Fawcett)

1 (nn) (16p) (gravure) US reprint   75p–£1.25
  (nn) (68p) (gravure)   £1.00–£2.00
– large format gravure   75p–£1.00
50 (Apr 1951)–134 (28p)   50p–75p

TOM PUSS COMICS
1949 (1)
Birn Bros
1 (700) (16p) (gravure) Marten Toonder   £2.50–£5.00

TOM THUMB COMIC
193– (3)
'British Manufacture'
1 (4p) (small) Harry Folkard   £1.00–£3.00
2–3   £1.00–£2.00

TOM THUMB'S OWN
1933–14 Nov 1933
Yorkshire Evening News supplement
1 (4p)   £2.00–£2.50
2–   £1.00–£1.25

TOM WEBSTER AMONG THE SPORTSMEN
1920 (1)
Daily Mail reprints
1 (nn) (100p) (first *T.W. Annual*) oblong   £2.50–£7.50

TOM WEBSTER ANNUAL
1921–1939 (19)
Daily Mail reprints
2–19 (nn) (shape varies)   £2.50–£5.00

TOMAHAWK
1954–1957 (40)
Strato (DC Comics)
1 (68p) US reprint   75p–£1.00
2–40   50p–75p

TONS O' FUN COMIC
Sep 1947 (1)
Philmar (Marx)
1 (nn) (16p) Ern Shaw   50p–£1.00

TONTO
1953–1955 (32)
World (Dell)
1 (28p) US reprint   75p–£1.00
2–32   50p–75p

TONY TRENT COMICS
1951 (1)
Streamline (Columbia)
1 (nn) (28p) (2C) US reprint   50p–£1.00

TOO GREAT A RISK
1972 (1)
Family Planning Assoc
1 (nn) (6p) promo for contraception   10p–25p

TOO MUCH PRESSURE
1984 (1)
Peace News
1 (52p) Brick strips   50p–£1.50

TOOTSIE SLOPER
14 Jan 1899 (1)
Dalziel
1 (20p) (magazine) (adult)   £5.00–£10.00

TOP CAT'S TV COMIC SHOW
15 Sep 1983–26 Apr 1984 (33)
Marvel
1 (28p) (4C) US reprints   15p–25p
2–33   10p–20p

TOP CAT'S CHRISTMAS SPECIAL
Nov 1983 (1)
Marvel
1 (52p) US reprints (4C)   30p–50p

TOP HOLE COMICS
Dec 1943 (1)
PM (Marx)
1 (nn) (16p) Frank Jupo   50p–£1.00

TOP MARK ADVENTURES
1947 (1)
Foldes
1 (12p) Rex Hart   50p–£1.00

TOP NOTCH COMIC
Sep 1947 (1)
Apex
1 (nn) (8p) Stanley White   50p–£1.00

TOP NOTCH COMIC
1947 (1)
Saward
1 (nn) (16p) Bob Wilkin   50p–£1.00

TOP SECRET PICTURE LIBRARY
Jul 1974–
IPC
1 (68p) *Wings of Death*   30p–50p
2–   15p–20p

TOP SECRET PICTURE LIBRARY HOLIDAY
SPECIAL
May 1976–
IPC
1 (196p) (reprints)   30p–50p
2–   20p–30p

TOP SPOT
25 Oct 1958–16 Jan 1960 (65)
AP
to: *Film Fun*
1 (32p) Geoff Campion   25p–75p
2–65 Hugh McNeill   20p–35p

TOP THREE
1961–1966 (124)
Famepress
1–124 (68p) (4C) (small)   20p–35p

TOPICAL FUNNIES
Apr 1940–Jan 1951 (42)
Swan
1 (68p) William Ward   £2.50–£5.00
  (also as two 32p editions)   £1.50–£2.50
2–12 (36p) Harry Banger   £2.00–£2.50
13–23 (20p) John McCail   £1.25–£1.50
24 (16p) D. L. West   £1.00–£1.25
25–34 (16p) format change   £1.00–£1.25
35–36 (20p) M. Stimpson   £1.00–£1.25
specials:
Spring/Autumn/Winter 1941 (52p)   £2.00–£3.00
Summer 1942 (36p)   £2.00–£3.00
Special 1943 (36p)   £2.00–£2.50
Double 1946   £1.50–£2.00

TOPIX
195– (4)
Grafton (Catachetical)
1–4 (28p) US reprint   25p–50p

TOPPER
7 Feb 1953–
Thomson
& Sparky: 23 Jul 1977
& Buzz: 11 Jan 1975
1 (12p) (tabloid) Dudley Watkins   £1.00–£3.50
1953–1959 Allan Morley   50p–£1.00
1960–1969 Paddy Brennan   25p–50p
              (16p from 17 Oct 1964)
1970–1979 Bill Holroyd   10p–25p
1980–29 Aug 1980 (last tab)   10p–15p
6 Sep 1980–(small)   5p–10p

TOPPER SUMMER SPECIAL
Jun 1983–

Thomson
1 (32p)   25p–35p

TOPPICK
Sep 1970 (1)
Finchglade
1 (8p)   25p–50p

TOPS
10 Oct 1981–28 Jan 1984 (121)
aka: *T.V. Tops*
Thomson
to: *Suzy*
1 (32p) (gravure) (TV strips)   10p–20p
2–121 Bob Dewar   10p–15p

TORNADO
24 Mar 1979–18 Aug 1979 (22)
IPC
to: *2000 AD*
1 (32p) Kevin O'Neill   15p–35p
2–22 Bellardinelli   10p–20p

TORNADO SUMMER SPECIAL
Jun 1979 (1)
IPC
1 (nn) (64p)   30p–40p

TORRID
Oct 1979–1982 (12)
Gold Star
1 (52p) foreign reprint (adult)   £1.00–£2.00
2–12   £1.00–£1.50

TOT AND TINA
Oct 1962–Jan 1964 (16)
Standbrook
supplement to *Trio* magazine
1 (8p) (2C)   50p–£1.00
2–4 (8p) (2C)   35p–50p
5 (8p) (large) (4C)   25p–50p
6–16 (8p–4p) (small) (2C)   15p–25p

TOTEM PICTURE LIBRARY
1961–1967 (102)
Famepress/Award
1 (68p) (4C) (small) foreign reprints   35p–50p
2–102   20p–25p

TOYTOWN
7 Oct 1972–17 Mar 1973 (24)
Williams
to: *Pippin*
1 (16p) Larry the Lamb   25p–35p
2–24   10p–25p

TOYTOWN COMIC
1948 (1)
PM (Marx)
1 (nn) (8p) Frank Minnitt   50p–£1.00

TOYTOWN HOLIDAY SPECIAL
May 1980 (1)
Polystyle
1 (nn) (48p) John Donnelly reprints   25p–40p

TRACY
6 Oct 1979–19 Jan 1985 (277)
Thomson
to: *Judy*
1 (32p)   10p–20p
2–277   5p–10p

TRAFFIC LIGHT
1946 (1)
ROSPA
1 (nn) (8p) Fred Robinson   £1.00–£2.00

TRAFFIC ROUNDABOUT
1950 (1)
ROSPA
1 (nn) (8p) Bob Wilkin   50p–£1.00

TRAMPS IN THE KINGDOM
1979 (1)
Hodder & Stoughton (*Daily Express* reprints)
1 (nn) (124p) Roland Fiddy   50p–£1.00

TRANSFORMERS
20 Sep 1984–
Marvel
1 US reprints   15p–25p
2–   10p–15p

TREASURE
19 Jan 1963–
Fleetway
to: *World of Wonder*
1 (24p) (magazine)   50p–£1.00
2–   25p–50p

TREASURE COMIC
1949 (1)
Martin & Reid (Gower)
1 (nn) (8p) Harry Banger   50p–£1.00

TREND AND BOYFRIEND
19 Mar 1966–7 May 1966 (8)
to: *Boyfriend & Trend*
City
352–359   15p–25p

TRIALS OF NASTY TALES
1973 (1)
H. Bunch
1 (nn) (36p) (adult) Chris Welch   75p–£1.50

TRIGGER
see: *Roy Rogers' Trigger*

TRIPLE TERROR
1949 (1)
Peters (United Features)
1 (20) (20p) (gravure) US reprint   50p–£1.00

TRUE COMPLETE MYSTERY
1950 (1)
Streamline/United Anglo-American (Atlas)
1 (nn) (28p) US reprint   50p–£1.00

TRUE LIFE ADVENTURES
Nov 1953–Apr 1954 (6)
Mans World (Atlas)
12–17 (28p)   50p–£1.00

TRUE LIFE LIBRARY
1955?–197–
AP/Fleetway
1 (68p)   20p–25p
2–   10p–15p

TRUE LIFE PICTURE LIBRARY HOLIDAY
SPECIAL
May 1973–
IPC
1 (224p) (small)   25p–30p
2–   20p–25p

TRUE LIFE SECRETS
1952 (20)
Miller (Charlton)
1–20 (28p) US reprint   25p–50p

TRUE LIFE SPORTS
Jun 1953 (1)
Sports Cartoons (Miller)
1 (28p)   50p–75p

TRUE LOVE
1983 (1)
Fontana (Collins)
1 (nn) (52p) (oblong) Posy Simmonds   £2.00–£2.95

TRUE LOVE CONFESSIONS
1954 (1)
Cartoon Art (Premier)
1 (68p) US reprint   25p–50p

TRUE LOVE ROMANCES
1953 (12)
Trent
1–12 (68p) US reprint   25p–35p

TRUE LOVE STORIES
1953 (12)
Trent
1–12 (68p) US reprint   25p–35p

TRUE MYSTERY
1953 (1)
Streamline/United Anglo-American (Fox)
1 (nn) (28p) US reprint   50p–£1.00

TRUE POLICE COMICS
1950 (1)
Cartoon Art
1 (36p) Paddy Brennan   50p–£1.25

TRUE SECRETS
1955
Miller (Atlas)
1– (28p) US reprint   50p–75p

TRUE 3-D.
1954 (1)
Streamline/United Anglo-American (Harvey)
1 (28p) (stereo glasses)   £1.00–£2.00

TRUE TO LIFE ROMANCES
1954–1955 (16)
Swan (Star)
1–16 US reprint   15p–25p

TRUE WAR
17 Jun 1978–19 Aug 1978 (3)
IPC
1 (40p) Keith Watson   10p–25p
2–3 Ian Kennedy   10p–15p

TRUE WAR EXPERIENCES
1953 (1)
Streamline/United Anglo-American (Harvey)
1 (28p) US reprint   35p–75p

TRUE WESTERN
195– (1)
Thorpe & Porter (Marvel)
1 (nn) (36p) US reprint   50p–75p

TRULY AMAZING LOVE STORIES
1977 (1)
Beyond the Edge
1 (nn) (52p) (adult) A. Ghura   £1.00–£1.50

TUMPY STRIP BOOKS
1952–1953 (3)
Sampson Low Marston (Enid Blyton)
1: *Mr Tumpy Plays Trick on Saucepan*   £1.00–£1.50
2: *Mr Tumpy in Land of Wishes (oblong)*   50p–£1.00
3: *Mr Tumpy in Land of Boys & Girls*   50p–£1.00

TUPNEY
see: *Paget Tupney*

TUROK SON OF STONE
see: *Giant Comic*

24 PAGES FILLED WITH JUST A COLLECTION
OF AMERICAN UNDERGROUND COMICS
undated/no imprint
1 (nn) (28p) US/UG reprint   40p–50p

21 YEARS OF ANGUS OG
1981 (1)
Daily Record (Scotland)
1 (100p) Eric Bain strips £1.00–£1.50

TWINKLE
21 Jan 1968–
Thomson
& *Little Star*: 24 Jan 1976
& *Magic*: 3 Mar 1979
1 (20p) Bob Dewar (gravure) 35p–50p
2– 10p–15p

TWINKLE FOR LITTLE GIRLS SUMMER SPECIAL
1969–
Thomson
1 (32p) (gravure) 25p–35p
2– 15p–20p

TWINKLE'S NURSE NANCY SPECIAL
Jun 1977–Jun 1978 (2)
Thomson
1 (nn) (32p) 20p–45p
2 15p–20p

TWINS SERIES
1948–1950 (3)
Brockhampton
1: *Twins at Peepoday Farm* (oblong) 50p–75p
2: *Twins on Holiday* 25p–50p
3: *Twins in London* 25p–50p

TWO FISTED TALES
1951 (1)
Cartoon Art (EC)
1 (28p) US reprint 75p–£1.00

TWO GUN KID
1950
World (Atlas)
1– (36p) US reprint 50p–75p

TWO GUN KID
1955– (38)
Miller (Atlas)
1 (28p) US reprint 75p–£1.00
2–38 50p–75p

TWO GUN WESTERN
1951 (1)
Streamline/United Anglo-American (Atlas)
1– (28p) US reprint 50p–75p

TWO GUN WESTERN
1952 (1)
Arnold (Atlas)
1 (28p) US reprint 50p–75p

TWO RONNIES COMICBOOK
Sep 1978 (1)
Carousel/Transworld
1 (100p) George Parlett (small) 50p–75p

2000 AD
26 Feb 1977–
IPC
& *Starlord*: 14 Oct 1978
& *Tornado*: 25 Aug 1979
1 (32p) 'Dan Dare' Bellardinelli £2.00–£5.00
2 'Judge Dredd'; origin £2.00–£3.00
3– Dave Gibbons 25p–75p

2000 AD SCI-FI SPECIAL
May 1978–
IPC
1 (nn) (64p) 'Dan Dare' Leach £1.00–£1.50
2– 75p–£1.00

2000 AD SUMMER SPECIAL SUPERCOMIC
June 1977 (1)

IPC
1 (nn) (64p) 'Judge Dredd' O'Neill £1.00–£1.50

UNCANNY TALES
May 1963–
Class (Atlas)
1 (68p) US reprint 50p–£1.00
2– 35p–75p

UNCENSORED LOVE
196– (1)
Class
1 (68p) US reprint 25p–35p

UNDERCOVER
1964
Famepress/White
1– (68p) (small) reprints 35p–40p

UNDERCOVER GIRL
1949 (1)
Streamline/United Anglo-American
1 (36p) (4C) US reprint 75p–£1.25

UNDERWORLD
1951 (1)
Locker (DS)
1 (36p) (4C) US reprint 75p–£1.25

UNSEEN
1962 (1)
Cartoon Art
1 US reprint 50p–£1.00

UNUSUAL TALES
196–
Class (Charlton)
1 (68p) US reprint 50p–£1.00
2– 35p–75p

UNUSUAL TALES
1959 (1)
Moring (Charlton)
1 (36p) (4C) US reprint 75p–£1.50

UP AND UP
1981 (1)
Picture Lions (Collins)
1 (nn) (36p) Shirley Hughes 50p–£1.00

UP-TO-DATE
14 Jan 1893–7 Jul 1894 (63)
Sisley
1–14 (magazine) (no comic interest)
15–29 (newspaper)
30 (12 Aug 1893) (8p) (tabloid) £5.00–£7.50
31–63 £2.00–£2.50

UP TO-DATE COMIC
17 Sep 1928–20 Apr 1929 (28)
Ransom (*Golden Penny* reprints)
1 (8p) (tabloid) Reg Carter £3.00–£5.00
2–28 Louis Diamond £1.50–£2.00

VALENTINE
19 Jan 1957–9 Nov 1974 (927)
AP/Fleetway
& *T.V. Fan*: 6 Feb 1960
& *Serenade*: 16 Feb 1963
& *Roxy*: 21 Sep 1963
& *Marilyn*: 25 Sep 1965
to: *Mirabelle*
1 (28p) 35p–50p
2–927 15p–25p

VALERIAN SPATIOTEMPORAL AGENT SERIES
1984 (2)
Hodder Dargaud/NEL
1: *Welcome to Alflolol* (52p) (4C) 95p–£1.95
2: *Ambassador of Shadows* (French reprint) 95p–£1.95

VALIANT
6 Oct 1962–16 Oct 1976 (730)
AP/Fleetway
& *Knockout*: 23 Feb 1963
& *Smash*: 10 Apr 1971
& *T.V. 21*: 2 Oct 1971
& *Lion*: 25 May 1974
& *Vulcan*: 10 Apr 1976
to: *Battle*

1 (32p) Eric Parker	£1.00–£2.00
2–730	20p–30p

VALIANT BOOKLET OF THRILLS
5 Oct 1974–26 Oct 1974 (4)
IPC

1 (4 pts) (giveaway)	25p–35p

VALIANT PICTURE LIBRARY
Jun 1963–May 1969 (144)
Fleetway

1 (68p) *War Eagle*	35p–50p
2–144	20p–25p

VALIANT STORY OF THE WEST
Apr 1966 (2)
Fleetway

1–2 (36p) reprints	50p–75p

VALIANT SUMMER SPECIAL
1967–1980 (14)
Fleetway/IPC

1 (nn) (96p)	50p–75p
2–7 (96p)	35p–50p
8–9 (80p)	30p–40p
10–14 (64p)	20p–35p

VALOUR
5 Nov 1980–11 Mar 1981 (19)
Marvel
to: *Future Tense*

1 (32p) US reprints	15p–25p
2–15	10p–15p

VALOUR WINTER SPECIAL
Nov 1980 (1)
Marvel

1 (64p) US reprints	25p–40p

VAMPIRELLA
Feb 1975–May 1975 (4)
IPC (Warren)

1 (48p) (4C) US reprints	25p–50p
2–4	15p–25p

VARIETIES
12 May 1894–25 Jul 1896 (127)
Henderson
to: *Garland*

1 (32p) reprints	£5.00–£7.50
2–24: *Story Varieties* supp.	£5.00–£7.50
25–127: *Pictorial Varieties* supp.	£2.00–£2.50

VAULT OF HORROR
1954 (1)
Arnold (EC)

1 (68p) US reprint	£1.50–£2.00

VENTURE COMIC
1948 (1)
PM (Marx)

1 (nn) (16p) Reg Parlett	50p–£1.00

VIC FLINT
1955
Miller

1– (28p) US reprint	50p–£1.00

VIC TORRY AND HIS FLYING SAUCER
1950 (1)
Miller (Fawcett)

1 (32p) US reprint	75p–£1.25

VICTOR
25 Feb 1961–
Thomson
& *Hotspur*: 7 Feb 1981
& *Wizard*: 31 Jun 1978
& *Scoop*: 10 Oct 1981
& *Buddy*: 13 Aug 1983

1 (32p)	50p–75p
2–	10p–35p

VICTOR FOR BOYS SUMMER SPECIAL
1967–
Thomson

1 (32p) (gravure)	35p–50p
2–	25p–35p

VICTORY FUNNIES
Nov 1944 (1)
Fulton

1 (8p) Bob Wilkin	75p–£1.00

VIEW FROM THE VOID
Aug 1973 (1)
H. Bunch/Cozmic Comics

1 (nn) (36p) (adult) Paul Simmons	50p–75p

VIZ COMICS
Dec 1979–
Viz Comics

1 (12p) Newcastle adult comic	25p–50p
2– (16p)	20p–30p
1983 *Best of Viz 1–4* (20p)	20p–30p

VOODOO
1961 (8)
Miller (Atlas)

1 (68p) US reprint	75p–£1.00
2–8	50p–75p

VULCAN (Scottish Edition)
1 Mar 1975–20 Sep 1975 (30)
IPC

1 (32p) (4C) (reprints)	25p–50p
2–30 Don Lawrence	20p–30p

VULCAN (National Edition)
27 Sep 1975–3 Apr 1976 (28)
IPC
to: *Valiant*

1 (32p) (4C) (reprints)	20p–40p
2–28 Don Lawrence	20p–30p

VULCAN HOLIDAY SPECIAL
Jun 1976 (1)
IPC

1 (64p) Don Lawrence	30p–50p

VULCAN MINI-COMIC
10 Apr 1976–24 Apr 1976 (3)
IPC

1–3 (supplement to Valiant)	5p–10p

WACKY WAYS
4 May 1973 (1)
Cardineller
supplement to *It* magazine

1 (nn) (4p) (tabloid) Chris Welch	25p–50p

WAGS
1 Jan 1937–4 Nov 1938 (88)
Powers/Boardman (US import comic)

1 (32p) US reprints) (4C) (tabloid)	£2.50–£15.00
2–15	£2.00–£5.00
16 Eisner/Bob Kane start	£2.50–£10.00
17 (28p) Briefer start	£2.50–£10.00
18–23	£2.50–£5.00
24 Eisner: Spencer Steel	£2.50–£7.50
38 Brenner's Clock	£2.50–£7.50
46 Meskin's Sheena	£2.50–£7.50
64 Kirby's Monte Cristo	£2.50–£7.50
NB: 31 numbered 32; 32 numbered 32A	
Special Edition (inc fiction)	£2.50–£3.50
(continues publication in Australia)	

WALLESTEIN THE MONSTER
1974 (3)
Top Sellers
1–3 (128p) (small) foreign reprint (adult) 25p–50p

WALT DISNEY SERIES
1956– (52)
World (Dell)
1: *Mickey Mouse* (36p) (4C) US reprints 50p–75p
2: *Donald Duck*
3: *Goofy*
4: *Lady & the Tramp with Jock*
5: *Mickey Mouse*
6: *Donald Duck: Annual Vacation*
7: *Goofy Playing It Safe*
8: *Lady & Tramp Album*
9: *Mickey Mouse Mammoth Adventure*
10: *Duck Album*
11: *Goofy: Inside Job*
12: *Chip 'n' Dale*
13: *Mickey Mouse: Mysterious Smoke Signals*
14: *Donald Duck: Rainbow Rendezvous*
15: *Goofy: Success Story*
16: *Jiminy Cricket*
17: *Donald Duck*
18: *Goofy*
19: *Pluto*
20: *Chip 'n' Dale*
21: *Mickey Mouse: Giant Pearls*
22: *Uncle Scrooge*
23: *Pinocchio*
24: *Scamp*
25: *Scamp: Bone Trouble*
26: *Brer Rabbit*
27: *Mickey Mouse: Tortoise Shell Treasure*
28: *Donald Duck*
29: *Walt Disney's Comics*
30: *Covered Wagons*
31: *Chip 'n' Dale*
32: *Grandma Duck's Farm Friends*
33: *Bambi*
34: *Scamp*
35: *Mickey Mouse: River Pace*
36: *Goofy Adventure Story*
37: *Donald Duck: Secret of Glacier*
38: *Chip 'n' Dale Flying High*
39: *Pluto: Polka Dotted Poocheroo*
40: *Mickey Mouse: Lost Mine*
41: *Snow White & Seven Dwarfs*
42: *Cinderella*
43: *Dumbo*
44: *Bongo & Lumpjaw*
45: *Scamp*
46: *Perri*
47: *Donald Duck: Daredevil Deputy*
48: *Tinkerbell*
49: *Pluto: Dangerous Diggings*
50: *Chip 'n' Dale: Big Top Bedlam*
51: *Mickey Mouse: Flying Rock Mystery*
52: *Uncle Scrooge: Golden River*

WALT DISNEY'S MICKEY MOUSE
4 Jan 1958–19 Jan 1959 (56)
Disney/Holding
to: *Walt Disney's Weekly*
1 (12p) (gravure) 50p–£1.00
2–56 35p–50p

WALT DISNEY'S MICKEY'S WEEKLY
see: *Mickey Mouse Weekly*

WALT DISNEY'S NOW I KNOW
7 Oct 1972–13 Oct 1973 (54)
IPC
to: *Disneyland*
1 (20p) (gravure) 10p–20p
2–54 10p–15p

WALT DISNEY'S PICTURE SPECIAL
1976–1979 (6)
IPC
1: *101 Dalmatians* (4C) (poster) 25p–50p
2: *Bambi* (4C) (poster) 25p–35p
3: *The Rescuers* (4C) (poster) 25p–30p

4: *Cinderella* (4C) (poster) 25p–30p
5: *Pete's Dragon* (4C) (poster) 25p–30p
6: *Fantasia* (4C) (poster) 25p–45p

WALT DISNEY PICTURE TREASURY
1972–1976 (5)
IPC
1: *Snow White* (32p) (4C) 25p–50p
2: *Robin Hood* (32p) (4C) 25p–35p
3: *Peter Pan* (32p) (4C) 25p–35p
4: *Lady and the Tramp* (48p) (4C) 20p–30p
5: *Jungle Book* (32p) (4C) 25p–35p

WALT DISNEY'S PUZZLE MAGAZINE
Sep 1981–
London Editions
1 (52p) (reprints) 15p–25p
2– 10p–20p

WALT DISNEY'S PUZZLE TIME
Aug 1979–Dec 1980 (17)
IPC
to: *Mickey Magazine*
1 (40p) Colin Wyatt 25p–35p
2–17 Basil Reynolds 15p–25p

WALT DISNEY STORYTIME COLLECTION
9 Jun 1984–20 Apr 1985 (24)
Whinfrey Strachan
1 (4C) (with cassette) £1.00–£2.00
2–24 £1.00–£1.50

WALT DISNEY STORYTIME SPECIAL
1983–1984 (2)
Whinfrey Strachan
1–2 (48p) (4C) with cassette £2.00–£2.75

WALT DISNEY'S UNCLE REMUS
1947 (1)
Collins (Dell)
1 (nn) (16p) (4C) US reprint £1.00–£2.00

WALT DISNEY'S WEEKLY
26 Jan 1959–24 Apr 1961 (118)
Disney/Holding
to: *Harold Hare's Own Paper*
1 (16p) (gravure) 50p–£1.00
2–118 25p–50p

WAMBI JUNGLE BOY
1951 (1)
Locker (Fiction House)
1 (68p) US reprint £1.00–£2.00

WANTED COMICS
1948 (3)
Arnold (Orbit)
1 (nn) (12p) (gravure) US reprint 75p–£1.00
2 (nn) (12p) (letterpress) 50p–75p
3 (nn) (36p) 50p–75p

WAR
1961–1962 (11)
Miller (Atlas)
1–11 (52p) US reprint 35p–50p

WAR AT SEA
1958–
Miller (Charlton)
1 (28p) US reprints 50p–75p
2– 25p–50p

WAR AT SEA PICTURE LIBRARY
Feb 1962–Jul 1963 (36)
Fleetway
1 (68p) *Devils Cargo* 25p–35p
2–36 20p–30p

WAR COMIC HOME JOURNAL
25 Nov 1899–10 Feb 1900 (6)
Harmsworth

Boer War editions of *Comic Home Journal*:
238; 240; 243; 244; 245; 249   £1.50–£2.00

WAR COMICS
Apr 1940–Dec 1943 (25)
Swan
to: *Kiddyfun*

1 (36p) William Ward	£2.50–£5.00
2–11 (36p) John McCail	£1.50–£2.00
12 (28p) Murdock Stimpson	£1.00–£1.50
13–20 (20p) Harry Banger	£1.00–£1.25

specials:

Summer 1941 (52p)	£2.00–£3.00
Winter 1941	£2.00–£2.75
Summer 1942	£2.00–£2.50
Spring 1943	£2.00–£2.50
Special 1943 (36p)	£1.50–£2.00

WAR COMICS
1951 (3)
Streamline/United Anglo-American (Atlas)

1 (nn) 2 (nn) (28p) US reprint	35p–50p
3 (nn) (68p)	35p–50p

WAR HERO
1970
World

1– (68p) reprint (small)	15p–20p

WAR PICTURE LIBRARY
Sep 1958–Dec 1984 (2103)
AP/Fleetway/IPC
& Action Picture Library

1 (68p) Fight Back to Dunkirk	25p–45p
2–2103	15p–20p

WAR PICTURE LIBRARY HOLIDAY SPECIAL
Jul 1963–
IPC

1 (224p) reprints	25p–35p
2– (192p)	15p–20p

WARLORD
28 Sep 1974–
Thomson
& Bullet: 9 Dec 1978

1 (36p)	25p–40p
2–	10p–15p

WARLORD PETER FLINT SPECIAL
1976 (1)
Thomson

1 (32p) (tabloid) (gravure)	25p–45p

WARLORD SUMMER SPECIAL
1975–
Thomson

1 (32p) (tabloid) (gravure)	25p–40p
2–6	20p–30p
7– (36p) (small)	15p–25p

WARPATH
1955 (3)
Streamline/United Anglo-American (St John)
aka: *Indians On The Warpath*

1 (nn) (28p) US reprint	50p–75p
2 (nn) (68p)	35p–50p

WARPATH WESTERN COMIC
195– (1)
Miller

1 (28p) US reprint	50p–75p

WARRIOR
1974 (1)
Skinn

1 (16p) reprints; Don Lawrence	25p–50p

WARRIOR
Mar 1982–
Quality

1 (52p) John Bolton	50p–75p
2– Dave Gibbons	50p–60p

WARRIOR SUMMER SPECIAL
May 1983 (1)
Quality

1 (52p)	35p–60p

WARRIOR WOMEN
Jun 1980 (1)
Marvel

1 (52p) US reprints	40p–50p

WASTEFUL FAMILY (WASTEFUEL FAMILY)
1980–1984 (6)
British Gas (giveaway)

1 (8p) (4C) gas economy promo	10p–25p
2–6	5p–10p

WEDDING RING LIBRARY
196–
World (Atlas)

1– (68p) US reprint	10p–15p

WEE CHUMS COMIC
1949 (1)
Philmar (Marx)

1 (nn) (8p) Bob Wilkin	50p–£1.00

WEEKEND FUN
8 Jul 1983–
Wakefield Express supplement

1 (4p) (2C) US reprints	10p–20p
2–	5p–10p

WEEKEND MAIL COMIC
13 Jan 1955–20 Oct 1955 (41)
Associated Newspapers
supplement to *Weekend Mail* magazine

1 (4p) (tabloid) Tom Kerr	25p–50p
2–16 Jun (4p) Jesus Blasco	20p–25p
23 Jun–20 Oct (2p)	5p–10p

WEEKENDER COMIC
6 Mar 1981–8 May 1981 (10)
aka: *The Comic* (1)
      Free Weekender Comic (2–3)
Free Weekender
supplement to *Free Weekender* newspaper

1 (8p) (4C) Toni Goffe	10p–25p
2–10 (some 4p only) Paul Sellers	5p–10p

WEEKLY BUDGET COMIC SUPPLEMENT
16 Oct 1910–28 Dec 1913 (167)
Hearst
supplement to *Weekly Budget* newspaper
(printed in US for UK distribution)

1 (4p) (4C) (large) US reprints	£2.50–£5.00
2–167	£1.50–£2.00

WEENY COMIC
1944 (5)
(no imprint)

5 folded strips in package (small)	50p–£2.00
single copies	35p–50p

WEETABIX OK
1982–1983 (3)
Weetabix giveaway

1 (nn) (12p) (4C) cereal promo	10p–25p
2–3	10p–20p

WEIRD PLANETS
1962–1963 (21)
Class (Atlas etc)

1 (68p) US reprint	50p–75p
2–21	35p–50p

WEIRD SCIENCE ILLUSTORIES
1962 (1)
Cartoon Art/Magazine Enterprises

1 (52p) (small)	£2.00–£5.00

WEIRD WORLDS
Mar 1953
Thorpe & Porter (Atlas)
1– (68p) US reprint   50p–75p
2–   35p–75p

WEREWOLF
Oct 1981 (1)
Marvel
1 (nn) (52p) US reprints   25p–50p

WES SLADE
1979 (1)
Express Books (*Sunday Express* reprints)
1 (nn) (68p) (small) George Stokes   50p–£1.00

WESTERN ADVENTURE LIBRARY
15 Feb 1963–
Micron/Smith
1: *Secret Witness* (68p)   15p–25p
2–   10p–20p

WESTERN BUMPER ALBUM
1972 (3?)
Top Sellers
Rebound remainders (coverless):
Bonanza; *Gunsmoke*; *Lone Ranger*   10p–25p

WESTERN CLASSICS
Feb 1958–
World (Dell)
1 (36p) (4C) *Gunsmoke* US reprint   25p–50p
2–   25p–50p

WESTERN CLASSICS
1972–
Top Sellers (Dell)
1– (36p) (4C) US reprints   25p–35p

WESTERN DAYS
1951 (1)
Scion
1 (nn) (28p) King-Ganteaume   50p–£1.00

WESTERN FIGHTERS
1951 (2)
Cartoon Art (Hillman)
1–2 (28p) US reprint   50p–£1.00

WESTERN FIGHTERS
1951–1953 (4)
Streamline (Hillman)
1 (nn) (36p) (4C) US reprint   75p–£1.00
2 (nn) (32p)   50p–£1.00
3 (nn) (28p)–4 (2C)   50p–75p

WESTERN FUN COMIC
1953–1954 (6)
Swan
1 (8) (36p) John McCail   50p–£1.00
9–13 William Ward   50p–75p

WESTERN GUNFIGHTERS SPECIALS
Jun 1980–Oct 1981 (3)
Marvel
1: *Summer Special* (52p) US reprint   35p–40p
2: *Summer Special 1981*   25p–35p
3: *Winter Special 1981*   25p–35p

WESTERN HERO
Sep 1950–1959 (100)
Miller (Fawcett)
to: *Heroes of the West*
1 (50) (28p) US reprint   50p–£1.00
51–149   35p–75p

WESTERN KID
1955 (12)
Miller (Atlas)
1 (28p) US reprint   75p–£1.00
2–12   35p–75p

WESTERN OUTLAWS
1954 (2)
Miller (Marvel)
1–2 (28p) US reprint   50p–75p

WESTERN OUTLAWS
1954 (8)
Swan
1–8 (36p) US reprints   50p–£1.00

WESTERN OUTLAWS
1953 (3)
Streamline/United Anglo-American (Prize)
1–3 (nn) (28p) US reprint   35p–75p

WESTERN PICTURE LIBRARY
Oct 1958–Jul 1959 (20)
Pearson
series: *Jim Bridger Mountain Man*   25p–45p
        Mustang Gray   25p–45p

WESTERN PICTURE LIBRARY
Jan 1979–
1 (501) (small) reprints   10p–15p
502–   5p–10p

WESTERN ROUGH RIDERS
1955 (2)
Streamline/United Anglo-American (Stanmor)
1 (nn) (28p) US reprint   50p–75p
2 (nn) (68p)   35p–75p

WESTERN ROUNDUP COMIC
Jan 1955–1958 (39)
World (Dell)
1 (28p) US reprints   35p–75p
2–39 (28p) (68p)   35p–50p

WESTERN STAR PICTURE LIBRARY
May 1965–
MV Features
1– (68p) *Showdown*   15p–20p

WESTERN STARS COMIC
1952–1958 (17)
Miller (Fawcett)
1 (68p) US reprint   75p–£1.00
2–17   50p–75p

WESTERN SUPER THRILLER COMICS
195– (49)
World
1 (34) (24p) James Bleach   50p–75p
35–77 (24p) Terry Patrick   50p–65p
78–82 (68p) Gerry Embleton   50p–75p

WESTERN TALES
1955 (1)
World (Harvey)
1 (28p) US reprint   50p–£1.00

WESTERN TALES
1956 (2)
Streamline/United Anglo-American (Harvey)
1–2 (28p) US reprint   50p–75p

WESTERN TALES
1962–
Brugeditor/Holding
1– (68p) foreign reprints (small)   20p–35p

WESTERN THRILLER
1955 (1)
Streamline/United Anglo-American (Prize)
1 (68p) US reprint   35p–75p

WESTERN THRILLERS
1950 (1)
Streamline/United Anglo-American (Fox)
1 (28p) US reprint   50p–75p

WESTERN TRAIL PICTURE LIBRARY
Jan 1966–
Famepress
1– (68p) (small) foreign reprints   20p–25p

WESTERN TRAILS
1957 (5)
Miller (Atlas)
1–5 (28p) US reprints   50p–75p

WESTERN WAR COMIC
Jun 1949–Nov 1950 (5)
Swan (3d series)
to: *New Series*
1 (20p) John McCail   50p–£1.00
2–5 Harry Banger   50p–£1.00

WESTERN WAR COMIC NEW SERIES
1952–1953 (7)
Swan (6d series)
to: *Western Fun Comic*
1 (36p) John McCail   50p–£1.00
2–7 Ron Embleton   50p–£1.00

WESTWORLD FOURSOME COMIC
195 (14)
Westworld
1–14 (68p) foreign reprints   35p–50p

WHACKY RODEO
1947 (2)
Transatlantic/Funnibook (Cartoon Art)
1 (8p) Dennis Reader   50p–£1.00
2 (8p) Denis Gifford   50p–£1.00

WHAM
20 Jun 1964–13 Jan 1968 (187)
Odhams
to: *Pow*
1 (24p) (gravure) Leo Baxendale   £1.00–£2.00
2–187 Don Lawrence   35p–75p

WHAM!
1977 (1)
Scouts Association
1 (nn) (44p) Cub Scouts   25p–50p

WHAT A ROTTEN WAY TO TREAT YOUR TEETH
1980 (1)
Health Education Council (giveaway)
1 (nn) (8p) (2C) promo   5p–10p

WHEELS
Jun 1978–1979
Byblos
1 (nn) (preview) (52p) foreign reprint   20p–30p
1 (Oct) (52p)   15p–30p
2–   10p–25p

WHITE RIDER
see: *Blue Bolt Series*

WHITE WARRIORS
1981–1982 (2)
Norman
1 (12p) Nationalist propaganda   50p–£1.00
2   50p–£1.00

WHIZ COMICS
1945–1959
Miller (Fawcett)
1 (nn) (16p) (small)   75p–£1.50
60–70 (16p) (gravure)   75p–£1.50
71– (16p) (letterpress)   50p–£1.25
50–70 (large) (gravure)   75p–£1.00
71–128 (28p)   50p–£1.00

WHIZZBANG COMIC
1947 (1)

Philmar (Marx)
1 (16p) Frank Jupo   50p–£1.00

WHIZZER AND CHIPS
18 Oct 1969–
IPC
& *Knockout*: 30 Jun 1973
& *Krazy*: 22 Apr 1978
1 (32p) Mike Higgs   25p–50p
2– R. Turner   10p–15p
see: *Best of Whizzer & Chips Monthly*

WHIZZER AND CHIPS HOLIDAY SPECIAL
1970–
IPC
1–3 (96p) Reg Parlett   35p–50p
4–6 (80p) Cliff Brown   30p–40p
7– (64p) R. Turner   25p–30p

WHIZZER COMICS
1947–1948 (5)
Cartoon Art
1 (12p) Dennis M. Reader   50p–£1.00
2–4 (16p) Dennis M. Reader   50p–£1.00
5 (36p) Crewe Davies   50p–£1.25

WHOOPEE
9 Mar 1974–
IPC
& *Shiver & Shake*: 12 Oct 1974
& *Cheeky*: 9 Feb 1980
& *Wow*: 2 Jul 1983
1 (40p) Reg Parlett   10p–25p
2– Brian Walker   10p–15p

WHOOPEE COMIC
1949 (1)
Philmar (Marx)
1 (16p) (reprints)   50p–£1.00

WHOOPEE HOLIDAY/SUMMER SPECIAL
1974–
IPC
1 (80p) Arthur Martin   35p–50p
3– (64p) R. Turner   25p–35p

WHOOPEE'S FRANKIE STEIN HOLIDAY SPECIAL
May 1977–May 1982 (6)
IPC
1 (80p) Robert Nixon   35p–50p
2–6 (64p)   25p–35p

WHOPPING COMIC
1945 (1)
International
1 (8p) Denis Gifford   50p–£1.00

WHOSE CHOICE
1977 (1)
National Abortion Campaign
1 (8p) abortion promo   10p–25p

WHUSSH
1966 (1)
Shell Mex/BP
1 (12p) (4C) oil promo   75p–£1.00

WIDE WORLD COMICS
Dec 1949–Jan 1950 (2)
Apollo
1–2 (8p) Eulalie   50p–£1.00

WILBUR COMICS
1950
Swan (Archie)
1 (36p) US reprint   50p–75p
2–   25p–50p

WILD BILL ELLIOTT COMICS
1954–1955 (18)

World (Dell)
1 (28p) US reprint   50p–£1.00
2–18   35p–75p

WILD BILL HICKOK AND JINGLES
1959–1960 (14)
Miller (Charlton)
1–14 (28p) US reprint   50p–75p

WILD BILL HICKOK COMICS
Dec 1952–1953 (14)
Thorpe & Porter (Avon)
1–14 (68p) US reprint   50p–75p

WILD BILL PECOS THE WESTERNER
1953–1958 (63)
Pemberton/World (Wanted)
1 (36p) US reprint   50p–£1.00
2–63   50p–75p

WILD FRONTIER
1955–1956
Miller (Charlton)
1 (28p) US reprints   50p–75p
2–   25p–50p

WILD WEST COMIC AND DRAWING BOOK
1946 (1)
Bairns (Marx)
1 (nn) (8p)   50p–75p

WILD WEST FLICKER BOOK
1948 (1)
Philmar (Marx)
1 (oblong) Reg Parlett   50p–£1.00

WILD WEST PICTURE LIBRARY
May 1966–
Fleetway
1: *Gun Rule* (68p)   20p–35p
2–   15p–25p

WILD WEST PICTURE LIBRARY HOLIDAY
SPECIAL
1973–
IPC
1 (192p) (reprints)   20p–45p
2–   15p–25p

WILD WEST PICTURE STORIES
May 1960–
Pearson
1 (68p) (small)   25p–50p
2–   15p–20p

WILD WESTERN
1951 (1)
Streamlined/United Anglo-American (Prize)
1 (28p) US reprint (*Prize Western*)   50p–75p

WILD WESTERN
1955 (7)
Miller (Atlas)
1–7 (28p) US reprint   50p–75p

WILL ROGERS WESTERN COMIC
1950 (2)
Streamline/United Anglo-American (Fox)
1–2 (nn) (28p) US reprint   50p–£1.00

WILLIAM SHAKESPEARE
1982–
Sidgwick & Jackson/Oval
1 *Macbeth* (136p) (4C)   £2.50–£4.50
2 *Othello*   £2.50–£4.50
(prices for paperback editions)

WILLIAM TELL
28 Feb 1959–13 Jun 1959 (3)
Pearson (*TV Picture Stories*)
1 (TVP 1) (68p) *Assassins*   25p–£1.00

2 (TVP 10) *Bear*   25p–75p
3 (TVP 16) *Prisoner*   25p–75p

WINDJAMMER
1950 (1)
Martin & Reid (Gower)
1 (nn) (16p) Mick Anglo   50p–£1.00

WINGS COMICS
1950 (1)
Cartoon Art (Fiction House)
1 (nn) (4C) US reprint   75p–£1.25

WINGS COMICS
1951 (2)
Streamline/United Anglo-American (Fiction House)
1–2 (nn) (28p) US reprint   50p–£1.00

WINGS COMICS
196– (3)
Trent (Fiction House)
1–3 (68p) US reprint   50p–£1.00

WINNER COMIC
Sep 1947–1948 (2)
Jeffrey/Burnside
1 (nn) (16p) John Turner   50p–£1.00
2 (nn) (16p) Frank Minnitt   50p–£1.00

WIZARD
14 Feb 1970–24 Jun 1978 (435)
Thomson
& *Rover*: 20 Jan 1973
to: *Victor*
1 (32p) Martin Asbury   50p–75p
2–435   15p–20p

WIZARD MIDGET COMIC
11 Sep 1954 (1)
Thomson
1 (nn) (32p) (*Wizard* giveaway)   25p–50p

WOMAN'S REALM STORY TIME
see: *Story Time*

WOMBLES HOLIDAY SPECIAL
Jul 1983 (1)
Polystyle
1 (48p) TV series   25p–35p

WOMBLES SPECIAL
Aug 1974–Aug 1978 (5)
IPC
1 (48p) TV series   30p–50p
2–5   25p–35p

WONDER
30 Jul 1892–27 Jan 1893 (27)
Harmsworth
to: *Funny Wonder*
1 (4p) (broadsheet)   £7.50–£10.00
2–27   £2.00–£2.50

WONDER
1 Jun 1901–9 Nov 1901 (24)
Harmsworth
1 (110) (8p) (tabloid)   £2.00–£2.50
111–133 H. O'Neill   £1.50–£2.00

WONDER
16 Nov 1901–3 May 1902 (25)
Harmsworth
to: *Wonder & Jester*
1 (16p) (tabloid)   £7.50–£10.00
2–25 Tom Wilkinson   £2.00–£2.50

WONDER
4 Jan 1913–21 Mar 1914 (64)
AP
to: *Halfpenny Wonder*

1 (16p) (tabloid) (story-paper)	£7.50–£10.00
2–64	£1.75–£2.00

WONDER
30 May 1942–12 Sep 1953 (317)
AP
to: *Radio Fun*

1 (1444) (8p) Roy Wilson	75p–£1.50
1445–1760 Ron Embleton	50p–75p
22 Nov 1952: weekly 12p issues	

WONDER AND JESTER
10 May 1902–17 May 1902 (2)
Harmsworth
to: *Jester & Wonder*

26–27 (16p) (tabloid)	£1.50–£2.00

WONDER BOX
29 Jul 1909–22 Oct 1909 (4)
AP
Card box containing comics, magazines, books, games

1 includes *Boys & Girls* 1	
Jack & Jill 1	
Scrap Book 1	
Story Book 1	£10.00–£25.00
2 includes *Boys & Girls* 2	
Jack & Jill 2	
Scrap Book 2	
Story Book 2	£5.00–£10.00
3 includes *Boys & Girls* 3	
Jack & Jill 3	
Scrap Book 3	
Story Book 3	
School Book 1	£5.00–£10.00
4 includes *Boys & Girls* 4	
Story Book 4 & 5	
Children's Story Teller	
Only My Fun (comic)	£5.00–£10.00

WONDER BOY
1955 (3)
Miller (Ajax)

1–3 (28p) US reprint	50p–75p

WONDER DUCK
1950 (1)
Streamline/Anglo-American (Atlas)

1 (28p) US reprint	50p–75p

WONDER HEROES
1981–1984 (2)
Sunburst

1 (12p) John Cooper	15p–25p
2 (24p) Harold Johns	25p–50p

WONDER PACKET OF ENGLISH COMICS
1938–1940
rebound remainders:

4 Target Publications	£2.00–£5.00
2 Soloway Publications	£2.00–£2.50

WONDER STORY COMIC
1944 (1)
Newton Wickham

1 (16p) John R. Turner	50p–£1.00

WONDER WEEKLY
5 Jul 1968–27 Jun 1969 (52)
Esso

1 (16p) (gravure) George Parlett	25p–50p
2–52	20p–35p

WONDERFUL WORLD OF DISNEY
11 Oct 1975–14 Feb 1976 (19)
IPC
to: *Mickey Mouse*

1 (20p) (4C)	20p–30p
2–19	15p–20p

WONDERFUL WORLD OF DISNEY CHRISTMAS SPECIAL
Nov 1975 (1)

IPC
1 (48p) Colin Wyatt	25p–40p

WONDERLAND
15 Sep 1961–23 Dec 1966 (275)
Wonderland/Beaumont

1 (16p)	35p–50p
V1 N2–V7	25p–30p
V8 N1 (2 Sep 66)–N17 (magazine)	10p–15p

WONDERLAND TALES
1 Jun 1919–30 May 1920 (46)
AP
to: *Wonderland Tales Weekly*

1 (24p) (oblong)	£2.50–£5.00
2–26 (oblong) Harry Rountree	£2.00–£2.50
27–46 (tabloid) H. O'Neill	£2.00–£2.50

WONDERLAND TALES WEEKLY
5 Jun 1920–26 Jun 1920 (4)
AP
to: *Wonderland Weekly*

47–50 (12p) H. O'Neill	£2.00–£2.50

WONDERLAND WEEKLY
5 Jul 1920–23 Jul 1921 (56)
AP
to: *Young Folks Tales*

51 (12p) (tabloid) A. White	£2.00–£3.50
52–106 Harry Rountree	£2.00–£2.25

WONDERMAN
1948–1951 (24)
Paget

1 (8p) Mick Anglo	£1.00–£2.00
2–7 (8p issues) Jack Bridges	50p–£1.00
8–15 (12p issues)	50p–£1.00
16–20 (16p issues) Dick Brook	50p–£1.00
21; 23; 24 (12p)	50p–£1.00
22: see *Oh Boy and Wonderman*	

WONDERMAN
Jan 1967–
White

1 (68p) (small) foreign reprint	20p–35p
2–	15p–25p

WOODLAND COMICS
Dec 1949–Jan 1950 (2)
Apollo

1–2 (8p) Eulalie	50p–£1.00

WOODY WOODPECKER
1972–1973
Top Sellers (Dell)

1– (36p) (4-col) US reprint	20p–30p
2–	15p–20p

WORLD ADVENTURE LIBRARY SERIES
see: *Bonanza; Flash Gordon; Man from Uncle; Mandrake; Phantom; Batman; Superman*

WORLD FUN
1948 (1)
Martin & Reid (Gower)

1 (8p) Harry Banger	50p–£1.00

WORLD ILLUSTRATED
1960 (36)
Thorpe & Porter (Gilberton)

1 (501) US reprint	25p–50p
502–536	20p–35p

WORLD OF ANDY CAPP
see: *Andy Capp*

WORLD OF SPACE
196– (1)
PR

1 (nn) (24p) Ron Embleton	50p–£1.00

WORLD OF WONDER
28 Mar 1970–
IPC
& *Treasure*: 1971
1 (32p) (magazine)   35p–50p
2–   25p–30p

WORLD'S COMIC
6 Jul 1892–10 Nov 1908 (855)
Trapps Holmes
& *Side-Splitters*: 8 Oct 1894
& *Larks*: 5 Jan 1907
to: *Funny Cuts*
1 (8p) (tabloid)   £5.00–£10.00
2–855 Will Spurrier   £1.50–£2.00

WORZEL GUMMIDGE (MONTHLY)
Oct 1981–Dec 1982 (15)
Marvel
to: *Worzel Gummidge (weekly)*
1 (36p) Bernard McGowan   25p–45p
2–15   20p–30p

WORZEL GUMMIDGE (WEEKLY)
9 Mar 1983–4 Aug 1983 (23)
Marvel
to: *Rupert Weekly*
1 (20p) (4C) Bernard McGowan   15p–20p
2–23   10p–15p

WORZEL GUMMIDGE SPECIAL
May 1982–Nov 1982 (2)
Marvel
1 *Summer 1982* (48p)   40p–50p
2 *Winter 1982*   35p–45p

WOW
5 Jun 1982–25 Jun 1983 (56)
IPC
to: *Whoopee*
1 (32p) Reg Parlett   10p–15p
2–56 Robert Nixon   5p–10p

WOW COMICS
1943–1950 (13)
Miller (Fawcett)
1 (nn) (68p) (gravure) US reprint   £2.00–£3.00
2 (nn) (16p) (gravure)   75p–£1.25
30; 42; 44; 45; 49; 55 (etc) (16p)   50p–£1.00

WOW HOLIDAY SPECIAL
May 1983–May 1984 (2)
IPC
1–2 (64p) Reg Parlett   35p–50p

WRECKERS
1948 (1)
Hotspur/*Secret Service Series 2*
1 (8p) (gravure) Bob Wilkin   50p–£1.00

WUFF SNUFF AND TUFF
1947 (1)
Rylee
1 (nn) (56p) (oblong) strip reprint   £2.00–£3.00

WUFF SNUFF AND TUFF ANNUAL
1951 (1)
Odhams
1 (nn) (68p) strip reprint   £2.00–£3.00

WYATT EARP
1957–1960 (44)
Miller (Charlton)
1 (28p) US reprint   50p–75p
2–44   35p–50p

XMAS COMIC
1947 (1)
Crayburn Neil/Algar
1 (nn) (36p) Walter Booth   75p–£1.50

X-MEN
see: *Original X-Men*

X-MEN POCKETBOOK
Jun 1981–Aug 1982 (15)
Marvel
1 (14) (52p) (small) US reprint   15p–25p
15–28   10p–20p
20 Xmas double number (100p)   25p–40p

X-MEN WINTER SPECIAL
Oct 1981–Nov 1982 (2)
Marvel
1 (52p) US reprints   30p–45p
2   25p–45p

YOGI AND HIS TOY
26 Feb 1972–26 Oct 1972 (35)
Williams
to: *Fun Time*
1 (16p) (gravure) (with gift)   15p–25p
2–35 (with gifts)   15p–20p
     (without gifts)   5p–10p

YOGI BEAR MINI-COMIC
27 Feb 1965 (1)
City (*Huckleberry Hound* supplement)
1 (16p) (*Mini-Comic No 2*)   20p–25p

YOGI BEAR'S OWN WEEKLY
27 Oct 1962–28 Mar 1964 (76)
City
to: *Huckleberry Hound Weekly*
1 supplement to *Huckleberry Hound Weekly*
   20 Oct 1962 (16p)   50p–£1.00
1 (16p)   25p–35p
2–75   15p–20p

YOGI BEAR'S WINTER EXTRA
1964 (1)
City (Dell)
1 (48p) (gravure)   25p–35p

YOGI'S SUMMER TIME FUN SPECIAL
1972 (1)
Williams
1 (48p) (gravure)   25p–35p

YOU AND ME
1970?
(no imprint)
1 (68p) (photos) (adult)   50p–£1.00

YOUNG BRIDES
1952 (10)
Arnold (Prize)
1 (68p) US reprint   25p–35p
2–10   20p–25p

YOUNG BRIDES
1953–1955 (38)
Strato (Prize)
1 (68p) US reprint   25p–35p
2–38   20p–25p

YOUNG EAGLE
1951–1956 (13)
Arnold/Miller (Fawcett)
1–4 (24p) (Arnold) US reprint   50p–75p
50–58 (28p) (Miller)   50p–75p

YOUNG FUN
Feb 1947–Apr 1948 (8)
Youngman
1 (4p) (supplement: *Basinful of Fun*)   25p–50p
2–8 (45–51)   15p–25p

YOUNG KING COLE
see: *Blue Bolt Series*

YOUNG KING COLE DETECTIVE TALES
1950 (2)
Miller (Star)
1–2 (28p) US reprint   50p–75p

YOUNG LOVE
1952 (10)
Arnold (Prize)
1 (68p) US reprints   25p–35p
2–10   20p–25p

YOUNG LOVE
1953–1955 (34)
Strato (Prize)
1 (68p) US reprints   25p–35p
2–34   20p–25p

YOUNG LOVE
1971
Shelbourne/Europrojects
1 (52p) (photos) (adult) reprints   50p–75p
2–   25p–35p

YOUNG LOVERS
1960–1966 (136)
Famepress
1–136 (68p) (small)   10p–20p

YOUNG LOVERS LIBRARY
1958–
Pearson
1– (68p)   10p–20p

YOUNG MARVELMAN
3 Feb 1954–Feb 1963 (346)
Miller
1 (25) (28p) George Parlett   £2.00–£3.00
26–370 James Bleach   50p–£1.00

YOUNG ROMANCE
1953–1955 (33)
Strato (Prize)
1 (68p) US reprint   25p–35p
2–33   20p–25p

YOUNG ROMANCE
Jun 1980 (1)
Marvel
1 (nn) (52p) US reprints   15p–25p

YOUNG ROMANCE POCKET BOOK
11 Sep 1980–12 Nov 1981 (13)
Marvel
1 (52p) (small) US reprints   15p–20p
2   10p–15p
3 (100p)   15p–25p
4–13   10p–15p

YOUR FAVOURITE FUNNIES
1948 (1)
Valentine (Mallard)
1 (nn) (16p) Sam Fair   50p–£1.00

ZANE GREY'S STORIES OF THE WEST
1953–1954 (31)
World (Dell)
1: *Riders of the Purple Sage* US reprint   50p–£1.00
2–31   50p–75p

ZAZA THE MYSTIC
1956
Miller (Charlton)
1– (28p) US reprint   50p–75p

ZETA
Oct 1967–
Gassman
1 (64p) (4C) (adult) photos   50p–£1.00
2–   50p–75p

ZINGA COMAG
Aug 1982 (1)
Zinga
1 (20p) (2C) 'black' comic   15p–25p

ZIP
4 Jan 1958–3 Oct 1959 (92)
Odhams
to: *Swift*
1 (12p) (gravure) Ron Embleton   50p–£1.00
2–92 Don Lawrence   25p–50p

ZIP-BANG COMIC
1946–1947 (2)
Forshaw/Ensign
1 (8p) W. Forshaw   50p–£1.00

ZIP COMIC
1946 (1)
Forshaw W.
1 (nn) (8p) Forshaw   50p–£1.00

ZIP COMIC
1948 (1)
PM (Marx)
1 (nn) (16p) Colin Merritt   50p–£1.00

ZIP COMICS
May 1973 (1)
H. Bunch/Cozmic Comics
1 (36p) (adult) Dave Gibbons   50p–£1.00

ZIPPER RIPPER COMIC
1946 (1)
Funnibook (Cartoon Art) (see: *Zippy*)
1 (nn) (8p)   50p–£1.00

ZIPPY COMICS
Nov 1947 (1)
Cartoon Art
1 (12p) Dennis Reader   50p–£1.00
   (inset: *Zipper-Ripper Comics*)

ZOMBIE
196 (8)
Miller (EC)
1 (68p) US reprints   £1.00–£1.25
2–8   75p–£1.00

ZOOM
1947 (1)
Childrens Press
1 (12p) Hugh McNeill   50p–£1.25

ZORRO
Feb 1952–1954 (38)
SNPI (Miller)
1 (50) (24p) foreign reprint   35p–50p
51–87   25p–35p

ZORRO
1955– (6)
World (Dell)
1: *Return of Zorro* (28p) US reprint   50p–85p
2–6   50p–75p

Reference Books for the Collector

The British Comic Catalogue 1875–1975: Denis Gifford
Alphabetical listing of all British comic publications with publishing histories, details of characters, and artists index. Mansell Books (1975)

British Comics and Story Paper Price Guide 1982: Denis Gifford
Alphabetical listing of all British comics, story-papers (for boys and girls), juvenile magazines and 'penny dreadfuls', with values. ACE (1982)

The World Encyclopedia of Cartoons: Maurice Horn (ed.)
Alphabetical entries on cartoonists and their characters (British entries by Denis Gifford). Chelsea House (USA) (1980)

The World Encyclopedia of Comics: Maurice Horn (ed.)
Alphabetical entries on comic artists and their characters (British entries by Denis Gifford). Chelsea House (USA) (1976)

Books of Interest to the Collector

The Comic Art of Roy Wilson: Alan Clark & David Ashford
Biography of the greatest 'Golden Age' comic artist with many illustrations. Midas Books (1983)

The Best of Eagle: Marcus Morris
Illustrated history of the most famous 'modern' comic by its editor (strips compiled by Denis Gifford). Michael Joseph/Ebury Press (1977)

The D. C. Thomson Bumper Fun Book: Paul Harris (ed.)
Collection of essays by many writers on the Thomson publishing house of Dundee. Paul Harris Publishing (1977)

D. C. Thomson Firsts
Facsimiles of eight Number One issues of D. C. Thomson comics and story-papers. Chimera-Posner (1978)

Discovering Comics: Denis Gifford
Concentrated history of comics in illustrated paperback. Shire (1971)

Happy Days: A Century of Comics: Denis Gifford
Pictorial history of British comics, many reprinted in colour. Jupiter Books (1975)

The International Book of Comics: Denis Gifford
World history of comics with over 1100 illustrations, many in colour, from the author's collection. Dean International (1984)

Masters of Comic Book Art: Peter Garriock
Examines ten major talents including Frank Bellamy. Aurum Press (1978)

Penny Dreadfuls and Comics: Kevin Carpenter
Illustrated history of British comics and story-papers published as the catalogue to an exhibition. Bethnal Green Museum of Childhood (1983)

Stap Me! The British Newspaper Strip: Denis Gifford
Pictorial paperback surveying newspaper strips. Shire (1971)

Tiger Tim's Own Comic Collection: W. Howard Baker (ed.)
Reduced size facsimiles of 16 pre-war comics. Baker/Greyfriars Press (1977)

A Very Funny Business: Leo Baxendale
Illustrated biography of the influential comic artist. Duckworth (1978)

Victorian Comics: Denis Gifford
Illustrated history of the earliest comics. George Allen & Unwin (1976)

Magazines for the Collector

There is no professionally published magazine about comic collecting. Although the titles listed here are of high quality, they are all basically 'hobby' publications and as such tend to be irregular as to publishing dates. As prices per copy or per subscription may change, a letter of enquiry to the editor/publisher, preferably enclosing a stamped addressed envelope, is recommended.

BRITISH COMIC WORLD
Serious, well-researched illustrated quarterly covering the whole spectrum of comic history. A. and D. Coates, 12 Inglehurst Gardens, Redbridge, Ilford, Essex 1G4 5HD.

COMIC CUTS
Newsletter/magazine of the Association of Comics Enthusiasts, full details of which will be found on page 224. Subscription £5 per annum. D. Gifford, 80 Silverdale, Sydenham, London SE26 4SJ.

COMIC JOURNAL
Magazine combining comic nostalgia with research. A. Cadwallender, 63 Green Street, Middleton, Manchester M24 2HU (discontinued 1984).

EAGLER MAGAZINE
Concentrates on artists and characters from *Eagle*. A. Whitehead, 2 Feathers Lea, Flint, Clwyd CH6 5BZ.

ESCAPE MAGAZINE
Professionally produced illustrated magazine mainly concerned with present-day comics and artists. P. Gravett, 156 Munster Road, London SW6 5RA.
GOLDEN FUN
Irregular, approximately annual, illustrated magazine mainly about artists and comics of the golden age. A. and L. Clark, 24 Arundel Road, Tunbridge Wells, Kent TN1 1TB.

The Association of Comics Enthusiasts

Known as ACE, or Ace for short, the Association of Comics Enthusiasts was formed in March 1978. It was the first, and remains the only, organization for collectors of British comics and those interested in the history and development of strip cartoons. Members receive a regular mailing of ACE material which is published in a unique loose-leaf format designed for filing under such headings as annuals, artists, characters, comics, free gifts, publishers, story-papers, and so on. These fully illustrated fact sheets form an ongoing Encyclopaedia of British Comics which members may assemble in the way which suits their individual needs: alphabetically, chronologically, by subject matter, etc.

Members also receive the Ace News-and-Viewsletter, *Comic Cuts*, which features current and forthcoming information on every comics-related publication in the UK, in detail and in handy reference form as 'The Comic Calendar'. New publications are reviewed, as are comic art exhibitions, conventions, festivals, awards, and visits to events abroad. Members may also advertise their wants, sales and exchanges at low cost, and their letters, comments and queries are also featured.

Among the several continuing series we research and publish for Ace members is 'The Comic Chronology' which lists in chronological order every juvenile comic, story-paper and magazine together with start/stop dates, publisher information, special editions, amalgamations, supplements, free gifts, etc. Already the years 1900 to 1939 have been completed. Another continuing series is the 'A to Z of British Newspaper Strips' which reproduces one selected example of every strip published. A special extended feature on a classic strip is included when the occasion arises, such as an anniversary or an exhibition.

Collectors who specialize in comic annuals are also catered for in our identification indexes to those published by D. C. Thomson and Amalgamated Press. These are especially useful as they describe the cover designs of undated issues. Our detailed lists of free gifts are also unique, being the first attempt to date, detail and identify these elusive collectors' items.

Another popular and unique series is devoted to the reminiscences and autobiographies of veteran artists who worked in comics. These are serialized with vintage illustrations. Occasional facsimiles have also been presented to members, including the Weary Willie and Tired Tim Club Membership Certificate, and the original leaflets issued to advertise the first publication of *Dandy* and *Beano*.

The Association also sponsors the annual Ally Sloper awards for veteran comic artists and newspaper strip cartoonists.

The current annual subscription, which runs from March to February, is £5 ($8) or by airmail £8 ($12). The address is AGE, 80 Silverdale, Sydenham, London SE26 4SJ.